ALSO BY WILF NUSSEY

The Hidden Third
  Published by Rebel ePublishers 2013

Salvation City: A collection of Lowveld tales
  Published by Stephan Phillips (Pty) Ltd in 2002.

South Africa, a Wonderful Land
  Published by Central News Agency, 1997.

Majestic South Africa
  Published by Central News Agency, 1997.

The Crowded Desert, on the Kalahari Gemsbok National Park, Published by William Waterman, 1993.

Kruger: Portrait of a National Park, with David Paynter. Published by Southern Books, 1987.

The Hidden Third

Wilf Nussey

Rebel ePublishers
Detroit New York London Johannesburg

Rebel ePublishers
Detroit, Michigan 48223

The Hidden Third
© 2013 by Wilf Nussey

ISBN-13: 978-0-9869871-7-5
ISBN-10: 0-9869871-7-4

Cover design by Mandie van der Merwe, *Love & Sweat*
Interior design by *Caryatid Design*

To Doreen, again

AUTHOR'S NOTE

After the 1994 general election which brought democracy to South Africa and swept Nelson Mandela's ANC into power, South Africans were intoxicated by euphoria. The widely predicted civil war had not happened. The crushing burden of apartheid had gone. Black and white celebrated together.

But the slate of hate had not been wiped clean. Under the sunny surface was a layer of white extremists utterly opposed to blacks in power. They were unseen but everyone suspected they were there: the Third Force, the Hidden Third.

This is a story of what could have happened after the election.

PROLOGUE

Jakes Mabuza guessed he was in trouble the moment he climbed into the taxi outside the hotel in Hillbrow. He knew it after he ducked his head through the low door, slumped into the seat, and saw someone already there, against the other side, a big white man, his face indistinct in the half dark.

Jakes turned and grasped the door pillar to heave himself out, but the heavy body of another man blocked him. The newcomer pushed him back inside and sat down. He was firmly sandwiched between them. All his mental alarms went into high decibel.

"This him?" the man on his left asked curtly, as the taxi swept away from the curb.

It can't be happening, Jakes thought, not even right here in decrepit Hillbrow in the heart of Johannesburg, teeming with the crowds on a warm summer evening.

"Don't know him by sight," the one on his right replied. "Looks like what they said." Without warning, he pinned Jakes hard against the seat with one arm across his chest and thrust the other into the inside pocket of Jakes' jacket.

He pulled out envelopes, a chequebook, an identity book, and scanned them.

"It's him," he grunted.

Oh Jesus! Jakes remembered. Ngwenya's things. Jakes had borrowed the jacket from Temba Ngwenya that afternoon because a waning few Hillbrow hotels, trying to prop plunging standards, barred cocktail bar visitors in shirtsleeves.

"I'm not Ngwenya!" he shouted. "This is his jacket. I just borrowed it!"

"Shut up," said the man on his left and rammed the barrel of a gun into his ribs.

It hurt. Jakes' heart sank. On both sides, pedestrians and cars blurred past. He thought of screaming, of trying to jump out, but the two men were big and nobody would give a damn in this sump of booze, sex, drugs and crime. And there was the gun.

***

When the computer games in a grubby arcade in Hillbrow's mindless swirl of noise and neon lights swallowed the last of their coins, the two bored boys walked down Claim Street towards the grubby apartment block, encrusted with small balconies in garish colours, they called home.

They strolled past plane trees deformed by pollarding, kicking at fallen seed balls. Near a corner, they paused to look at a small brick building down a side street hunched between faceless high-rises, a seedy Art Deco relic of days when Hillbrow was a select suburb. Paint hung from its front like dead skin. Dirty curtains suggested the apartments were still occupied but, in fact, nothing in Hillbrow was unoccupied; the new South Africa had brought a tidal wave of humanity into Johannesburg in the years since apartheid ended.

"C'mon, let's go an' have a look," said one, a gangling fair-haired boy of about ten, in jeans and T-shirt, "We haven't been for ages."

His companion, a thin Indian with skin like milk chocolate, shook his head in doubt. "It's getting late," he said.

"Nah. It's happy hour, they're still boozing. Won't be home before seven."

The Indian boy glanced at his Swatch.

"Okay, but not for long. Ma said she'd be home at six."

Exploring a year ago they'd found a basement in the old building, a private place where, by the light of the single bare ceiling bulb, they could play cards, smoke pot and pick through discarded refrigerators and other junk.

They loped, as light as alley cats, down the street and pushed the broken doors, which opened into a dim foyer smelling of urine and damp rot. Six battered wooden mailboxes clung to a side wall. At the back of the foyer, a flight of bare steps with a chipped concrete banister led upwards. The door to the basement was in the dark corner beneath the angle of the steps.

Treading gingerly because the place was spooky, they moved to it. The blond boy twisted the handle and pushed. The door swung open, hinges creaking. A strong, unfamiliar, sick-sweet smell gushed through the gap.

The Indian boy stopped.

"Come on," the other said in a fierce whisper, tugging his arm.

They felt their way down three steps into blackness. The strange smell became stronger. The blond boy patted the wall to find the light switch and flicked it. Weak yellow light flooded the room.

The Indian boy screamed, a cutting screech of pure horror. The blond boy's mouth opened wide but panic froze his voice. Shock rooted them to the floor, their eyes huge.

Right below the naked light bulb a corpse lay on the rubbish-littered floor. Glazed, half-open eyes stared at them from a swollen black face. Lips puffed by decay leered from shining white teeth. The bloated body, in a light houndstooth jacket over an open-collar shirt, now taut as a sausage skin, lay with limbs outspread. Right in the centre of the forehead was a dark hole. A revolver lay next to the corpse, gleaming blue in the light.

The rising stench of decay overwhelmed the boys. They turned and ran. In the foyer the Indian boy stopped and vomited. His friend shouted and pulled his arm, frantic to escape.

"What the fok's going on!" a voice bellowed from the staircase. "What the hell you little buggers up to?"

A big old man in a collarless shirt and stained tracksuit pants stood halfway down the stairs, glaring at them. The white boy stared in shock at him, desperate to flee but unwilling to leave his friend.

The old man stepped around the splashes of bile with distaste and saw their terror.

"What you doing?" he demanded.

"In there," the blond boy answered, pointing a shaking finger at the light streaming from the cellar door.

The old man stepped to the door and went in. Seconds later, he rushed out and sprinted up the stairs, ignoring them.

The boys ran for home. Closer to the apartment block they recovered their poise, embarrassed by their mutual display of fright. The basement scene seemed unreal ... a weird dream. They would not tell their parents, they decided, because they would get hell for going there.

CHAPTER ONE

Jeffrey Ballance braked the VW Jetta with care on the wet road at the first set of traffic lights on the outskirts of Johannesburg. He glanced at the cars on either side of him and checked that his doors were locked. In this crime-ridden city, it was wise to be always alert for hijackers.

The air was washed clean by the afternoon thunder-storm and on the horizon, the palisade of high-rise office blocks stood in glinting silhouette against the red glow of sunset. He stretched to ease the tiredness in his muscles. When the light flicked to green, he accelerated slowly, letting the other traffic flow ahead.

It had been a difficult three days in Maputo, the hot and sticky capital of Mozambique, still redolent of its former Portuguese colonisers after twenty years of independence. He had helped to negotiate a new aid agreement for the country with European benefactors who were reluctant to put more money into Africa because so much had been wasted or stolen. Having at last learned their lesson, they now wanted every cent and pfennig accounted for. A specialist in negotiation, Jeffrey worked hard for his fees setting up deals, which satisfied donors without offending recipients.

The Frelimo were as hypersensitive as were all new black governments with their prestige at stake, he mused as he followed the familiar route from the airport to his townhouse in Sandton. His task had been smoothed by his fluency in Portuguese: when tempers ran high and pa-tience ran dry, he was able to soothe with words. He worked hard for his money.

What he needed now was a large scotch and soda, a beef sandwich and sleep.

The swift political and social change in South Africa, even in the few years since the collapse of apartheid rule, and only two years after the first democratic elections, had produced so large a crop of impasses between trade unions, business, government and foreign benefactors, that at thirty-five Ballance was much in demand as a mediator or facilitator or arbitrator, depending on who was hiring ... he was never quite sure how to describe himself. A visiting lecturership in labour relations at the University of the Witwatersrand left him little time for diversions. Three times a week he played violent bouts of squash. Once a week, he treated himself and a female companion to a dinner at a top restaurant, a different companion each time. Easy in Johannesburg where ambitious young women came and went like shooting stars.

Women entered his ambit and left when they discovered they were little more than equipment for sexual athletics, like gym apparatus, because his preoccupation with work left no room for lasting relationships. Female students drawn by his rumpled good looks wanted to take care of him. Female colleagues found him intimidating.

Ballance stopped the Jetta in front of the entrance to the high security complex and touched his remote control to open it, and then his garage door. Driving into it, he saw a faint strip of light beneath the door from the garage into the kitchen. He must have left a light on.

Two men, one black, one white, both large, rose to their feet, saying nothing; one from the couch near the picture window, the other from an armchair. They wore dark suits, white shirts, dark ties and brown shoes, the unofficial uniform of officialdom.

"Who the hell are you?" he demanded, dropping his travel bag on the floor.

"Police, Mr Ballance," the black one said in a soft throaty voice. He was a head higher than Ballance, with an athlete's taut body. "I am Captain Ndzimandze and this is Sergeant Greeff."

Captain Ndzimandze did not offer to shake hands and stood with his own clasped in front of him. He looked ill at ease amid Ballance's expensive furnishings, paintings and objets d'art.

The sergeant, short and broad, reached inside his jacket, startling Ballance, and stepped forward, holding nothing more sinister than a plastic card with a small photograph of himself next to the new sunburst-and-aloes emblem of the South African Police Service.

"You have no right to enter my home without permission," Ballance admonished them. "What do you want?"

"The caretaker let us in, sir," Ndzimandze said and went on without preliminaries. "Do you know a man by the name of Temba Ngwenya, from Tzaneen, a teacher and a senior official of the African National Congress, who lived in Zambia until 1990?"

Ballance continued to glare, feeling curiosity overcoming his indignation.

"Of course I know Ngwenya," he said. "He wasn't just a teacher. He was a senior lecturer in education and a colleague before he went into exile. When he came back, he was a member of the ANC constitutional negotiating team and now he's one of their senior education advisors, far as I know. Why?"

"Wasn't he a friend of yours?" the big policeman persisted.

"He still is, though I haven't seen him for some time." He looked from one to the other, unable to read their stolid faces. "What's all this about?"

"Sir, we are investigating a case of murder," Ndzimandze replied.

"Murder?" The ugly word hung in the air. "Temba's not a murderer," Ballance said.

"No, sir. Are you the owner of a Smith and Wesson .38 revolver, manufacturer's number 7327089?"

Ballance felt a worm of worry. "Yes, I have one, but I can't remember the number. I inherited it."

"Can we see it, please, sir?"

He led the way down the passage to his study with the two police officers close behind him. His father's big old rolltop desk stood against a wall covered with snapshots and visiting cards. He grasped a corner of the desk and pulled; it rolled forward on castors, revealing a small steel safe sunk into the wall. He inserted a key and swung the door open.

It was empty save for a white cloth stained with oil. His face drained of colour.

"I don't understand," he said, "it was locked. I have the only key ..."

Sergeant Greeff knelt to examine the lock and the inside of the safe, taking care not to touch anything. There was nothing to indicate it had been forced.

The captain stared at Ballance.

"Ngwenya was found dead in a basement in Hillbrow two days ago," he said. "Your gun was lying next to the deceased."

Shock stunned Ballance. Temba dead? *His* gun? He groped for his swivel chair and sat down.

Ndzimandze drew a brown envelope from his inside pocket and extracted a sheaf of postcard-size photographs. He selected several and lined them up on the edge of the desk in front of Ballance.

They were colour pictures of a swollen corpse lying on its back with arms and legs outflung, head twisted to one side. The harsh glare of the photographer's flashgun threw highlights on the taut black skin and cast dark shadows beyond it. The dead man was wearing a sports jacket, casual shirt, and slacks. Close-ups showed a bullet hole in the middle of the forehead and the vacant back of the head where the bullet had emerged in fragments.

Ballance been in the presence of death several times in his life and it had not bothered him, but these photographs made him feel sick.

"The remains are not in good condition," the captain said, apologetic, "but do you recognise him?" He kept his gaze on Ballance's face.

"No," Ballance answered, staring at the grisly pictures, "not for certain, although it might be him. How do you know it's Ngwenya?"

"Fingerprints, sir. And we know he was hiding in Hillbrow for a week or more before he was killed."

Fingerprints were conclusive. Ballance's mind was in a whirl. Why would Temba be in hiding? Respected in political circles, he was known for quiet moderacy and an inoffensive low-profile persona. Since the end of apartheid, he had worked hard behind the scenes, helping to integrate and expand education. He was a private man who never sought the limelight. Who would want to kill him?

He turned to the policemen.

"Who killed him?"

The captain and the sergeant exchanged a glance.

"Maybe you can help us answer that, sir," the captain said.

"Me? How? I haven't spoken to him for months and I haven't the foggiest idea who'd want him dead."

"You have been seen in Hillbrow in the past week near the scene of the crime—"

"I have *what!*" Ballance yelped in astonishment.

"The deceased was killed by a bullet from your pistol, which had your fingerprints on it."

"You're accusing *me* of murder? Are you out of your mind? That's absolute rubbish!" Ballance was shouting now and waving his arms.

"Please come with us, sir."

"Are you *arresting* me?"

"No, sir. We are asking you to come with us for questioning, sir."

He went like an automaton, unable to credit what was

happening. He sat silent in the back of a Toyota Corolla beside the sergeant, while the captain drove through the evening traffic to the Murder and Robbery Squad headquarters.

They led him to a room that smelt of Jeyes fluid and lit by a strong ceiling lamp. It had a single window giving a depressing view onto decrepit houses in the dim streets of old Johannesburg. A framed portrait of the new Minister of Police hung on the otherwise bare walls. The furniture comprised an empty table with a chair on either side.

A man in a plain grey suit who appeared to be in his late fifties, walked in behind them and sat in the chair without saying a word. His face commanded attention, angular and etched by experience, the grey hair cut short and a thin pencil moustache clung to the upper lip of a hard mouth. Wintry black eyes examined Ballance. He looked like a man of little patience.

"I want to speak to my lawyers," Ballance demanded.

"There is no need for that yet, Mr Ballance." The man's voice was gruff and Afrikaans-accented. "You have not been formally charged. I am Superintendent Louw and I'm leading the investigation into the Ngwenya murder. There has to be a rational explanation for your involvement and the sooner we can find it the sooner we can finish. Sit down, please."

The superintendent questioned him while the captain and the sergeant stood and listened. How long had he known Temba Ngwenya? Did he know of anyone who might want to kill Ngwenya? Why did Ngwenya not keep in touch with him, since they were old friends? Whom else did he know in the ANC? What was he doing in Hillbrow last week? Could he account for his movements in the seventy-two hours before Ngwenya's death? When last did he use his pistol?

Ballance reined in his temper and answered with patience, in spite of the superintendent's peremptory tone and the absurdity of the situation. No, he had no idea who might want to kill the man. He was certainly not in Hillbrow last week and hadn't been there for months. He'd just returned from three days in Maputo. He hadn't used the Smith and Wesson for years ... wasn't even sure now how to use it. The questions went on and on.

Ninety minutes later, Superintendent Louw swivelled his chair to stare out of the window for a minute, sighed, and turned back.

"I don't think you murdered Ngwenya," he said.

"I *know* I didn't!" Ballance snapped.

"All right, Mr Ballance, relax." He raised a conciliatory hand. "You're not off the hook because your gun was used and until there's an explanation for that you are, *ipso facto*, the prime suspect. I'm inclined to believe you because you can account for most of your movements and because I don't think you're the type to carry out a well-planned murder."

"Damn right," Ballance said, relieved, "Now can someone take me home?"

"The captain will take you back, later, but consider this before you go: if you are not the murderer, then somebody wants us to think you are. Who?"

Ballance, who had been rising from his chair to go, lowered himself again, bewilderment chasing anger across his face.

"You mean someone's trying to frame me?"

Louw winced at the Americanism. "Maybe. This was a planned killing but for no obvious reason. Can you think of anybody who might want to do this to you, any political or professional enemies?"

"No." Ballard shook his head. "I've had disagreements with some people, like anyone else. It goes with the territory, but nothing so big anyone would want to pin a murder on me."

The superintendent leaned back in the hard wooden chair and folded his arms across his chest. He studied Ballance for a few moments before he spoke again.

"Mr Ballance," he said, "there is a chance your predicament could be part of a larger scenario. You are aware, of course, that assassination has been an everyday thing in South Africa for several years now, since De Klerk took the lid off the political can."

"That's not strictly true," Ballance interrupted, "murder was a favoured tactic of the old regime for years."

"You misunderstand me. I am not saying the government has a policy of assassination. I mean that killing has become a commonplace method of covering up past sins and of silencing noisy opposition. Do you believe the butchery between ANC and Inkatha supporters in Zululand was not politically motivated? Or that all the dirt and mayhem of the previous ten, twenty years has been revealed?"

"No, of course not, but—"

"Do you think all the people responsible for it were exposed, or have miraculously turned into lily-white non-racial angels?"

Taken aback by the vehemence in the superintendant's tone, Ballance said nothing and waited while Louw, frowning, rubbed the bare surface of the table with the palm of a broad, sinewy hand.

"There are scores of unsolved murders, Mr Ballance. I don't mean open-and-shut cases like the shooting of Chris Hani. I'm talking about all those clever murders where the killers just disappear into thin air. Most victims are low-profile but often quite important local party people who don't always make the headlines."

Louw rested his forearms on the table. "Many of the killings have one thing in common. They point a finger at some particular person or party. Luckily for us, it's been a bit too obvious in several cases. Yours may be one of them."

"But why me? Ballance's voice rose a notch. "I'm not a political activist. I'm a lecturer and arbitrator. I help people and organisations to resolve their differences, not aggravate them."

"That's reason enough for some troublemakers who don't want differences resolved and would rather foment conflict, so they can pick up the pieces. And on top of that you are rather well-known for your liberal beliefs."

Louw stood up and looked at Ballance with cold eyes. "But all this is speculation. It's possible though very improbable you did kill Ngwenya."

Ballance rose too. He was taller than the superintendent but not as wide.

"We have your gun and we have witnesses. I'm not the judge so I'm afraid we have no option but to charge you and let the law take its course. Meanwhile, if you will cooperate with us until we can get to the bottom of this, we'll let you go on your own recognisances, Mr Ballance. Just keep what we have discussed to yourself please, and do not try to disappear."

A gruff Sergeant Greeff drove him home in silence. Exhausted by the gauntlet of questions on top of a hard-working trip, Ballance drank a large neat whisky and collapsed on his bed.

**

Tight-skirted hips swinging, the young receptionist led the way past a clatter of typists to a cloth-panelled door, opened it, and stood aside to let him brush by her amply-filled shirt. Ballance stepped into an office with two walls lined with books and box files. On one side, a tall sealed window showed a slice of Johannesburg's glass-and-cement forest from seventeen floors above the crawl of traffic. On the opposite wall, in sharp contrast, hung a serene Voigt oil of the Namib Desert's sinuous orange dunes. There was nobody in the office.

"Please have a seat. Your attorney will be with you in a minute," the receptionist said and smiled.

He sat in a leather armchair and picked up acopy of a morning tabloid from a tiny glass table. Its fat black headline screeched 'PROF SLAYS ANC MAN' and added in smaller type below 'Police Allege'.

Ballance's spirits drooped as he read it. Such publicity, good or bad, was a new experience for him.

"Good morning."

He looked up to see a tall woman walk in, slender in a severe tailored charcoal suit and plain white blouse. Pale fronds escaped from the mass of blonde hair drawn back and tied at the nape of her neck. Bright, cobalt-blue eyes looked at him.

He stood up hastily.

"Mr Ballance?"

"That's right."

"I'm Penelope Fox and I'm handling your case," she said, squeezing past the clutter in the office to go behind a leather-topped desk beneath the Voigt. "Sorry I'm late but some mindless idiot parked his car in my bay in the basement."

Oh hell, thought Ballance, it's mine. He had parked in a hurry, not seeing any names on the bays and anxious not to be late himself.

"Anyway, it's not a problem," she went on as she settled into a swivel chair and picked up a file. He sighed with relief until she added, "The garage manager had it towed away and the owner can fetch his fancy Jetta from the city pound. Please take a seat."

His spirits sank. It had to be his car; not a good start to a legal relationship. He lowered himself into the chair.

"I'm pleased to meet you," he said.

"I'm sorry it had to be under such circumstances."

"Me too. I think it was my car."

The blue eyes widened and she stared at him in surprise, then blushed with embarrassment.

"Oh dear ..." She slumped back in her executive chair and looked at the ceiling, the books, anywhere but at Ballance.

"No, please, I'm sorry ... it's my own stupid fault,"

14

Ballance stammered. "Really, it's no problem ..."

She laughed a clear bell-like peal. He grinned.

"Oh dear." She struggled with her smile, conquered it, and rearranged papers on the desk. "I'm very sorry. I don't always treat my clients like this."

Ballance felt better.

"Forget it. It means things must get better. I must admit I'm rather scared ... no, that's wrong, I'm very scared." He picked up the tabloid and showed her the headline. "And that doesn't help. They can't even get it right. I'm a lecturer, not a professor."

Her smile became businesslike.

"Mr Ballance, what happens now is that first you tell me exactly what happened and then I brief our advocate, Max Adelman. We're lucky to get him, he's one of the best. Then we'll go over it with him."

"That's fine. I'm sorry to put you to all this trouble."

"There's nothing to be sorry about. It's not every day one is charged with murder."

"I have to go before a magistrate in a few days. That doesn't leave much time."

"Don't worry about it. The case will be remanded to the Supreme Court because it's a murder charge. I don't expect it to come to trial for a month or two."

"Two months! But won't the magistrate throw the whole case out when he sees how ridiculous it is?"

"It doesn't work like that. The Attorney-General has decided to prosecute even though the police have nothing more than circumstantial evidence. Did they take your passport, by the way?"

"Yes, a Superintendent Louw at Murder and Robbery has it."

"That's odd."

"What?"

"The CID security section phoned to ask if you still have it. If Frans Louw has it, they should know."

"The security police? Why?"

15

"I've no idea. We'll have to find out." She cocked an elegant eyebrow at him. "Did you kill Temba Ngwenya, Mr Ballance?"

The question surprised him, coming from his lawyer, then he realised it had to be asked and shook his head. "Good Lord, no, we're old friends. We've known each other since we were kids ... or rather, knew each other. We grew up together on the same farm. I didn't even know he was dead until the police told me, then arrested me."

"I suppose academics are not the murdering type."

"I suppose not, except of each other's professional reputations." He began to relax. "I guess we'll be spending a lot of time together on this, Miss Fox, so please call me Jeff."

"Thank you. I'm Penny. Can we make a start now?"

She leaned forward to push keys on a recording machine. The movement drew her suit tight and he decided she had a good figure, if a little lean. Her name had a nice resonance to it: Penelope Fox.

"Everything that's said from here on will be taped," she said. "You don't mind?"

"Not at all. Anything to clear up this mess."

"Good, now please tell me what happened right from the beginning. I may interrupt you with questions."

Ballance settled in his seat and thought back to the event that had turned his life upside down.

***

Penelope studied him while she waited. He was a big-boned man, a little over six feet, tall with the sculpted spareness of an athlete, wearing a loose, somewhat creased grey suit. Untidy brown hair grown too long fell across his forehead and curled around his ears. A rather typical academic, she mused, no doubt interested in himself and his theories. The one distinctive feature in an otherwise ordinary appearance was his eyebrows, startling black bars above deep-set grey eyes, now focussed inward in recall.

"I'd been to Mozambique for a few days," he said, "when I got home there were these two large men in my living room, cops bulging out of their plainclothes. They asked if I knew Temba Ngwenya and when I'd last seen him, and they wanted to see my gun."

"When did you last see him?"

"Oh, months ago. Temba quit South Africa in frustration in 1987 and went to the African National Congress in Zambia. We met from time to time, for a drink or a meal when I went there on business. Maybe that's why the security police are interested, they had spooks everywhere in those days, before the Nationalists rediscovered God and dropped apartheid.

"I didn't know what Temba was doing then, except that he was involved on the ANC's education side. We talked about home and friends and old times and what's happening in South Africa, but seldom about his work."

"Why not? It seems odd, given your friendship?"

"I don't think he wanted me to know and I wasn't going to embarrass him by insisting. If I had, doors would have slammed in my face. Anyway, then came F W de Klerk and the great South African reboot and Temba returned home with the ANC hierarchy and all the other bureaucrats. He became very busy as a backroom boy for their negotiating team right up to and through the elections, so I haven't seen as much of him as I used to, although I was an advisor in the constitutional conference."

"Isn't it a bit unusual for a lecturer to travel so much and become so involved in trade union affairs?"

"Not at all. Archeologists and anthropologists and astronauts have to travel to get information at first hand, so why not me? What better way to study events than being right there? My students seem to appreciate it and it pays well. So," Ballance continued, "when I found these policemen making themselves at home in my place I was pretty annoyed, and when they started quizzing me about

Temba I became a bit short with them."

"You don't trust the police?"

Ballance showed surprise. "Well, I am a known liberal, though of the conservative variety, and I'm at Wits University, that celebrated stronghold of liberalism. So I thought they were harassing me, which South African policemen have always done very well. Then they told me Temba was dead, murdered, and took me away, just like that. They said he'd been shot with my pistol and it had my fingerprints on it."

Ballance spread his hands in a gesture of bewilderment. "It was a hell of a shock, the news of Temba's death and then being called his killer. When I last saw him, he was fit as a fiddle and elated by the Great Leap Forward and the African Renaissance and all the other clichéd policies."

"You sound rather cynical."

"I am a bit, I suppose. Even as a liberal, one gets tired of all talk and no action." He shrugged. "They've had plenty of time to enjoy their euphoria, satisfy their greed, and work out how to run a country."

"Mr Ballance … Jeff … I want you to tell me every last detail of what happened that night with the police."

"Do you mind if I take off my jacket?"

"Please do."

He stood up to drape it on the back of his chair, at the same time glancing down at the verdigris dome of the Supreme Court across the street, surrounded by a forest of concrete and glass. The sun was setting, mantling the city in twilight.

"Superintendent Louw was pretty fair, I suppose." Ballance recounted the superintendent's theories about assassination. "He let me go on my own recognisances."

Penelope leaned back and swivelled her chair from side to side while she thought. "That's odd behaviour for Superintendent Louw," she said. "He's been a very tough cop for more than thirty years. He's known as a hard hunter of criminals and doesn't give them a millimetre.

18

I'm surprised he didn't put you in a cell."

"Well, last night he sounded quite apologetic when he said he had no choice but to charge me because of the weight of evidence."

"Hmmm." She shook her head as if dismissing a doubt. "Jeff, they say they have these witnesses, what were you doing in the two or three days before the murder?"

"Apart from a day working on a lecture in my office, I was in Maputo."

"Can anyone vouch for that day? Did you have visitors who could say where you were and when? Students? Friends?"

"No," he said, thinking back. "Maybe someone saw me on the campus. There were no visitors, no students, no girlfriends."

She switched off the tape recorder and reached up with both hands to pat back strands of hair, in an unconscious movement Ballance found attractive.

"Can we continue this over dinner tonight?" he asked on impulse.

Surprised, she stood up and began putting away her notepad and pencil.

"Thank you, Jeff, but no. Maybe some other time. Tomorrow I want you to go back to the beginning ..."

"Not again!"

"I'm afraid so. Somewhere we might find something useful. You want to stay out of jail, don't you?"

She pressed a button on her desk. The receptionist appeared in the doorway and stood, hip cocked, waiting to show Ballance out.

"Have a good night, Jeff," Penelope called after him.

19

CHAPTER TWO

"Lucky, what do you think of this Ngwenya case?" Superintendent Louw asked.

"How do you mean, sir?"

"You don't think there's something funny about it?"

Captain Ndzimandze shrugged. "I am not sure. It *is* Ballance's gun. How could it get there if he is not involved?"

They were in the lounge of the superintendent's home, a small house he had bought twenty years earlier on Melville Ridge, when prices were still within a policeman's reach, before it was tarted up as a fashionable pseudo-Chelsea, and twelve years before cancer claimed his wife, leaving him rattling around in it alone.

The furniture had been her conservative choice; heavy, carved wood armchairs and settee with ball-and-claw feet and floral upholstery matching the carpet. Sepia family photographs in oval frames and a single painting, a Pierneef print of stylised umbrella thorn trees against infinite clouds, hung on the walls.

The house was worth a lot now but he refused to sell it. It was his museum of memories. He planned to refurbish it when he retired in two years, to be replaced by one of the up-and-coming black police officers. Affirmative action, they called it, but it meant dumping quality for expediency, Louw believed. He was fortunate in having in Lucky Ndzimandze, a policeman of fifteen years' experience.

The two men were in shirtsleeves and loosened ties, talking over sundowners. It was a regular ritual between the superintendent and his current Number Two, so they could discuss work away from the formality of the office.

"I'm not happy with cases that rely so much on circumstantial evidence," Louw said. He reached for his brandy, flavoured with lime juice and drowned in soda, a taste picked up in his army days before he switched to the police.

"Yes, but we've also got those witnesses," the captain pointed out. He sipped at his beer.

"Mmmm. All we have are two witnesses who can't pin him with certainty to the crime scene, only to the general area, the gun lying conveniently near the victim, lots of lead fragments too small for ballistic evidence, and nice clear fingerprints on the butt, trigger and trigger guard. No other prints, no smudges."

"Well, Ballance can't account for his movements at the time of death, when the witnesses say they saw him."

"It's too *vlot,* too slick," the superintendent sighed. "What did they say again?"

Captain Ndzimandze frowned into his glass, recalling their statements from memory. "Two men were in that area at different times, about an hour apart. Both said they noticed a man wearing a thick car coat, because it was unusual on a hot day. He must have worn it to hide the gun, an old Smith and Wesson with a five-inch barrel. Both described him in some detail, the coat, the blue sports shirt, jeans, blue socks and blue and white running shoes, all similar to clothes we found in his wardrobe afterwards.

"One saw him walking down the hill along Claim Street about two blocks from the building where Ngwenya was shot, and the other an hour later on the next corner, walking uphill. Both identified him from photographs."

"Their descriptions tally exactly, even down to the socks?"

"Yes."

"Isn't that a little strange, Lucky?"

"I don't think so, Superintendent. They're quite bright guys, young black men. One's a medical student at Wits and the other's the manager of a pop music shop up in Kotze Street in Hillbrow. He keeps the accounts and everything."

"And the time they saw him, it fits into the district sur-
geon's time of death?"

"Yes. The time span was quite wide, about twelve hours
because the corpse was pretty ripe after a couple of days
down there, maybe longer. Ballance was seen right in the
middle of it."

Superintendent Louw heaved himself up from his chair,
swallowed the last of his drink, and crossed the room to an
ornate teak sideboard to pour a fresh one, picking up the
captain's glass on the way.

"*Ja*, well." He sighed again as he poured himself a large
measure, dropped in ice from a plastic bucket in the shape of
an oak barrel labelled Richelieu, and splashed in lime juice
and soda. He uncapped a bottle of Windhoek lager, poured
it and handed it to the captain.

"So our Mr Ballance managed to be in two places about
six hundred kilometres apart at the same time. His times,
places, flights and so on all check out, though we haven't
talked to anybody yet who saw him in Maputo. Without an
obvious motive and harder evidence, I figure the chances of
a conviction are slim, but the Attorney-General insists we go
ahead with it. I smell something political, Lucky."

"Heh, no, Superintendent. Ballance is a soft-headed liberal but that's no crime nowadays. Where's the politics?"

"Maybe that's the point … the Attorney-General wants to
show the world what a fair fellow he is, by nailing the
murderer of an ANC man."

The captain mulled this over. Following political convolu-
tions was not his strong suit.

"Lucky," the superintendent asked, "how did Greeff find
these witnesses?"

"He was tipped off about them, sir."

"Tipped off? Who by?"

"I think it was one of his pals in the CID, Superintendent,
fellows who were with him in the old Security Police and
now work for special investigations. You remember he used
to work for the SP before it was disbanded and made part of

the CID? He was transferred to Murder and Robbery."

"Special investigations?" About to sit down, Superintendent Louw turned around in surprise. "What the hell have they got to do with it?"

"It wasn't them officially, sir, just some guy who works there. He found out about the witnesses and passed their names on to Greeff because he'd heard he was on the case. Greeff checked them out and took their statements."

"Where's Greeff now?"

"I don't know. Out with the boys tonight, I guess." Seeing the expression on his chief's face, Captain Ndzimandze looked at him with concern. "Why, sir, what's wrong?"

"Ballance comes up in the magistrate's court first thing tomorrow for remand, right?" The captain nodded. "You make sure Greeff's at the courts half an hour earlier. I want to talk to him."

Five minutes later Superintendent Louw drained his glass and thumped it down on the sideboard.

"Okay, Lucky, let's call it a night. I'll see you in the morning." He moved towards the front door.

Captain Ndzimandze realised he was being dismissed with unusual haste. The superintendent was irritated. He tipped the last of his beer down his throat, shrugged on his jacket and left with a brief "Goodnight".

Superintendent Louw locked the front door and switched off the light on the little porch, where he used to sit every evening with his wife, watching their small world stroll by. He moved to the sideboard to pour himself a last drink and slumped into his chair.

The damned special investigators again, he thought with irritation. Those cocky bastards, who breathed politics into everything, were interfering once more. He suspected they were manipulating him again, like a bloody puppet. But for what, this time?

CHAPTER THREE

"Isn't it unusual for an advocate to appear in a magistrate's court?" Ballance asked.

"It is, but we do our best for academia," Max Adelman said, cheerful as always. "After all, Wits is my *alma mater.*"

They stood with Penelope Fox in a bleak bench-lined corridor, outside the row of courtrooms waiting for Ballance's case to be called. As usual, the hearings in the overcrowded Johannesburg Magistrate's Courts, an unattractive brick and concrete building spanning most of a block, were running well behind schedule.

Adelman puffed at a curved pipe with a huge bowl, sending aloft streams of smoke as grey as the halo of untidy hair fringing his bald crown. He was a pinch-shouldered gnome, no higher than Ballance's armpit, with gold-rimmed spectacles balanced on a De Gaulle nose.

His reputation in criminal cases was formidable. Ballance worried how much it was costing him to have Adelman standing there, waiting, like a taxi with its meter ticking. Enough to keep the man in tobacco for life, he thought.

"I'm just up for remand and I'm sure Penelope here can handle it, Mr Adelman. Aren't I wasting your time?"

Adelman removed the pipe from his mouth. "No," he said, breathing smoke, "we must get the charge dismissed right now to avoid a long Supreme Court trial, which would cost you about ten thousand a day. Their case is so ridiculous and circumstantial it should never go beyond this court. Anyway," he grinned like a monkey, "you're paying my retainer whether I'm here or not."

Penelope smiled reassurance. She looked very businesslike today in a well-cut navy suit with her blonde hair drawn high into a soft crown.

"We might as well sit," she said and they found a wooden bench outside the room where the State intended to begin the procedure of sending Ballance to prison.

Less than thirty paces away in a borrowed prosecutor's office, Superintendent Louw stood with his back to the window, glowering at the stocky form of Sergeant Greeff, who stood rigid at attention although he was not in uniform.

"Why in God's name didn't you tell me that in the first place?" he said in exasperation. "From your report I thought you found the witnesses yourself, by doing some honest legwork in Hillbrow."

Greeff was indignant. Not very intelligent and destined to be a low-ranker all his career, he was surprised and hurt at being hauled over the coals by his chief. After all, it was his witnesses who had pinned the accused to the scene at the time of the crime. What the hell more did the superintendent want? What mattered was a conviction, not where or how he had found them.

"I did do the legwork," he said, resentful, "and all I could get was a bunch of blacks and Hillbrow fairies who saw nothing. Or so they said. Those people never help us."

"So you dug up a pair of convenient eye-witnesses from your own sources?"

"No, sir. It was not like that. I just mentioned to this CID inspector that I was on this case. I worked with him when we were in the SP and he said he knew of two blacks, who'd read about the murder in the papers and come forward because they were in the area then, and had seen a man."

Superintendent Louw aimed a withering glare at him. It was idiots like this who gave the force a bad name.

"So you questioned them and they both happened to have seen the same man in the same place at about the same time, behaving suspiciously?"

"*Ja*, Superintendent. It was good luck we found them."

"Did your ex-SP friend also tell you that both those men work for the security division?" he demanded. "That the medical student is a paid spy at Wits and the other one is paymaster for a whole bloody spy network in Hillbrow?"

Greeff was flustered, obviously wondering how the superintendent had discovered that. "Well, *ja*, I know that, sir, but so what? Shit, those guys are policemen too and it will make their evidence even stronger in court."

"Policemen! Greeff, don't you know the difference between a real policeman and a bloody spook?"

"Sir, Ngwenya was a terrorist and the man who killed him is a commie. We've got to fix those bastards." To many cops, every ANC member was a terrorist and every liberal a communist.

"Don't be a damn fool! This is an ordinary criminal case, not bloody politics. You're working for the State, not a political party! Can't you see that if the defence finds out that the two witnesses work for security, they'll tear the prosecution into little pieces?"

"No, sir." Still standing firm, at attention, Greeff retreated into warrant officer stolidity. "May I go now, sir?"

"*Ja*, get out of here!" Superintendent Louw gestured towards to the door. "You go back to Hillbrow and question everybody who lives or moves in that area, and this time do the job properly! Do you understand?"

"Sir!"

Greeff turned about as if on parade and stalked out with stiff shoulders.

The superintendent sat on the edge of the battered

26

wooden desk, drained by his outburst, depressed by the aura of despair left in the bleak little office by the passage of thousands of tawdry criminal cases.

There was no way the prosecution could go ahead, he thought. It was too late to call off today's remand hearing; the magistrate would be angered by the waste of his time and lambaste the police. He decided to speak to the Attorney-General about it later in the day and persuade him to suspend the charge until he could investigate further.

He closed the door behind him and walked to the courtroom, his footsteps echoing on the tiled floor.

Turning a corner, he was in time to see Ballance and the lawyer Fox entering the room, halfway down the next corridor. The superintendent recognised Adelman with them, which deepened his gloom.

Why would one of Johannesburg's toughest advocates attend a simple remand hearing in front of a magistrate? Did they know about the witnesses?

He followed and found a seat on the tiered wooden benches near the back. Adelman and Penelope settled themselves with books and files at one of the lawyers' tables in the well of the court, Ballance between them. The youthful prosecutor was already at the other table with Captain Ndzimandze at his side. Six reporters lazed at the Press bench against a wall.

People began to file in, almost filling the spectators' gallery, men and women, some well dressed, most in working clothes without jackets or ties, reminding Superintendent Louw that the victim in the case was an ANC man.

He didn't recognise any party organisers among them; they would turn up in force at the full hearing. It occurred to the superintendent that, as the accused killer of an ANC official, Ballance's life might be at risk.

"Order in court!" the orderly, an ageing uniformed constable, called in English and repeated in Afrikaans,

Zulu and Sotho. Shoes scraped and clothing rustled as people stood. The magistrate entered through a door in a back corner, a middle-aged brown man whose hair was graying from the pressures of dispensing mass justice, much of it to people who did not understand it.

He settled himself into the high-backed chair behind the wide bench and everybody sat except the prosecutor.

"Your Worship," the prosecutor said at a nod from the magistrate, "this is an application for a postponement in the case of the State versus Ballance on a charge of murder. We request remand to the Supreme Court for summary trial."

"Bail?"

"No bail, sir, the accused has been released on his own recognisances."

The magistrate's eyebrows lifted and he swung his gaze to the defence table. "I see we are graced by the presence of silk," he observed when he saw Adelman, "I assume, Mr Adelman, this means the defence intends to oppose the application?"

Adelman rose to his full five foot two and rested his fingertips on the table, peering over the rims of his glasses. "Indeed, sir. We wish to put forward testimony and argument at this stage to show that the charge against the accused has so little foundation that it verges on the frivolous, could well be deliberate harassment, and should be summarily dismissed. We submit that the evidence the prosecution state they will produce is so flimsy and leaves so much room for doubt that the lordships of the Supreme Court would take offence if it were brought before them."

"Good for you," Ballance muttered under his breath.

The magistrate sighed at the prospect of a long and perhaps complex hearing. His roster was already crowded. He looked at the prosecutor.

"I cannot accept that, your Worship," the prosecutor said. The defence move had caught him unprepared.

"The defence is wasting the court's time with delaying tactics. We have considerable circumstantial evidence which links the accused straight to the murder, supported by at least two witnesses who will testify to his presence in the area at the time of the crime. The Attorney-General is satisfied that this justifies prosecution."

"We propose to dispute the Attorney-General's assumptions here and now," Adelman interjected, ready for battle, eyebrows bristling.

The attention of everyone in the room focussed on the prosecutor and the advocate. A heated courtroom battle seemed imminent.

Ballance was concentrating so hard, he at first ignored the tap on his shoulder. When it came again, harder, he swung around in annoyance and saw an arm reaching towards him from the front row of black spectators, right behind the defence table.

Annoyed, he looked into its owner's bearded face and his eyes widened in astonishment. "Temba!" he gasped, and then said again so loud the whole courtroom heard, " *Temba!* "

He scrambled to his feet, knocking over his chair with a crash, and seized the outstretched hand in both of his. "Temba! Good God ... you're supposed to be dead! What the hell ..." Lost for words, he spread his arms wide and spun around to face the magistrate. "Jesus, man, they're saying I killed him and here he is!"

The bearded face split wide in a grin, flashing white teeth.

The crowd of spectators rose in a rumble of astonishment to peer at Temba Ngwenya, supposed to be a corpse, standing at the front of the courtroom. The reporters watched, sensing sensation.

"Your honour," Ngwenya said, speaking clearly in a resonant voice, "I am very much alive in spite of allegations to the contrary."

The courtroom exploded with excitement. Spectators

clambered on seats to see better. Women in ANC colours shrilled ululations. The court orderly looked around for help, but there were no other policemen in sight.

"Order! Order in court!" he bellowed through the uproar. Nobody paid any attention. Everyone watched the white murderer hugging his black victim.

The magistrate rose to his full height on the dais, frowning and angry. "SIT DOWN," he roared.

Nobody sat.

He raised his gavel high and slammed it on the bench. The bang, like a pistol shot, cut through the racket and the clamour subsided.

"Silence or I will clear the room!" he thundered, crashing the gavel down once more. "The next person who makes a sound will be arrested for contempt of court!"

He glowered at the defence table. "Mr Adelman," he said, his tone acid, "I suppose you have an explanation for this ridiculous disturbance?"

The advocate, blinking like an owl over his glasses, switched his gaze from Ballance, still gripping Ngwenya's hand, to the magistrate.

"Your Worship, I haven't the foggiest idea what is happening but if you'll give me a few moments I will try to find out."

"Be quick about it!" the magistrate ordered and sat.

"This is the fellow I'm supposed to have murdered," Ballance said to Adelman in a fierce whisper heard by the whole room.

"Have you proof that you're Temba Ngwenya?" Adelman asked.

"Here," Ngwenya said and handed Adelman an ANC membership card and a South African passport, both with his photograph. "I couldn't speak out earlier because someone out there is trying to kill me."

Adelman studied Ngwenya's face, examined the photographs in the two documents before giving both to the orderly, who put them on the bench in front of the magistrate.

"Why didn't you notify the police or the Attorney-General, or Mr Ballance here, that you were alive?" the magistrate demanded.

"I could not, sir, I have been in hiding. I'm taking a risk coming here today, that's why I brought friends." He glanced at six large men grouped behind him. "I think the poor guy who was murdered, was mistaken for me."

"Do you know who he was?" the magistrate asked.

"A comrade, sir, Jakes Mabuza."

"Who murdered him?"

"I don't know yet." He turned to Ballance. "Sorry you had to go through this, Jeff. I can't trust anybody. There was no other way to get you out of the mess."

"Temba, what the hell's going on?"

"Somebody's trying to fix us both. I must go. You look out. They can't nail you for murder now but that won't stop them. Watch your back."

"Damn it, Temba, you can't just leave—"

"Why? I've done nothing wrong. Can I have my documents back, please?"

The magistrate pondered for half a minute. There was no valid reason to withhold them. He gave them to the orderly, who carried them to Ngwenya as if they were infectious.

"See you," said Ngwenya. His human shield moved him along the aisle. The door swung shut behind them.

The spectators swarmed out in a chattering mass.

Two white men in open-neck shirts, sports jackets and RayBans, seated against the back wall of the courtroom, glanced at each other and followed them.

Superintendent Louw sat quite still staring into space, numbed by what he had seen and heard, the foundations of his ordered police world shaken. He felt a deep rage simmering within him. The magistrate's chill voice jerked him back to the present.

"Mr Adelman, I take it you wish to formally apply for

31

the dismissal of the charge?"

"Yes, your Worship. There is no case to answer."

The magistrate fixed an icy gaze on the young prosecutor. "Have you an explanation for this?"

"No, sir." Grey-faced, he shuffled his papers. "I ... there's nothing I can say. I don't know how this could have happened."

"It is obvious that the police made a grievous mistake that might well have had tragic results," the magistrate snapped, staring at Captain Ndzimandze. "I want a full report because I intend to take this matter to higher authority. Case dismissed. This court is now adjourned." He stalked from the dais.

The orderly rushed to open the door for him.

"God!" Penelope said with feeling. "That's left me absolutely wrung out." She gave Ballance an impulsive hug.

"Jeffrey, something very peculiar is going on," Adelman broke in, gathering his papers, his mobile face serious. "Have you any ideas about it?"

"Max, I know as much as you. I'm baffled. But thank heaven Temba made his appearance."

"Take my advice, son. He'll no doubt be in touch with you. If there's any truth in what he said, you could be in danger. We're in very strange times, so be careful. And keep in touch, you might need some help. I won't charge you, today's show has more than paid for it."

The courtroom was empty when they walked out, save for one man seated near the back with his head in his hands. In his elation at being free, Ballance did not recognise him as his interrogator, Superintendent Louw.

CHAPTER FOUR

The two men in open-neck shirts trotted down the broad steps outside the courts and shouldered their way through the crowd of people milling on the sidewalk. They climbed into a small white Ford, illegally parked between the yellow lines of a loading zone.

A traffic ticket was stuck under the windscreen wiper. One of them plucked it out and tore it into strips, which he dropped in the gutter. The car's plates were false. He reminded himself to change them.

They wove through the teeming morning traffic, taking the one-way streets for speed, dodging the aggressive minibus taxis swooping across lanes to snap up passengers on the sidewalks. They turned into Oxford road and travelled for ten minutes before descending into the basement parking of a hotel in Rosebank.

Minutes later, one pushed the bell button on a varnished door on the top floor. They waited, big-chested, thick-muscled men in their late twenties or early thirties, boasting almost identical Sundance moustaches.

A small plain man opened the door; either of them could have lifted him with one hand. They stood while he looked at them and entered when he gave a curt nod. One clicked the door shut and they followed him into a room furnished in Swedish stereotype. Hands in his jacket pockets, he stood with his back to windows screened by vertical plastic louvres and studied them with cold, unblinking eyes.

"Well?" His accent was very BBC British.

"Temba Ngwenya is alive, sir," one said without preamble. "We saw him in the magistrates' court today."

The plain man frowned. "Explain."

"Ballance came up for remand to the Supreme Court. He had an advocate with him, Adelman, and they were going to fight it. The court was full of ANCs. One of them stood up and identified himself as Ngwenya. There's no doubt. The magistrate threw out the case. Ngwenya's gone back into hiding. We couldn't do anything, it was too public and he had a bunch of ANC goons around him."

The plain man's face remained expressionless and he continued to stare at them without comment. Unnerved, they stood almost at attention.

They knew him as Smith, which meant nothing, and by reputation, which meant a great deal. He was a formidable killer, a specialist, who for twenty years had made his living by dispatching, with the detached efficiency of a rat-catcher, the opponents of those who paid him.

He used many methods, including hits by hired killers, letter bombs and other cruder explosive devices, poison, the sniper's rifle and straightforward frontal assassination by shotgun, pistol and knife.

Sometimes, when the challenge appealed to him and he wished to keep his hand in, he did the work himself. He disdained torture, leaving that to the lower orders, and like a gun, he killed whatever he was pointed at.

Born in Britain, raised in Kenya, Smith gravitated to South Africa via Rhodesia, staying ahead of the slow tide of African independence and, to his thinking, the resurgence of the Stone Age. He had learned his trade in Africa and polished it in the political and criminal cesspools of southern Europe. He was a thin, unremarkable figure in subdued clothes, at whom nobody would look twice. He always wore some inconspicuous club tie, perhaps a subconscious symptom of the status to which he aspired, and his grey moustache was always clipped, military close.

Now he considered the information, prolonging the

unease of his visitors under his steady gaze, and formed his plan.

"So Greeff and Basson bungled the job by taking out the wrong man. You," he aimed a forefinger at one of the men, "find out what went wrong. Do it with care, they'll know by now they cocked it up and I don't want to alarm them. You," he said, pointing at the other, "start a trace on Ngwenya. Use our black operators and tell them to find him, nothing more. Set up a watch on Ballance too, phone tap and a tail. Ngwenya must make contact with him and we should eliminate Ballance as well, because any further attempt to compromise him will be pointless after this.

"Both of you report back to me as soon as you have made your arrangements. Thank you."

The two left in haste, relieved to be out of his presence. One went back to his desk in a well-known bank and the other resumed his interrupted leave from his job in the Department of Home Affairs.

Both useful men, the specialist mused when he was alone. Former reconnaisance unit fighters in Angola, though with not much experience in his kind of action, they showed promise. Both had access to useful information.

He picked up a telephone on a blonde-wood stand, a relic of Swedish fashion, and called an out-of-town number. "Let's have lunch today," he said. "A problem has cropped up in our accounting system and I'd like to talk it over. One o'clock then? The usual place? Fine."

He replaced the phone and pondered the problem. Greeff and Basson, the bloody fools. More enthusiasm than competence. Their error was stupid but not irretrievable.

Driving north out of Johannesburg at a sedate speed in his Mercedes Benz 280, a solid, old 123 model with the muted suggestion of a fishtail, he considered how to turn the mistake to advantage.

The objective had been to kill two birds with one stone.

Murder Ngwenya, who could become a serious threat, and leave enough evidence to incriminate and thereby discredit Ballance, whose peacemaking in labour disputes was becoming a nuisance.

At Midrand, he turned off the freeway, drove along the Blue Gum-lined avenue of the old Johannesburg-Pretoria road and turned into a walled-in cluster of buildings. One was a pseudo-French restaurant with Moulin Rouge décor, the garish artificiality masked in the evenings by dim nightclub illumination.

It was a place where people could talk in privacy. Tables were placed well apart and nobody could overhear neighbours through the mixed hum of muzak and conversation diffused by the high ceiling.

The man he was meeting sat with his back to the wall, watching the movement of customers and waiters. A glass of water stood on the red-checked tablecloth in front of him.

Smith ordered a gin and tonic and a plain salad; the other man a glass of house wine and an omelette. Smith described what had happened in the magistrate's court earlier.

The other man, whom he addressed only as Doc, listened with impassive calm, banana-like fingers wrapped around the bowl of the thin-stemmed glass. He was tall and heavy with a thick neck, broad shoulders and crumpled ears that revealed a past on the rugby field. Although in his sixties, with grey streaking his thinning hair, his body, in an expensive suit, exuded physical strength.

A doctor of economics and an influential industrialist, he was well known in South Africa's inner business circles. He had been an advisor to the new government in the years following the transition to democracy. It had been a low profile rôle but a powerful one.

They discussed the problem as if talking about the weather while they ate. Over small cups of black coffee, Doc summed it up. "Basson, the CID inspector, is a simple oaf, a strong-arm man who'll do what he's told and is not expected to think. The weak link is Greeff, he should not have been brought into that assignment. His heart's in the right place but he hasn't the brains. He should have thought like a policeman when he did that job, but he made a mess of it because he's not even a good policeman. He must be pulled out of there and given a task where he can be used without risk, weapons training, or something else harmless."

"We gave him the job because he's been pressing for more responsibility," Smith said. "He's as keen as a bitch on heat and he is, after all, a sergeant. He refuses to quit the police. He likes it and insists that he's the right man in the right place for us. Greeff has a rather inflated view of his own importance, however."

"One of those, hmm? Too big for his boots." Doc lifted a bushy eyebrow. "He knows the rules and he knows what's at stake. And he's dispensable. If he won't do what he's told, then demote him. We can't risk prima donnas in this business, the kind who makes mistakes."

"Demote him?"

"Yes, get rid of him if necessary," said Doc, sipping coffee, "with as much lateral damage as possible."

"All right," Smith said, unruffled.

"And thank you. I'll tell the committee."

Doc paid the bill and stayed to finish his coffee. He was playing a dangerous game, he mused, watching Smith pause at the desk to take several peppermints on his way out. So be it, the game had to be played to whatever conclusion fate decreed.

***

Ballance was feeling a mild tipsiness when he let himself into his home late in the afternoon, feeling merry after a long lunch with Penelope Fox to celebrate his unexpected release from a murder charge.

Max Adelman had cried off, pleading work, age and a

sensitive stomach. He preferred to let the younger people do the celebrating without the damper of his age. The jolt the prosecution had received was sufficient satisfaction for him for one day.

The lunch had gone well. Both Ballance and Penelope had time on their hands, having kept the day free for the court hearing, and agreed to meet at an Italian restaurant in Sandton.

At about the same time as Smith was meeting his employer, Doc, in Midrand, Penelope walked into Francesca's trattoria, her hair loosened from its severe office style and falling free to her shoulders. It shone gold in the sunshine spilling through the arched brick doorway. She had changed into a cool blue summer dress and at sight of her, Ballance felt an unexpected lift in his already good spirits.

She saw him wave from a booth against the far wall and picked her way between the crowded tables with a lithe swing of stride that made men look at her.

"Sorry I'm late," she smiled, slipping on to the bench facing him. "Whew! I could do with a drink, it's hot out there."

"I've just arrived myself," Ballance said. "What would you like? They have more or less everything, though I recommend their house wine because it comes in a stemmed glass the size of a jug. Or there's this ..." Triumphantly, he hauled a bottle of Clos Cabriére sauvignon blanc from an ice bucket. "… one of the best."

"Wine later," Penelope said, fussing with a tissue, "right now I'd love a VCB."

"A what?"

"A viciously cold beer," she laughed. "I'm dying of thirst."

Ballance ordered the beer from a passing waitress and poured it into an ice-frosted glass. Penelope drank down a third of it and licked her lips with a pink tongue tip.

"Aah ...!" She sighed with pleasure. "Why are you staring? Haven't you seen a woman drink beer before?"

"Sure," Ballance grinned, "but never with such voluptuous enjoyment. I thought you were the type who likes men to ply you with martinis, Moët and Martell."

"Me? Heavens no, I'm a simple country girl at heart and anyway, there aren't any men to ply." She drank down the rest of the beer.

"What!" in mock surprise. "None?"

"None I'd allow to ply me with that kind of stuff. Jeff, I'll have some of that lovely wine now. What are we going to eat?"

They chose thin slices of veal in a sauce of cream, mushrooms and herbs, and raised their glasses over the steaming plates in a toast to victory.

"You vindicated my instincts," she said. "I didn't think you looked the murderous type."

He reached to touch the back of her hand.

"I needed someone to believe in me. It wasn't a very pleasant episode."

They ate in silence, enjoying an easy familiarity after the courtroom tension. The wine dwindled and Ballance ordered another bottle.

Penelope opened her eyes wide in mock surprise. "You realise you'll have to finish most of that or I'll become drunk and disorderly?" she said, faking a frown.

"Fine. Then I'll commit myself to the care of my lawyer."

Penelope paused and the humour left her face. "Jeff, being serious, you remember what Ngwenya said to you in court this morning, and Max too. I don't know what's going on but it worries me. You must take care, watch your back. The murder rate in this benighted country is frightening enough, but that there are people who do it to pin the blame on others, is singularly evil."

In spite of the sunlight and cheerful chatter surrounding them, the atmosphere in the restaurant felt chill. In Penelope Fox's company, Ballance had forgotten the

39

reality out there. Someone had tried very methodically to have him taken out of circulation, and to do it had killed an unknown man, without compunction.

With a small shock, he remembered that his revolver was still in the possession of the police. He would have to fetch it. "Penny, I can't run away and I can't just forget it. I have to make an effort to find out what's behind all this. Who can I go to for help?"

"Why not talk it over with the police?" she said, suprising him. "They can't drop the matter either. They still have a murderer to find remember and, by rights, they should give you protection. Go and see Superintendent Louw."

Ballance's face expressed doubt. "Hell, it could have been the police who set me up."

"I don't think so, Jeff," Penelope said. "They're a rough and ready bunch and those of the old guard who survived the transition, were brutalised by the apartheid laws they had to impose for so long. But the SAPS is still all we have and it's improved a lot since the thugs were weeded out. There are many good cops around and I think Louw's one of them."

Ballance considered this. It was an avenue, perhaps the realistic one, but to go back to those stolid men in that dreary headquarters ... "I'll think about it. Can you help me?"

"Of course, Jeff, if possible." Penelope smiled and put her hand on his. "I'd like to but I can't see how, except on the legal side."

"Okay, let's forget the horrors now and celebrate some more."

Later he walked her to her car and she kissed his cheek in quick thanks before she opened the door to get in.

The scent of her subtle flowery perfume lingered as he drove home. Humming, he pushed the latchkey into the front door. At its touch the door moved.

Oh, Christ, not again! he thought and then remembered

the warning: watch your back. Adrenalin flooded his arteries.

He watched the door slowly swing wide. The passage lights were on, warm and welcoming. Moving in silence, he stepped forward and reached for an old naval shell case, used as a stand to hold an umbrella, a walking stick and a golf club, a putter.

He slid out the putter and walked forwards on tiptoe until he could see most of the living room. It looked empty. He charged in, the club held high to smash down on an intruder.

"Ah, there you are," said a voice behind him. Ballance whirled to see a figure walking towards him in the half-lit passage from the bedrooms. "I'm sorry. I had to use your bathroom. I was expecting you much earlier."

The figure came into the full light. It was Superintendent Louw. He eyed the raised club, faint amusement twitching his moustache.

"That's a very big backswing for putting," he said.

Ballance exhaled and lowered the putter, feeling temper replacing his tension.

"The police seem to think this is an open house," he said with distaste. "What the hell's it for this time?"

Louw was unperturbed. He reached for a briefcase lying on the couch. "I brought your passport and your firearm," he said, placing the document and the Smith and Wesson on the coffee table. "I've had it cleaned and oiled. It was the least I could do. The chambers are loaded, by the way."

Ballance looked at the gun and back at the policeman, not knowing what to make of the gesture. "Don't you need it for evidence? You still have a murderer to catch, don't you?"

"If we do, we can always collect it," the superintendent said, ignoring the sarcasm. "The problem is we don't know for certain that this is the gun that fired the fatal shot, because the bullet was so fragmented ballistics can't tell."

"And on such damning circumstantial evidence you charged me with murder?"

Louw felt uncomfortable. Ballance was making it difficult for him but he supposed the man couldn't be blamed for that. "Mr Ballance, can we sit down, please? I would like to talk to you, off the record."

With reluctance, Ballance replaced the putter in the shell case and moved to an armchair. The superintendent perched on the front of the settee and leaned forward with his elbows on his knees.

"I can understand your anger," he said, "but please realise this is not easy for me either. I assure you that if the magistrate had not dismissed the case against you today, I would have asked the Attorney-General to withdraw the charge. I had real doubts, which is why I released you without bail. Ngwenya's somewhat melodramatic appearance confirmed them."

Ballance opened his mouth to speak.

The superintendent held up a hand. "Please hear me out. What I am saying is confidential and I trust you to keep it so. I was never happy with this case because it was too circumstantial, but," he shrugged, "the Attorney-General was insistent. Then this morning, a few minutes before you went into the court, I learned something that gave me a strong suspicion the evidence against you was fabricated."

"What was it, Superintendent? What made you suspect?"

"I can't tell you that."

"Superintendent, it's *me* who was up there in the dock facing years in bloody prison! I have a right to know."

The cynical old policeman looked at the idealistic intellectual for a few moments then made a decision. He clasped his hands and frowned at the fist. "How much can I trust you? You're an outspoken liberal, with no reason to like the police, even if they are accountable to an ANC government now."

Ballance recalled what Penelope had said, "They're not all bad, go to Louw."

"I'm a South African, Superintendent, like you. Like you, I'm very worried about the killing, criminal and political, upsetting our fragile stability. If you're trying to do something about it, you can trust me."

"Thank you." Louw spoke as if reading a statement. "This afternoon I was able to confirm what I suspected this morning. The two witnesses who said they saw you in Hillbrow are both paid agents for the security division of the Criminal Investigation Department, and they were told what to say. They've never seen you and neither of them were in that part of Hillbrow on that day."

The sheer effrontery brought Ballance to his feet. He was so angry he wanted to lash out. He paced across the room. "The fucking security police!" he hissed.

"No," Superintendent Louw said, "not the security police. They were closed down long ago. The CID—"

"And you know they're up to their same old tricks under another name!" Ballance interrupted.

"The CID have already begun investigating the witnesses," the superintendent went on. "It was somebody inside the security division who put them up to it."

"Well, who the hell was it? And why?"

"That's among the things I want to find out. Will you help me?"

Ballance flopped into an armchair. The day had been too full of shocks. What he needed, he decided, was a stiff drink. He stood up and walked to a rosewood cabinet in the corner, poured himself a large whiskey and was about to sip it when he realised he was being discourteous. "A drink, Superintendent?"

"Brandy and soda with a dash of lime, thank you."

Ballance clattered ice into a squat crystal glass, mixed the drink and gave it to him, then slumped back into his armchair, still simmering.

"I don't see how I can help you," he said. "I'm a mere businessman and lecturer, not a private eye and I have no access to the CID."

"You also have an inquiring mind and two other things which give you a head start. You want to know, as much as we do, who is trying to fix you, and nobody else but you and Ngwenya can work out why they want to. You're also the one person Ngwenya might contact and I very much want to talk to him."

"What are you looking for, Superintendent? What do you expect to find?"

"I don't know for sure. I think we might find some worms in the security apple, diehard radicals using official resources for their own ends."

"What ends?"

"Sabotaging the new set-up, the multiracial government ... your guess is as good as mine, but they don't seem to like the way things are going here. Maybe they just want to put a scare into the left. Maybe they want to squash them. Next, it will be the moderates. They could become big trouble."

"You mean a third force, Superintendent? The right-wing underground whose existence everybody connected with the old government has been strenuously denying for decades?" In spite of his anger, Ballance felt a prick of professional interest.

Superintendent Louw rolled the tumbler between the upright palms of his large hands and stared into it for a moment. He looked up at Ballance from under bushy brows. "*Ja*, maybe so, Mr Ballance. There's no proof but there have been just too many unexplained killings for an old policeman like me to ignore, going right back to Robert Smith, Rick Turner and David Webster. Now there's this fresh run of assassinations and multiple shootings in the townships for no rhyme or reason. A lot of it is by gunmen who just vanish like mist. How?"

"Policemen from the old guard?"

The superintendent stared back. "Could be. Maybe. Some at least. Maybe army people too. You remember the army's admission back in the Goniwe inquest, that targeting politically difficult citizens was made official policy?"

"Yes, and I remember how they went on supporting the Renamo rebellion against the Mozambique government for years after they were supposed to stop, and how they mounted a farcical coup attempt in the Seychelles. There was the so-called Civil Cooperation Bureau. Then there were those hit squad raids into Lesotho and Botswana and Zimbabwe and those never-explained murders on that secret police base on a farm north of Pretoria, Vlakplaas. I could go on and on ..."

Louw's face twisted with disgust at the mention of the CCB, the undercover unit with an incongruous title, which became a monstrous law unto itself under the apartheid regime: prosecutor, jury, judge and executioner rolled into one. He emptied his glass in one swallow. "You're right," he said, "there's a lot still to answer for but believe me, Mr Ballance, however crude the police force sometimes is, there are still honest professional policemen. They are frustrated as hell. Every time there's a case that smells of insider politics, left or right, we're blocked. Some fat general, or commission of inquiry, is appointed to investigate and soon the file starts gathering dust. Most of us just want to start operating like a real police force again."

He sounds sincere, Ballance thought, and he is experienced. Anyway, do I have a choice? No. "One thing," he said, "if Temba does get in touch with me and agrees to see you, what will you do with him? I mean, will he be safe or will you detain him or something?"

"Detain him? No, we won't do anything like that." Superintendent Louw shook his head. "He hasn't done anything wrong, as far as I know."

"Right. Fill in the background and tell me what I should do."

Chapter Five

A week after Superintendent Louw's visit, Ballance had pushed his brief wrestle with the law to the back of his mind under the pressure of making up for lost time on the eve of a long university vacation. The newspaper fuss over the murder mystery and his dramatic release had drifted to the inside pages. No word had come from Ngwenya and he was nagged by worry about his friend's safety.

For his own reassurance, Ballance slept with his pistol on the bedside table, though he doubted he would ever be able to shoot anyone. He had fired the thing once and hoped that if he had to fire it again, the noise alone would scare any intruder as much as it had scared him.

Marking papers late into the night, the memory of Penelope Fox, her sharp mind and her physicality, distracted him. He was diffident about calling her, telling himself he had to clear his backlog of work, knowing it was an excuse.

He did not want to become involved. There had been a succession of women, all of whom moved on, to his relief, when they discovered he preferred independence to serious emotional ties.

Penny was different though; none of the usual flirtation, no seductive body language. She was attractive without seeming to be aware of it, without exuding sex appeal. There would be no quick fun and games with her, Ballance decided. A relationship would be as serious as the law and that meant a commitment he did not want. He wanted a few more years of freedom before anchoring himself, if ever.

***

For several days, Penelope Fox wondered about her ex-client's failure to resume contact, then tried to shrug him into her past and concentrate on her career. It left no time for anything more than casual friendships.

It was not easy she found, with exasperation. He stuck in her mind like a burr in fur, the smile pulling down a corner of his mouth, the thatch of tousled hair, clear grey eyes beneath startling black eyebrows.

The man was intriguing but he didn't look like a long-term prospect, she thought. She sought stability and a career, with a husband if possible but single if necessary, and she wore a businesslike manner like a shield against men who wanted her slim body.

Several affairs lay behind her, one of such intensity it had left her disillusioned, the others passing dalliances, more to satisfy physical need than from affection. Now she tried to avoid them even when her body urged her on, because they made her feel tarnished.

I'm stuck in a classic bloody female dilemma, she told herself. If I keep on cold- shouldering the men, I might pass up the genuine one I can live with. If I don't, I'll get a reputation as tawdry as a hotel mattress.

Though drawn by Ballance's obvious intelligence and easy amiability, she saw no future there. He looked a confirmed bachelor, destined to grow old in the dull corridors of business and academia. Either the good ones were married or on the shelf, she commiserated with herself. There must be something wrong with me.

***

Twelve men gathered in a farmhouse halfway up the northern slopes of the Zoutpansberg range of mountains in the Limpopo Province. Outside the air was soggy with heat and humidity. Indoors, beneath its high-pitched thatch roof and deep eaves resting on massive log beams,

47

the house was deliciously cool. The stone walls were old and thick and layered with many coats of whitewash.

They sat at a long pine table, worn with use, on a wide stone-flagged stoep in the shade of sweet-smelling thatch. From here they could gaze out over the sun-bleached vista of baobab-studded bush stretching to the Limpopo River in shimmering heat waves. On the rough walls behind them hung trophies of the hunt, mounted heads of kudu, nyala, bushbuck, tusked boar, lion, leopard, and a rhino with a record-length horn.

Two hundred yards down the slope a young white man, with a hunting rifle slung from his shoulder, patrolled inside an electrified security fence. Out of sight, behind the house and on either side, other young men patrolled.

The twelve were farmers, businessmen and other professionals from many parts of South Africa. Five were English-speakers and the others Afrikaners, all fluent in both languages. All were past middle age and all had risen to prominence. Some were national figures. One was a Member of Parliament who avoided the limelight and was regarded by the public as a mild conservative. He looked much younger than his sixty years, a small black-haired, black-eyed man with sharp features. Another was the Doctor, now dressed in the everyday garb of the Bushveld farmer, *velskoene*, khaki shirt, long khaki trousers.

They relaxed in comfort, some smoking pipes, or cigarettes, like any meeting of countrymen discussing the weather, crops, prices and the greed of the market agents, switching from English to Afrikaans. They had been talking revolution and now they were listening to the Doc describing the bungled attempt to liquidate a senior ANC backroom figure and compromise a liberal academic in a single killing.

"We have spent a lot of time on little brush strokes like that," added their chairman, a man with a penchant for analogy, "We must move to the big canvas now and start painting with bold strokes. That incident has generated a lot of unwanted publicity in the media and aroused the interest of the police. Now they suspect there's more behind it and that's not good. Not yet."

"We cannot stop targeting individuals just because one job went wrong," said another man. "It is very much part of the whole operation. It's worked like a charm so far, they're scared stiff because they don't know who'll be next."

"True, but it's not our main thrust and it absorbs a lot of money and effort. It is time now to start the main-stream operations."

"That man must be disciplined," an ascetic, rake-thin farmer broke in, an ultra-conservative in everything from sex to religion. "The man who buggered up the Jo'burg liquidation. He put us all at risk with his stupid failure."

"We've enough to do without ..." the Chairman began, then hesitated and turned to Doc, "... what do you think?"

"I have already given instructions to the operative in charge to discipline him. The bungler can't point back to us, the cell system is intact," Doc said.

Airy-fairy idealists, Doc sighed to himself. They couldn't make a pot of tea without a woman to fill the kettle. With more leadership experience than any of them, he resigned himself to prodding them into action without ruffling their egos. All were needed for their influence and connections, but they had to work faster.

"Good. Then let's get on with other matters," the Chairman said.

"What's the overall picture at this moment in time," the MP asked. "How far have we got?"

The Chairman paused to collect his thoughts, gazing out over the bushveld, part of the Canaan that would be theirs before much longer. It had to be before the ANC further consolidated its power.

49

"Most of the actors are on stage and some are performing with great success," he said, forging another analogy, "the big scene, the final act, is still being prepared and so far we have encountered no insurmountable difficulties. I foresee a successful launch but cannot yet tell you when. I hope quite soon."

He came down to details. "As you know, the first stage, eliminating movers and shakers among the opposition, has been in progress for some time. It has gone well apart from this latest one. Targeting some people on the right as well as the left, in all race groups, works because it generates insecurity right across the political spectrum.

"In the second stage we have had great success in stimulating the inherent enmity between ethnic groups and urban factions. The Inkatha-ANC feud is the best example. It has slowed down in the past few years but our agents are about to fan it back to life."

The Chairman paused to scan the faces around the table. "Watch the media," he said. "In the next few weeks you will see a sharp rise in violence in the townships, the urban areas and elsewhere. It will be maintained until the country is in a state of near anarchy."

"Isn't it risky using white agents in black areas?" one of the twelve asked. "Won't it give us away if one is caught?"

The Doctor cut in, "We use whites where their presence is unremarkable. For the rest we use black agents. They're all mercenaries who cannot be traced to us because of our cut-off cell system."

"For the third stage," the Chairman continued, "we are distributing large quantities of weaponry, including assault rifles, rockets, grenades and explosives among the black population.

"We are not doing it from charity, I assure you. They're paying for it but they pay less than the going rate because we can get so many cheap weapons from across the border. Distribution is easy. We let the agents take a good commission and AK-47s are so much in demand, they have almost become a factor in the Mozambique economy."

His comment drew smiles and a few chuckles from the assembly. They were ready to pay for their political ambitions but it was nice to know some of their money was coming back.

"We also have good friends in the United States and Europe, most in Germany, France and Belgium. You'll be pleased to know that they are supplying us with some of the most modern arms available. They are shipped to us in containers under cover of various manifests and our members in Customs and Excise will see they get through unchecked.

"An important spin-off from giving guns to blacks is the spread of violent crime from black into white areas. We have seen that as more blacks discover how easy robbery is in white suburbs, they expand it to political action.

"It plays straight into our hands with a panicked white retreat into conservatism and a backlash against black rulers who cannot control crime. The police will not able to stop it because the government has let the police force run down so far. It doesn't have the manpower, money or organisation to do its job any more. Anyway, many policemen are with us."

He paused for several minutes while the host's wife and two maids placed coffee and rusks on the long pine table. White independence will continue to need black servants, Doc thought, but that would be arranged. The servants left and the Chairman continued.

"The last stage of undermining this bastardised government will be an uprising of anarchy, so widespread they will be forced to declare martial law. Our supporters in the security forces will push hard for it and some are of such high rank they cannot be ignored. That," he aimed a finger at the MP, "is where you and our brothers in parliament come in."

The MP nodded.

"The imposition of martial law with black and white troops and police being dragged into the fighting and shooting both ways", the Chairman went on, "will disrupt the economy, create public disillusionment, scare away foreign investors and set the ANC, PAC, Inkatha and all the other black fanatics and communists at each other's throats. It will do much damage to government's reputation, such as it is. Nobody will want to touch a South Africa beginning to look like another Angola or Algeria.

"All of this sets the scene for us," he said, "I cannot say too much yet though I can tell you we have strong allies who, like us, want their own independent fatherland. They are black, but no matter. Once this is over, each will all be in his own republic."

He stood to stretch cramped muscles and favoured his colleagues with a benign smile, anticipating their reaction to his next statement. "There's just one more thing. Our revolution is making money."

The others looked at him in surprise.

"Our Mozambique friends need certain goods we can supply when most of their backers have deserted them. They are paying us in ivory and some rhino horn. We have found an international outlet and our profit is about a thousand per cent."

They laughed. All that and a Canaan too.

They talked until it was time to move into the cool of the house for lunch. Afterwards they departed for their homes one by one to avoid attracting undue attention.

***

Some fifteen minutes by road from Jeffrey Ballance's home, but less than two miles away as the crow flies, Temba Ngwenya pondered his unknown enemies, his safety, and what he might do about both.

Although so close, the two men could have been continents apart. Ballance's home was in an elegant townhouse complex in select Sandton, the satellite city favoured by Johannesburg's commercial aristocrats. It was ringed by a high security wall with manicured hydrangeas and clipped lawns on the sidewalks outside, along two quiet side streets shaded by many trees. Inside the complex, the townhouses shared a large secluded garden. Each had its own off-street entrance and a garage protected by electronic doors. By night, an armed watchman backed up by rapid response security guards guarded the complex. It had cost a small fortune and Ballance was still paying.

From where Ngwenya stood, moodily thinking, with his hands thrust deep into the pockets of his tattered trousers, he looked out on a stinking view of garbage-strewn streets and open sewers between dilapidated buildings and flimsy shacks.

The old house he stood in bore the scars left by fire. It was in a dirt road a few blocks from Times Square in Alexandra township, whose grubbiness belied its grandiose name. By day, the road was full of people and children played on either side of the runnels of filth flowing into a festering stream. By night, it was empty and silent save for a few drunks and daring stragglers. Alexandra was dangerous then and the police seldom ventured there.

The house was the home of a local ANC official. Ngwenya was indistinguishable in the mass of struggling people swelled by thousands of new squatters. He was safe for now but could not stay indefinitely. He had to go out to start looking for whoever was hunting him. He had no idea who they might be; there were too many options.

The memory of his close brush with death made him shiver. The man who had been helping him look at schools in Hillbrow, Jakes Mabuza, an ANC organiser there, had borrowed his jacket to meet a friend in a pub that insisted its customers wear them. Ngwenya had forgotten to take identifying letters and papers from the inside pocket. Mabuza had not come back. Two days later a body had been found and identified as him, Temba Ngwenya.

Ngwenya realised he had stirred a hornet's nest by denouncing, in public, several schools which were still trying to exclude black children by upping their fees and other tricks. He was in no doubt he had generated even greater fury with his brazen appearance in court.

He prayed he had lost his pursuers in spite of his appearance in court to get Ballance off the hook. Why had they picked on Jeffrey? He was sometimes outspoken, it was true, but an academic, not an activist and, in Ngwenya's opinion, his politics were flaccid. Maybe this kick in his academic arse would make him sit up and do something.

He had to contact Jeff, but how?

Whoever they were, his pursuers were obviously ruthless and organised. He assumed they were diehard rightwingers but in the political morass of present-day South Africa they could be almost anybody, even ANC stalwarts whom he had fingered for corruption. They must be watching Jeff like hawks in the hope of finding him, Ngwenya, maybe including a phone tap in his home. So approaching him there was out of the question.

Jeff was still in danger and had to be warned. Ngwenya recalled the courtroom scene and Ballance's two legal representatives, Adelman, the little advocate who quizzed him, and the woman lawyer.

They might well be watching Adelman too. The woman seemed the best bet. What was her name?

Ngwenya turned from the depressing view and rummaged through newspapers on the old kitchen table, the only piece of furniture in the room apart from an iron-and-wire frame bed. He found the tabloid he wanted and turned to the small type at the foot of the report of the dismissal of charges against Ballance.

"... instructed by Ms Penelope Fox of Farragher, Wolhuter and Dunkeld" he read.

At dusk, he left the house and picked his way down the road between the strewn paper, cans, plastic, slops and sewage. In a worn old overcoat too large for him, torn cotton trousers and a woollen balaclava rolled up to form a cap, he looked like any other impoverished black on Alexandra's streets. Nestling in a soft leather holster clipped inside his belt in the small of his back, was a small CZ semi-automatic pistol.

He appeared to wander without purpose while he made his way steadily towards the fast food shops, cafés and illegal shebeens in Wynberg, a tatty suburb of small factories, wholesalers, garages and second-hand stores locked up and abandoned by their white staff at night.

He was looking for a telephone booth that might still have a directory in it. Most were stolen for toilet paper.

CHAPTER SIX

Captain Lucky Ndzimandze was so nervous, sweat beaded his upper lip. He paused outside Superintendent Louw's door to take several deep breaths. What in hell did Sergeant Greeff think he was up to, the crazy white man. Whatever it was, Greeff was in deep shit now. He tugged at his jacket to smooth it over his lank frame and rapped on the door with his knuckles.

"*Kom binne.*" From the peremptory tone Ndzimandze guessed the boss was in a bad mood. His temper had been mean for the past week, since the fouled-up court case. He twisted the doorknob and marched in.

The superintendent looked up from a brown police file and noticed his captain's parade posture and carefully blank expression. It did nothing to improve his humour. "Yes?" in blunt Afrikaans.

"Sir, about the witnesses in the Ngwenya case ... I mean, the man we thought was Ngwenya."

"Well?"

"The two men who say they saw the accused have disappeared, sir."

"Disappeared? How can they disappear, man? They're bloody CID."

"Yes, sir. Not full-time, sir. They're agents. The CID say they can't find them. They've just ... vanished, not turned up at work and the university."

"But damn it, Lucky ..." Superintendent Louw smacked the top of his desk in irritation then reminded himself it was not the captain's fault, he was the messenger.

"Brigadier Hamman is very upset about it, sir. He's ordered a search and a full investigation." Hamman was the chief of the local security division.

"What about the man who tipped off Greeff to the witnesses?"

"Sir, they can't find him."

"You mean he's disappeared too?"

"No, sir. They don't know who he is. All of them say they know nothing about it. Greeffie won't tell us the man's name. Says he's damned if he's going help an investigation into himself on false suspicions, and drag an innocent man into it too."

Superintendent Louw rose to his feet like a gathering storm.

"Greef says that, does he? I'll have to have a word with Mr Greeff."

"Yes, sir. But that's not all, sir." Ndzimandze could feel the radiation of the superintendent's anger and his agitation grew. What he still had to say would make his chief positively torrid. The superintendent glared at him, waiting.

"It's about the dead man's fingerprints, sir."

"Well? What about them?"

"They were planted, sir."

"Planted? What do you mean, Captain?"

"They were planted in Ngwenya's file."

Superintendent Louw stared, stunned.

"How on earth could that happen? Those files are like the Bible, man, sacrosanct. Who planted them?"

"It couldn't have been Greeff, or those witnesses, and Brigadier Hamman swears it wasn't the security men. Someone took prints from Mabuza's corpse and filed them in Fingerprint Records as Ngwenya's and put a copy in the security file on Ngwenya. Security found out only when they double-checked the dead man's prints taken at the post mortem against Ngwenya's file."

"You mean they were already there when Greeff

checked the body after those kids found it?"

"Yes, sir. It must have been planned and done well in advance, before the body was found."

Superintendent Louw sat down as if his legs had lost their strength. The import of the captain's words shook him. Of all the things in his experience, of all techniques in solving crimes, the most infallible were fingerprints, inviolate. They were the most valuable investigation tools, more useful than DNA in his opinion. Nobody tampered with those.

Someone had. Someone cunning. Someone manipulating the police to do their work for them. Someone who knew police business inside out and more, because it was next to impossible to doctor fingerprint records. He noticed the captain still standing, sweating, and irritably motioned him to a chair. The captain perched on its edge, relieved the worst was over, or so he hoped.

"Where is Greeff now?" Superintendent Louw asked.

"I don't know, sir. Since you carpeted him he's been loafing around the station or going out for coffee."

"Find him, Lucky, and bring him here. Let's try to sort out this thing now, once and for all."

***

Sergeant Stefan Greeff was not in the Brixton station. A uniformed constable at the desk said he thought he had seen Greeff going out about an hour earlier, he did not know where to. Ndzimandze began the round of the cafés frequented by the police for their coffee and gossip breaks.

Greeff was sweating too. He was full of anger at having been rocketed by Superintendent Louw for his uncritical acceptance of the two witnesses' statements. He was bitter because of his growing suspicion that his friends had left him carrying the can.

But more than anything, he was worried.

At the age of 45, facing a bleak future on his pathetic

pay and pension, he was frustrated and full of resentment at the system that refused to acknowledge his talents. So when a former working acquaintance of the old Security Police days had approached him to do occasional deep cover assignments – "Nothing that will interfere with your normal work, Greeffie, might even help it" – he had jumped at the chance.

Being appreciated had hooked him, not the extra cash, although there was quite a lot of it. The man who had baited the hook had done his job well: he knew Greeff had been transferred out of the old SP because he could not make the grade and he saw there could be profit from Greeff's injured dignity.

He told his connections, who reported to their local director, Smith, who added Greeff to a list of usable people in useful places. They tried him with several minor tasks, which he completed competently enough. Greeff suspected the work was somewhat irregular, but as it was aimed at nailing slippery bloody communists, what the hell. He pressed for more responsibility.

Now the chunky sergeant could not find the SP man who had enrolled him and pointed him to the witnesses. He wanted to warn him that Brixton's Superintendent Louw was on the warpath. He dared not ask about his contact's whereabouts more than casually for fear it might expose their liaison.

He went to the places where they met when he was briefed for a job, or to receive payment in crisp cash, in several downtown street bars and hotels. Nothing. His contact had faded like morning dew.

In a bar in Orange Grove, a grubby hole-in-the-wall once frequented by bus conductors and beer-and-malmsey drinkers in the apartheid days, he noticed two men in sports jackets and slacks, fit young fellows with Sundance moustaches and the hard stamp of heavy gymnasium work on their bodies. They looked familiar. They had glanced at him but Greeff did not find that unusual.His own physique often attracted interest, the powerful blocky build of a front row forward.

Two bars later, he saw them again over the rim of his beer glass, still glancing at him, and put it down to pub-crawl coincidence. When they strolled into the next bar he visited, he realised it might be more than coincidence. It did not bother him; he could handle himself in brawls and had the added reassurance of the pistol holstered under his left arm. He went home.

He was concerned the next morning when he slipped out to check at hotels in Rosebank and found the two young men already in the first one, sipping early beers in the lounge, just waiting. They pretended not to notice him.

He considered confronting them then thought better of it. He could not afford to draw attention to himself. He turned on his heel and walked out.

At the next pub, he settled his bulk on a bar stool and ordered a beer. Five minutes later, while he was wondering where next to look for his contact, one of the men peered over the bar's batwing doors and turned away.

Enough's enough, Greeff decided. He drained his beer and left the bar to confront them. They were not in the neighbouring lounge, a bleak room of veneered furniture and dark carpet, where prostitutes paraded in the evenings.

He strode out of the hotel to his old Ford Cortina parked in a nearby loading zone, worrying about this new complication. Who could those guys be? Cops sent by Superintendent Louw to tail him, or CID men? Maybe he should go to the superintendent and tell him the whole story, or to his former SP chief.

He opened the driver's door, swung in behind the wheel, and fastened the seat belt.

Before he could insert the ignition key, the passenger door and a rear door opened and the two large men climbed in very fast, one next to him, the other right behind. He reached for his shoulder holster but the seat belt strap hampered the movement. Then he saw the pistol half hidden in the hand held low at his side, a little black .25 automatic popgun but more than lethal enough this close.

"Drive," the holder of the gun said, smiling.

Greeff could not believe what was happening. He looked at the pedestrians passing by on the sidewalk but nobody gave him a glance. In Johannesburg, people refused to become involved. His brain, trained for emergencies, sped through the options: wait for the opportunity, let them think I'm scared, let them relax.

"Who are you? What do you want?" he demanded, trying to sound frightened.

"Just drive," the man commanded.

Greeff edged the Cortina into the traffic. He considered pushing his foot flat to reach a speed at which they dared not shoot the driver, but the streets were too busy.

"Where are we going?" he asked.

"To meet friends. Don't worry. Your pal from security wants to see you but he can't break cover. Turn left here."

Greeff felt a touch of relief. Just he and his contact knew of their link so the contact must have sent them. But why all the secrecy and the gun?

He turned left into a tree-lined street deeply shaded by tall apartment blocks.

"There." The gunman pointed to a curbside space beneath overhanging branches. Greef steered the Cortina in, switched off the engine and reached for the safety belt release. "Why the gun?" he asked to distract attention, his right arm tensed. "You know I'm also undercover."

The man behind him held a kitchen knife, whose eight-inch blade was honed, narrow and sharp. He had already made a half-inch slit in the vinyl behind the driver's seat and inserted the blade horizontally between the springs, so the needle-sharp point was poised next to

Greeff's lower back, with just the thin plastic cushioning between.

Now he rammed it the rest of the way with a short powerful thrust of his right arm. The blade slid through muscle into Greeff's spine. The knifeman jerked it sideways, severing the spinal cord, pulled it out and slipped it into an armpit sheath.

Searing pain overwhelmed Greeff, blinding him, robbing him of breath, wiping away all thought. The frayed tip of every nerve in his body seemed to focus on the small of his back. He flung his head up and his mouth gaped but no sound came except a clicking gurgle. He tried to arch his back and scrabbled to reach with his hands but his torso was rigid with shock and his hips and legs would not move.

The men climbed out of the car. One took something out of a pocket, dropped it in the tray between the front seats and closed the door. They walked away without haste under the concealing trees.

Through his massive agony, a small part of Greeff's consciousness detected the slight rattle of the object in the tray. His head lolled forward and he saw it, an obscene ovoid thing, chequered like a bar of chocolate.

With his last thought, he registered it as a hand grenade, fragmentation, Russian made, and stared at it, past fear.

CHAPTER SEVEN

Penelope Fox kicked off her shoes, dumped her fat legal briefcase on the couch and flopped down next to it. The case was full of papers she had brought to study in the uninterrupted quiet of her apartment. The last damned thing I want to do tonight, she thought. I'm tired and what I need is a drink, bath, supper and bed, with a good book. She heaved herself up and slouched into the bedroom, finding some consolation in its view over the outward end of the Wanderers golf course, a broad green belt between houses and apartment blocks. Having an address on Corlett Drive was almost more than she could afford, a bit rich for a country girl from the Cape, but she had decided to enjoy her money while it was still worth something.

If she was going to jog today, it had better be now or not at all, she thought. Any later would be too late; it was unwise for a woman to be alone on the streets after dark. A quick run would sharpen her mind for work.

Penelope stripped, slipped on a runner's bra and briefs, donned Nike shoes and a wool tracksuit of electric blue with vertical yellow stripes. In this town's traffic one had to be visible. She trapped her long hair behind her head with a rubber band, pocketed her small pepper spray and hung her apartment key on a string around her neck, inside the tracksuit top.

***

Ngwenya watched her emerge from the glass doors of the apartment block, cross Corlett Drive at a pedestrian light and set off uphill past the expansive greenery of the

Wanderers Club grounds. He had hoped to catch her attention near her apartment block but its entrance was too full of light. He followed at a trot to see where she was going.

She ran with a long easy stride and he was in time to see her turn left into Rudd. He thought she would run around the club grounds and come back to Corlett down one of the side streets. He strolled back and turned into Irene, thinking times had indeed changed. Not so long ago a passing police van would have picked up a black man looking as disreputable as he did. Now they couldn't care less, nor do much about it if they did.

He was on a corner when he saw her coming, coasting on the downslope, and waited under a tree by a gate.

"Miss Fox," he called out when she was about ten paces away.

***

Startled, Penelope glanced in the direction of the bearded, scruffy black man in an overcoat standing in the deepening shadow of a tree. Her immediate instinct was to run like hell and she veered away.

He called again, urgent now. "Miss Fox, please! It's me, Temba Ngwenya."

The name stopped her. She braked and peered back at the man from a safe ten paces, arms akimbo and her chest heaving.

"Ngwenya? You were the man in court, the one who was supposed to be dead?"

"That's right. Miss Fox, I'm sorry to approach you like this but I need your help."

"Why couldn't you come to my office? This is a hell of a way to ask for legal advice."

He came closer, moving out from beneath the tree into the pale twilight where she recognised the angular bearded face and keen eyes.

"I am very sorry, Miss Fox, but I dare not come into

the open. My life is in danger, as I said in the court, and Jeffrey Ballance's is too."

Penelope studied him, crossing her arms. She felt vulnerable standing in this empty darkening street.

"Do you know where I live?" she asked, reaching a sudden decision.

"Yes. I watched you leave just now."

"Follow me. When I switch off the hall lights, come in and up the stairs to the third floor. Don't use the lift, someone else might be in it."

She turned and jogged away at a slower pace, giving him time to follow. In the foyer, she switched off the ceiling lamp and waited at the foot of the stairs in the corner until he slipped in. She turned on the lamp and took the lift.

He was at her heels when she opened her door.

"You're not going to try to rape me or something, are you?" she said, half in jest as she closed the door.

Ngwenya grinned, displaying even white teeth.

"*Aikona miesies*, not at all, ma'am," he mocked, caricaturing the English accent of an uneducated African, "I em a good keffir."

She smiled back, embarrassed.

"Please come in, sit down. Would you like something to drink? Tea, coffee?"

He declined. She poured herself a glass of fruit juice and chose an armchair across the room from him.

"Let's have it, Mr Ngwenya. How can I help you?"

"Miss Fox, it's a long and complicated story and I'm not sure it would be good for your health to know it. I'm pretty certain they don't know I'm here but if they find out, you could be marked too—"

"Who are 'they'?"

"I don't know that myself yet. It seems to be some people trying to wreck the peace in South Africa, but my reason for coming to you is that I must warn Jeff. I didn't have time in the court and I don't think he took me seriously. I can't go straight to him; they're sure to be watching him to try to catch me."

Penelope listened with growing alarm. Ballance in danger? Some mysterious bunch of anarchists? Such melodramatic cloak-and-dagger stuff sounded weird here in the lamp-lit comfort of her living room. "What do you want me to do?"

"Set up a meeting for me with Jeff as soon as possible. Find a place where we can talk. Warn him to make very sure he's not being followed."

Penelope considered this without enthusiasm. The last thing she wanted was to become involved in politics or intrigue. Her thoughts returned to Ballance. He was her client, and she liked him. And Ngwenya was in dead earnest; he had already risked much to pluck Jeffrey out of trouble.

"The only place I can think of is here," she said. "He's never been to my flat and has no connection with me except as his lawyer, and that case is finished. I can pick you up somewhere in my car and bring you into the basement parking. You can come up the stairs again."

It was as good a venue as any. Ngwenya could not think of a better one. "Okay," he said, "you get hold of Jeff. Tell him it's essential we meet here. I'll call you every evening at about eight o'clock until you've contacted him and set a date."

She took him out of the flat through the service door. Concealed by darkness, he left by the outside fire escape and climbed over several garden walls to reach the street.

***

Superintendent Louw stood bent as if in pain, his shoulders hunched, which he was, but it was not physical pain. Hands thrust into the pockets of his suit jacket, he stared down at the mess and felt a deep, icy fury grow within him, filling his mind and making him clench his fists. He wanted to strike out and hurt and kill but there

66

was nothing tangible to vent his fury on.

He forced himself to be calm, to cut emotion out of his thinking and try to examine the thing before him dispassionately. He needed all the willpower generated by years of experience to persuade himself that it was just another victim, the corpse of another unfortunate caught in the wrong place at the wrong time. Not a Sergeant Stefan "Greeffie" Greeff.

They had been able to identify him first by his car registration after several telephone calls from anonymous flat residents reported an explosion and a smoking vehicle. When the police arrived, two traffic officers were holding back a small crowd and all the apartment windows overlooking the scene were closed.

They marked out a wide cordon with yellow police tape tied to stanchions. Confirmation came when a forensic investigator reached in to gingerly probe the pockets of the dead man's suit on the side away from the blast and withdrew a damaged wallet with Greeff's SAP identity card, still legible, just. Then they found his police pistol.

Greeff himself was almost unrecognisable. Shrapnel from the grenade a few inches from his left thigh had shredded that side of his body. The upholstery had disintegrated. The dashboard had been riddled, the glass of the windows blown into the street, and the punctured roof bowed up by the blast. Blood spattered the interior surfaces and pooled on the carpet under the seat. It was still warm and the smell was strong.

"One of yours, sir?" a gruff voice said beside him. The superintendent glanced up to see a heavyset man he recognised as a CID security division inspector, Donovan Bothma. They were always on the spot fast after explosions; part of their job.

"Yes. Stefan Greeff. One of my team."

"I'm very sorry, sir. It looks like a terrorist hit." He held out something like a small square of dark chocolate between his forefinger and thumb. "Piece of the shrapnel that came through the door on this side. A grenade, looks Russian."

Superintendent Louw straightened and stared into the man's eyes, as if seeking answers there.

"Why, Inspector? He was an ordinary, low profile policeman, not a politician. Why pick on him?"

The man shrugged, pulled down the corners of his mouth, raised his eyebrows and spread his hands at the same time in a demonstration of helplessness.

"Can't say, Superintendent, but it's a terrorist hit all right. Leave it to us, we'll find out."

"No."

The inspector was startled.

"No," Superintendent Louw repeated. "It's not terrorism. It's plain and simple murder. We'll handle it. Murder and Robbery, Brixton."

"But sir—"

"Go ahead with your investigation but don't get in my way. I want to know about everything you find and I'll do the same for you." He smiled to soften his words but it was bleak. "Two heads are better than one, right?"

The inspector shrugged again. "Okay, sir, if you say so. I'll have to tell my chief though."

"You do that. I'll speak to Brigadier Hamman too."

Gloved men in white were lifting the torn corpse from the Cortina to place it on a wheeled stretcher. They struggled with Greeff's weight and still loose limbs, despite the seat belts sheared clean from him by flying steel. They drew a plastic sheet over him and loaded the stretcher into the back of an ambulance, which drove away. Detectives worked meticulously around the car, picking up pieces of the grenade. One dusted what clean surfaces he could find inside for fingerprints.

"Death was instantaneous, he couldn't have known what hit him," Captain Ndzimandze said at the superintendent's shoulder.

"How could someone put a grenade right next to his left hand in a locked car without his knowing?" Superintendent Louw retorted.

Ndzimandze felt his ears burn. He hadn't thought of that. He decided to keep his mouth shut.

"Get extra men," the superintendent ordered, "Knock on every door in every block of flats within sight of the car and ask if they saw or heard anything. I doubt we'll get much joy out of these bloody troglodytes, but try, damn it."

"Sir."

"And tell forensics I want this job done with a fine-tooth comb. The doc must check out Greeff one thousand per cent for everything ... drugs, the lot. He may have been a fool but he was not downright stupid. I don't believe anyone could plant a bomb next to him and walk away. He must have been doped or something."

"Sir."

"Well, get on with it, man!"

"Sir!" Ndzimandze spun on his heel and strode to their car to use the radio, glad of something positive to do.

I don't know who the hell you are, Superintendent Louw promised himself, but I'll have you. I'll have you dead or alive for this. This has to be mixed up with the Ngwenya business. Greeff and the missing witnesses, the mystery SP contact, Hillbrow ... it's all too much for coincidence.

Ballance, he thought. Ballance is the link. I must see him.

CHAPTER EIGHT

On a sunny Thursday morning, two twenty-ton horse-and-trailer trucks laden with glazed face bricks rolled on their multiple wheels across the border from Swaziland, the little mountain kingdom trapped between Mozambique and South Africa.

One left from the Oshoek customs and immigration post in the western escarpment and headed across the bleak Highveld towards Johannesburg, three hundred and fifty kilometres away.

The other crossed at Jeppe's Reef in north-east Swaziland, followed the highway along the steaming Crocodile River Valley as far west as Nelspruit, then turned on to the northern route to Louis Trichardt more than six hundred kilometres distant.

They moved at never more than eighty kilometres an hour, the legal limit for heavy vehicles. They were well tended and the big chrome ERF logos on their broad radiator grilles glinted in the bright day, the paintwork polished, the multiple double tyres almost new, the massive loads packed tight in straw under lashed tarpaulins.

The drivers of both were white men, which with the trucks' clean appearance, gave them a seven-in-ten chance of the police or army waving them through the roadblocks sometimes set up to check for everything from roadworthiness to smuggled weapons.

Not that the drivers were worried about being stopped. Obvious freight loads were seldom examined even at top security roadblocks, and who would want to unload and look at thousands of bricks?

Their main worry was a breakdown or accident that might make it necessary to transfer the cargoes to other vehicles. They closed their minds to the nightmare thought of overturning and drove with exemplary care.

The freighter going north started first, passing the document check at Jeppe's Reef when the border post opened, and made good time until stopped at a road-block almost halfway along its route in hot, hilly country north of Bushbuckridge.

Orange plastic cones marked the entry to a zigzag in the highway, marked by mud-coloured military trans-ports to prevent vehicles speeding through. Soldiers with R1 and R4 rifles at the ready, stood guard well off the road at either end and watched the policemen check each vehicle.

The driver braked and changed down, slowing the truck with a throaty blare of the engine. A policeman signalled him to pull up on the verge and took the truck's registration number to a van to be verified by computer.

Another policeman walked around the long horse-and-trailer, peered underneath and climbed up behind the cab to look at the load. Satisfied, he paused to chat to the driver.

"Bricks from Swaziland?" he said. "Man, that's a helluva long way to bring bricks when we make them here."

"Cheaper," the driver explained, offering the constable a cigarette. "We sell them for about half what you pay here. Remember that when you build a house some day."

"That so, hey? Hell, we get ripped off in this country."

A man at the computer van gave the thumbs up and the policeman stepped to the ground.

"Okay," he called, waving the truck on. "Drive with care, hey."

The driver negotiated the zigzag and the ERF's growl rose to a whine as it gathered speed.

Hours later, after the painstaking haul up the Drakensberg escarpment from Tzaneen, he turned east near the entrance to the dozing town of Louis Trichardt, nestled picture-pretty against the Zoutpansberg mountains.

Night had fallen when he reached Thohoyandou, the ramshackle capital of what was supposed to be an independent homeland until brought back into South Africa after the fall of apartheid. He travelled at low speed until he found a dark side road in the random urban scatter along the highway, turned down it and drove the truck into a large warehouse, well back from the road.

Tall doors swung shut behind him and his shoulders sagged with relief and fatigue, his part done. Now the tricky work would begin.

By this time, the other driver's work had also ended, abruptly.

He had left Oshoek at two o'clock in the afternoon and followed secondary highways to join the multilane N4 freeway at Middelburg. From there he hummed along in the company of other freighters and cars, glancing often at his watch, until just after sunset when he reached Benoni. There he turned off into the grubby necklace of gold mines, towns, suburbs and industrial parks of the East Rand, near Johannesburg.

He checked his watch for the last time as he approached a set of traffic lights between a sprawl of darkened factories. The ERF grumbled along, the lights changed to red and he stopped with hissing brakes.

The cab doors jerked open and two men jumped in without a word, one from each side. They were right on time. The driver nodded a greeting to them and slid to the middle of the seat to make space for one of them, who engaged the gears and pulled away when the lights turned to green.

Both the newcomers were black and wore dark clothing and balaclavas, the ubiquitous headgear of the South

African underworld.

The new driver took the freighter on a circuitous route through deserted streets to a small bluegum plantation at the foot of an old mine dump.

There all three stepped down from the high cab.

"Sorry," said the driver, "we have to make this look good, but you'll be okay."

They tied the white driver's hands behind his back around the trunk of a gum tree, lashed his ankles to it, and gagged him with an oil rag from the cab, leaving it loose.

One of them stood in front of him and hit him solidly in the face, breaking a tooth and hammering his head against the tree. Fury and pain shone in the man's eyes as he tasted his own blood, and then fear. This wasn't in the plan.

"Sorry, sorry," the black man said and hit him again, now on the side of the head. The driver sagged in the ropes that held him. The black hit him once more, an open-handed smack on the other side of his face that made his cheek swell red.

They left him there and drove away.

It took him minutes to spit out the gag together with pieces of tooth and start yelling for help. He shouted for more than half an hour before a passing mine patrol heard him, freed him and called the police.

"Another bleddy hijack," said the corporal to the desk officer when they brought him to the police station, "They jumped him at the lights on the way to that construction site down the road. Beat him up when he tried to fight them off and tied him to a tree."

"Hey, you're damn lucky to be alive, man," the desk officer grinned at him, "Most times they just kills the drivers."

"But why bricks?" the corporal asked, "Who wants bleddy bricks?"

"*Ag*, man, don't be so dumb," the desk man retorted,

73

"You know the price of bricks nowadays? Or maybe they just want the truck."

That night, at about the same time in the darkened warehouse at Thohoyandou, and in another on the outskirts of Germiston between Benoni and Johannesburg, teams of twenty men, working fast, unloaded bricks from the trailers by the light of dimmed torches.

They ignored the stacks at the sides to concentrate on lifting out those in the centre, passing them from hand to hand with practised skill and stacking them on the floor.

When they had removed two levels of bricks, a deck formed of wooden crates lay exposed, the lids stencilled with Cyrillic lettering.

Inside most of them were Kalashnikov assault rifles packed in grease and layered between oiled paper. Hundreds of them.

Other cases contained ammunition, Scorpion machine pistols, Makarov and Tokarev semi-automatic pistols, land mines and hand grenades. Several held RPG-7s, the cone-tipped rocket-propelled grenades that can punch a hole in a tank, with their launching tubes.

In less than an hour, the crates were spirited away by a succession of mini-buses and cars with doused lights, which came and went, one by one.

In less than another half hour, the bricks were stacked back into the trailers, the warehouses locked and the workers and the men who had stood guard outside, AK-47s cocked and ready, had gone.

CHAPTER NINE

As soon as the House rose for the midday recess, the deputy leader of the right-wing Freedom Front Party hurried into his office overlooking the avenue of old oaks in tranquil Gardens, next to Parliament. An erect, raw-hide-tough farmer from the North West Province, who carried his beard trimmed to the bony line of his jaw like a flag of defiance, he relished the cut and thrust of political debate but disliked cities. He was impatient to quit crowded Cape Town for the familiar hot thornveld of home.

His middle-aged secretary saw his harassed expression and hastened to his help, notebook in hand. "Is there anything you need, sir?" she asked, in Afrikaans. He never spoke anything else.

"No," he said, patting his pockets to make sure he had his wallet, pen, pipe and tobacco, "No thanks. I have to meet Lena in five minutes. She's taking me to lunch."

He frowned. He would much rather eat in the House dining-room with his colleagues, denouncing the behaviour of the Cabinet Ministers and their crazy ideas, than at some restaurant of his wife's choice, much as he respected her taste.

"Shall I call for your car, sir?"

"*Ag*, no, leave it. She's picking me up in Church Square."

He walked down the steps from the mezzanine floor overlooking the thick-carpeted lobby, with its portraits of politicians, and pale rectangles where some had been removed, and went out of the security entrance, nodding at the immaculate policemen in immaculate uniforms. In the sunshine of Parliament Street, he clamped a Homburg on his head and strode past the spearheaded iron railings towards the little square behind the Groote Kerk with the pigeon-flecked statues of politician Jan Hofmeyr and church leader Andrew Murray.

His wife had parked her white-and-yellow Citigolf, the prized runabout she kept in Cape Town, in the middle of the square. He found her leaning into its open hatchback, loading her morning's purchases.

The deputy leader was pleased he had not kept her waiting. After forty years of marriage, he was very fond of her. "Hullo, my dear," he greeted her in Afrikaans.

She turned to smile up at him, a matronly woman with blue eyes in a sweet round face, all floral print and cologne, and stretched to kiss his cheek. "Hullo, my husband. On time as always. I've a surprise for you today. French cuisine."

He glanced at his watch. "We must hurry then, my dear. I have to be back in the House by two-thirty."

"You drive. It's at the Waterfront, not far, and I've already ordered for us to save time."

He unlocked the passenger door and held it open for her. Sliding in behind the wheel, he moved the seat back to accommodate his long legs, fastened the safety belt and turned the key in the ignition.

The blast shattered all the windows around the square, blew the leaves off the trees behind the Groote Kerk, and sent the surviving pigeons racing away in fright, and hoisted a giant melon of grey-black smoke skywards.

It flung pedestrians flat on the sidewalks, cut and bruised. None was seriously hurt because the mangled cars around the Citigolf bore the brunt of the explosion. The statues of Hofmeyr and Murray, anchored on their heavy plinths, were scored and chipped by flying debris.

Of the Citigolf itself, almost nothing recognisable was

left, except twisted wheels and chassis and the engine block in the middle of a street thirty metres away.

Of the deputy leader and his wife there was nothing at all where the little car had stood. Police later found a blackened bone they identified as human on top of a five-storey building.

The needle wail of an alarm pierced the pall of silence that followed the blast, joined within minutes by the ululating sirens of ambulances. Uniformed and plain-clothes police officers rushed to the square. Instant security reaction sealed off the Houses of Parliament.

It was an hour before anyone realised that the Freedom Front's deputy leader was absent and connected this with the bombing.

Driven to unaccustomed effort by terrorism so close to the legislature and by the rank of the victim, the police discovered within minutes that the blast was caused by a large package of plastic explosive fastened to the chassis underneath the Citigolf, right between the front seats, and triggered by a radio signal.

In the House, feelings ran high. A grim-faced President stood up during the afternoon sitting to announce that no stone would be left unturned in the hunt for the perpetrators of this awful double murder, and urged the members to react with the responsibility and calm that behoved them as the nation's leaders.

The Freedom Front was not to be calmed. When one enraged member could no longer restrain himself and stood up during debate to shout for immediate action against the African National Congress and its trade union and communist partners, all his colleagues rose in support. Bedlam ensued.

The Speaker told the angry member to sit down and await his turn. He refused. The Speaker ordered him to leave the chamber. All the Freedom Front members stalked out with him.

Cape Town was taut as a bowstring that night and

white, brown and black people on the streets trod warily around each other.

***

Though his job as a local organiser was low on the ANC Youth League totem pole, it gave Moses Manxaba much pride. It marked him as one of the rising young men in the seething human cauldron of Soweto, with prospects of rising to influence and wealth when the old guard leadership at last faded away.

He had once shaken the hand of Nelson Mandela at a pre-election rally in the stadium, not far from Manxaba's boxy little brick home in Orlando township, part of the vast sprawl of townships south-west of Johannesburg. Designed by the creators of apartheid as a black dumping ground, it had evolved into the focal point of black political activism and urban culture.

The rally had not impressed him as much as he had expected. He was one of scores introduced and he doubted Mandela would remember him.

He respected Mandela's fortitude, intelligence and charisma, but in his youthful opinion the man was too old and too moderate, a relic of an outdated policy of appeasement.

Manxaba was one of the ANC's hungry young lions who scorned talk and wanted to flex their muscles now. Black power was firmly in place, why not use it now to take over everything, why wait?

He had already tasted what he thought was victory, watching once-feared policemen in blue retreat from his advancing mob of bobbing, bouncing, banner-waving demonstrators. He did not realise then that his victory was because change had left the police in leaderless disarray, with few of their old powers.

But the incident had enhanced his image in the alleys of Orlando.

Tonight Manxaba was leaving his home for an ANC

district meeting. They were going to discipline some local kids who had quit school and turned to petty crime to buy liquor. The ANC was determined to restore order to schools.

His two companions, semi-literate ex-guerillas he adopted as 'bodyguards' when they returned from Tanzania under amnesty, waited beside his Honda Civic at the gate of his small dusty garden. The car had been 'liberated' in Johannesburg a year before but had been so well 'recycled' its owner would not recognise it. One guard climbed in the back, the other next to Manxaba.

The headlamps cut bright tunnels through the dim streets on the way to Orlando High School. There was little traffic at this hour, when few people ventured out. Warm light glowed from the windows of the houses they passed.

Manxaba turned a corner to find all the lamps in the street ahead were dead, which happened often in Soweto. His headlight beams spotlighted figures ahead, a dozen men prancing towards them waving knobkieries, axes, iron bars and bush knives.

All wore red bands around their foreheads, the emblem of Inkatha, the powerful political movement among the Zulu people, which sometimes collaborated with, but more often opposed, the ANC.

He rammed his foot on the brake, which was a mistake because it threw his guards off ballance as they reached for their pistols. By then it was too late.

A high-velocity rifle bullet came through the windscreen and struck the front guard at the base of his throat, killing him and passing on through the rear window.

A second bullet tore through the radiator and the engine clattered and died.

The guard in the back seat flung open the door and dived out. Muzzle flashes from an AK-47 at the roadside illuminated him in staccato flashes. His riddled body jerked in a macabre dance and toppled into the dirt at the roadside.

At the first gunshot, all the lights in nearby windows flicked out. In Soweto, shots were the signal to lock up and stay low.

The man with the high-power rifle stepped into the headlight beams, holding it one-handed with his finger still hooked round the trigger, and looked straight at Manxaba. He was all in black and a balaclava revealed just his eyes.

Manxaba saw with shock that his hands and the little of the face he could see were white.

The shock flowered into rage. He pushed open his door. A big black man next to the car kicked it shut and swung an axe against the window.

Flying glass stung Manxaba's face. He fell across the gap between the front seats. A rain of heavy blows shattered the remaining windows and caved in the thin metal of the roof. The sharp point of a pickaxe penetrated it and stopped centimetres above his head.

Half-blinded, blood trickling down his face from small cuts, Manxaba knew this was the end. He was more angry than frightened until, through the din of metal beating on metal, he heard splashing and smelt petrol. Terror overwhelmed him.

One of the red-banded men shouted at the others to step back. He struck a match, pushed its burning head among the rest and, when the whole box flared, tossed it through the gaping windscreen.

The petrol-soaked car *whoofed* into brilliant orange fire, so hot the men were forced back.

They stood watching in silence while the flame-limned figure inside straightened in agony, head thrown back and for a second, haloed by his burning hair. As the ferocious heat began to incinerate his skin and lungs and shrink tendons, the dead Manxaba hunched forward until his forehead rested on the blackened dashboard, as if tired.

The rifleman barked a sharp order. Two of the attackers lifted the body of the dead guard from the roadside, approached as close as the heat would allow, and heaved it into the inferno, creating an eruption of smoke and sparks. The rank smell of burning flesh tainted the air.

The killers turned and ran into the Soweto night.

***

While Manxaba roasted in Soweto, five hundred kilometres to the east, near Pietermaritzburg, two Toyota minibus taxis navigated winding roads between steep green hills encrusted with small houses, huts, shanties and other pustules of overcrowded humanity.

Neither drew a second glance because they carried local numberplates, which the drivers had screwed on when they crossed into KwaZulu-Natal, and such taxis were commonplace.

The drivers were jittery. They knew the area well enough but people and loyalties shifted fast in the ebb and flow of political and factional fighting and yesterday's sanctuary might well be today's slaughterhouse.

It took them more than an hour to circumvent Inkatha strongholds and reach their destination, an old abandoned farmhouse surrounded by flimsy mud and tin shacks halfway up a bushy hillside. The dull light of a paraffin lantern glowed through gaping holes, doors and windows long since stolen.

They stopped, switched off lights and engines and stepped into the dust road, stretching to relieve tired muscles.

"*Sanibonana*, we see you," a soft voice greeted them in Zulu from the velvety humid night. "Who do you seek?"

With eyes still recovering from the glare of headlights, they could not see the voice's owner.

"We seek our comrades," said the driver of the first taxi, praying that this was still ANC territory.

"What do you want of the comrades?"

"We want nothing of them, *bangane bethu*, our friends. We have been sent to bring them something."

"Who are you?" The voice was neutral, like a judge's.

Moving with care, the men drew driving licences from pockets and paused, unsure what to do with them. A small torch flicked on, into their eyes, and a disembodied hand took the papers. They heard voices muttering on the other side of the taxis.

"Inside," the voice said, polite but firm. The drivers climbed the short steep slope to the house and entered. Three men came in close behind them, each carrying a honed cane knife. In the dim yellow lantern light, the drivers did not recognise any of them.

"There are more comrades outside," one of the trio said when they turned around, "so you must stay here please while we look." He cupped his hand over the lantern and blew out the flame, leaving them in pitch darkness.

The drivers sighed with relief. Had these people been Inkatha they would have been dead already. They heard scratching and an occasional thump and clank from the direction of their vehicles, but this was expected. Their cargoes were being taken from behind panels and beneath false floors.

It seemed like a lifetime before the soft voice spoke from the dark again, so close they jumped.

"*Siyabonga bangani,*" its owner said. "Thank you, friends. You have done well. We have much use for your gift."

"Thank you, comrade, it is nothing," they both replied. "*Amandla awethu!* Power to us!"

"You may leave now. *Hambani kahle,* go well."

"*Salani kahle,* stay well," they responded together.

They walked out of the old house and stumbled on the slope, until someone snapped on a torch and aimed its beam on the first taxi so they could see their way.

When they started up there was nobody to be seen in

their headlights. They drove away with relief and sped as fast as the tortuous roads would allow towards the distant glow of Pietermaritzburg's lights.

Near the abandoned house, in a shanty constructed of old corrugated iron sheets on a lumber frame, Comrade Veli Bhengu squatted on his haunches and examined the gift under two lanterns. Thick blankets covered the shanty's one window so not a sliver of light could escape.

It reflected from the greased blue-black metal and green plastic of thirteen new AK-47 rifles and their spare magazines. To one side lay several rope-handled wooden boxes of ammunition.

Bhengu's eyes shone with admiration. Laying there in an inanimate row, the AK-47s created a sense of menace. These efficient guns, more than anything else, were the symbol of power in Africa.

He touched one and lifted his fingertip to his nostrils to sniff the distinctive smell of gun oil, savouring it like a perfume.

Satisfied, he rose to his feet and the men crowding around watched.

"You," he said, pointing, "and you, and you ..." He picked out thirteen men, all former ANC exiles who were trained in Tanzania or Angola. Each took a gun.

They loaded the magazines and spares, which gave them sixty rounds each, and checked the action of the breeches with the ease of familiarity.

The six men without guns looked disappointed.

"I, too, have no gun," Bhengu told them, "but our time will come." He turned to the armed men. "You all know what you must do?"

"*Yebo.*" They nodded. "Yes, we know."

"Come, let us go."

They doused the lights and left the shanty one by one, invisible in the darkness. The time was ten o'clock.

***

In the early dawn, when the first pale light filtered through coils of night mist still wreathing the gentle valleys, men started gathering on a hilltop opposite the old farmhouse.

Silhouetted by sunrise, they formed a moving frieze. They carried a variety of weapons, most of them traditional kieries and assegais, and brandished them in the curious and distinctive manner of the Zulu warrior, holding them vertical and swinging their hands so the knobs and blades seem to hang still in the air, while the hafts beneath swayed from side to side.

Most wore strips of red cloth tied around their heads, marking them as Inkatha. In half an hour their number grew to over two hundred and as the crowd swelled, they moved their bodies in unison, lifting and placing their feet in rhythm to a deep-voiced Zulu chant.

Working themselves into a fighting mood as their ancestors had done for centuries, their purpose was revenge. The previous day an Inkatha supporter had been ambushed, chopped to death and set alight on the road through the valley below. Their objective was the hill opposite: ANC territory.

One man ran forward and spun to face them, thrusting high a long-stemmed axe in the air. He shouted a string of words and the frenzied mob streamed like raiding ants down the hillside between huts and hovels and small, tilled fields.

A third of them had crossed the winding dirt road, slowing on the uphill opposite, when the shooting started.

Bhengu had placed his thirteen gunners well behind bush cover in a wide arc, about fifty metres up his side of the hill with a clear view of the road itself and with broad fields of fire between and over the flimsy shanties.

They triggered short bursts, selecting their targets with care, aiming first at running clusters of Inkatha men for maximum effect, swinging their sights to shoot again.

The road was a death trap, the central mass of attackers caught when crossing it. In seconds, it was strewn with their torn bodies, some writhing and screaming in agony. Blood puddled in the powdery brown dust.

The oncoming mob stopped in confusion, at first not knowing where the shots came from, then blundering into survivors fleeing the gunfire lashing the road.

The gunners ignored them to pick off men who had crossed and were labouring uphill towards them, or frantically trying to hide from the invisible bees buzzing past their heads.

Some crept behind shanties and were killed by bursts fired right through the thin walls. Others turned to run and were shot in the back.

When the Inkatha rearguard realised what was happening, they threw aside their puny traditional weapons and fled in panic, but the retreat was uphill and slow. The ANC marksmen put in fresh magazines and picked off one after another until the range became too great.

It was all over in a few minutes. Corpses littered the area on both sides of the road with crying wounded among them, until jubilant ANC men and women appeared with knives and axes to still the crying.

From the centre of a second line of men armed with hand weapons behind the riflemen, Bhengu watched with satisfaction.

"*Phelile*!" he shouted. "It is finished! *Yizani*, come!"

The defenders leaped from their hiding places and ran past him up the hillside. Over its crest, they split up and went in many directions carrying their AK-47s.

The guns would be cached as soon as they reached home, wrapped in plastic and buried beneath hut floors, in tilled fields, under the dung of goat kraals.

They did not care that people saw them carrying the rifles. ANC comrades would never talk.

***

Three hours later the police arrived in a convoy of small yellow trucks behind a Casspir armoured personnel carrier. It had taken over an hour for the first report of a fight to reach them and they had struggled with poor directions through the maze of roads and tracks to find the place.

The time was not yet ten o'clock but already the bodies were bloating in the sun's heat and the smell of blood and flesh hung thick in the air.

The scene on the ANC-controlled hillside was of bucolic tranquillity. Women bent over their hoes, tilling their tiny patches of maize and vegetables. Old men sat in the shade. Children played in the dust.

Police with shotguns scoured both sides of the valley and found hundreds of AK-47 shellcases on the ANC side. They questioned the women and the old men. All shook their heads. They knew nothing about these things.

And all those dead men, where did they come from?

Oh, there was fighting in the night. We saw nothing, master. When we heard shooting, we were too frightened to look.

The police gave up. They took names and such addresses as could be defined, knowing there would never be usable witnesses, knowing that somewhere in this maze of hills, where hundreds of thousands of people lived, guns had been hidden for use another time.

A heavyset black police officer carrying a pump-action shotgun watched the corpses being dragged from the scrub and laid in rows beside those on the road.

"How many?" he asked another policeman.

"Fifty-eight so far, sir, and still counting."

"Jesus," he muttered under his breath. "Zulu against Zulu."

CHAPTER TEN

In colonial times, it was a game reserve where Portuguese elite and wealthy clients from Europe and America indulged their lust for killing wild animals in the guise of trophy hunting.

Now the Parque Nacional de Banhine was a park in name only. The years of civil war after Mozambique gained independence had returned it, and a far larger area around it, to the raw wilderness of centuries earlier. It was not an exception; much of inland Mozambique inland had retrogressed the same way.

The modern difference was that guns were almost as common as spears. In the Banhine region, the few remaining tribespeople lived almost like wild animals, often in flight from others with guns, who stole their manioc and maize, raped the women, beat or butchered the men, and sometimes took away the children.

Just within the former Parque Nacional de Banhine, some forty kilometres east of the derelict outpost of Sao Jorge de Limpopo, the Chairman and the Doctor stood in the hot brassy sunlight, watching a parade.

The temperature was well over one hundred and twenty degrees and the humidity so high, sweat saturated their khaki shirts and trickled down their faces and necks.

The heat did not appear to affect the men on parade, fifty small sinewy blacks in mottled or striped camouflage, strutting up and down a clearing the size of a football field, to orders from a young officer. They carried AK-47s at the port and lifted their knees and free arms high with each step.

"Very smart, brigadier, very smart, but can they fight?"

the Doctor asked. He and the Chairman looked at the stocky Mozambican in well-pressed camouflage fatigues standing next to them. Three small brass stars glinted on his brown beret.

He peered up at their faces, his thoughts impenetrable behind dark glasses.

"Of course, *senhors*," he replied in stilted, Portuguese-accented English. "They are very experienced. They fight better than they march."

Experienced in chopping up unarmed peasants, Doc thought cynically. What kind of army does that make them?

Colonel Simião Manjacane (they called him brigadier for flattery) sensed the doubt in his guests. He stepped forward and gave orders in a language they could not understand. "Now you will see," he told them.

The young officer shouted new commands. The marching men broke ranks and sprinted off the clearing into the knee-high grass and scrubby trees at the far end, crouching low. Doc and the Chairman heard the *click-clack* of cocking and selector levers as they ran.

In less than ten seconds, they had vanished. There was nothing to indicate they had existed, except light dust hanging in the muggy air.

"Good, no? They are there and you cannot see them." Colonel Manjacane glanced at the visitors and gestured towards the bush. "They have you in sight now, all of them."

Doc grunted.

"You don't believe? I show you."

The little colonel clapped his hands and called out. Fifty men rose out of the grass and from behind scrub in an arc around the far end of the clearing. Every one was aiming down the barrel of his gun, with every gun aimed at the white men.

It was a chilling sight. Doc was impressed. In spite of the heat, the Chairman shivered.

"Good," said Doc, "very good, brigadier. Can they shoot as straight as they aim?"

"Sim, amigo," the colonel said, reverting to Portuguese. "Yes, my friend. You forget I was a soldier for Salazar. I have taught them well. You wish to see?"

"No thank you, Colonel, I believe you." Wanting to get out of the sun, Doc had no desire to listen to the rattle of small arms fire. He knew that even half-trained soldiers spraying bullets from automatic weapons were formidable; they had to hit something.

He and the Chairman had come to this dismal wilderness by a devious route, across the Limpopo River at night, into the southeast corner of Zimbabwe and through it to Mozambique.

They were escorted for the last few kilometres to the camp on foot by a patrol, who handled their AK-47, Simonov and G3 rifles like extensions of their own arms.

The camp seemed to appear out of nowhere. One minute they were in featureless bush, the next in a clearing beside a large village. Rows of small, neat rectangular huts of trimmed and woven saplings roofed with reed thatch, stood beneath the trees. Straight paths edged with stones ran between them.

Several huts were longer than the others. Over the door of one hung a board with the word *"Hopita"* hot-pokered into it. Beneath a palm-frond roof with no walls stood rows of tables and benches of lashed poles, the mess hall. Another hut they recognised as the headquarters because two sentries stood outside.

The Chairman and Doc paused at the edge of the clearing to mop the sweat from their faces and examine the oasis.

"Aren't they exposing themselves to attack?" the Chairman asked. "They must be as visible as a town from the air."

Doc, who had not visited this former Renamo base before but seen others, shook his head.

"Frelimo and Renamo have made peace now, remember, and Frelimo never had an air force worth speaking of."

Manjacane had met them on arrival with two young officer aides at his side.

"*Boas dias, amigos*, good day, friends," he greeted in Portuguese. "Welcome to the *Acampamento Banhine*, Banhine Camp."

"We are honoured that you can receive us," Doc replied in the same language with a genial smile. "This is the head of our organisation," indicating the Chairman. "I regret he does not speak Portuguese."

Manjacane spoke to him in English.

"I am delighted to meet you, sir. You are welcome in our simple home and I hope you will be comfortable."

"It is an honour to meet you, Brigadier Manjacane, and I am sure it will be a pleasure to stay here," replied the Chairman, who was accustomed to much more primitive camps on his hunting expeditions.

"You will wish to wash and rest after your long journey, *senhors*, then I show you what you have come to see."

An aide led them along paths through the trees and drew aside a canvas screen that served as the door of a hut.

Inside were two low beds of lashed poles with light blankets on mattresses of sacking, stuffed with grass. Mosquito nets hung above them and a washstand with an enamelled basin, a tall tin jug of water, a bar of soap and two towels, stood against a wall. The aide gestured to another open doorway. Inside was a simple shower made of a twenty-two-litre drum with a hole in the base opened by pulling a string that worked an overhead lever.

"All mod cons," the Chairman said. "Real one-star accommodation. Where's the shithouse?"

"Probably a long drop, in a nearby hut." Doc lowered his voice and switched to Afrikaans. "One thing, don't forget there's no privacy here. The walls are see-through. Anything we say can be heard for yards around, so be careful."

The Chairman lifted an eyebrow at him without comment.

Thirty minutes later the colonel paraded his troops, ending with the fifty men hoisting their guns high in salute.

Manjacane excused himself, pleading work, and the

South Africans spent the afternoon in their hut and strolling around the camp, followed at a discreet distance by a soldier.

When the aide fetched them near sunset, he took them not to the mess hall but to a spacious room inside the headquarters hut where, to their surprise, a table had been laid with a clean white cloth, glasses, cans of South African beer, bottles of Portuguese wine and brandy, and one of Johnny Walker Black Label.

"You see, we have amenities of civilisation in the bush," Manjacane said while aides poured drinks and soldiers proferred plates of *petiscos*, small pieces of unidentifiable meat, chicken or goat, on crude toothpicks in a reddish sauce. The white men swallowed their doubts and ate, feeling fiery *piri-piri* singe their mouths and consoling themselves with the thought that germs were not likely to survive it.

Manjacane, still wearing his dark glasses and beret, drank neat Constantino brandy, half a tumbler at a time, the first three rapidly. The visitors also sipped their drinks neat, not eager to risk the local water. In the background, they heard the thump of a diesel engine starting up and bare bulbs under the thatch roof pulsed into weak life.

Dinner was roast bushpig and cane rat stew with strong-smelling boiled manioc, maize and the tubers of water lilies from the nearby swamp.

The Chairman was impressed, except by the manioc, which stank, and the white wine, which was warm. What strange bedfellows the exigencies of politics demanded, he thought. Thank God they'll be no more than neighbours, not partners.

At the end of the meal, Manjacane stood up and proposed a toast. "To our future," he said, holding aloft a full tumbler of red Dão wine. "May we long be good friends and allies in freedom."

The Chairman responded, "To Renamo's president, Afonso Dhlakama, and a homeland free of communists and fellow travellers."

Manjacane grimaced with distaste and drank, then banged his empty glass on the table.

While an aide refilled it the Chairman and the Doctor stayed silent, caught unawares by this show of temper.

Manjacane swallowed wine and resumed his usual wide smile.

"*Pfah!*" he said, waving a dismissive hand. "Dhlakama is a fool."

The Chairman and the Doctor glanced at each other with raised eyebrows.

Manjacane thought for several moments and went on, "*Senhors,* Afonso Dhlakama plays stupid political games. He makes peace with Joaquim Chissano. They hold elections. Today Dhlakama talks war, tomorrow he talks peace, the next day war again. *Pfah!*" he spat again. "It is nonsense. We cannot go to bed with the Devil."

"But what if it works, if there is peace?" the Chairman asked.

"It will never be!" Manjacane said, his voice vehement. "Dhlakama is nothing here! He sits in Gorongosa, or Maputo, or wherever he thinks he is safe! He does not know what the people think! He is too frightened to come here to find out! They will throw him out.

"*We* are the true Renamo in Gaza and even farther!" He rose to his feet, leaned on the table with one hand and smacked it with the other. "*I* am Renamo's leader here, my friends, not Afonso Dhlakama! It is what *I* say that is done! No," he sat down and went on, "there might be a peace for a week or a month or a year, but there will be war again." His smile beamed down on them.

"Yes, of course," Doc said, rising to his feet to tower over the rebel and raising his glass high over his head. "I give you a toast to Brigadier Manjacane, ruler of Gaza, your future country!"

The little man's face softened. "You are good friends," he said. "I look forward to collaboration with you."

"Brigadier," the Chairman said, seeking to approach a subject without offending his mercurial host, "I congratulate you on the excellence of the troops we saw today, but may I ask, how many do you have? How strong are your forces?"

"Hundreds, *amigo,* I have hundreds more."

"Of course, you have command over a very large and important area so they must be spread far and wide," said Doc, coating his words with sugar. "I suppose they are all as experienced as those here."

"Yes," Manjacane waved a hand airily. "Although, I have not trained every one myself. I have good officers who fought with the Portuguese or with Machel."

"How many can you muster?"

"Here? Oh ... hundreds. No problem. Do not worry."

Manjacane's speech was slurred and, when an aide re-filled the colonel's glass, the Doctor thought, this is a weak reed but there is no other.

"Enough to hold the ground you take?"

Manjacane frowned. "Enough!" he hissed. "I said I have hundreds, all experienced, all have good weapons. Do not concern yourselves." He leaned forward and stared at them, his dark glasses reflecting the twin bulbs overhead. "And you? You will help us? We will need many things, *senhors,* experts and vehicles and money, much money."

"You will have them, brigadier," the Chairman said, "but first we must make sure that everything is correctly pre-pared. When we are free, so will you be. Nothing must go wrong."

"*Não problema,* no problem." Manjacane swallowed the rest of his wine, almost a full tumbler, and leaned against the back of his chair. Behind the dark glasses, his lids drooped shut and he slid lower, until just his face showed over the edge of the table.

Without saying a word, the two aides hoisted him up, hooked his arms over their shoulders, and carried him out of the room with his feet dangling inches above the ground.

The Doctor and the Chairman watched this performance

with cynicism.

"You handled him well, Doc," the Chairman said in Afrikaans. "He's a pompous little arsehole. Brigadier ... my God! He wouldn't make a damned one-striper in our army."

"Unfortunately, he *is* the boss of this whole region. His word is life or death. We don't have a choice."

"Just because he has guns and the locals have nothing, the murderous little bastard."

"And also chief, because the Frelimos were too bloody scared to come out of their barracks to take on Renamo. That's the ace card, remember. One company of decent troops could send this lot running like hares."

"Maybe, Doc, but don't write them off altogether. The men we saw today didn't look so bad."

The Doctor's mouth twisted in contempt. "I bet they're the only ones he has real control over. The rest out in the bundu are just bloody *tsotsis*, wastrels who'll do what he asks if it suits them."

The Chairman walked to the table with the liquor, broke the seal on the bottle of Black Label and poured two stiff tots.

"This is to clean out the muck," he said, handing one to the Doctor. "What's the programme tomorrow? We have to sign some sort of agreement, don't we?"

"Yes. It's all written up in both languages on expensive paper full of blue ribbons and sealing wax. The Portuguese drummed red tape so deep into their heads, they won't agree to a thing without lots of ceremony and impressive documents."

"Pieces of paper!" the Chairman grunted. "Let's hope the agreement's worth more than that."

94

CHAPTER ELEVEN

Smith was depressed. As a career killer, he preferred to eliminate single people and plan accordingly. On rare occasions, when his clients insisted, he had arranged the assassination of two or three in one operation but he disliked it because the chances of error, of something unpredictable happening, thereby endangering the operation, multiplied with each additional target.

Capture was not his main worry; it seldom entered his mind. Rather, he was a skilled professional who sought perfection and a speck on his record caused him painful self-examination.

The botching of the Ngwenya-Ballance job was the first for a long time. It was not directly his fault but he carried the responsibility of leadership and it rankled. I'll finish that one, he promised himself. I'll clean it up.

As a purist hunter – one shot, one trophy – Smith listened without enthusiasm while the Doctor talked of the mass operations the committee were launching. A messy business. Putting truckloads of guns into the hands of primitives lusting to kill, was as crude as tossing a match into gunpowder, he thought. The results were spectacular but lacked finesse and were uncontrollable.

"It started off well in Soweto and Natal," the Doctor said, "and it's taking off in the Witwatersrand and the Cape. Wherever there are townships and squatter camps, Jo'burg, Pretoria, Cape Town, Port Elizabeth, Bloemfontein, you name it, that's where the blacks will massacre each other and put the fear of God into the liberals."

"What's happening up north?" Smith asked. "Won't it

look suspicious if everything's quiet up there?"

The Doctor mulled over this for a few moments. Smith was a hired instrument, a cog; he did not need to know the rest of the machine, the big picture in detail, but he was too useful to be rebuffed.

"There will soon be enough taking place up there to convince everyone we're in the middle of an undeclared civil war. Our friends in Venda are arranging a night of long knives for the ANC, and everything is ready in Mozambique, just across the border."

He remembered his doubts about the abilities of Manjacane and his ragtag army. No point in telling Smith.

"The committee is using the axe," he went on, "your job is with the stiletto. The security forces already have their hands so full trying to stop the blacks killing each other and at the same time fighting urban crime, they can't investigate each and every death. Now we must force their hand, and that's up to you.

"The committee want you to step up the ..." the Doctor fastidiously avoided the word 'killing' , "... the elimination of prominent people. The public outcry will force the police to divert manpower and, we expect, will force the President and Vice President to declare a state of emergency, which they're so reluctant to do."

"How high can I aim?" Smith asked, his professional interest stirred. "The President? The Cabinet? The Archbishop?"

"No, not the very top, yet. Threaten them and they might, for once, take positive action. Leave them alone and they'll argue over what to do, and leave the top churchmen. The more those mealy-mouthed muddlers pontificate, the more the public will panic. Stick to people like that Freedom Front deputy leader you bombed in Cape Town the other day, an excellent piece of work, by the way."

"*I* bombed?" Smith lifted a quizzical eyebrow.

"Whoever. Focus on top businessmen, senior civil servants, leading blacks, academics ... you know the kind."

"Perhaps you're right. The President has very tight security anyway. The others are easy, but there's one piece of work I must finish."

"What's that?"

"Those two we tried for and missed, Ngwenya and Ballance." Smith felt a twinge of self-disgust at the memory. "There's also a police officer asking awkward questions."

"A police officer? How senior?"

"A superintendent. One of the old guard, tenacious as the devil. It was his sergeant we had to demote for botching the Ngwenya job, remember?"

"All right. Finish it, and this time no loose ends," the Doctor said. "Do you have the right men for it?"

"Oh yes," Smith exposed teeth in a rare smile. "Since the Civil Cooperation Bureau and some other covert operations were shut down, it's been a hirer's market."

"I hope you can trust them."

"I don't. That way I can be sure of them."

***

"Come in!" Ballance snapped when the double knock on his office door was repeated. He was sitting with his shirtsleeves rolled up, ploughing through a small mountain of examination papers. Books and documents littered the desk and spilled on to the carpet. His hair was mussed from running a hand through it in exasperation, brought on by student ignorance. He did not look up when the door opened.

"Yes?" he said, curt.

"Hullo, Jeff, you're not easy to find."

He jumped up in surprise, scattering more paper.

"Good grief, Penelope!"

"I hope I'm not interrupting ..."

"Of course not! You caught me by surprise, I wasn't expecting you. Here, have a seat ..." Flustered, he looked for a chair, saw they were all stacked with papers, and lifted a heap from one.

Penelope Fox sat on it, taking in the disorder. "Makes me feel at home," she smiled, "it looks like my place."

97

"Yeah," he smiled back, "it seems a mess but if anyone tried to organise it I wouldn't be able to find a thing. To what do I owe this pleasant surprise?"

"To Temba Ngwenya," she replied, and went on when he looked up in surprise. "He came to see me. I didn't call before coming here because I promised him I would see you in person. He needs to talk to you, Jeff, but he won't contact you direct because he thinks your phone is tapped and that you're being watched."

"Isn't he being a bit paranoic?"

"I don't think so, Jeff." She told him what Ngwenya had said. "He's convinced that he and his ANC friends are on to something big and dangerous. So dangerous he wouldn't tell me for fear it would get me into trouble. They don't have any faith in the police. You're his one hope."

I'm a negotiator, not an action man, Ballance thought, disliking the sense of being dragged into something outside his pleasant, ordered life, but he wanted to help Temba. He also wanted to see Penelope again.

"Okay, where and when?" he asked with a sigh.

"My flat, tomorrow evening at eight." She stood up and gave him a card with her home address. "Is that okay? I'll make us supper if you'll bring a bottle of that wine we had the other day."

"Done. I'll sneak unseen out of my house somehow like a John le Carré spy. Penny, I'm glad you came, I've been wanting to call you, but ..." he waved his hands at the pile of work around him, "... this has to be finished before the terrorists get back from vac."

"Terrorists?"

"Students."

"Oh." She smiled.

"Would you have dinner with me, later this week perhaps?"

"Let's talk about it tomorrow, Jeff. Park in the basement and take the lift."

She let herself out of the office and closed the door behind her. Ballance stood and stared at it, test papers forgotten.

***

That night Ngwenya called Penelope as he had every evening at the same time without giving his name.

"Tomorrow, eight," she said.

"Good. And many thanks."

***

Ballance found himself torn between his distaste for the cloak-and-dagger melodrama of the meeting in a little over an hour, and his desire to see Penelope again. He had just poured himself a consoling whisky and soda when the soft chimes of his doorbell dinged. He frowned. He was not expecting anyone and lately that door had admitted nothing but trouble. Glass in hand, he opened it.

Trouble. Superintendent Frans Louw stood there blinking in the bright light, hat in hand, grey suit buttoned. Ballance stared at him.

"That's a change," he said, "you ringing the bell. Why didn't you let yourself in as usual?"

"Good evening," the superintendent said, ignoring the barb. "Do you mind if I come in? I must talk with you and it's difficult from here."

Ballance opened the door wide and walked ahead into the living room.

"Brandy and soda with a dash of lime, wasn't it?"

He was thinking as he mixed the drink; last time they met, he had tentatively agreed to bring him and Ngwenya together, and forgotten about it. He would be seeing Ngwenya in about an hour. Awkward.

Superintendent Louw might have been reading his mind. "Has Mr Ngwenya been in touch with you yet, Mr Ballance?" he asked, taking the glass. He held it in both hands, like a chalice.

"Yes."

"And what did he say? I am sorry to be so abrupt but the matter has become very urgent."

99

"Why the urgency?"

"You must have read about the murder of Sergeant Greeff, one of the two men who detained you? He was killed by a hand grenade in Hillbrow."

"I think I did see something. I've been so busy I haven't been following the news. I'm sorry, I didn't realise it was the same man. A terrorist attack wasn't it?"

"Yes, but not the usual. I think it was the same people who killed that unknown man in mistake for Ngwenya and tried to blame you."

Ballance felt a sudden chill between his shoulder blades. "Why do you think so?" he asked. This damned business wouldn't go away.

The superintendent sipped and placed his drink on a side table.

"It's hard to say. Chiefly instinct, backed by a few facts, and it's never let me down. I want to speak in confidence … can I ask you to keep it so?"

"You have my word."

"Greeff seemed to be mixed up with a fellow in the police force, a former Security Police operative who was working to his own agenda, or someone else's, I don't know. I don't even know the man's identity, but it was he who used Greeff to plant false evidence against you."

"That's about what I'd expect from a Security Police spook."

"Please, Mr Ballance. Let's not start off on the wrong foot. The SP did terrible things but it's history now—"

"Are the SP people history too?"

Louw shrugged. "Maybe not all."

"Go on."

"Well, I'm assuming Greeff was killed because he was a weak vessel and the business he was mixed up in would have come out into the open, had I or the CID questioned him. When people don't hesitate to knife a policeman to silence him they must be very worried indeed."

"Knife him? You said he was killed by a grenade?"

100

"He was. But just before that, I think less than a minute before, he was knifed in the back to immobilise him. They stuck it in here ..." the superintendent half-turned and put his fingers on the spot on his own back "... and severed the spinal cord."

He picked up his drink, sipped and continued. "We didn't find out until the post-mortem. The killers wanted it to look like a terrorist hit and the grenade made such a mess of Greeff, the injury might have gone unnoticed had I not asked the doctor to examine him with special care."

Ballance shivered with revulsion. What kind of people would stoop to such brutality?

"We backtracked Greeff's movements as best we could. It appears he had been on a pub-crawl, not drinking, perhaps looking for somebody. We found the last bar he was in and spoke to a newsvendor who saw him drive away with two other men. The vendor said they were whites but he couldn't see them too well inside the car."

The superintendent swallowed the rest of his drink and put the glass on the table, holding it in his fingertips.

"Mr Ballance, I'm sure in my own mind these are the same people who are looking for Mr Ngwenya. Now you see why I must talk to him. He must know what they're after, why they want to eliminate him. He might even have some idea of who they are."

Ballance finished his own drink, glanced at his watch and refilled both glasses. He shivered again, his mind picturing a long blade slipping into a man's lower back like a knife into a cheese.

"Okay, superintendent. I said I'd help if I could. Temba didn't get in touch with me until yesterday and then by devious means. The truth is I'm seeing him tonight. I'll try to persuade him to meet you and I'll let you know tomorrow. Okay?"

Superintendent Louw fixed penetrating eyes on Ballance. "Rather take me with you now," he said. "This is no time to play games. It is imperative that I see Ngwenya now. I can't wait for him to make up his mind."

"You know what he thinks of the police."

"Man, that doesn't worry me. It's lives I'm worried about, including his! God knows what lies behind these killings and we must find out fast. These people have infiltrated the police force and you know what that means. They *must* be uncovered!"

Ballance swore to himself and thought, I shouldn't have told him. "I'm sorry, I can't take you. Temba was very insistent about meeting in a safe place with me alone, nobody else. I can't let him down. He won't trust anybody else, least of all the police. He believes I'm being watched too."

"You'll be letting him down if you don't let me see him. I could follow you, you know."

"Oh, for Christ's sake, do you have to play the heavy when I'm trying to help you!"

"I'm sorry." Superintendent Louw wagged his head from side to side. "This is too serious for niceties."

Ballance threw up his hands in despair, mentally kicking himself for mentioning the meeting. He would call everything off but Temba had said it was urgent.

"Oh, hell," he said, "I don't suppose I have much choice."

"It's for his own good. Yours, too."

"Okay. In case I'm being watched, I'm borrowing a car from a neighbour and you can follow me. When we get there, let me do the talking."

"Sure, but ride with me. I'll drive away from here. You go out through the garden and I'll pick you up in the street on the far side of the complex."

Ballance considered this and agreed. The time was a quarter to eight. Louw left by the front door. Putting on a black polo-neck shirt and a dark jacket, Ballance went out through the patio door, leaving the inside lights on.

He waited in the darkened porch of his neighbour's entrance until an ageing Peugeot 504 sedan came down the street and paused in the shadow of a tree for him to climb in.

"Corlett Drive," Ballance said. Louw nodded.

Chapter Twelve

Temba Ngwenya slipped through the night like cloud shadow. He had ridden a minibus taxi from Alexandra with fifteen other passengers, crammed so tight they swayed as one when the driver hurtled around corners.

He stepped off into the evening bustle of the shops and pubs in lower Corlett Drive and strolled along a side street that brought him to the end of the Wanderers golf course. Glancing up and down the street to make sure nobody was watching, he clambered over a fence on to the tree-lined course and made his way through pools of darkness to the street where Penelope Fox lived, stopping often to check whether he was being followed.

He climbed a wall into the backyard of her apartment block. A dog barked next door. Nobody paid attention. It was seven thirty.

For twenty-five minutes, he sat immobile in an angle of shadow and watched. A few cars came and went into the parking basement, flashes of headlights illuminating the entrance.

Five minutes before eight o'clock, he slipped into the basement and pressed the button for the elevator. When the doors clanked open, Ngwenya took the stairway nearby and ran up to the third floor two steps at a time, pausing at each floor to make sure the way was clear.

Penelope Fox must have been waiting at the door; she opened it before the second tap of his knuckle and hustled him inside.

"Whew," he puffed, leaning against the wall. "Hello, Miss Fox. I'm not as fit as I thought, or you have more stairs than I thought."

"I guess both." Penelope smiled, eyeing his battered clothing, bushy beard and general air of township dereliction. "Welcome back to the Fox mansion, Mr Ngwenya. I'm sure you need a drink."

"I could do justice to a beer, thanks. Is Jeff here yet?"

"Not yet. It's just on eight. He said he'd be on time but he's an academic and you know them."

"Miss Fox, before he comes, I want to apologise for involving you and to thank you for what you've done. I hope after tonight you can forget all about it."

"It's no trouble, Mr Ngwenya. I'm glad I could help."

"Please call me Temba. You've been a big help. This business is more important than you realise."

Penelope heard the tap on the door and opened it. Ballance stood there.

"Hello, Penny. Temba," he said, looking embarrassed, "I've got a surprise for you."

Behind him, half obscured until he was inside, came another man and Penelope's eyes widened in surprise: it was the policeman, Superintendent Louw.

"Good evening, Miss Fox," he nodded gravely.

Ngwenya saw Ballance and the stranger at the same time and for a moment thought of the window, then remembered it was three storeys up. Instead, he reached for his belt. Superintendent Louw stopped, Ngwenya's pistol pointing at his stomach. He stood still, his face impassive, arms hanging straight down, one hand holding his hat.

For what seemed an aeon, the four stood in rigid tableau. Penelope held her breath, her mind frozen. Don't, Ballance prayed. Ngwenya's fist was rock steady.

"I am pleased to meet you at last, Mr Ngwenya,"

Superintendent Louw said. "I'm sorry for intruding like this but you're a difficult man to find. I made Mr Ballance bring me."

"Jeff, what the hell *is* this?" Ngwenya demanded, his voice taut with suspicion.

"He's Superintendent Frans Louw of the police, Temba, but put away that gun, please. He's wants to help. Believe me."

Recognition glowed in Ngwenya's eyes. "Ah, yes, the policeman in the back of the court, the one investigating my 'murder', right?" he said with heavy sarcasm.

"Right. I was investigating your 'murder', now I'm trying to discover who arranged it and why, for your sake as much as mine."

"Bullshit. It could be you who set me up. You guys have been killing us for forty years, why stop now." It was a statement, not a question.

He edged towards the door, still holding the gun but with the muzzle lowered. He looked at Penelope.

"I suppose you're in this too?" he sneered.

Penelope frowned at him in silence. Then her temper flared.

"Put that gun away!" she snapped. "Stop being so bloody precious! Can't you see Jeff's trying to help you? Why don't you trust him? Because he's white? This is my *home*, damn it! Put that thing away!"

The words stung Ngwenya. He looked at her in surprise and felt his own temper rising.

"Will this convince you?" Louw asked.

Moving slowly, he put his hat on a chair, unbuttoned his suit jacket, opened it wide with his left hand and, with the fingertips of his right, withdrew a nine-millimetre Walther parabellum pistol from a shoulder holster.

Holding it by the butt between forefinger and thumb, he held it out to Penelope, who took it as if it

105

was red hot and put it on the sideboard.

Ngwenya tucked the Tokarev automatic back in his belt. "Sit down everybody," he said.

Penelope lowered herself onto the sofa and Ballance slumped beside her. She glared at the policeman and Ngwenya. Louw sank into an armchair.

"Okay, I'm listening," Ngwenya said.

"I'm a policeman not a politician—" Louw began.

"Skip the crap. Why do you want to see me?"

"I had to say that because you have to know it. I'm not apologizing to you, I don't need to. Somebody arranged for you to be murdered and for the crime to be pinned on Mr Ballance here, then killed the wrong person. I found that out before your theatrical appearance in court, so the charge against Mr Ballance would have been withdrawn anyway. I think the people who set you up are linked to the murder of one of my officers, and that they have connections inside the police force."

In a few dispassionate words Superintendent Louw told them what had happened since a corpse was found in a Hillbrow basement and how evidence had been manufactured and its planting arranged by an unidentified security policeman manipulating Inspector Greeff. He described Greeff's death in detail, as if testifying in court.

Ngwenya listened in silence without any softening of his expression.

"So you see why I'm in a hurry to find out who the murderers are and what they are trying to do," the superintendent continued. "At this stage I can but guess, and my fear is they could be working to a political agenda.

"You know how volatile South Africa is right now, how delicate the balance between stability and anarchy. If there is some party or movement, or whatever, trying to tip the balance, we are facing big trouble.

They have to be stopped, I don't care who they are."

"Maybe they *are* the police," Ngwenya interrupted.

"Could be some are. Policemen have beliefs like everyone else. It's quite possible some haven't been able to change direction as easily as De Klerk did. It's just as likely that some of your ANC comrades are behind it. That's why I want to talk to you. You must have some idea who these people are who want to kill you, and why, or you wouldn't be running. If we put our heads together maybe we can come up with answers."

Ngwenya snorted. "Typical," he said, "blame the ANC when it's the bloody Afrikaners behind it."

Louw's face tightened.

Ngwenya grinned, white teeth flashing. He moved across the room, picked up the Walther pistol and handed it back to the superintendent, butt first. "For now I'll take you at your word, Mr Policeman. But don't expect me to trust you."

"Thank you," Louw said, slipping the gun back into its holster. "I'm trying to forget why I don't like the ANC so I can look ahead, Mr Ngwenya. You should try it too."

"A philosophical cop, hey?" Ngwenya said. "I hope you can persuade the men who want me dead to forget too."

Louw's face was wooden with the effort of self-control. "Look," he said, "I have told you what I am doing and why. I admit I do not like being ruled by people whose sole practical experience is in terrorism, but I have no option. You're not making it easier."

Ngwenya turned to Ballance. "Jeff, why do you trust this guy?"

Ballance picked his words with care. "I don't know anything about him except that he's been tough, but fair and frank in admitting he made a mistake. My instinct tells me he's a cop, not a political animal. We have to trust somebody, Temba, and he's all we've got.

107

Something's going on that's too big for you alone to handle, or you wouldn't be in hiding or here. It's way over my head, I've no idea what it's all about. There's nowhere else we can find help."

Ballance was right. There were no options. "Okay, superintendent," Ngwenya said, "I'll play along. But understand this, I am not making statements or identifying people or appearing in court. If I think for one moment you're conning me, it's over, understood?"

"Understood. How will we keep in touch?"

"Through Jeff here. Okay Jeff?"

"Sure. We can work out how later."

"Or through me," Penelope said and when they looked at her in surprise, added "I'm in this now whether I like it or not. Can we take a break now, gentlemen? I could do with a drink and I'm sure you're all starving."

"How on earth can you think of food at a time like this?" Jeff wondered aloud as the tension eased and he set about pouring drinks.

***

"When I was in Harare about three months ago, a friend in Zimbabwe's Central Intelligence phoned me at the ANC office and said they had something that might interest me," Ngwenya said.

He was pacing as he spoke, exuding restless energy. The others were sitting around the coffee table, Penelope's finger supper of Italian bread, cold meats and salads hardly touched.

"I went over and the 'something' was a man, a pretty unsophisticated Manica from Mozambique. He'd had the stuffing beaten out of him and he was still bruised and stiff and puffy in the face. They said he was a bandit picked up south of Chimoio a couple of weeks earlier, by Zimbabwean troops helping to train Mozambicans. He was drunk when they found him. He and two others had raided a small kraal at gunpoint, raped some of the women and helped themselves to food and drink.

"The villagers filled them up with home-made booze, and when the three were very drunk they slit his friends' throats and delivered him like a trussed chicken to the first army patrol to pass their way, which luckily for him was Zimbabwean, because he wouldn't have lived long with the Frelimos.

"The Zimbabweans beat him up to make him talk. They wanted information about bandits raising hell there, but he couldn't tell them much. He'd just come up from the south. So they beat him up some more for good measure and he began to babble about a bunch of Renamos who were unhappy about making peace with Frelimo and wanted to declare their own government. Well, you know the Zimbabweans ... mention a unilateral declaration of independence and they bristle like porcupines.

"They thought it was important but didn't know how to handle it, so they wrapped him in chains and sent him back to Harare, which is where Central Intelligence came in."

Ngwenya stopped pacing and sat down. "They flushed his brain with drugs and found nothing in it of particular interest to them," he said, "but there was quite a lot concerning Mozambique and South Africa, and that's when they called me. You remember the long-standing relationship between the South African army and Renamo in the apartheid days?" Ngwenya looked at Superintendent Louw. "Well, it didn't die with apartheid, it still exists, secret as ever."

"That's not so," Ballance interrupted. "It ended when the ANC took over and pressured Renamo into making peace with Frelimo."

"Remember the army diehards who helped set up Renamo and kept it going?"

"They were fired after the elections."

"Most of them," Ngwenya conceded, "but a covert few are still in the army and police, Jeff, and the others didn't just fade away. They're still around, as militant and nationalistic as ever, and I bet they're the ones who set us up and who killed our superintendent's man."

Superintendent Louw lifted an inquiring eyebrow at Ngwenya.

"What makes you think so?"

"What the captured bandit told us. He said the Renamo dissidents down in Gaza were sending arms into South Africa, AK-47s, RPGs, handguns, grenades and so on. In return the South African side sends money, materials and other kinds of help. They're being pressured to make some sort of declaration of independence."

"A breakaway state? But by whom? And where?" Ballance asked, puzzled.

"He was vague on detail but as far as I could make out, many of the Renamo down there are fed up with their top leaders. They don't want to integrate with the Mozambican forces under Frelimo's command. They want to go their own way. The Gaza leader is a colonel who has the loyalty of the troops, or terrorists, or whatever you want to call them, in that area. They want to carve a large slice out of Mozambique and set up their own government there."

"How on earth do they think they can get away with that?"

"Hell, I don't know, Jeff, but it might not be so difficult. For a start the area they're in, between the Save River and Maputo port, is Shangaan territory with a few Swazis in the south, and the Shangaans and their neighbours cordially dislike each other. It's wild, empty country with no towns, a few villages, and primitive communications. The world doesn't give much of a damn about what happens in Africa after the fiascos in Somalia, Nigeria, Rwanda, the Congo and all the others."

Spreading his hands in question, he went on, "Who's to stop them? Not Frelimo. They barely function outside the main centres. Not the Renamo bosses. They're so clueless they can't find their own shadows. Their men are out of control."

The prospect of a breakaway state in Mozambique disturbed Ballance; it would wreck the negotiations he was working on there and send trouble rippling far and wide. He recognised the twisted reasoning behind such a scheme; it was more and more familiar in Africa.

Ethnic consciousness was straining the arbitrary borders the colonisers drew a century earlier. Political parties were shaping more around groups than ideologies and more tribes were demanding autonomy.

"It would set them back centuries," Ballance said, "How do they think they can survive in that desolation with nothing, not even roads?"

"The 'how' doesn't enter into their thinking," Ngwenya replied, "they're backward people – what some of you Afrikaners would call 'bush kaffirs', Superintendent – and they've never advanced much beyond subsistence living, except for sending their men to work on the mines."

"Mr Ngwenya," said Louw, who had been listening with silent attention, "leaving aside this UDI for a moment, you say this prisoner spoke of weapons being sent here. Who are they going to, and what kind of support are the Mozambicans expecting?"

Ngwenya shrugged. "That, Superintendent, is what I tried to find out. The captive couldn't tell me, except that the arms are fetched by white people. It worries my chiefs because they must be going to some undercover organisation, which presupposes a rebellion."

"You know anything to back up that theory?"

111

Ballance chipped in, "It makes sense, superintendent. When Pretoria was supporting Renamo, the guns were going from here to there. Now the flow is the other way. You can't go out and buy what you need for a revolution so, like the ANC during apartheid, you're forced to smuggle weapons in."

The three men and woman were silent for a moment, digesting the implications. Ngwenya resumed his pacing.

Louw added Ballance's logic to the little information he already had and perceived the vague shape of something that frightened him.

Separate incidents began to click into place. A series of inexplicable killings in the townships, for which all sides denied responsibility; the bomb assassination of a senior parliamentarian in Cape Town; the shotgun killing of a prominent insurance company executive in a Durban suburb; the destruction by arson of a black businessman's luxury home in Soweto; the rash of bank robberies by well-organised gangs with automatic weapons. Violent incidents were happening almost daily.

"You said you tried to find out," he said, looking at Ngwenya, "What did you get?"

"Wait, let me finish." Ngwenya helped himself to a can of beer and snapped open the tab. "I told my superiors what the captured man said. It put them over a barrel. The African National Congress, and I'm speaking frankly now, does not want to make a fuss yet because we have too little hard fact to go on. Without hard evidence we'd have egg on our faces, our credibility would be shot."

Ngwenya sipped his beer before going on. "We tried everything but we couldn't get confirmation at this end."

"Well, you can't go around asking people if they're going to start a revolution," Ballance interjected.

"We didn't even know where to start asking, except that former spook who spilled everything at the Truth and Reconciliation Commission and was jailed for several murders. He said he heard about a covert organisation some of his mates belonged to. Nothing detailed, no more than casual talk among friends, and remembers it because it wasn't one of those fanatical right-wing movements like the *Wit Wolwe*, the White Wolves, or the Afrikaner Resistance Movement, the AWB."

"That's very little to go on," Superintendent Louw said.

"Yeah, it is. He said they sometimes used certain hotels in Hillbrow and I was asked to do some digging. It was a mistake." Ngwenya lifted his hands in resignation. "I'm no sleuth. I talked to comrades living in Hillbrow and asked around the hotels and all it did was draw attention to me. In one pub a hulking great white brute asked me who the hell I thought I was, what the hell I wanted and why the hell didn't I ... excuse me, Miss Fox ... fuck off before I was thrown out.

"So I did. Then the comrades warned me I was being followed. So I kept a very low profile. And that's the whole story, up to my bungled murder."

Superintendent Louw rose from his armchair, his back stiff. God help us, he thought. "Thanks, Mr Ngwenya," he said, "It fits what little I know. At least we're getting a faint picture of what we're up against."

"What do you plan to do now? You're the detective."

"I don't know yet. What we've heard here must not go beyond the four of us." He sighed a gusty sigh and smiled. "Things have changed, hey? I never thought I'd work with an ANC man. The problem is the dissidents must have infiltrated the police, the army and other government departments. How do we find them

113

without tipping them off?"

"There must be a way," Ballance insisted.

"I'll think about it. I know policemen I can trust but I might need your help."

"Jeff, you have the contacts in government," Ngwenya said, "can't you get action by going right to the top?"

"Huh! Apart from the President who can we trust? How will *they* know who to trust if we tell them?"

"We're wasting time," Penelope said, "I mean, we should stop looking for answers now. It's late. Let's all sleep on it and meet here again when we do have something."

"Miss Fox is right," Superintendent Louw said, retrieving his hat, "I'll drop you near your home, Mr Ballance. Mr Ngwenya, do you want a lift?"

"No thanks. I'll leave the way I came."

"Temba, you keep in touch through Penny," Ballance said. "Meanwhile keep your head down."

"You too. Take care."

The three men left the flat together, Ballance last. He gave Penelope a quick kiss on the cheek before she closed the door and locked it.

CHAPTER THIRTEEN

Ephesias Mutale was not sleeping well. Uneasy dreams of being scorned and humiliated by some of his own people disturbed him. They sprouted from depressing experiences in promoting the cause of the ANC among the Venda people, a hard and thankless task.

Mutale was a local chairman of the ANC in Venda, which until the coming of democracy, was a black homeland in the far north of South Africa then became part of the new Northern Transvaal province. Remote from all but a few other tribes, living at the opposite end of the country from the ANC's spiritual home in the Transkei and wrapped in a very different culture and traditions, the Venda were insular and reclusive to Mutale's permanent frustration.

Many of them he could not even reach, sprinkled as they were through the wild mountains of the homeland stretching north, almost to Zimbabwe. With fervent oratory and subtle talk, he had drummed up some support among the people working the fields and orchards in the fertile valleys south of the Zoutpansberg range, in the settlements scattered along the tarred main road and in the tongue-twisting capital, Thohoyandou, a mishmash of shacks, shops and sheds.

They know more about witchcraft than politics, he told himself, and sometimes his dreams were invaded by witches, turning them into nightmares.

Spreading the ANC gospel had drawn the baleful gaze of the Venda police to him, before the homeland returned to the national fold. They had taken him in several times for questioning but to his surprise, despite their reputation, they had never laid a hand on him.

Now they had gone or been absorbed into the South African Police and no longer bothered him because the ANC was the government. What did worry Mutale was that the harder he tried to penetrate the community, the more he encountered a wall of silent resistance, as if the people were frightened.

"Be careful, Ephesias," a nervous supporter once warned him, "there are many who hate the ANC. They want their independence back. The Venda do not like the Shangaan and the Sotho and the Zulu. They do not like being small fish in a big South Africa."

"Independence was an old divide-and-rule trick of the racists," Mutale had replied in scorn. He was a gentle man but he was losing patience with the people's stubbornness.

"But it made them their own masters," the man retorted.

Woken by his dreams, Mutale curled up and pulled the blankets closer, feeling the midnight cold descend on him through the ceiling from the corrugated iron roof. His home was a small house of unpainted cement blocks, high on the hillside above Thohoyandou. The rent was low and he had little furniture. He was seldom here and used the bedroom and sometimes the small kitchen.

Still he felt cold. He raised himself on one elbow and felt a soft chill breeze. Faint against the glimmer of stars, he could see the square outline of the window through the thin curtain. It was closed. Puzzled, he turned over to reach to the floor beside the bed for a box of matches and a candle stuck in the neck of a bottle. Then he saw a slim vertical strip of pale stars where there should be none: the bedroom door was open and, beyond it, the front door.

Mutale came wide-awake in alarm because he knew he had locked the front door before he went to bed. He could see nothing in the absolute blackness inside the house.

He was not a coward and had been trained as an Umkhonto we Sizwe fighter but now he felt the icy tickle of fear flutter down his spine.

Moving like a cat, his hearing attuned for the slightest sound, he slid the blankets off his naked body, not noticing the cold through the insulating rush of adrenalin. He placed his feet on the bare cement floor and bent to reach beneath his bed for the short-handled axe he kept there.

He had it in his right hand and as he rose to his feet, muscle by muscle, the metal bedframe, freed of his weight, creaked. The noise seemed deafening.

A light flashed into his eyes, blinding him, and before he could raise the axe something hard and heavy slammed into his solar plexus, driving the breath out of him. He toppled back on the bed and something crashed against the side of his head. He lost consciousness.

***

A man holding a torch walked from behind the half-open door and shone it down on the slack body. Another man came from the foot of the bed gripping a long, heavy kierie with which he had hit Mutale in the stomach and on the head. He pulled the axe from Mutale's grip and tossed it aside.

They grasped him by his upper arms and dragged him from the room, feet trailing and head flopping like a rag doll. Outside they bound his wrists and ankles with electric flex. A third man came out of the dark and together they carried Mutale some thirty paces to a black Volkswagen panel van and dumped him inside. He fell on other prone bodies.

The three men climbed into the front and the driver released the handbrake, letting the van roll on silent tyres some way downhill, before he started the engine by engaging the clutch in second gear. He switched on the headlights at the outskirts of sleeping Thohoyandou and drove east on the main road, lit by a few feeble street-lamps until they left town.

Mutale awoke when the van turned north off the tar on to a bumpy gravel road. Pain pulsed through his dizzy skull. The road climbed into a jumble of steep-sided hills, bulking against the stars like ships at sea. For some time he wondered what was happening to him and then remembered the attack with a rush of fright.

He felt bare skin against his own and the warmth and pressure of other bodies jolting against his where he lay on his face. The sour smell of stale sweat filled his nostrils. He tensed his body to rise and felt the wire bonds trapping his feet and hands. The fear in him flamed into anger.

"What are you doing with me!" he shouted. "Who are you! Where are you taking me!"

"Be quiet!" a voice growled in the Venda tongue. The toe of a shoe kicked his shoulder.

Mutale struggled to draw up his legs beneath him and heave himself into a kneeling position. Peering forward, he could see three heads and shoulders against the glow of the headlights beyond the windscreen. The middle man sat on a box between the front seats, facing backwards.

"Do not move closer," he ordered. "I will shoot you."

A keening wail came from a body cramped against the side of the van, rising in volume and pitch to a near scream.

"We are dead!" the man cried. "We are dead already!"

"SHUT UP!" bellowed the driver, swivelling his head to glance behind. "Shut that man up!"

The middle man leaned forward and struck down with something that gleamed. It smacked hard against flesh. The wail quietened to a whimper.

Mutale eased away until he felt the rear door against his spine. He pushed against it with as much force as he could muster with his feet braced against soft bodies but it stayed firm. Kneeling, he could peer ahead through the windscreen, down the tunnels of light bored by the headlamps.

The van climbed in low gear with its engine straining, descended into a valley where the lights carved through thick bush and overhanging trees, and rose up the next mountainside. As they climbed higher, the bush thinned and gave way to ranks of man-high aloes like an army frozen in flight.

The track crossed a saddle between the dark bulk of two mountains and fell again into a wide flat valley. Half way across the driver stopped, changed into first gear and turned off along two deep wheel ruts with tall grass growing between them. He stopped after a hundred yards, leaving the headlights on, and the three captors got out.

They made no effort to conceal themselves now. One unlocked and jerked open the rear doors and pulled Mutale out by his wrists. He fell hard on his back, winded again. The captors dragged out seven more men by the wire binding their ankles and tumbled them into the dust. Most were partially clothed, but some were naked like Mutale.

Four more vans and several medium trucks stood nearby, parked in haphazard fashion in a space half the size of a football field, covered in knee-high grass. At its far end, the headlights of the vehicles fell on a crumbling brick building with no roof and, just beyond it, the lattice of an old mine headgear, whose timbers were rotting away from the rusting steel frame.

Mutale recognised it as a long-abandoned small mine, one of hundreds pockmarking the landscape of northern and northeastern South Africa.

Torch beams flickered over about a hundred men huddled together on the other side of the clearing. Some blinked into the glare, while others stared from vacant faces, grey and slack with fright.

Mutale shivered with shock. He recognised most of them in spite of the blotchy light: they were ANC supporters and some office-bearers.

Someone knelt behind Mutale to free his ankles. The wire burned his skin as it was pulled off. A fist slammed between his shoulder blades, making him stumble forward.

"Move! Move!" a voice shouted in Venda. His three captors hauled his fellow captives to their feet and shoved them across the field. Nearer the crowd, Mutale counted about thirty men holding torches. All carried weapons that glinted in the light, shotguns and pistols, pangas and bush slashers.

He could not identify any of their captors. They were dressed for the cold in ordinary clothes, a few wearing items that might be army issue.

They began to herd their shivering prisoners towards the derelict building at the end of the clearing, pushing and prodding them, swearing at the stragglers.

An elderly man in a blue dressing gown, white hair haloed by the torchlight, stopped, drew himself erect and faced the herders, letting the others stumble by him.

"What do you want of us?" he shouted. "Who are you men? We demand to know!"

All the captives stopped and turned to look at him and their moans and whimpers died into silence. Mutale watched from the side of the group.

The men with torches stopped too, forming a silent ring of illumination, past which the prisoners could see nothing. One of the torches moved closer to the old man, who screwed up his eyes trying to see beyond its dazzle, and stopped a few feet from him.

From his angle, Mutale saw the movement of the torch bearer's arm drawing back. The broad blade of a cane knife flashed sideways into the torch beam and struck the old man at the base of his thin neck. His head jumped off his shoulders and a spout of shining blood jetted straight up in the air from the stump of his neck. The man with the knife stepped back hastily to avoid the splashes.

The headless corpse stayed erect for two or three seconds then crumpled to the ground in a shapeless blue and crimson heap.

Shouts and screams of panic came from the other prisoners. Immediately the guards closed round them and they looked into the black snouts of guns. Nobody tried to run. All eyes stared in horrified fascination at the guns or at the killer, who was lifting the severed head from the grass by its white hair.

The shock cleared Mutale's mind and the discipline of his training took over. He had seen killing before as a guerrilla, but nothing as vicious and cold-blooded as this. He knew now exactly what was happening.

This was a mass liquidation of ANC in Venda, an unmistakeable warning to anyone else who might think of joining the movement.

Nobody would ever be able to prove anything, the place of slaughter might never be discovered, but everybody in Venda would soon know what had happened here tonight. The message would travel as fast as always in Africa: join the ANC and you die.

The captors closed in, prodding with gun barrels and blade points. A low keening sound rose from their prisoners but they moved. The bloody execution had terrified them into helplessness.

They moved like sheep past the crumbling mine building towards the old headgear stark in the headlight beams. There Mutale saw what awaited them.

Under the short skeletal tower, the mineshaft had once been capped with iron beams overlaid by logs. The wood had long since rotted and been eaten away by termites, and the heavy iron had been pulled away to the sides, exposing a black hole some three metres square.

Mutale thought fast. He edged towards the outside of

the press of prisoners as they approached the shaft, on the shadowed side farthest from the headlights.

He glanced about to see if anyone else was poised to act. He saw nothing but grey faces emptied by dread, slack mouths, vacant eyes.

A man with a revolver stepped ahead of the prisoners, bent to peer down the shaft and tossed in a stone. It clattered hollow against the sides of the shaft for a long time before it plunged into water with a distant smack.

The armed men lined up around the prisoners, cornering them against the shaft. The prisoners nearest to it looked down into death and tried to push back against those behind and their keening swelled to an animal howl.

A twelve-bore shotgun boomed behind them. Its blast of buckshot flailed into the men at the back. Three died outright and more fell wounded. Screams shredded the air.

The shotgun levelled again. The men close to it pushed forward in panic. The whole crowd swayed under their frantic pressure. Four men at the front toppled over the brink and fell into pitch blackness. For long appalling seconds their yells of terror bugled from its mouth and then ended in a great washing splash.

Terror seized the rest and they tried to run. Mutale dived flat and felt the bare feet of fleeing people thudding on his back. Guessing what would come, he wriggled ahead, like a snake into the knee-high grass.

Killing frenzy erupted in the captors. A roar of gunfire met the fleeing men, scything them down and blasting back those behind. In their panic and blinded by the headlights, many turned and ran straight into the shaft. Some dodged past the guns to be felled by slashing knives.

Mutale slithered and rolled away from the slaughter towards the farthest side of the headgear. The blood-crazed assassins, eyes alert for running men, did not see his black skin against the dark earth in the blacker shadows cast by the headlamps. He heaved himself around a leg of the headgear and behind a heap of iron beams.

Frantic, he rolled on to his side, felt behind him for the rust-rough edge of a beam and sawed the plastic-covered flex binding his wrists against it. In less than a minute, his hands were free.

Behind him the night was agonised by the staccato sound of gunfire, the gurgles of the wounded and the ear-piercing shrieks of men falling down the shaft. The air stank of fresh blood. Stray bullets whispered over his head.

Mutale gasped with fear. Pressed close to the ground, he paused for a moment in the concealing shadow then started to snake away from the shaft through the thickest grass as fast as his arms and legs could drive him. The roughness cut and sandpapered the soft underparts of his arms, his chest, his stomach, legs and, most painful of all, his naked genitals, but he dared not stop.

His skin prickled with the expectation of a bullet or a panga slicing into his flesh. He dared not look back because the whites of his eyes might be seen.

He had been crawling for what felt like a lifetime when the ground dropped away beneath his torso and he tumbled forward, legs flailing the air, into a donga, a shallow dry watercourse.

Face down at the bottom, he gulped air with great shuddering heaves of his chest. The gunfire was dwindling, becoming more sporadic as the targets became fewer. If they come after me now, I'm dead, he thought in exhaustion, I can't run.

Nobody came. After several minutes, Mutale dragged himself a few yards along the donga until he found a place on its edge, between two stones to conceal his head, where he could look back.

He was more than fifty yards from the mine shaft. Luck had been with him, he had unknowingly crawled along the widening cone of shadow thrown by a corner post of the headgear.

The killers were moving about the slaughter ground at a more leisurely pace now, their frenzy over. They were checking for life in their victims, finishing off the living. A man bent forward and Mutale saw the flicker of a descending panga blade. He heard the soft *chunk* as it bit into some unseen body.

Several of the killers moved back and forth, dragging limp corpses to the edge of the shaft and dropping them in, like so many sacks of coal.

He had to get away from here. When they had mopped up the slaughtered, they might spread the search wider.

He had no idea where he was, except that it was somewhere in Venda well east of Thohoyandou in wild and empty country. The donga must follow the bed of the valley, he knew, and most of the valleys ran east-west.

He dared not stand because the donga was only a metre deep. He moved on all fours, ignoring the rasp of gravel and stones on his knees and hands; he hoped eastwards. If they came for him, they would expect him to go west, back towards the town.

After some ten minutes, he again peeped over the rim of the donga. The killers were about two hundred yards away now, still looking for anyone who might be alive. Search beams probed the dark outside the reach of the vehicle lights. They would soon find the donga. He had to move faster.

He rose to his feet and walked, crouched almost double, with his arms extended in front of him. His breath wheezed. He blundered into the donga's walls and tripped over the small boulders littering its bed but he kept a steady pace.

After another ten minutes, he could no longer see the killers or their vehicles, nothing more than the distant glow from their lamps.

His eyes, now accustomed to the faint light of the myriad stars massed in the Milky Way, could make out obstacles. He stood up straight, his back aching from strain, and walked on, slow at first then quicker as his vision gave him confidence.

Hours later, when a faint tinge of pink touched the eastern horizon, the donga petered out into flat sandy terrain between rocky hills blanketed in a low forest of thorn, marula and mopani trees and shrub. They'll never find me here, he thought with relief.

Three times he crossed fences. One was barbed wire, four feet high. The others were two- and three-metre fences of meshed wire, topped by barbed strands. They scratched his bare skin as he scrambled over.

When the first thin shafts of light pierced the sky, Mutale was still travelling towards the sun, staggering from fatigue and chilled by the pre-dawn temperature drop. Sleep, he thought, I must sleep, I can't go on.

He lay down in a body-sized clearing, pressed in thick grass beneath a mahogany tree on the edge of a gully, too exhausted to care that it had been made by an animal, and fell into oblivion.

He slept, dreamless, until a toe nudged his naked back several times, tugging him back to consciousness. He opened his eyes and froze in fright.

Three feet away, a black man squatting on his haunches stared into Mutale's face. The man was propping himself with a long rifle in his right hand, butt on the ground.

"We have caught you," the man said and Mutale felt sick. "Who are you and which way did you come?" He spoke Shangaan and repeated the question in Afrikaans.

Mutale sat up but said nothing.

"Come on, talk!" a gruff voice ordered from behind him in Afrikaans. He spun around and his worst fear evaporated. He felt a huge rush of relief and fell back on

125

his grass bed, laughing.

The man behind him was white. He wore the khaki clothes, green epaulettes and brass shirt badge of a game ranger in the Kruger National Park.

"He's crazy," the black ranger said.

"Not surprising. But he's made it almost all the way through the park from Mozambique without being eaten, poor bugger."

"Must have come close though, sleeping on a lion's bed. Look how badly he's scratched and cut. Wonder what happened to his clothes."

Mutale's laughter climbed into hysteria.

Chapter Fourteen

"No!" The Chairman smacked the glossy yellowwood table with his palm, an unusual expression of vehemence for him. "No. We cannot ease up now! We must increase the pressure. We are too close. Slow down and we could lose everything, including, may I add, our freedom."

The little Member of Parliament glared back at him, his black eyes cold. "Why the devil did you have to pick on the deputy leader of the Freedom Front?" he demanded, "He was also fighting for partition."

"Partition for some vague Boer autonomy in the indeterminate future," the Chairman retorted, "We seek better than that. He meant nothing to us and he would have opposed us. What better way to bring matters to a head between right and left?"

"And to bring us perilously close to exposure," the MP retorted. "I mean, right there next to Parliament. My God, it was like kicking a nest of wasps. The police, National Intelligence – everybody is hunting, asking questions, looking for somebody to crucify."

Doc, who had been watching the exchange without comment, pushed himself to his feet from the chair at the end of the table. His bulky presence dominated the gracious living room. The other six men fell silent.

All seven were members of the twelve-man committee, which had met in the farmhouse near Louis Trichardt, those who could come at short notice when the MP called the meeting.

They were in Doc's home on Waterkloof Ridge in Pretoria, a comfortable Dutch-gabled house, filled with

South African antiques collected in his lifetime, delicate, carved yellowwood and stinkwood furniture, Cape silver and glass, Baines and Bowler originals and, his prize, some fine VOC porcelain in a leaded-glass cabinet.

The Doctor realised with sadness that he would have to leave the house and Pretoria for an indefinite time when the crisis came, but comforted himself with the knowledge that he would take all its contents to safety with him. When it was all over, he would return. "If we lose courage and faith and fight among each other, we lose the battle," he said. His strong sonorous voice calmed tempers. "We have advanced too far to retreat or change our direction or tactics. Perhaps it was a risk to target a Member of Parliament so close to the House, and a senior one at that. However, the target and place were my choice, the risk was calculated, and it has had the desired effect. Parliament is in uproar, as our colleague here has demonstrated ..." nodding at the still glowering MP, "... the government is in confusion and all the parties are excoriating each other."

"Not everybody suspects the lunatic left of planting the bomb," the MP interjected.

"Good," Doc replied, unruffled, "that is what we want. As the Book says, sow confusion amongst thine enemies. The deed is done, there can be no undoing. Do you accept that?"

The MP hesitated for a moment then nodded, his sleek black hair glistening in the lights from the crystal chandelier above the table.

"Fine. Now, as we have a quorum here, we can be briefed about the situation as it stands."

He sat down and the Chairman rose at the opposite end of the table, levering himself up with his hands on the arms of the blackwood and yellowwood carver. Over six feet tall, in his youth a rugby player, in his sixties, he was thickening a little in the middle. With his mass of senatorial white hair, he was an imposing figure.

"Gentlemen," he said in Afrikaans, "I am able to assure you that not very much more water must pass under the bridge before we can make our final, definitive move.

"You are, of course, aware that fighting has resumed among blacks in the Durban, Witwatersrand and Eastern and Western Cape regions, and is spreading. Not all of it was started by our agents.

"We have received sufficient arms from our collaborators in Mozambique for our needs and they are ready to act in support of us when we give the word. They continue to supply us with weapons for distribution to the blacks.

"We have also received some sophisticated weaponry from our conservative friends in the United States for our own men. It came in containers with shipments of machinery."

"Isn't that very risky?" a man down the table asked. "It could be picked up by Customs."

"Each container was marked so our people in Customs could clear it without inspection." The Chairman smiled. "All have arrived. I can also tell you that in Venda, the independents have all but eliminated the local ANC. How they did it, I don't know and do not wish to know.

"The next few weeks will see further action to silence or discredit our opponents. We are fully prepared. It will not be long before the government will be forced to declare a state of emergency or martial law. Then we will make our move.

"And then, gentlemen, we will be our own masters, independent of South Africa, free of black rule."

The others clapped. The meeting ended with a prayer by the Chairman for success for the righteous.

***

By coincidence, nine other men met in Cape Town on the same day.

They gathered in the warm, wood-panelled and leather-furnished billiard room of a gracious old Cape Dutch house, in the sheltering lap of mountain behind Devil's Peak. It was the home of the Vice President in the Groote Schuur complex, the historic presidential estate bequeathed to the nation by Cecil John Rhodes.

The Vice President put down his glass, clasped his hands and looked at the others gathered at the small bar in the cosy room. They were a strange political mix but all had one thing in common: he had complete trust in them. Some were members of the Cabinet, some old friends, two of them leaders of Opposition parties.

They had worked very hard behind the scenes to steer the country away from the explosion of violence the world had anticipated when apartheid collapsed. They had ridden out nation-wide turbulence to achieve the election in 1994, which ushered in non-racial government.

Now, inexplicably, mass violence and assassinations were erupting again and threatening to shatter the precarious peace.

The Vice President's imperturbable manner hid deep worry. Choosing his words with care, he outlined his suspicions based on disconnected pieces of information reaching him from many quarters. Some of it they had heard themselves but the picture he pieced together unnerved them.

"A third force," the Minister of Finance pondered aloud, "but whose? We shut down the CCB and the other covert units long ago and we've rooted out the militants in the army and police, or at least those we know."

"It can't be the CP or the lunatic fringe, those secessionists and AWB and *Wit Wolwe* people," said one of the Opposition party leaders. "They're altogether discredited and don't have the organisation for it."

"Yet there is no doubt a third force is operating," the Vice President said. He lit a pipe and breathed blue smoke towards the low-slung copper lamps, casting yellow light on the baize table.

He had to be very careful of what he said or his words might be misconstrued and give offence. "The evidence is too strong to ignore. Look at this – we all agree violence is futile and self-destructive. The security forces' presence in trouble spots has been radically increased, yet, far from declining, violence worsens. Look at the volume of firearms coming into the country. The police have seized tens of thousands, not so?"

The Minister of Police nodded.

"And at a generous estimate, that may be ten per cent of the total. Look at the spate of assassinations: white, black and brown businessmen, opinion-makers from across the board, dozens of township leaders, and the deputy leader of the Freedom Front almost on the steps of the House. Why him, of all people? And why here when it would have been much simpler to shoot him at home or on his farm? The pattern is the same. It is deliberate, high profile destabilisation."

"Are we quite sure it wasn't by Pan African Congress radicals?" asked an advisor, a prominent ANC policymaker. Since the PAC had fared so badly in South Africa's first free elections, the ANC had dismissed it.

"I think we can be," said another minister, a short, impatient man with a mouth like a rattrap. "They're too committed to the constitution to risk destroying it and their own image. There is no evidence pointing to them."

"That's the problem," the Vice President said, "there's no evidence pointing to anyone."

"So where do we go?" asked the Minister of Finance. He was anxious about the economic effects of upheaval. "Shouldn't we be discussing this with the Cabinet? Shouldn't the National Intelligence Service, the police and the security committee be consulted?"

"We should," the Vice President sighed. He drew on his pipe and sipped from his glass. "I cannot, yet. There's so little to go on I wanted to hear your views in private first. As for the NIS and the rest, I don't know who to trust any more, who might be involved with this third force or fifth column or whatever you want to call it."

The Minister of Police bridled. "I trust the police. We have cleaned out the racists."

The advisor fixed him with a cynical eye. "How many policemen does the department have?" he asked. "A hundred thousand? Two hundred thousand? Can you vouch for each one?"

"It's not for us to go into that detail," the Vice President said, sensing dispute. "There may be bad apples among them, just as there might be in the Defence Force and the civil service and even in Parliament. If we start doubting everybody we're sunk before we start."

The Finance Minister put down his wine glass and faced his colleagues.

"What is needed," he said, weighting each word, "is an independent investigation. Define a small group of men who can be trusted absolutely. Free them of all other duties and put a strong man in command. Tell them to use all their energy to expose this third force. We don't require Cabinet approval for that."

"An excellent idea," an Opposition party leader said, then smiled.

"I think so too. Will all of you please look for such men for me," the Vice President said.

Satisfied, he relit his pipe. He had not told them everything, of course. His plans were too devious and delicate. He could not yet reveal his own very secret source among the country's radical dissidents.

CHAPTER FIFTEEN

"*Ag*, let's call it a day, Lucky, there's nothing here that can't wait until tomorrow."

Superintendent Louw tied the red tape around the cover of a file, tossed it into a wire tray and stood up to stretch, feeling his years. He could take early retirement now if he wanted, but what the hell would he do with himself?

"*Ja*, it's been a long day," Captain Ndzimandze said, straightening the stack of files in the tray. "All this shit routine, I don't know why we bother."

The remark irritated Superintendent Louw but he let it slide.

"Still nothing new on the Greeff murder?" Ndzimandze asked.

"Nothing," the superintendent grunted, frowning, "It's been two weeks now and the trail's grown cold. We can't keep three men on it full time for much longer."

"We must, sir, they mustn't get away with killing a policeman."

"*Ja*, well. Come round for a drink, Lucky. There's a lot we should talk over." Superintendent Louw felt the need for company in his empty home.

"Sorry, sir, I can't tonight. My wife's bought tickets for some film."

"Maybe tomorrow, then. You better be on your way, it's late."

"Goodnight, sir." The captain shrugged on his suit jacket and left.

Carrying his worn old briefcase of thick leather and

brass clasps that seemed to last forever, Superintendent Louw walked down the corridor, painted in the traditional government brown. The building was almost empty at this time of evening and the dominant smell of dust and old files depressed him.

On the way out, he paused at the charge office counter to tell the duty officer where to find him if needed. Young policemen in blue fatigues lounged about – mostly black and brown, some whites, all fit and brash with bulky automatic pistols on their hips. They nodded in respect to him. Silly buggers, he thought, behind my back they think I'm a relic.

He climbed into his Peugeot looking forward to his first brandy of the day. Maybe two or three and then off to the Portuguese restaurant down the road for a meal, knowing it was an excuse to escape loneliness. Tonight he wanted people around him.

Melville's shopping centre was as lively as usual. People strolled the sidewalks between cafés and restaurants and the still open shops. Most of them were younger than him, the new generation of go-getters, who had taken over and remodelled the small old Melville houses.

He parked the car against the kerb in front of his darkened house instead of in the garage. As he inserted his latchkey into the front door, Louw felt some hidden nerve jangle; his sixth sense honed by his life in police work, its antennae on full alert.

His left hand was holding the briefcase and his right the key. He did not hesitate, because a pause in the small sounds of opening the door would be a giveaway, and turned the key in the lock. The door swung open. He dropped the key in his pocket and reached in to flick the switches that turned on the porch and hall lights.

Nothing. Everything in its place as it should be, undisturbed, silent. He walked towards the hatstand-cum-telephone table where he always put down the briefcase, resisting the temptation to peer into the darkened living room or dining room doors as he passed them.

The dining room! his sixth sense shouted and in confirmation, a voice behind him spoke in Afrikaans.

"Stand still, superintendent. Don't turn around. I have a gun pointed at you and I will shoot."

He froze; his pistol was in the shoulder holster under his left arm. The carpeted floorboards in the middle of the passage gave a faint creak and the front door clicked shut behind him. The boards creaked again, steps coming back to him.

"Look straight ahead and don't move," the voice said, a young man's.

"What do you want?" Every muscle in Superintendent Louw's body taut but he was as calm as if offering the man a drink.

"You'll see, superintendent, you'll see. Now shut up."

The voice was familiar.

The floor creaked again, very close now, and Superintendent Louw felt the hardness of a gun muzzle jab into the small of his back.

That was a mistake.

He spun around clockwise with bewildering speed, his right forearm slashing down and back, ahead of his body movement. It struck the intruder's gun hand in the instant he pulled the trigger.

The nine millimetre shot crashed like a cannon in the narrow passage. The bullet passed through the superintendent's jacket and ploughed into the top of the table, just missing the telephone.

The intruder staggered back and tried to line up the gun again. Before he could pull the trigger, the superintendent completed his fast turn, swinging the briefcase in his left hand with all the force of his broad shoulders.

The edge struck the man square on the ear. The weight slammed him off balance and bounced his head hard against the wall. He stumbled back, dizzy, still trying to aim the gun.

The superintendent sidestepped and kicked high. His shoe hit the underside of the man's wrist. Another shot roared in the confined space. The bullet went into the ceiling and the pistol flew free.

Before the intruder could regain his balance, Louw was on him. He hit him twice with short powerful forearm jabs, both beneath the stomach. No Queensberry rules now.

The man folded forward, gasping. The superintendent brought up his right knee below the intruder's chin and heard bone crack. The man's head snapped up and he toppled over backwards on the passage carpet, unconscious.

Superintendent Louw leaned his shoulder against the wall, sucking in deep breaths. He was not as fit as he liked to believe and the eruption of energy had drained him.

Sharp knocks on the front door echoed in the passage. He picked up the fallen pistol and switched off the hall light. Holding the gun down at his side, he opened the door a few inches.

A fat little man in jeans and an open-neck shirt stood there, knuckles raised to knock again, with a frowsy woman peering over his shoulder. The neighbours. They stared at him, wide-eyed.

"Are you okay, Superintendent?" the man asked, looking him up and down as if expecting to see blood, "We were walking past when we heard shots. Is everything all right?"

Superintendent Louw tried to look apologetic. "I'm sorry, the maid left the television turned up far too loud and I switched on in the middle of one of these crime shows." His smile was disarming.

The man relaxed. "*Ag,* hell," he said, "there's too much of that crap on the telly these days. If you need anything, just shout, hey."

"Many thanks."

They walked down the steps and he closed the door.

136

The intruder still lay on his back, mouth slack and half-open eyes staring, unfocussed, at the ceiling.

He grasped the man by the armpits and dragged him along the passage to the kitchen. There he threw back the cord carpet and lifted a trapdoor to reveal wooden steps leading down into a shallow empty cellar, the store room in the days when the house was built. Holding the intruder by the wrists, he eased him legs first over the edge and let go.

The man bumped on his back to the bottom of the steps and lay in a heap. The superintendent pushed a switch beside the kitchen door to turn on a ceiling light in the cellar and followed, pulling the trapdoor closed over his head.

He sat on a step, turned the stranger with a toe until he flopped over on his back, and studied him. He knew that face but he could not place it: about twenty-eight, curly black hair, an athletic, muscled body in dark shirt, slacks and windbreaker.

The man's pockets yielded a canvas and Velcro wallet with a few banknotes but nothing else, no ID, credit cards, receipts, or address. No holster. He had carried the gun, a Beretta, under his belt or in a pocket.

Superintendent Louw settled down to wait and think. His prisoner snored.

Five minutes later, the man stirred and groaned. Coming to, he screwed up his eyes against the glare of the ceiling light and raised himself on one elbow.

"You can sit up if you like but stay right there," the superintendent said. "This is your gun and you know it works."

The man shook his head to clear it and a spasm of pain twisted his face. Gingerly he felt his jaw. He opened his mouth to talk and found it did not function as it should.

"My jaw," he said, his voice thick. "You broke it." He sounded indignant.

"Better you with a broken jaw than me dead."

137

The intruder's gaze shifted from Louw's face down to the hands resting on his knees, where the Beretta dangled from the right one, forefinger around the trigger.

Louw watched the man guage the distance – three paces – and decide it was too far to jump him. Louw had shown how fast he could move for such an old man.

Louw dredged a name from the back of his mind. "Who are you?" he asked.

The intruder stared back in silence.

"No matter, I think I remember you now. Basson? Warrant Officer Theo Basson? You were with the Security Police until it was disbanded and you left the force, right?"

The man raised himself into a sitting position, wincing as pain stabbed him in his bruised stomach. He clamped his lips tight and looked at the walls and ceiling.

The superintendent sighed.

"Basson, you forget I've been a policeman for over thirty years. I can get the information out of you, it will just take longer than if you use your head and tell me now. To save you time, I think you were Stefan Greeff's contact. You manipulated him, you planted the faked evidence in that Ngwenya murder case, and you might have had a hand in killing him. Maybe did it yourself."

Now the man stared straight at him and the superintendent thought he saw a flicker of anxiety in the dark eyes.

"What I want to know," he went on, "is why you did all those things. Who are you working for? What are they trying to do? And why did you try to kill me?"

Basson drew up his feet as if to stand.

"Sit down!" Superintendent Louw ordered, the Beretta pointing straight at Basson's chest, the hammer back.

Basson straightened his legs out on the floor and pushed himself until his back was against the wall of the small cellar. He stared, sullen, saying nothing.

The superintendent rose to his feet, trying not to feel a

new stiffness in his hips and shoulders, and walked closer. He stayed beyond reach of Basson's legs and kept the pistol trained on him. "Have it your way then," he said in a voice now hard. Anger made him impatient. He had to know now what lay behind the attack.

"This is what will happen. You will be charged with one murder, an attempted murder, defeating the ends of justice and God knows what other crimes after we look into your activities. But before you reach the charge office, Basson, you will hurt. For instance, who will doubt me when I say I shot you in self-defence?"

His wrist twitched and the Beretta roared. The copper-jacketed bullet grazed the skin and muscle of Basson's left calf and buried itself in the cement floor.

Basson's whole body jerked taut like a puppet on strings. His eyes rounded in shock and he opened his mouth to yell. The pain of his fractured jawbone stopped the movement and the scream came out in a high, baby wail. His face turned pale. Blood welled through the hole in his trouser leg and made a small glistening puddle on the floor.

"Of course, me being an old man and you a fit young bastard I might have had to wound you twice to stop you, even three times ..." The superintendent's right arm straightened and the Beretta's muzzle rose a fraction to point at Basson's thigh. His forefinger curled tighter around the trigger.

Basson reared back in fear and tried to press himself into the wall. He stretched out an arm with fingers splayed as if to ward off a bullet. "*No!*" he shouted, "No! Please!"

Louw lifted the gun's muzzle to the vertical. "Talk then!"

Basson slumped and gulped in air. Sweat beaded his face and neck. His Adam's apple bobbed and his gaze flicked in desperation around the small cellar, seeking hope. There was none, just this cast-iron nemesis standing over him. He hung his head.

"It's the Free Staters," he mumbled. "They made me do it."

"The who? What the hell are you talking about, man? The province?"

"No, no. It's some people who want to break off from South Africa because they don't like a government of primitives and commies."

"Who are they?"

"I don't know."

"Bullshit, man! You don't kill for people you don't even know!" The Beretta's muzzle dropped.

"Honest, Superintendent, I don't know them! They came to me when things began to change and asked me to help."

"And you agreed because you're another of these *Boerestaat* crazies?"

"Not a *Boerestaat,* superintendent, a republic run by civilised people."

Louw studied the young man with a tinge of pity; that anyone could be so bloody naive ... "Well, who *did* you work for?"

"One man ... there's a cell system, so if one is caught the others are still safe. That's why I can't tell you. Honestly."

Basson sat up straighter and bent forward to squeeze his right calf above the wound. The blood was not flowing very fast, the bullet had cauterised a furrow through flesh. The muzzle of the Beretta followed his movement.

"Who is this one man?"

Basson peered up at him with his face screwed up by the anguish of his situation as much as the pain in his leg.

"Superintendent, if I tell you I'm dead. They've got people everywhere. They'll get me even in prison."

The Beretta boomed again. The shot smacked into the cement between Basson's legs, six inches from his crotch, spraying dust and chips. He rammed himself back against the wall in fright.

"You're dead if you don't tell me, mister. The next one might be right in your balls."

"Jesus, you're mad!" Basson gasped.

"Mad as hell. Who is he, damn it?"

"Someone who calls himself Smith, I don't know his real name. He stays in a hotel in Rosebank, I don't know which one. I've seen him once. He sends other guys to pass on orders. I don't know their names."

"Could you identify them if you saw them?"

"*Ja*, but if I'm caught they'll disappear. You'll never find them."

"Hmmm." Superintendent Louw changed direction. "What were you supposed to do to me tonight?"

Basson had the grace to look embarrassed. "Eliminate you. My instructions were to set up a gas explosion in the kitchen. Easy enough. Leave a two-kilo liquid petroleum gas canister on a hot plate on the stove and the explosion would wreck the whole house."

"Why?"

"Because you were beginning to sniff around too much, after that ballsed-up Ngwenya murder."

"Who did kill that man?"

"Not me. I just arranged the evidence."

"And after you've blown me to hell tonight, who else is in line for a visit?"

Defiance crept into Basson's eyes. His lips closed in a thin line. Louw recognised it as an indication Basson's leg and jaw were beginning to throb.

"Okay. It's your choice," said the superintendent. He took careful aim with the Beretta.

"Oh shit!" Basson cursed. "That fucking red lecturer, Ballance."

The pistol's muzzle lowered. "Well, he's safe now."

"No, Superintendent," Basson's mouth twisted in a lop-sided grin, "it's too late. Smith is already there."

The words stung Louw. Galvanised, he stepped forward, grabbed Basson's shirtfront in his left hand and shook him so hard, his head banged against the wall. "Where!" he shouted. "Where is the hit, damn you!"

"At his house. He's dead already." Basson grinned as his two hands shot forward and clamped on the breech of the pistol, over Superintendent Louw's fist. He wrenched it towards him, at the same time trying to lever himself up on his good leg.

The superintendent tugged back, felt his finger being forced against the trigger, and let his arm relax a fraction to avoid firing. Basson jammed a thumb inside the trigger guard over the superintendent's finger and pushed hard. Louw tried desperately to hold off the pressure but it was too strong. The Beretta jerked and went off.

The bullet struck Basson in the mouth. It fragmented and splashed a mess of grey and red on the wall behind his head. His body quivered for a moment and slumped like a wet sack.

Louw let go of the pistol as if it were red hot and stepped back, stunned by Basson's action. The man had deliberately killed himself. Rage at letting it happen overwhelmed him and he spat curses. A young man, albeit a killer, was now an inanimate lump of meat because of his lapse.

Ballance. He leaped up the steps, banged back the trapdoor, and ran to the telephone.

There was no reply from Ballance's house. He telephoned the Brixton station, issued rapid orders, and dashed out of the house to his car. The front door slammed behind him.

Ballance's home was across town, some fifteen minutes driving at this time of night, when Johannesburg's streets were busy with evening traffic.

He shoved the gear lever into first and swung the Peugeot into a U-turn. The rear tyres squealed and trailed blue smoke as he accelerated, making a passing couple look up in surprise.

Chapter Sixteen

Ballance steered north on Jan Smuts Avenue with the stream of commuters abandoning the city centre to another night of crime, their headlights a glittering stream of sequins on the black ribbon of road.

He was tired but content, the heap on his desk levelled, papers marked, the syllabus for the coming term prepared and his next negotiation contract lined up.

Nearly a week of relaxation lay ahead, before he had to confront the rows of faces in the tiered benches of the lecture room to try to inject some knowledge into them.

Almost a week; he would take Penny Fox to dinner. The thought was pleasant.

It also reminded him of Ngwenya and the menace that had brushed them. That brought a sudden wave of depression; skilled mediator though he was, he felt his objectivity crumbling to personal fears and prejudices.

It's time I got out of the ivory tower, he thought as he turned up Bompas Road towards Oxford Road. Had I done so earlier, I might have been better prepared for what happened.

It was no surprise some whites, so opposed to sharing society with other races, were plotting secession. South African history, littered with the cadavers of breakaway republics, demonstrated one common characteristic: the exclusion of people of other colours except as menials.

The same kind of warped minds had to be behind the current plotting, but who were they? It would be foolish to dismiss them as blind fanatics, however crude and bloody their tactics. A great many adult whites were familiar with weapons and explosives, thanks to conscription and two years of national service. Thousands had first-hand battle experience in Angola, Namibia, Rhodesia and Mozambique. Many, like the kind the CCB had used, were utterly devoid of conscience or compassion and skilled in the dark arts of covert warfare. Born killers, fit for nothing else.

It struck Ballance that if the white supremacists wanted to start a revolution, now was as good a time as any. They had capable, intelligent leaders and a public disillusioned by rocketing crime, rising living costs and corruption in high places. South Africa was on a tightrope. How in hell to prevent revolution?

The puzzle was exercising his mind as he drove the last few hundred yards through the peaceful wooded avenues of Sandton's suburbia, towards his home.

He turned into his street and saw a dimmed red flashlight waving at him from the middle of the road. Police. Must be a stolen vehicle check, he thought, and drew to a stop at the kerbside. The red beam of the torch flashed across his face and switched off. He lowered the window.

"Mr Ballance," said Superintendent Louw's gruff voice, "I'm glad to see you."

"Superintendent Louw ... what are you doing here?" Ballance asked in surprise.

"Leave your car and come with me. It'll be quite safe."

Ballance switched off, climbed out and locked the car. They stopped under a leafy jacaranda tree. Darkness was falling and the air was sweet with the allure of night flowers. Fifty metres away, the lamp above his front door cast a welcoming yellow glow.

"What's happening?" Ballance was aware of another man standing in silence nearby, a vague figure in the filigreed shadow of streetlights through the foliage.

"I am afraid you cannot enter your house yet," the superintendent said.

Ballance felt the now familiar blend of fear and irritation return. "Why not?"

"Because someone is trying to kill you."

"Oh, for God's sake!" Ballance exclaimed, throwing wide his arms in exasperation. "Aren't you being a little melodramatic?"

"Please keep your voice down. You didn't honestly think those people would try once and then forget you, did you?"

"But ... how the hell do you know? What's going on?"

"A man tried to kill me just over thirty minutes ago. Before he died, he said a professional assassin was on his way to kill you. It's lucky you're late."

Louw's dispassionate tone made the statement more chilling. Ballance shivered in spite of the evening warmth. He looked up and down the quiet street and moved into a deeper patch of shadow.

"Two Murder and Robbery men are watching your front door," the superintendent went on, "and a third is on the other side of the townhouses. We don't know the assassin by sight but we can see anyone coming or going."

"I thought professional assassins existed only in paperbacks."

"He's real enough. Name's Smith but that means nothing. He works for some secessionist group. It ties in very well with what Ngwenya told us."

"What if he's already in my place? Everybody else walks in there, why not him?" Ballance remarked with a tinge of sarcasm.

"I considered that." Louw shoved his hands deep in his trouser pockets and hunched his shoulders. Ballance remembered the bleak eyes and was glad it was dark. "If he is inside we have to wait until he comes out. It could be a long time."

"I can't wait here all night, I have to go home, I ..." Ballance felt the unseen gaze on him and was embarrassed. "Sorry," he said, "I didn't mean to sound un-

145

grateful."

They stood in silence with their own thoughts, watching the innocent entrance to Ballance's home, a solid carved door in the warm red and brown brick. Several cars cruised past and one appeared to slow outside the property, causing the superintendent to stiffen until it moved on. A small man in a tracksuit puffed along the far side of the street, towed on a leash by a black and white Border Collie, sniffing every flower bed. He glanced at them as he passed.

"What other entrances are there?" Superintendent Louw asked.

"This one and the sliding glass doors to the garden, the way I went out the other night when you met me on the far side."

"Can we go in that way?"

"Yes, through a friend's house on the far side. I have a key for the garden door."

Louw was silent for a minute while he considered options. He hoped he had reached Ballance's house ahead of the assassin, assuming that Basson had told the truth, but if the man was already inside, extracting him could be messy.

Waiting all night to prise him out by daylight would be even messier. Reinforcements would have to be called in, the whole complex vacated and the job done in an unavoidable glare of publicity he did not want. He made up his mind.

"Give me the keys, please, and ask your friend to let us through."

Ballance fished out his keyring and unclipped the brass front door latchkey and a chromed key for the inner sliding door. Louw pocketed the chromed key and handed the brass key to his man standing nearby and gave him instructions. The man nodded and strolled down the street.

"Do precisely what I tell you when we're inside," the

superintendent said, "I don't want you in the way if there's shooting."

Shooting. Ballance had not thought of that. "What about the other residents?"

"I hope they'll all be indoors watching TV or having dinner. The detective at the front door will open it ten minutes from now."

Ballance saw two men move towards his front door, keeping in shadow. They melted into the blackness on either side of the light.

Louw and Ballance walked to the far side of the townhouse cluster, where a detective in a brass-buttoned blazer joined them. Ballance knocked on a door and a middle-aged man in shirtsleeves appeared with a glass of red wine in his hand.

"Jeff," he said, smiling, "This is an unexpected surprise. We're just having a drink, come in. Who're your friends?"

"Ben Cartwright, Superintendent Louw," Ballance introduced them. "Ben, I'm sorry but this isn't a social call. They're police. There's a burglar in my place and they want to catch him by surprise. Do you mind if we go through?"

Cartwright's smile vanished and he stepped back.

"Good God, a burglar in here? It shouldn't be possible."

"But it's happening," Louw said. "Please ask your family to move out of the living room, if the man sees someone watching he might panic and run."

"Go on through, you know the way."

Ballance led the way down a short passage and through a small laundry room, the same as his own, to a door opening into the inner garden.

The superintendent stopped Ballance with a hand on his shoulder.

"Stay here and leave this to us," he whispered. "Keep out of sight."

The two policemen edged through the door and crept close to the wall past large picture windows and glass doors. The houses were in darkness or their curtains were drawn.

Ballance's curtains were wide open and from the glow from the decorative lampposts in the garden, he could just see the inside his lounge.

Louw and the detective paused next to his sliding door. Louw reached under his jacket and drew an automatic pistol, pointing it skywards. There was still no visible movement inside.

Louw stepped to the door, flattened himself against the wall next to it and inserted the key. The detective hunched behind a prunus bush.

The second hand on Ballance's watch ticked away the last moments.

Right on time, on the other side of the townhouse, a detective inserted the front door key and turned it.

A brilliant blinding flash bathed the garden in intense white light, etching every detail. A blast shook the cluster. Ballance's picture window and sliding door burst outward, into the garden, in an explosion of sparkling shards. Nearby windows cracked and collapsed. Pieces of invisible debris buzzed past him.

On the street side, Ballance's front door blew off its hinges and splintered. It struck the policeman with the impact of a truck, smashing him into the street, fracturing bones. The blast lifted his partner and dumped him metres away flat on his back.

Silence followed the explosion. Then sounds began, small at first, querulous voices, a baby's cry, dogs barking, a woman's voice sharp with fear. The bang of doors. Running feet.

Ballance sprinted across the lawn, feeling glass crunch beneath his shoes. The detective in the blazer was on his hands and knees, hanging his head and shaking it like a tired hound, blood dripping on the grass.

"Shit," he said with quiet vehemence. "Shit."

Louw propped himself with his left hand against the wall and wiped his watering eyes with the back of his gun hand.

"Superintendent, are you all right?"

"*Ja*, I'm okay." He blinked to clear his sight and saw his partner, still kneeling.

"Pieter!" Superintendent Louw went to him, stumbling, to examine him. The detective's hair was thick with blood from cuts in his scalp caused by flying glass, but they were superficial.

"Get help," the superintendent ordered Ballance, "An ambulance, fast!"

Ballance ran to the Cartwright house while Louw returned to the shattered townhouse. Louw raised the key, remembered he didn't need that now, and stepped through the gaping frame of the sliding door.

At the front door, he found a detective sprawled on his back on the front path, with the wreckage of the heavy door on top of him and heaved it off. A brief check of his pulse confirmed he was dead. The other man was out cold but seemed unhurt. The superintendent rolled him on to his side.

People peered from windows and front doors up and down the street. Several offered help. The superintendent declined. The wail of ambulances approached from Rosebank.

Deep gloom descended upon him. We fucked it up well and truly. How the *hell* did we miss him?

Ballance emerged from the shattered front doorway. Inside was destruction: walls gouged, paintings torn, furniture churned up. He felt a seething anger that someone could do this to him. "What was it, Superintendent?"

"I'm not certain. A small bomb, for sure."

"Wired to the latch?"

"Had to be."

"Why in hell did we walk right into it, Superintendent? Shouldn't you have thought of a bomb?"

Louw looked up from where he knelt beside his unconscious officer and cast a bitter look at at Ballance. He was in no mood for amateur criticism. "We're only human," he replied.

Ballance saw eyes still watery and bloodshot from the scorch of the explosion and regretted what he had said.

An ambulance hurtled around the corner and stopped with a diminuendo howl nearby. Men leapt out with equipment.

"This one needs urgent help," the superintendent told them. "That one's dead. There's another man inside with multiple cuts."

Two attached an oxygen mask and a drip to the injured man. Two others ran into the house with a stretcher.

Louw turned to Ballance. "Where will you go?"

Ballance had not thought of that yet. "I don't know. I doubt I'm going to be very popular among my neighbours."

An idea came to him. "I'll see if Miss Fox can put me up," he said. "It should be safe enough."

"You might be drawing danger to her."

"I'll make sure I'm not followed. At least I'll be able to give her some protection. Is it okay for me to take some stuff?"

Louw grunted. "If she agrees, let me know and I'll assign a man to protect both of you. Phone her now. I'll see you tomorrow. I'll want a statement from you anyway."

Ballance returned inside as a blue and white police van with flashing headlights and a police car lurched around the corner and pulled up behind the ambulance. Men boiled out of them, those from the van in uniform, one with an Alsatian on a leash. Louw sighed; it would be a long night with lots of publicity.

***

150

In his room in the hotel Smith sipped from a tall glass of beer while he peeled off the tracksuit. He had cooled off on the drive back but still felt sweaty.

The Border Collie lay on a corner of the thick carpet and watched him with intelligent eyes, its panting drawing up the corners of its mouth in a satisfied smile.

Smith smiled too. He liked dogs. He would take this one back to the SPCA tomorrow and say he was very sorry, he couldn't keep it after all, the residential hotel he was living in wouldn't allow dogs. A few rands should make them happy.

He knew his muscles would be stiff in the morning, although he had jogged no farther than twice around a block. It exasperated him that it had all been for very little; a suburban explosion would sow fear, but his target had escaped. Luck of the devil.

Unlocking Ballance's door with a master key, placing the limpet mine and battery on the floor inside, inserting the prepared connector into the back of the lock and departing had taken him less than thirty seconds. He did not think anyone had seen him. Anyway, who would suspect a grey-haired old jogger of planting a bomb? Minutes later, as he had neared his car, policemen began to appear. He blessed his luck.

Passing his car, he made a second circuit of the block to test his cover and see what they were up to, and chuckled to himself when they ignored the old man and his dog; his real satisfaction of the night, he reflected.

He knew he had failed when he saw Ballance standing with the policemen. How had they known? It must have come from Basson, which meant they had caught him.

Smith tipped the last of the beer down his throat and decided he would leave this hotel tomorrow to move to an alternative base.

CHAPTER SEVENTEEN

"Jeff! Come in." Penelope's face was full of concern as she freed the safety chain and opened the door wide for Ballance, who was carrying a small nylon suitcase and looking more rumpled than usual, his tie loose and his hair tousled.

He put down the case in the small passage and smiled at her, pleased at seeing her again. She looked fresh and scrubbed, without make-up.

"Penny, this is very kind of you. I didn't know who else to call. A hotel's too public and my university mates would pester me with awkward questions when the papers come out tomorrow."

"Don't worry about it. When in trouble, always come to your lawyer. It pays my keep." She laughed. "I'm joking, Jeff. Take your bag through to the guest room and make yourself at home. Is that all you have?"

"Enough for a week. The rest is still at home but the police are all over the place."

"You parked in the basement?"

"No, I parked underground in Rosebank and came by cab. After tonight, I didn't want the risk of being traced through my car. They might bomb that next."

The sobering remark brought home to both of them why he was here: someone had tried to kill him.

When he had unpacked, he returned to the lounge.

Penelope held out a large cut-glass tumbler filled with amber liquid and tinkling chunks of ice. "Johnny Walker and soda," she announced. "It's your favourite, isn't it?"

"And boy, do I need it!" He sighed in gratitude.

She sat on a couch and crossed her long legs, still tracksuited from her evening jog.

"Jeff, what is happening to you, to us? One day we're going about our business then ... *wham!* ... both of us are up to our necks in some spooky business full of policemen and assassins and bombs."

"Mine is, not yours to the best of our knowledge."

"Let's not kid each other, Jeff," she said, "It's very obvious that anyone around you, or Temba Ngwenya, or Superintendent Louw, is also in danger and the connection has in all likelihood been made to me. If I believed otherwise I wouldn't have let you come here but as the risk already exists, I feel safer with someone around."

"I brought my notorious gun, by the way, and Superintendent Louw says he'll have someone keep an eye on this place."

"I know. He phoned before you arrived. He also said you'd tell me what happened tonight."

Ballance described arriving home, finding the police, the attempt to enter the house, the appalling shock of the explosion, the injured men ... and the angry remonstrations of his neighbours.

"I've decided to take leave of absence from varsity," he said. "I want to work with Temba to get to the bottom of this so I don't expect to bother you for more than a day or two."

"It's no bother, Jeff. The guest room's there and it's never used. Where will you go?"

He leaned forward and rested his elbows on his knees, thinking. He had been asking himself the same question since he had made up his mind.How and where do you start to expose an organised undercover movement that will stop at nothing to prevent that happening?

"I don't know. I haven't worked it out yet but there are several options I want to discuss with Temba. One is to start digging from outside the country. It should also be safer, because digging here sets you up like a bloody

153

duck in a shooting gallery. We can leave that to the superintendent and his merry men."

"Don't forget I'm in this too. I'd like to help if I can, perhaps on the legal side ..."

"Sure, Penny, but don't go asking questions around town," he said. "Look what happened to that man they mistook for Temba, and to Sergeant Greeff, and almost happened to Superintendent Louw himself. You'd draw attention to yourself and that could be fatal."

She shivered involuntarily and for something to do, she rose to pour Ballance another drink.

"Have you had anything to eat?" she asked.

"No, I forgot all about it, but I'm not hungry."

"Nonsense. You must have something."

She left him watching television while she scrambled eggs and made toast. She was unsettled by his presence in her home, a feeling she had not expected. Perhaps I shouldn't have let him stay here, she thought, and was embarrassed by the thought.

The whisky and food eased Ballance's tension and he felt fatigue invade his body. He stood up and stretched like a cat.

"Penny, it's been a hell of a day. Do you mind if I use the bathroom and head for bed? Good heavens, it's past midnight!"

"No, go right ahead, you must be worn out. There's a shower if you like."

"Thanks, Miz Lawyer." He bent and gave her a light kiss on the forehead. "You're a star and I'm enormously grateful to you."

Penelope looked into the grey eyes, creased at the corners with laugh lines, and wanted to hold him. Instead, she patted the lapels of his jacket.

"And my considered legal advice to you, sir, is to go to bed and have a good night's sleep. You look as though you need it."

While she tidied the small kitchen, she heard the

shower running and the small bumps and rustles of a man settling down for the night, comforting and familiar sounds that her choice of independence had shut off a long time ago.

She found the bathroom empty and clean, the towels racked and the basin surround adorned by razor, shaving brush, toothbrush and toothpaste tube. The mat next to the shower door was damp. Typical male, she thought, they never remember to use the bathmat.

When she had showered, Penelope shook her hair free of her cap and let it tumble down her back in a pale glossy curtain. She stood in front of the full-length mirror and considered her reflection on its steam-misted surface. A bit thin, she mused, but not bad.

Her legs and thighs were long, slender and firm, from running. A small behind and rounded hips recurved into a narrow waist and flat stomach. Her skin was tanned a pale brown except for a small triangle of pure white left by a cutaway bikini, a memento of her last vacation.

She sucked in breath and the action hollowed her stomach and expanded her chest, thrusting out small firm breasts with wide pink areolae.

Studying her body, she thought of Ballance on the other side of the wall. No, she told herself, he's very nice and good-looking and I haven't slept with a man for a year, but it won't work.

The pensive mood broke. She patted on powder, shrugged into a long terrycloth robe and swept out of the bathroom to her bedroom. She donned a short cotton nightgown and climbed into bed. The radio clock said a quarter to one, too late to read. She turned out the light.

In the dark, she saw through her open door, a narrow shaft of pale light across the passage. It came from the slightly ajar door of the guest room.

Damn, he'd fallen asleep with the bedside lamp on. It would disturb her sleep and might disturb his. Irritated, she got out of bed and pulled the robe over her nightdress.

He lay flat on his back on top of the bedclothes wearing a pair of tennis shorts, mouth open, one arm lying across his stomach and the other flung out sideways.

Penelope paused just inside the door to look at him; lean, hard and almost hairless, with flat chest muscles, a stomach corded even in repose and the shoulders and arms of an athlete.

She tiptoed to the bedside table and reached to press the button on the lamp base. The side of her robe brushed his arm and his eyes opened.

Ballance stared at the ceiling for several seconds, bewildered by the unfamiliar room, while she stood stock still, annoyed at herself, embarrassed that he might read meaning into her presence.

"Penny?" His voice fuzzed by sleep.

"Yes," she whispered back. "I'm sorry I woke you. You left the light on and I came to turn it off."

His hand rose and rested on her forearm. "I'm glad you did."

Wide awake now, Ballance rolled on his side to face her and raised himself on his elbow. He took her hand in his. "Penny, stay."

"Jeff, I can't ..."

He stroked her arm. She felt a sudden warmth suffuse her, as if she were blushing with her whole body.

"Please."

She slowly sat on the edge of the bed, as if her knees had a will of their own. "Damn," she said, shaking her head so the golden hair spread across her shoulders, "I want to, but ..."

"But what?" He sat up.

Penelope lowered her head and the curtain of hair screened her face. "Jeff, I hardly know you. This is not very professional, is it?"

Ballance leaned forward, wrapped his arms around her shoulders, and drew her to him. She resisted for a moment, then the tautness in her melted.

"Jeff?" A muffled voice.

"Yes?"

"Yes!"

She gripped his shoulders and pulled him hard against her, feeling the firmness of muscle under her fingers, pressing her warmth against his chest. Their lips touched and their tongues probed.

She pulled free abruptly and stood up. She dropped the robe and with a quick lift of her arms, pulled off the nightgown. She stood straight and still, legs together and arms hanging. The body that had seemed gaunt in clothes was slim but strong and well rounded, a blend of curves and satiny planes.

A half smile curled the corners of her mouth. "Seen enough?"

In answer, he reached forward and pulled her to him. She lay on top of him and kissed him hard, her body startling him with her fervour. With quick strength, he rolled her on to her back and held down her arms.

Penelope's long legs parted and he slid his body down hers, touching with his tongue, first her breasts then tracing a line lower. She gasped and gripped his shoulders so hard it hurt.

"Ah, Jeff ..." she whispered, her hands finding and caressing his hair, "... Jeff ..."

He bent his head and worked until her hips rose against him in quickening rhythm. Then he lifted himself and hung over her, looking at the beautiful face with closed eyes and open wet mouth, hearing her fast breathing, until she could wait no more and pulled him down. They joined as if made for each other, lunging hard, conscious of nothing except the ecstasy generated by their clamped bodies. She locked her limbs around him and they moved faster until they reached the crest together and there was nothing else on earth. For long delicious moments they hung poised there, exhausted, then let their muscles relax and they lay still.

Ballance traced the line of her throat and breast with a fingertip. "You're bloody marvellous and you're mine," he whispered.

She stroked his cheek and smiled. "And you're mine."

They slept and awakened and this time it was better, a deeper satisfaction.

***

Ballance woke up with sunlight shining into his eyes through the net curtains. He disentangled himself and stood to look down at the sleeping woman lying on her side under a sheet. Her curves were tantalising.

Oh hell, he thought, it's more than sex. I'm in love.

***

"Three policemen dead, two injured, the house of a man acquitted of a political murder bombed, those precious rich *Engelse* in the northern suburbs in uproar, and not a word of explanation from us. No wonder the media are screaming for blood, and they haven't heard about the second dead man yet."

Assistant Commissioner Mike Miller tilted back his chair, folded his hands across the ample waist of his impeccable tunic and raised a bushy eyebrow at Superintendent Louw across the desk top, empty save for a pen stand and a blank sheet of paper.

The superintendent sat erect in the hard guest chair and listened to his boss, police chief for the Witwatersrand, without expression. They were old friends, had been since the superintendent joined the police. That Miller was several years younger did not bother Louw. A self-admitted dogged plodder, he respected his friend's drive and university degrees. Miller's principles had cost him promotion under the old regime; he had risen fast under the new one.

This visit was business, permitting no familiarity on Louw's part. He had been summoned the second day after the Sandton bomb.

"Frans, I have good news and bad news," Miller said. "The bad news will be made public but the good news must not go further than this room. Do I have your word on that?"

"Yes, sir."

"Well then, the bad news first, as I suppose you'd prefer." He swivelled his chair to look out of the window high in police headquarters and spoke in a formal tone. "Superintendent Louw, you are suspended from all official duties with immediate effect, pending the conclusion of a departmental inquiry into the performance of your duties in the Ngwenya murder case and subsequent events, leading to the murder of Sergeant Stefan Greeff and the death of one officer and wounding of two others in an explosion.

"You will not be required to resume normal duties before proceedings have been completed but must remain available to assist in the inquiry."

Miller swivelled his chair back. Louw's face was impassive but his mind was seething with curiousity. Why had he left out the death of Basson?

"Okay, Frans? You must please sign this form acknowledging your suspension." He leaned forward to push the sheet of paper towards the superintendent.

"And the good news, sir?"

Miller grinned at him, an action that made the twinkle of his grey eyes all but disappear behind heavy lids.

"Frans, what I tell you now must remain absolutely secret. It must stay in your mind, nothing written, nothing on record anywhere. The President has asked me to set up a special unit to uncover this third force they believe is stirring so much trouble. I believe it too, now, though for a long time I didn't.

"From here on you are part of the unit. You will head an investigation into all the deaths including Basson's, and into whatever lies behind them."

Miller saw the questions queueing on the superintendent's face and held up his palm. "No, wait until I finish. You are not the alone in your suspicions. Your report this morning points in the same direction as a number of others, some from very high up. What this ANC man Ngwenya told you and what Basson said before he died look like two pieces of the same ugly jigsaw. The attempt to discredit your Mr Ballance was another part. And you haven't seen this ..."

The Assistant Commissioner opened a drawer and passed Superintendent Louw a blue folder stamped in bold red letters "Top Secret / *Uiters Geheim.*"

"You can read it just now but in this office, it mustn't leave here," he said. "In short, it's an eye-witness statement by an ANC regional boss, Ehpesias Mutale, who the Kruger Park rangers found naked and aslseep in the bush up near Punda Maria. He'd escaped from a massacre of ANC people in Venda.

"We've confirmed it. So far, sixty-seven bodies with gunshot and panga wounds have been pulled out of an old mine shaft and there are still more in there. It's very obvious that these killings are also part of the jigsaw. It's your job to help find the rest of the picture, and fast."

"It's a big order, why not someone more senior?"

"Because it's the kind of work you're good at, because we trust you, and because if we put some top officer in charge it would be too high profile and attract unwanted attention."

"We?"

"Professional policemen who serve the State, not some sectional ideological interest."

"Do you know those who don't, sir?"

"If we did, Frans, there wouldn't be a need for this special unit. Outside of yourself and a handful of others, none I know well enough to be certain of. Most are okay but there are many worms in the apple, plus many more people too weak or dumb to make up their own minds and who'll wait to see which way the wind blows.

"We have to play our cards close to the chest while we check out the rest. You can second a few men to work with you, but you must be very sure of them and give me their names first."

Louw felt satisfaction. At last he had backup, people he could turn to, talk the thing over with. The weight of his burden of worry lightened.

"Where do I start, sir?"

"You fly to Cape Town," Miller glanced at his watch, "in ninety minutes, tourist class, as just another civilian. So shave off your moustache or something and try not to look like a policeman. I'll announce your suspension when you've gone so the vultures can't pester you. And Frans, wear a decent suit, you're meeting the President at lunch time."

CHAPTER EIGHTEEN

Wishing he could keep it, Smith scratched the soft fur behind the Border Collie's ears while it wolfed down the slices of beef he had brought from the delicatessen. We'd make a good team, he thought, smiling at the memory of the pair of them jogging right past the noses of the policemen.

"Sadly, old boy, it's not on in my business," he said to the dog, whose tail swung at the sound of his voice. "You'll have to go back, but I'm sure someone else will fall for you."

He gave the dog water in the Styrofam dish the meat had come in, broke the dish into small pieces, and dropped them in the waste bin in the bathroom. He would do a thorough clean up later.

The dog came to him, tail wagging, when he took the short leash and choke chain from his pocket. It had been trained and he could not imagine why anyone who had raised a dog like this would want to get rid of it.

He opened the door and checked the corridor. It was empty; the chambermaids finished on this floor by ten thirty.

Smith walked the dog to the end of the corridor and pushed open the door to the seldom used fire stairs. They went down five flights to the basement, where he'd parked his old Mercedes Benz close to the stair exit, backed in, as always, so he could leave in a hurry if necessary.

The Collie jumped on to the back seat and sat there gazing regally at the passing scene as he drove south.

The staff at the SPCA received him with reluctance when he said he was giving it back. They were locked in an unending and depressing struggle to find homes for abandoned pets before fate in the form of euthanasia overtook them. He explained that the residential hotel he had moved into had neglected to tell him dogs were not allowed.

A hundred rands mollified them and they agreed that the collie's chances of beguiling a new owner, being such a likeable animal, were better than most.

Back in his hotel apartment, Smith considered his decision to leave this hotel. Tomorrow. That would give him time to have his laundry and dry-cleaning done.

***

"Maybe now you'll listen, you stubborn old bugger. I told you, Penny told you, that cop told you but still you wouldn't believe me and they damn near got you yesterday. Jesus, man, you're born lucky."

The humour in Ngwenya's eyes took the sting out of his words, as he stood looking down at Ballance's lanky figure slumped on Penelope's sofa with legs outstretched, hands thrust deep in pockets, chin on chest.

"I think you're doing the right thing," Ngwenya went on, "You'll be safer in decadent Mozambique than here. We can maybe go tomorrow."

Ballance glared up at him from beneath lowering black brows.

"No, not tomorrow. I'll think about it."

"Think about it! What's there to think about? Your home's trashed, the bastards are after your blood, you never know when the next bullet or bomb will come. You're too nervous to start your car. You want to live like that? No way, man! No way!"

Ngwenya waved his arm with such energy, a dollop of beer slopped out of his glass on to the carpet. He looked around but Penelope was in the kitchen, clattering the

163

supper plates in the sink.

Something had changed, his instincts told him, the aura in the flat was different tonight. Jeff wasn't his familiar animated self and Penelope was withdrawn.

"What's the problem, Jeff?"

Ballance hoisted himself off the sofa and stalked across the small room, turned and stalked back, his long frame tense. "It's Penny," he said. "She refuses to go with us."

"Why should she?"

"She's in danger too, man. They must know she's tied up with you and me."

"You maybe, not me, and the longer you hang your ass around Jo'burg the more likely you'll get it shot off, and Penny's too. Be sensible, Jeff," Ngwenya said. "So far she's linked to this business as your former lawyer, they're not likely to go after her for that and there's no reason they should suspect she knows anything, but if they find out you're staying here ..." He drew the edge of his hand across his throat.

"He's right, Jeff." They had not heard her come up behind them. "I'm sure I'll be quite safe once you're gone. And I can't walk out of my job just like that."

Ngwenya detected a tone in her voice that made his suspicion flower. It was confirmed when Ballance put a comforting arm around Penelope's shoulders.

Oh hell, he thought, they're involved. Of all the complications we need now, this is the last. Aloud, he said, "It's more than Penny's safety, isn't it?"

"Yes." She looked him in the eye. "It's just one of those things, it's happened. I don't want him to go but he must. He's in far more danger than I am. He'll be back, I can wait."

"Jeff?"

Ballance dropped his arm and paced some more before he replied. "I suppose you're right," he growled, slumping back on the sofa, "Go ahead, set it up."

Ngwenya sighed with relief and changed the subject

because it was patently painful to Penelope. "How did the bastards get into your house, Jeff?"

"Picked the lock, I suppose. The limpet mine was on the floor inside and wired to the lock so that when the key turned, it completed a circuit."

"And nobody saw a thing. Jesus, don't you whiteys ever know what goes on in your own streets?"

"No. We lock ourselves into our little fortresses every night and don't give a stuff. Do you know, just minutes after the bomb went off, my bloody neighbours were bitching at me – *me* – as though I was responsible! Selfish twits. I've become an undesirable tenant overnight, as if I'd brought the hounds of hell to crap on their door-steps."

"Dogs of war more probably."

"Yeah ..." Ballance gave a sour smile and then his face lit up. "That's it!"

"What's it?"

"The dog ... by God, it must be!" He jumped to his feet and shook Ngwenya by the shoulders.

"What the hell are you going on about?"

"A dog of war!" Ballance chortled and rushed to the telephone. "It has to be!"

He dialled, shifting from foot to foot in impatience while he waited. "Superintendent Louw? Hi, it's Jeffrey Ballance. No, nothing's wrong. Listen, you've got to find a Collie, a Border Collie ..."

"A *what?*"

***

Superintendent Louw dropped the telephone in its cradle on his bullet-gouged hall table and wondered whether he was getting too slow for this game. Or whether Ballance was jumping at shadows. He was weary after the journey to Cape Town and back.

A Border Collie? He struggled to wrestle up an image in his mind. Not the long-nosed Lassie kind, with hair like a film star's and eyes that would melt stone; a smaller black and white dog, darting about herding sheep, like the one in the TV ads.

The image clicked into place: the little old jogger panting past while they waited under the tree near Ballance's house. He was being towed by a black and white dog sniffing every flower, tree and bush.

That fellow? The superintendent's mind resisted the thought. He was just one of thousands out for a trot every evening in Johannesburg. It was not in character with how he imagined the bomber to be. They had not seen him anywhere near the house ... but then, they hadn't seen him at all until he was trotting past them ...

He lifted the telephone and dialled.

"Lucky? Sorry to trouble you so late, but would you come around? Yes, it's quite urgent. *Ja,* man, I know I've been suspended but I'll tell you all about that when you get here. Thanks. I'll have a drink waiting."

Captain Lucky Ndzimandze would win no prizes for a high IQ, the superintendent knew, but he was honest and loyal and had that indefinable something that made a good detective, a certain doggedness born from a determination to prove he was as good as any man.

Ten minutes later when he had seated the lanky officer with a drink in his hand, Louw told him what had taken place since his suspension.

"All this is for your ears only, Lucky, or I'll pin them both above the mantelpiece. Yes, I have been suspended but that's a smokescreen. Today I saw the President in Cape Town ..." Ndzimandze's eyes grew wide "... and I've been put under cover to help dig out this third force raising hell everywhere.

"It's far more serious than the public knows. There are clever people out there sabotaging stability and they're doing a good job. We don't know them. They seem to be all over the place, inside the public service and security forces and in commerce and industry.

"I saw statistics and charts showing eruptions of violence all over the country in a pattern which could be planned, not spontaneous. They coincide with batches of illegal firearms coming across the border. Some black-on-black fighting has been provoked, started by people who vanish. Blacks believe whites are behind it. Maybe they're right. If we don't nail them soon, the violence might spill over into civil war, Lucky.

"So the President has created this special unit to find them. Most of us are police, some are army and a couple are from National Intelligence. I'm in charge here. Do you want to join me?"

Ndzimandze did not hesitate. "What must I do, sir?"

"You can start by looking for a dog."

"A *dog?*"

"It might be a wild goose chase but I can't afford to ignore anything."

He told the captain about Ballance's telephone call.

"If that jogger we saw was in fact this mysterious Mr Smith then he's nobody's fool. A professional killer wouldn't burden himself with a dog, so there's a thin chance he bought or borrowed one for the job. Basson said Smith lives in a Rosebank hotel, so check the pet shops there and the nearest SPCA for anyone who took a Border Collie, you know what they look like?"

"Yes, I've seen them on TV."

"Good. Report back to me here, Lucky. I won't be using my office for a while."

***

Captain Ndzimandze did it the other way around. He went to the SPCA first, reasoning that pet shops sold puppies, not adult dogs. The notion paid immediate dividends.

"Yes, that's right," the white-coated young woman behind the desk said with a bright smile. She had the dishevelled appearance of people who work with animals. In one arm she cradled a pink piglet. "A man brought back a Border Collie yesterday, a very nice one about two years old. Would you like to see him?"

"Do you know his name?"

"We call him Chips."

"No, ma'am, I mean the man."

"Oh, pardon! I can't remember offhand ... hang on." She placed the piglet on the counter, where it piddled as she reached below to rootle in a shoebox. Her hand came up with a slip of paper.

"Here it is ... oh, blast you, Piglet!" She handed the slip to Ndzimandze, placed the pig on the floor and mopped the counter with a sheet of newspaper.

"Jones," he read. It was as original as Smith. "Did he leave an address?"

"No. He said he was moving." Her brows drew together. "When he brought Chips back he said it was because his residential hotel wouldn't allow dogs."

"So you have no idea where he is?"

"Oh, we made sure we could get in touch with him." She brushed back straying hair and smiled up at him. "We never place animals without being able to check on them later. He gave us a telephone number ..." She turned over the slip of paper and pointed a fingertip, "... and because he said he didn't have his new address yet, we wrote down the number of his car, there."

Ndzimandze sighed, suspecting both the phone number and the car registration would be dead ends. The man was a pro, after all.

"He didn't mention his old address by any chance, the one he was moving out of?"

"No... " she hesitated and Ndzimandze sighed again, "... but he used a ballpoint pen to write down the phone number and there was a hotel name on it. The Rose." She grinned.

Ndzimandze returned her smile with admiration.

"Many thanks, madam, you've been a big help."

"Has he done something wrong?"

"No, it's a routine inquiry."

"Are you sure you don't want a dog or a cat, Captain?" She fixed large green eyes on him. "Or a pig, they make very good house pets, you know?"

"Madam, I have kids and that's enough."

A few minutes on the police radio in his car confirmed Ndzimandze's suspicion that the telephone number was false, it belonged to a diaper cleaning business. The registration was for a BMW from Natal wrecked months ago.

He drove straight to The Rose off Oxford Road and parked in its basement. About thirty cars stood in the subterranean gloom.

Ndzimandze strolled around and found the registration. It was on an ageing but well-groomed Mercedes Benz parked in a back corner.

My luck's running, he thought.

In the hotel foyer, he fed coins into a public telephone and dialled. Superintendent Louw could hear the suppressed excitement in his voice.

"I think we have him," Ndzimandze said, "I traced him here from the SPCA ..." Ndzimandze gave the name, "... and his car's here now. Must I pick him up?"

"No, he's not the top man. He's our one lead to the top. Stay there and if he moves, follow him and keep in touch by radio. I'll be there as soon as I can."

"Okay. I'll be in my car in the basement."

The superintendent reached the hotel in less than ten minutes and parked in a loading zone. He walked down the basement ramp and joined the captain in his Toyota Corolla.

"That's the one," Ndzimandze said, pointing through the windscreen at the Mercedes Benz on the far side. He described his morning's work.

"*Mooi*, Lucky, nice work, you've done well. This is the first real break we've had. You don't know what he looks

169

like?"

"The SPCA lady said he was shortish and grey-haired, that's all. I didn't want to ask about him at reception because they might be in it with him."

"From the little we saw the description fits but he could change his appearance easily enough. So we sit and wait. He must come down some time."

***

Smith telephoned the front desk for a porter to take his suitcase down to the car. While he waited, he examined the living room. It was as blank as the personality he had adopted. He had brought nothing into it except himself, his bag and, for one night, the Border Collie.

The dog had slept on the bedroom carpet. He had taken meticulous care to ensure that nothing was left to reveal the dog's presence; the hotel manager would not be charmed and Smith had no wish to draw attention to himself.

After packing his clothes, he had brushed stray hairs off all the carpets and flushed them down the toilet, cleaned out cupboards, drawers, wastepaper bins and emptied ashtrays. He would leave the room as he found it, a characterless box for transients, its one human touch the Gideon Bible.

The porter, a young black man in a chin-high blue tunic with red piping, bobbed his head in thanks when Smith gave him a five-rand coin and ordered him to take the case to his car.

Smith told the receptionist, accustomed to his comings and goings, he would be away a few days on business. He paid his bill for a month in advance so the room would be held for him.

The two policemen had been waiting almost an hour. A few cars had come and gone. Nobody took notice of them; in this city, people minded their own business.

They almost missed the young porter because he

emerged from a door behind the Mercedes Benz and stood there, waiting, half hidden. Then the lift doors opened and out stepped Smith, a small unobtrusive man in a tweed sports jacket, his grey hair in a spikey brush cut.

"That's him!" Louw hissed and slid lower in the seat until he could just see over the dashboard. "That's our jogger. Get down, Lucky, he mustn't see us."

Smith unlocked the boot of the Mercedes Benz for the porter to put in a suitcase, nodded thanks and climbed behind the steering wheel. He drove past the Corolla without a glance and up the ramp into Twist Street.

"Give him space, don't get too close."

Ndzimandze followed into the street in time to see the Mercedes Benz swing left into Oxford Road and then right into a cross street which took him to Orange Grove. He drove with caution in pursuit, staying four or five cars behind in the busy traffic.

***

Smith travelled north on Louis Botha Avenue to a small house in Orange Grove. Built by an Estonian Jewish tailor in the 1930s, it boasted a low concrete and picket fence, a cement gnome on the miniature front lawn and a postbox on the fence. The narrow street was lined with similar houses, most of them inhabited by the elderly.

He parked in the garage at the side, lowered its roll-down door and carried his bag into the house through the front entrance. He noticed a small white Toyota drive past while he was unlocking the door but did not give it a second thought. Corollas were everyman's car in suburbs like this.

The house was stuffy from non-use. He opened windows in the spacious back section, overlooking a cemented yard. Rummaging in the refrigerator, he found a bottle of cold beer, uncapped it and drank straight from the neck.

Smith was not particular about where he lived but he had a soft spot for this place because it was so improbable a base for his kind of work. He could leave it for long periods, assured that its contents would be safe with the sophisticated silent alarm system linked to a very efficient security service with headquarters a hundred metres away, around the corner in Louis Botha.

He had better see the Doc, he thought, finishing the drink. Doc would be as unhappy as he was about Ballance's escape, but that was history.

***

Thirty metres from the house on the other side of the street the policemen sat in the Corolla and watched the house. Louw was worried because he had nobody to spell them in watching the house.

"Sir, I know a good man we can bring in," Ndzimandze said, guessing the dilemma, also not wanting to stay the night here.

"Who is he?"

"Detective Inspector Stramm, Joe Stramm. He's on a desk job at headquarters and bored to death."

"How well do you know him, Lucky?"

"For years, sir. He's Jewish." The comment implied he and Stramm had shared injustice.

"Can you get me through to Assistant Commissioner Miller by radio?"

"Sure."

"Go ahead."

CHAPTER NINETEEN

Like bushfires after long dry heat, when the grass is so desiccated it crumbles to powder and the seed pods rattle in the trees, killing flared simultaneously in separate parts of South Africa.

On Red Friday men calling each other 'comrade' descended on mourners at a Zulu funeral in KwaMashu near Durban with axes, knives and handguns. When they had passed like a cloud of locusts, thirty-seven people lay bleeding and crying in the hot dust of the cemetery and nine more were dead. Two were old men in their shiny best suits; four of them fat matrons, whose blood stained the glossy taffeta and satin flounces of their formal dresses; three were children in their teens, chopped through the backs of their necks as they tried to flee.

The same evening, near Pinetown, continuous fire from four automatic weapons raked a minibus with sixteen black passengers as it travelled through a shallow cutting. The shooting was good: the gunners triggered when the driver reached the point where their fire converged, held their aim and let the taxi ride through it as if through a car wash.

By the time it was past them, swinging from side to side with the roll of the driver's corpse against the steering wheel, everyone inside was riddled and dead. It swerved for fifty metres before it canted off the edge of the road and tumbled down a slope, scattering bodies like obscene seeds.

While police collected the bodies, two more taxis were attacked on side roads between Durban and Pietermaritzburg, one full of Inkatha supporters, the other of ANC.

At about the same, time a crude bomb of Russian plastic explosive detonated behind cases of beer in Tshab's Tavern, a popular shebeen in Soweto. A scything hail of broken glass slashed patrons and passers-by, regardless of their political beliefs, vaporised a large quantity of liquor and blew Tshabalala into bankruptcy.

Tempers in Soweto reached boiling point. Armed vigilantes roamed the streets with improvised weapons, stopping anyone who looked suspicious. Many people fled, some died. Most locked themselves indoors.

In Tembisa, east of Johannesburg, a white Hi-Ace taxi turned into a street full of people walking home from the railway station. Four men thrust AK-47 muzzles out of the open windows and fired long bursts while the driver cruised down the street, leaving seven dead and forty wounded lying in their blood in the dust. Wailing went on late into the night as relatives identified the victims.

The police and paramedics came fast but too late. The Hi-Ace had melted away amid the scores of others on the roads. Nobody took its number.

In Johannesburg's opulent northern suburbs, there was no hint of the bloodshed and tension in the black townships a few kilometres away. The evening began with the Friday ritual of socialising in pubs, clubs and restaurants. The shopping and cinema malls bustled with activity.

At the corner of Jan Smuts Avenue and Tyrwhitt in Rosebank, an elegant middle-aged blonde in a short black cocktail dress stopped her BMW 535i at a traffic light, between a Mercedes Benz 500 SE and a Saab. She was on her way to join her husband in a restaurant in Hyde Park.

A shadow passed her on the right and the upper half of a man's body reared over the windscreen. A huge black face leered at her from two feet away. A hand lifted an iron bar.

Years in Rhodesia during the UDI war had taught her to react in reflex. She plucked an Astra pistol from the small handbag on her lap and fired through the windscreen, straight into the face.

The man lurched back, eyes and mouth open in shock. The iron bar clanged on the bonnet. She stamped on the accelerator and felt a thump as the surging car threw the body aside. Someone screamed.

Heart pounding, she drove and squealed to a stop at the floodlit entrance of the restaurant. A uniformed black security guard opened her door. She collapsed in tears into his arms.

She was lucky.

The driver of the Mercedes Benz 500SE, while listening to Mahler on his tape deck, heard a tap on the window and turned in irritation to look straight into the muzzle of a revolver.

It was the last thing he saw. The gun went off about eight inches from his eyes and the .45 calibre bullet split his head.

The gunman pulled open the door and heaved him into the street, jumped into the car and drove off at high speed.

At the same time, a brick smashed in the Saab's windscreen, showering the driver and his woman companion with pebbles of glass.

She loosed a piercing scream as the brick thrower jerked open the unlocked door, dragged her out by her hair and flung her into the gutter, her tight skirt riding high up her legs.

On the other side, a man swung a baseball bat through the gaping windscreen and hit the driver on the forehead, concussing him.

At that moment, two cars stopped behind the Saab and the drivers leaped out, one waving a gun. The two attackers fled in different directions. Nobody gave chase.

A few kilometres east, a chanting, prancing mob of

more than two hundred swarmed across Louis Botha Avenue near Corlett Drive, tangling traffic and panicking motorists, and spread like ants through the genteel streets of Bramley suburb.

They hurled stones and petrol bombs at houses, beat up anyone they found in the street, and yelled "VIVA!" as they slipped away. A few householders fired pistols into the dark.

It lasted no more than ten minutes. The raiders melted back into Alexandra township. They left behind several housemaids, attacked and wounded in their servant's rooms, a wife burned when her panelled living room went up in flames and three of their own lying shot in the street.

Police rushed to Tyrwhitt, to Jellicoe and to Bramley. They reached one scene and only to be called to the next. They were too few to cope.

Fifteen hundred kilometres to the south, the late afternoon Metro suburban train returning from Simon's Town to Cape Town picked up holidaymakers going home from the False Bay beaches, more than usual because the schools were on holiday. Sun-sated vacationers filled the coaches, laden with bags, towels, umbrellas, hats and the other paraphernalia of a day on the beach. Children played in the aisles.

The lucky ones left the train at Retreat, Heathfield, Plumstead and Deep River and at the busy Wynberg station, to amble homeward. The destinations of most were ahead, Kenilworth, Claremont, Rondebosch, Rosebank, Mowbray, Observatory ...

In the few seconds before the automatic doors hissed closed at Wynberg, a dozen men slipped aboard, six at each end of the train.

It was gathering electric speed for the short dash to Kenilworth when they struck. They drew clubs and knives from their clothes and walked along the aisles slashing, beating and stabbing startled passengers at random on both sides.

They made their way towards the middle of the train. A bedlam of screams marked their progress and drowned the click of the wheels on the track. The noise went ahead of them; passengers heard and leaned out of windows to look. On both sides they saw people scrambling through windows to escape the horror inside, some bloody, falling, bouncing on the hard embankment, rolling until they flopped still and were left behind.

The terror in the coaches swelled into panic. Men stood up to defend families with bare fists and beach spades only to be hit and hacked in the frenzy.

The conductor, a plump Coloured man, proud of his rank, pulled open a door to cross a narrow rocking walkway between two coaches. Another brown man in the other doorway lunged forward and thrust a knife blade upwards into his body, just beneath his ribs.

The conductor stood poised on the toes of his polished black shoes for long seconds, held there by the strength of the knifeman's rigid arm. The killer jerked back the blade and the body toppled sideways over the guard railing and fell between the wheels of the moving train.

The steel wheels screeched as the driver braked for Kenilworth. The train slowed to approach the platform. People waiting to board it heard the tumult and watched in astonishment as it stopped, with yelling passengers hanging out of the windows.

The attackers forced open the sliding doors on the other side, jumped down between the tracks, clambered onto the opposite platform and ran away.

The horrified driver, unaware of the mayhem until he stopped, signalled an emergency. Many passengers fled in fear, not caring how far they were from home. Others stayed to help.

Police talked to victims but none could give clear descriptions of the raiders. Some said they were brown men, others said black, others white. The victims were all colours.

Then they missed the conductor and went to look for him. They foundhim in two pieces. Beyond him they found passengers who had jumped, all with broken bones.

***

At seven o'clock, an antique grandfather clock chimed the hour in the living room of a large, opulent home above Newlands Avenue in Rondebosch. The small black-haired Member of Parliament checked his wrist-watch, a reflex so automatic he seldom noticed the time.

He dropped the pages of the evening paper on the floor beside his armchair and stood up to switch on the radio.

The news was a litany of bloodshed: a massacre at a Durban funeral, minibus taxis ambushed, trouble at this moment in Johannesburg, no further information yet.

The next item made him frown. Killers attacked passengers on a train from Simon's Town this evening ... details not yet known ... special bulletins will be broadcast as news comes in.

Their planning was producing results, he thought. He did not object to violence as a necessary tool, but he did not like it too close to home.

Erratic hammering on the front door pulled him from his reverie. Surely that could not be one of the dinner guests, it was too early. He was about to answer the knock when the old Coloured manservant crossed the yellowwood floor to open the door.

The MP heard him gasp.

"Master!" the old man shouted. "Master, come quick!"

The MP rushed into the hall and froze in horror.

Jannie, his fourteen-year-old son, lay slumped against the oak door pillar. Darkening blood covered his face, yellow and white beach shirt, bermudas, and even his Adidas running shoes, and oozed through the towel wrapped around his head.

"*Jannie!*" he screamed and ran to him. The boy collapsed into his arms.

The elderly servant took charge. He was used to blood from the knife fights in the ghetto where he grew up. "Call the doctor, master!" he ordered in Afrikaans and picked up the boy in his arms.

The MP's wife came running down the staircase to the foyer, wearing evening dress for the dinner. She saw her son soaked in blood and fainted in a heap on the Bokhara.

The doctor arrived in minutes, cut the clothes off Jannie and examined him on the floral couch where the manservant had laid him down, ignoring the blood smearing everything. When he had finished, the doctor stood up looking relieved and wiped his hands with cotton wool.

"His worst injury is that slash," he said. "It runs almost the length of his head and he's lost quite a lot of blood. He'll have a scar for life under his hair but the knife, or whatever it was, scored the skull and didn't penetrate. He's very lucky."

He gave the boy a sedative injection and a local anaesthetic, shaved and disinfected his head and used sixty stitches to close the gaping wound.

Jannie's mother, recovered, came into the living room struggling to regain her composure.

"Darling, please phone our guests and cancel the dinner," the MP ordered, hoping to distract her. She left the room and he heard her speaking on the telephone in the foyer, forcing her voice to stay calm.

"I'm so sorry ... there's been an accident ... no, no, we're quite all right ... next time then ..."

"I'm worried he'll have delayed shock," the doctor said to the MP. "It's a wonder he made it home. This cut happened an hour or more ago, judging from the bleeding. I think we'd better put him into hospital for the night."

"No!" the MP said. "We'll stay up with him. Just tell us what to do."

Jannie struggled to raise his upper body from the couch. He opened his mouth and tried to speak.

"Lie down, son, take it easy, there's nothing to worry about now, you'll be fine."

"Those men, those men on the train," Jannie said with a wobble in his voice, "it was horrible ..." He burst into tears and fell back.

The MP knew what he meant and felt the chill of fear.

When he had turned away guests they could not reach by telephone, he switched on the radio.

"Ten or more men rampaged through the train ... conductor thrown between the wheels ... four dead, scores battered and knifed ... may never know complete figure because so many fled ... fifteen found alive along embankment ... pushed or jumped, injuries serious ... reason for attack not known ... ANC and Inkatha deny ... blame mysterious third force ... pure anarchy ..."

"Is that where Jannie was?" He had not heard his wife enter the room. "Dear Lord, what is happening to us?"

He knelt at his armchair and prayed. Not like this, I never knew it would be like this. Oh God, what must I do?

CHAPTER TWENTY

Ballance made the parting quick. It was less painful

Ngwenya had slept in the guest room. Ballance had shared Penelope's bed; it was their third night together and they had not slept well, trying not to think of tomorrow.

Ballance had telephoned Superintendent Louw the day before to tell him he and Ngwenya were leaving the country before dawn.

"Don't leave Miss Fox's flat without me," the superintendent had ordered him, very conscious that the two of them together would be just what the assassins wanted. "We'll take you to the airport."

Ballance handed Penelope his Smith and Wesson in its leather holster.

"Keep this next to you at night and don't hesitate to use it," he said. "Hide it somewhere when you're out."

She locked it in the wall safe in her bedroom.

When the superintendent knocked on the door at five thirty, they were ready and waiting. Despite the hour, Penelope was already dressed in a dark business suit.

Ngwenya shook her hand. "Don't worry about Jeff," he said, "I've been looking after him since he was a farm brat."

She kissed him on the cheek. He hefted his luggage, a canvas tog bag, and led the way. Ballance hung back until Ngwenya was outside, pulled Penelope close and kissed her hard.

"Take good care of yourself," he said. "It's my property you're looking after now."

Penelope watched the three of them walk to the lift. When they were gone, she shut her door and leaned against it, wondering when she would see Ballance again. Her eyes were wet.

Captain Ndzimandze drove on the back roads through Bramley, Lyndhurst and Sunningdale. Louw broke the silence.

"We found Smith, your bomber, thanks to your brainwave about the Collie," he said. "He's moved to a house in Orange Grove. We have a full-time watch on him. We hope he'll lead us to the people behind all this." He tapped the front page of the morning tabloid with a forefinger.

'All this' had become a monstrosity, an eruption of bloody anarchy the evening before, in many parts of the country. South Africans woke up to a breakfast of tombstone headlines and gruesome colour footage on television screens.

The superintendent told them of his assignment to a special undercover unit to investigate the supposed third force.

"It's about damn time," Ngwenya snorted. "It might already be too late."

Louw twisted around in the front seat to face him.

"You can help make sure it isn't," he said. "Half the problem is the weapons from Mozambique. Find out who the suppliers are and we'll fix them."

Ngwenya studied the serious face, made more austere by the lack of the pencil moustache. *Eish*, he thought, me working with the cops. "We'll try. Don't expect miracles."

"I can't help you if you get into trouble over there. If you learn anything one of you must get out to bring back the information. And Mr Ballance, we'll keep an eye on Miss Fox."

"Thanks, I'd appreciate that."

Waving his police documents, Ndzimandze cut

182

through Johannesburg International airport's layers of security and steered the Corolla around one end of the terminal, an architectural monstrosity in glass and concrete. He stopped on the apron under the nose of the South African Airways Boeing 737. They went through neither customs nor immigration.

"Good luck," Louw said at the foot of the boarding steps, watched by an inquisitive stewardess at the top. His handshake was quick and strong.

***

The tan highveld and tumbled contours of the Eastern Escarpment slipped below like a rumpled carpet. Erratic silver threads wandered from west to east, the Crocodile and Komati rivers reflecting the sun.

"Feel good to be back?" Ngwenya asked forty minutes later as the plane taxied towards the low Maputo airport terminal.

"It's a derelict country but at least we can walk around without being shot at or bombed," Ballance retorted.

Ngwenya grinned without humour. "Mozambique was crawling with South African spooks before. There might still be some around," he said.

"You're a cheerful soul, *bra*. Thanks."

A few idle onlookers on the balcony watched the plane park with whining engines. It was still something of a novelty to see South African and Russian airliners sharing the same airport. Service crews, lethargic in the heat, moved around an Aeroflot Ilyushin parked in the next bay.

The Indian Ocean humidity hit them like a hot towel as they stepped from the plane. They were sweating by the time they walked into the terminal. An immigration officer stamped them through and a customs inspector pawed through their bags, leaving them to repack.

They rode in a rackety taxi to the city through its teeming slum fringe of reed and grass huts and shanties, exuding thin pillars of smoke from cooking fires. The approaching skyline of tall blocks against azure sky and sparkling sea, held the promise of clean tropical beauty until they entered the city and found the streets potholed, the buildings unpainted and the gutters full of litter. Big old Flamboyant trees on the sidewalks softened the marks of decay.

Ballance wondered how they should tackle their task. For many years since Mozambique's independence in 1975, Maputo had been a base for a kaleidoscopic collection of movements fighting UDI in Rhodesia and apartheid in South Africa. They in turn attracted a colourful variety of spies, saboteurs, and freelance agents, who sold anything to anybody if the price was right.

Many were still there, held by the easygoing life and laissez-faire attitude of the authorities. The city, Ballance thought, was a kind of African Saigon, place of intrigue. Whatever he and Ngwenya did, someone was sure to notice their presence and sell the information.

He decided to start with innocuous visits to a couple of friends in the government.

The taxi stopped beside the exuberant tropical foliage and lawns fronting the Cardoso, a broad, comfortable old hotel on the Polana bluff overlooking the wide river estuary to which Maputo owed its existence. Ballance preferred the Cardoso's understated luxury to the expensive hotel palaces favoured by the flock of diplomatic, foreign aid, UN, welfare and other visitors travelling on expense allowances that enabled them to live like royalty.

"I'll take the taxi on to see some friends," Ngwenya said after they checked in, "Let's meet here this afternoon, the downstairs bar at lunchtime."

"Noon it is. First round's mine."

***

"They've skipped the country," the voice on the telephone said.

"When? Where to?" Smith demanded.

"They took this morning's flight to Maputo."

"How did we miss them?"

"We didn't. Our Jo'burg International contact spotted their names on the passenger list after they made bookings yesterday but they gave no call-back number and we had no idea where they were staying."

"You mean this morning they just drove up, checked in before your eyes and boarded the plane?"

"No." The voice was respectful but not apologetic. It belonged to one of the burly pair with Sundance moustaches. "The cops drove them straight to the plane. They didn't go into the terminal or go near the passport and customs desks."

Smith assumed Ballance and Ngwenya had left because they were both prime targets in South Africa and he cursed the string of mistakes which had forewarned them.

On the other hand, it might be easier in Maputo where they would not have official protection and the police were, to say the least, inept.

"So what do you want me to do?" asked the man waiting at the other end of the line, breaking Smith's train of thought.

"For the moment, nothing. I'll call you when I need you."

Smith replaced the phone and considered his options in Maputo. The organisation had agents there, as it did in every Southern African capital. A quarter of an hour later, he dialled a number in Mozambique and for several minutes talked business, a discussion of freight shipments and prices which would have meant nothing to anyone who might have been eavesdropping.

***

Big plate-glass windows covered the full width of the main bar lounge at the Cardoso, giving an expansive view from the long bar of the curved swimming pool outside and beyond it, to ships passing to and from the harbour up the estuary. Actual war had never touched Maputo itself during the independence struggle, but it had felt the aftermath of war, the en masse departure of Portuguese colonials, the takeover by novice Frelimo rulers and the inexorable economic collapse.

Now the city was clawing itself back, emerging with a fresh African patina overlaying its legacy of colonial characteristics.

Ballance sipped draught beer from a tall narrow glass and savoured the view of bikini-clad shapes around the pool and of the sunlit sea beyond. It had not been a productive morning. His connections in government had been welcoming at first but when he obliquely began mentioning the arms trade, they pleaded pressure of work and hastened him out.

"Hi there." Ngwenya sat down on the stool next to him. Ballance turned and saw a stranger with him, a bony man of about thirty in a floral sports shirt and blue cotton slacks.

"Jeff," Ngwenya said, "meet Hannes Smart."

Smart shook hands, studying Ballance with intense blue eyes, and remained standing between them. He accepted a beer but seemed uneasy.

"Hannes is with the ANC office here," Ngwenya said. "If he looks nervous it's because he's still worried about being taken out by the fanatics and he doesn't know you. I had to twist his arm to come here."

"*Ag*, Temba exaggerates," Smart said, smiling nervously. His voice was deep. "But *ja*, being careful is a habit since I left South Africa back in '85."

"Hannes was an army conscript," Ngwenya explained. "He skipped the country when they wanted to send him into Angola because he's a conscientious objector and he's been with us ever since. I asked him around because part of his job was to keep tabs on arms shipments to Renamo. That right, Hannes?"

"Is it safe to talk in here?" Ballance asked, glancing at the few other people in the lounge.

"Yeah, but let's sit over there."

Ngwenya wove his way between tables to a corner where they slid on to leather-padded benches around an ornate, carved table. Ballance carried their drinks.

"I hope you can point us in the right direction," he said to Smart. "We're interested in the arms trade but I've been getting nowhere all day."

"Well, I dunno. I used to watchdog arms going to Renamo but that all changed after '94 when the ANC became the government. Since Renamo and Frelimo buried the hatchet there's been no point."

They paused while a white-jacketed waiter in a red fez placed a plate of hot-spiced *petiscos* on their table.

"But you must know the way the traffic is conducted, the people involved and the routes and so on?"

"Sure, I guess so. I haven't checked them out for a while so I can't say who's still around."

"Can you put us in touch with anyone who might know about arms being trafficked the other way, from Renamo into South Africa?" Ngwenya asked.

Smart looked puzzled. "Why would anyone do that? South Africa's awash with guns. Anybody who wants an AK can buy one across the border for the price of a bag of maize meal."

"We're talking about big shipments, hundreds at a time, maybe thousands."

"Jesus," Smart frowned. "What's this all about?"

Ngwenya glanced at Ballance, who nodded. Leaning forward and almost whispering, Ngwenya told Smart of their suspicions about a third force, giving little detail. When he finished Smart sank back against the padded leather and looked more worried.

"That's heavy, man, heavy," he muttered, "People in that game play rough, you don't want to get in the way."

"Okay, Hannes, we won't involve you at all," Ballance assured him, "Just tell us where to look, who to talk to."

"Man, I'm involved already by talking to you—"

"Come on, Hannes," Ngwenya's voice had an edge to it. "A bit of help and you can forget you ever saw us."

Smart's gaze shifted from Ngwenya to Ballance and back. He fiddled with his half-finished drink, then lifted the glass and drained it.

"Listen, I'm a bit out of touch," he said, coming to a decision, "Let me check around and see who's still in place. Don't call me, Temba, I'll call you."

Smart stood up. Ballance put a restraining hand on his arm. "When?" he asked.

"Maybe tonight, maybe tomorrow. Okay?"

They watched him hurry away, looking to neither side as if that made him invisible.

"He doesn't inspire much confidence," Ballance remarked.

"Give him a chance. He was good at his job."

***

Bob Thomlinson was in import and export, a ubiquitous category of business in Maputo, covering a broad spectrum of activities which often had nothing to do with moving goods in and out. His operation was legitimate and he was in good standing with Mozambique's new crop of black entrepreneurs and officials. A fat, jolly man always with a glass in hand and a ready chuckle, he often entertained Maputo's glitterati at his luxurious Polana home overlooking the vast bay.

An ex-Rhodesian, his private belief was that blacks had neither the wit nor the will to run a country and were interested in no more than self-enrichment, a conviction strengthened by his experiences in Mozambique. When the republican underground approached him, he agreed without hesitation to be their agent.

Swivelling his chair to look down from the window of

his fourth floor office at the old fishing harbour below, he considered what to do about the visitors from Johannesburg.

They had been easy enough to find after Smith's phone call – the taxi drivers plying the airport route sold information – and watched, as they went their separate ways. They did nothing that appeared out of the ordinary ... until midday when they met the traitor, Smart, in the Cardoso bar. That was no social call.

Smith's instructions had been specific. Thomlinson swivelled back to his desk and picked up the telephone.

***

Ngwenya knocked on the door of Ballance's room and walked in without waiting.

Ballance looked up from the small desk where he was making notes. "So? Any word yet?" He was in a bad mood after waiting the whole afternoon in the hotel.

"Yup. A note has come from Hannes. He wants us to meet him at five at the ..." he glanced at the piece of paper in his hand "... *Casa do Pescadores.*"

"Where's that? Never heard of it."

"According to the reception clerk it's a Portuguese-type pub across the estuary, somewhere in Catembe. We'll have to take the ferry." He glanced at his watch. "We better start moving, Jeff, it's past four."

"Damn." Ballance did not relish an excursion into the Maputo night. With a few exceptions, the city's cafés and restaurants were rundown and grubby. He wanted a quiet evening with a decent dinner but he sighed, reached for his jacket, and followed Ngwenya.

On the way out, he picked up a tourist brochure from the reception desk with a map of Maputo and Catembe.

189

CHAPTER TWENTY ONE

Detective Inspector Joseph Stramm was inured to monotony. He paged through the heap of unsolved vehicle theft files, looking for common factors, patterns that might point to the syndicates of thieves, chop shops and exporters.

Desk work others shunned, seemed to gravitate to him. He never complained and his senior officers turned to him when dull but necessary paperwork needed tackling. His career was in a cul-de-sac.

Nondescript in size, shape and age, with a knobby nose and cheeks pocked by childhood acne, Stramm was not the model of an action man. His brown suit was worn shiny, his manner defensive because of the incessant carping of his wife and two teenage daughters. He was dull in everything except intelligence.

Stramm's one idiosyncracy was his worn felt hat, the brim dark from years of fingering. He wore it all the time, in the office and out, in the police canteen and bar, even in bed, his colleagues sniggered, so he wouldn't have to kiss his wife.

Bent over a brown folder, 'Audi A6 with alarm and immobiliser stolen from city parkade', he lifted his head, surprised, when the station commander stopped at his desk and looked with distaste at the disarray of papers and coffee mugs.

Stramm raised his head to see first, under the brim of his hat, the chief's waist then chest and then the gaunt black face frowning at him.

"Stramm, you're being detached. The Assistant Commissioner wants you to report to Brixton Murder and Robbery right away."

"The Assistant Commissioner, sir?" Stramm was puzzled.

"Yes, Stramm, the Assistant Commissioner. If you've been pulling strings to land a cushy job, I'll have your balls."

"Yes, sir."

Asshole, Stramm thought, watching the man's retreating stiff back. He stacked the files and handed all of them to the duty officer. Shrugging on his jacket, he persuaded a police driver to take him to Brixton Murder and Robbery.

An hour later, he was in an unmarked, over-powered Mazda saloon in a side street in Orange Grove sixty metres from a small house with a small lawn behind a concrete and picket fence in need of a coat of white paint.

Superintendent Louw had met him around the corner in Louis Botha Avenue. They sat in the Mazda while the superintendent briefed him, finishing with the warning that if he let a word of this operation leak, he would spend the rest of his career ploughing through files as a constable, not an inspector.

Stramm permitted himself a rare smile, transforming his face. This was his kind of work.

"Thanks for bringing me into it, sir," he said. "He won't fart without me knowing it. I'll keep in touch on the hour." He patted the police radio below the dash.

"Good. I'll send someone to help you as soon as I can. This thing caught us on the back foot a bit. Here." He handed Stramm a small pair of binoculars and stepped out of the car.

Stramm drove around the corner, parked near Smith's house and reclined his seat just enough to see it over the dash, his hat brim shading his eyes.

There was no sign of life in it. The front window curtains remained closed. The afternoon was uneventful. At dusk, the porch and interior lights of the house came on.

***

"This is a disgusting business," Assistant Commissioner Mike Miller growled, glaring down the table, "but I suppose we have no alternative."

"None," the Minister of Police said from the opposite end. He was a young black man with a manner blunted by the necessity to exert his authority. "Rebellion against proper elected government is disgusting in all its aspects."

"It never got very far before," said the Deputy Director of the National Intelligence Service, Dawid Filander, a smooth-shaven man with an unusual ability for self-effacement, "I mean, De Wet, De la Rey, the Red Revolt, Leibbrandt ..."

He knew as he said it the comparison was idle. The earlier rebellions in South Africa's rough-and-tumble history had been more idealistic than practical and had fizzled. Most were all-white affairs born of Afrikaner nationalism and anti-British and pro-German sentiment.

The others around the table, a small cross-section of South Africa's top security structures, ignored the interruption.

"What I mean," Miller explained, "is that it's disgusting to be forced to suspect people I have trusted and worked with for years. Now I'm spying on friends. In fact, sir," he frowned at everybody, "how can I be sure I can trust everyone in this room?"

His words fell like slivers of ice.

The Commissioner of Police, a fat, sweaty man who had reached his rank through sycophancy, glowered at him. Everyone looked at the Minister.

"Your point is taken, Miller," he said, unruffled. "You will have to accept my word. I can vouch for each of you here today. The absence of others does not mean I do not trust them. I want to keep this project small and secret.

192

We must nip this subversion in the bud. On the President's instructions, a handpicked team is investigating and when they report, we will act, but we will do so as covertly as possible to avoid a public fuss. I am involving only those security sectors whose services are indispensable.

"Both the senior Cabinet members and the main Opposition leaders in Parliament are convinced that the great majority of whites are willing to give power-sharing a chance. I believe most blacks want the same.

"This secessionist group, however, appears to be exacerbating white fears and anti-black feelings by fomenting widespread trouble. They want to create a climate of fear and insecurity in which partition, carving out an independent white state, becomes an emotionally attractive prospect.

"The advocates of partition point to the fragmentation of the Soviet empire and Eastern Europe into ethnic components and argue that if it works there, it must work here, so let's do it before we become another Yugoslavia. But this is not Europe, it is Africa. Partition would plunge the whole country into civil war, which is an unacceptable option."

"That's what they want," the Defence Minister interjected. "Black against white. The Phoenix mentality ... burn everything and from the ashes shall arise—"

"That may be. Our information is sparse but points to these people as instigators of most of the current violence. When the investigation unit identifies them, your job will be to stop them. I do not care how, provided you do it without fuss because we must not panic the public. We will tell you when to move."

The Minister paused and looked around the faces watching him, black, white and brown: the new South Africa. He was very conscious of his youth beside their accumulated experience. "If in the process you find old friends and comrades on the other side," he said, "that is tough. They must be brought to book too. Do not under-rate the subversives. They are not fools and they have the capacity to wreak far greater damage than any rebellion in our history."

The Minister of Police bestowed a bland smile upon them. Nobody smiled back.

"Thank you, gentlemen. I expect action very soon. Commissioner Miller, stay a moment, please."

The rest rose to their feet and left the room.

"Whew!" the Minister sighed when they were alone, wiping his shining forehead with a handkerchief. "Mike, I want you in Cape Town where I can be in direct touch with you at any time. Put your deputy in charge on the Reef and be here by tomorrow. There's an office for you near mine. Don't worry about your family, I doubt it will be for long."

***

Colonel Simião Manjacane examined, with some distaste, the thirty or so men gathered before him in the shade of a wide-spreading ficus tree.

The officers from his headquarters camp were distin-guished by the cleanness of their weapons and camou-flage dress, and by their obsequiousness to him. The handful of commandants who had come to the meeting from camps scattered across the Gaza province, were sloppy in dress and behaviour and two or three dis-played a surliness verging on insolence. The guns they carried were battered and dirty, but worked.

He wished he could have them under his thumb at headquarters for a few weeks. He should have done so long ago, he thought with regret.

Manjacane's swagger disguised a hard leader, tough-ened by years of will-o'-the-wisp warfare. He had spent long periods living almost like an animal in the hostile Mozambican wilderness between brief and bloody clashes with first the Portuguese, then Frelimo.

The respect the men under his personal command held for him was built on fear, a tried and trusted African way of leadership. They knew he lived better than they did and that sometimes he drank himself into a stupor, but they did not hold it against him because in his position they would have done the same. This too was African.

The commandants of the outpost camps had enjoyed their autonomy too long to submit docilely to his word, although he was their nominal leader within the ramshackle command structure of Renamo. They lived more like feudal barons than military officers, exploiting their subjects, the long-suffering tribespeople, as black chiefs had done since anyone could remember.

Manjacane had to tread with cunning to impose his will without seeming to do so. He had the bait and in time, he would have his way. The leaders before him represented close to two thousand armed men, many no better than bandits but all necessary to his plans.

"*Camaradas,*" he addressed them, "I have called you here because the time is near to seize our own country. When we last met, I promised to tell you what progress has been made. We have fought the Frelimo Marxists for twenty years now and still we do not have power. They have the towns, we have the rest. That is not defeat but it is not victory, it is stalemate.

"There are two reasons. One is we have been abandoned by our allies. The South Africans have surrendered to the ANC and gone to the side of Frelimo. The other, *camaradas* ..." Manjacane paused. This was a delicate part, "... is our own leadership. President Afonso Dhlakama led us well and fought hard, but he is old and feeble and has joined hands with the communist dictator."

Manjacane raised his fist high like a club and his voice rasped with assumed rage. "That is surrender! It is defeat! He is a sell-out! We shall not accept it!"

195

He glared at the little assembly. The commandants shifted uneasily, all eyes fixed on him.

Manjacane let the anger fade from his face and spoke in a calmer voice. "But Renamo has some friends left. A few in the Middle East, Brazil and Portugal give us money. And we have other friends in South Africa, men of honour who reject their traitorous government. They help us, *meus camaradas*, and we help them.

"They do not wish to share the bed with the ANC. They will do as we do, declare their independence in their own country! We will stand together. Our new states will be born at the same time, as neighbours. We will fight together against the communists. We will start one week from today!"

A buzz of interest came from the listeners. Some raised their rifles aloft in half-hearted salute.

A wiry man wearing a peaked khaki cap and a torn and faded Portuguese camouflage jacket appeared unimpressed. He looked at Manjacane with sullen eyes. "How will the racist whites help us and how are we helping them?"

Manjacane gave him a benign smile. The man headed a motley group of more than a hundred men controlling a large area to the south-west, on the border, and they needed his support. "We have sent weapons we do not need ourselves from the stockpile. They give us money and equipment, they will help us to build our capital, a port and roads, and they will provide electricity. They will fight next to us."

"And who will be the head of our new state?"

This made the other men listened intently. Manjacane chose his words with care.

"*Amigo*, how can I say? There must be a democratic election, not so? We ... you and I and all of us here ... will govern our state until an election can be arranged."

The sullen man grunted, not committing himself. He might be a problem, Manjacane thought. I will have to resolve that afterwards.

"*O chefe*," one of his local officers asked with enthusiasm, "tell us what will happen next week."

"When you leave here," Manjacane said, "you will take with you extra supplies and equipment and the transceivers our friends have given us. When I give the signal by radio, simultaneous strikes will be launched against chosen targets."

One of his aides handed Manjacane a walking stick. In the sand beneath the mahogany tree, he drew a rough map of Mozambique between Inhambane on the Indian Ocean coast, the South African border in the west, the capital city of Maputo to the south and the Save River to the north.

"This, *camaradas*, is how we will have our own country at last ..."

For the next two hours he went over the plan with them, explaining, answering questions, stroking egos by agreeing to changes, repeating the phrases 'our new state' and 'our own country'.

CHAPTER TWENTY TWO

The Catembe ferry was a blunt-nosed wooden craft with rows of park benches covering its broad deck beneath a sagging canvas awning. It rocked and creaked against the old tyres fending it from the worn stone-block quayside of the fishing harbour as passengers clambered aboard, men going home from work in the city, women in bright cloth dresses carrying bulging bags and baskets, some with the heads of phlegmatic fowls protruding, a few tourists, small boys begging.

Ballance and Ngwenya found seats at the stern where smiling Mozambicans paused in animated chattering to make space. Behind them stood the small open box of the wheelhouse where the black skipper ,wearing an ancient, grime-encrusted cap, waited. Beneath their feet, they felt the slow vibration of an idling diesel and heard the burble of its exhaust.

"*O capitão,*" Ballance called up, "at what hour does the last ferry leave Catembe for Maputo tonight?"

Surprised when addressed in fluent Portuguese by a foreigner, the skipper grinned and bent down to them. "*A onze hora, senhor,* at eleven o'clock ..." he said above the engine's mutter, "... maybe, but if you are stuck you might find a water taxi. Ask at the cafe near the jetty."

"*Muito obrigad',* many thanks," Ballance replied, smiling back.

A barefoot boy, naked to the waist, loosened a frayed rope from a bollard and jumped with it to the deck. The engine's mutter rose to a growl and the ferry heaved itself backwards out of the harbour's narrow entrance. The estuary seemed to Ballance to be much wider than from the Cardoso's picture window. Catembe was visible as a ragged fringe of low buildings on the southern horizon. The journey across took twenty minutes and ended at a rickety wood and iron jetty.

They disembarked in a rush of passengers that left the ferry rocking. Ngwenya found a taxi at the end of the jetty; a rusting Fiat with loose pieces of body held together by baling wire. In ten noisy minutes, it carried them into the depths of Catembe, a short transition into a random spread of houses, huts, shops and shanties alongside meandering sand roads. There were no white faces.

Ballance was surprised when they reached the *Casa do Pescadores*: expecting some crude dive, he found it clean and pleasant, Caribbean-like with log poles and comfortable wicker furniture in the sun-speckled shade of a long low roof of untrimmed palm fronds. It begged relaxation, a vacationer's delight.

Smart waited for them, sitting at a table right at the back of the deep veranda against the reed wall, a tall glass of orange-juice-and-something close to his hand. Beside him sat another man. He was as heavy as Smart was lean, thick in shoulder, arms and waist, about middle age, with skin so black it reflected bluish highlights. He wore the Maputo fashion of casual shoes, slacks and loose shirt.

Smart did not stand but waved a languid hand at his companion. "Meet Armando," he said, introducing them. "Mr Ballance, Temba Ngwenya. You guys like a drink? Try this one, white rum and fresh orange."

Ballance and Ngwenya greeted him in Portuguese and ordered Laurentina lagers. Armando was not drinking.

"My friend here," Smart said, leaning forward and speaking in a low voice, although nobody was within earshot, "used to be the ANC eyes and ears inside Renamo when it was an instrument of the P W Botha government."

He paused for a nubile girl to place their drinks on the

table. "In those days he helped me keep track of the weapons going to them from South Africa. Right, Armando?"

Armando nodded. He seemed uneasy and kept looking around the veranda and the road outside.

"It wasn't easy," Smart went on. "Much of the stuff was air-dropped to them by the South African army, even long after Botha made friends with Frelimo and was supposed to have turned off the arms tap. I managed to keep tabs on what came through by road and sea and Armando kept record of the stuff that arrived at Renamo's headquarters, so together we got a pretty clear picture.

"Last night I told him what you said about arms going the other way and he made some inquiries. He has something interesting for you. I hope you appreciate it, because he's taking a risk by meeting us here, in the open, and certain people would still like to get their hands on him. Armando?"

The big man leaned closer, elbows resting on the table, his heavy-lidded eyes half closed. "Since Frelimo and Renamo made friends we have not kept a close watch on the movement of arms," he said, picking his words with care in English. "There is no more any reason. There always was some export of light weapons the other way, to South Africa for the ANC – everybody knows. When Hannes said somebody was buying in quantity, I checked. You are correct, it appears there is much crossing the border."

"How much?" Ballance asked.

"I cannot tell you in detail but it is not a few rifles hidden in the ceilings of the passenger trains, or under the floors of buses, or smuggled through the border fence. Now it is truck loads, thousands at a time."

"They can't be for the ANC!" Temba protested. "We've taken over a whole arms industry and don't need them. We're trying to stop the flow of guns, not increase it."

"How did you learn this?" Ballance asked Armando.

He was suspicious; shipments that size should have been noticed.

"*Senhor*, moving freight is everything in Maputo. It is why this port exists. It is easy to conceal anything from the authorities here or buy their eyes, but the people in the freight trade always get to hear in the end. All I had to do was ask old friends in the trucking business."

"Do you know where it's coming from and who's transporting it?"

"I am sure it comes from the Renamo stockpiles north of here. Renamo has plenty of weapons, plenty, all given to them by the old South African regime." Armando's lips curled in a wry smile. "Now somebody is selling them back to the South Africans ... AKs, mortars, RPGs, SAMs, grenades, ammunition.

"The transport? I do not know. Maputo is full of South African wheelers and dealers, most of them in transport. It could be any of them. Many have big trucks." Ballance and Ngwenya looked at each other, thinking the same questions: where were the arms stockpiles? Who was sending them? Who was buying them?

Armando shrugged when they asked him. "The stockpiles were in several places when I was in the north with Renamo," he said. "The biggest was in Gaza, another near Gorongosa. As for the rest, I do not know."

Ngwenya gave a grunt of exasperation. "That's great. You've confirmed our suspicions but it gets us nowhere. No wait," he said, when Smart frowned, "we're very grateful for what you and Armando have told us but unless we have names, places, that kind of detail, we can't do anything about the gun smuggling. You with me?"

They were silent. Armando was thoughtful, fiddling with a cigarette lighter, then he looked at Ngwenya. "I could show you the exact position of the Gaza stockpile if we had a map," he said. "It would not be difficult for us to monitor transport from there and you could follow it to the border."

"Not a bad idea," Ballance agreed, "but I can't go up there and nor can Temba, even if he is black, because he doesn't speak the local languages."

They all looked at Armando, who shook his head. "Ah, no," he said with finality, "they know me too well. They will suspect something the moment I arrive there, asking questions."

Ballance remembered the tourist brochure from the hotel in his shirt pocket. He plucked it out and unfolded it like a concertina on the table between them. It showed the city's main streets on both sides of the estuary. He turned it over; the other side carried a map of the southern third of Mozambique, from the Ponta de Ouro to Quelimane near the great Zambezi River delta. It was a chart of near emptiness except for the string of villages near the coastal road.

"It's a bit small," he frowned.

"No, it is fine," said Armando, pleased. He leaned forward to peer at it. "You see ... here?" placing a thick forefinger on the paper.

It touched an almost vacant space northeast of the Limpopo River and the railroad from Zimbabwe to Maputo. Small print on it read, Parque Nacional de Banhine.

"A game reserve? There?"

"*Não, senhor,* a hunting area in the old days for the rich and privileged, abandoned for many years. First because of Frelimo activity against the Portuguese, and then Renamo activity against Frelimo. It is very wild, very primitive."

There was nothing on the map except straggly lines indicating streams, a speckle of symbols denoting a swamp, the railroad and a few bush tracks.

Armando took a ballpoint pen from his shirt pocket and drew a small circle on the edge of the swamp. "The base camp is there. To send arms in quantity they must take it by road, so, from Machaila to the railway at Mapai and from there by train, otherwise by road from Chigubo, all the way to the coastal highway to Maputo and then on."

"What is there at the camp?" Ngwenya asked.

"A small town of wood and grass houses, maybe more than a thousand people, most of them soldiers, others cooks, medics, armourers. It is a big place, *amigo*, with its own electricity, a little hospital, barracks, kitchens ... and a powerful transmitter to talk to Pretoria."

"Any flying facilities? A landing strip?"

"Nothing." Armando spread his hands, palms up. "The way is by road and by walking through the bush. It is a very long way."

"Who is in command?"

"I do not know, *amigo*. It has changed since Renamo joined the government. Some of the soldiers there, they do not like Afonso Dhlakama because he has made friends with Chissano. They do not want to put down their weapons and leave there."

Ngwenya and Ballance looked at each other. This was all very interesting but they were not making much progress. Ballance made up his mind.

"Okay," he said in resignation. "Temba and I will keep snuffling around our friends here. We'd like you two to do the same through your contacts. You, in particular, Armando, because you are closest to the kind of people who can tell who is shipping the goods, and where they are going. Hannes, can you call us tomorrow to set up another meeting?"

"Fine. I'll leave a message at the hotel reception."

Ballance and Ngwenya found the clapped-out taxi waiting for them, custom being scarce at this time of night. They waved a goodbye to Smart and Armando, who went into the night in the other direction, and climbed in. There was plenty of time to make the ferry.

Behind them in the *Casa do Pescadores* a man rose from a table inside the restaurant close to the thin wall where he had listened to them, and stood in indecision for a moment, wondering which couple to follow. He decided to follow neither, he knew what to do tomorrow.

***

The clock on the kitchen wall of the house in Orange Grove said eleven p.m. Smith picked up the extension telephone and dialled a Pretoria number. "Good evening," he said

The Doctor at the other end of the line recognised the voice. "Yes?"

"Can we meet? An auditing problem has cropped up."

"It seems to be happening often."

"Yes, well, these things do happen in our kind of business." Smith added a touch of sarcasm, "I'm sure you've experienced it, too."

"When?"

"Now, if possible. That is, in half an hour, at your place."

"Why not tomorrow at the usual place? You know you are not supposed to come here."

"There is some urgency."

"Half an hour then." The line clicked.

Two minutes later, as Stramm noted the lights in the front rooms of the house being switched off, the radio under the dashboard of his car buzzed and a small red light came on. He picked up the handset and pressed the transmit button.

"Stramm," he said.

"Our man has just phoned Pretoria, somewhere in the Waterkloof area, we're checking. He's going there now. Stick with him and call on entering Pretoria. We'll have backup for you there. For their ears, when you talk to them, you're keeping tabs on a drug dealer. Got that?" The tinny voice was Captain Ndzimande's.

"Affirmative. Out."

Smith appeared a few minutes later from the back of the house. Through the binoculars Stramm watched him unlock and roll up the garage door, reverse the Mercedes Benz and get out to relock the door. Smith turned on the headlights when the car was in the street, so the beams would not swing across neighbours' windows and arouse their interest.

A careful man, Stramm realised.

The Mercedes Benz travelled west at a sedate speed to the M1 highway through Johannesburg and turned north to join the N1 national road to Pretoria. Traffic was light, so Stramm kept position several hundred yards behind it, dropping back up to a kilometre or more, and closing up again because staying the same distance might alert Smith.

Outside Pretoria, Smith took the Fountains turnoff and travelled halfway around the big traffic island with its lawns and jets of water, to enter George Storrar Drive.

Waterkloof it is, Stramm thought, the capital city's elite suburb, whose lush gardens and large homes bespoke old money, influence, and the diplomatic world. He was half right: the Mercedes Benz climbed straight up the steep slope of Crown Street, past security guards and ambassadorial residences, to Waterkloof Ridge where the money was younger.

Stramm followed as far behind as he dared in the well-lit streets with his own lights turned off. At the top of the ridge Smith turned right and four blocks on pulled into the driveway of an imposing house in the gabled Cape Dutch style, incongruous among its modern neighbours.

Stramm stopped at the kerb a block before the house and, using the binoculars, saw a lamp outside the front door come on for ten seconds and then extinguish. He waited five minutes and drove past to stop again a block beyond.

He picked up the radio handset and touched the button three times.

"Detective Inspector Joe Stramm," he said and waited. They answered in thirty seconds. He gave the address and ten minutes later two unmarked cars, help from the local police, entered the street on the ridge and parked two blocks on either side of the house. Two men sat in each.

Now nobody could leave the house without being followed, he thought with satisfaction.

***

Thirty miles away Superintendent Louw sat in the seldom-used front room of his home and read with astonishment the printout Captain Ndzimande had brought him.

"Well I'm damned," he said, "Gideon Van Geyssen's home. What the hell's Smith doing there?"

"Not killing him, they were too friendly on the phone," Ndzimande said, unimpressed.

Dr Gideon van Geyssen: farmer, industrialist, chairman of The Surety Bank, donor of millions over the years to charities, member of economic commissions, champion of financial reform, advisor to the government.

"I don't believe this," the Superintendent reflected, "but you never know. Lucky, do some more digging. Find out what other addresses he has. Check on any visits to Mozambique and links with any known rightwingers. Put someone on to it right now and you go off and get some sleep. Oh, and one more thing, tell Stramm he's done a good job."

***

When he walked into the spacious entrance hall of the Doctor's house Smith stopped in surprise.

The last time he was here, it was sumptuously furnished, now it was empty and his footsteps echoed. A large dull area of the yellowwood floor between the polished edges revealed where the Persian carpets had been. Every one a collector's item, he remembered. An irregular darker patch of wallpaper at one side showed where a tall bow-fronted armoire of blackwood and stinkwood had stood and opposite it, darker rectangles were left where three Cape seascapes by seventeenth century Dutch artists used to hang. The pendulum clock, the objets d'art ... all gone.

He turned to the Doctor with a raised eyebrow.

"It looks rather barren, doesn't it," the Doctor said, "Everything has gone to the farm."

"You're quitting this place?"

"No, taking the precaution of moving the contents out of harm's way. When matters settle down later, I may move back. But enough of that, please come through."

He led the way to a small reception room with a few armchairs and a coffee table. Smith accepted the offer of a glass of white wine and the Doctor poured a dark port for himself.

"Well, what is so urgent?" Doc asked. He hitched a hip on the sill of a wide casement window and looked down at the small assassin in the embrace of a deep armchair.

Smith frowned into his glass. He was as offended by having to admit failures as he was by the failures themselves. "We missed both Ballance and the policeman, Superintendent Louw, the other night."

The Doctor's expression remained impassive. "Why?"

"Basson under-estimated Louw ..."

"I told you Basson was a fool."

"Yes. The police are keeping it covered up but as far as I can establish from our connections, Louw overpowered him and managed to extract some information before Basson was shot in a struggle."

"And Ballance?"

"Oh, the hit was good but Ballance wasn't there. Somehow, Louw managed to find out that there was a hit and stopped Ballance from going into his house. The bomb injured a couple of policemen, however, and caused a great fuss—"

"I know. I read the newspapers. Did they see you?"

Smith flashed one of his rare smiles. "No. My cover was perfect." He remembered jogging past the unsuspecting Louw and Ballance. "It is impossible to trace it back to me."

"Are you certain?"

"Absolutely."

"Good, because it would be most unfortunate if you were linked to me," Doc said and Smith knew any such misfortune would be his.

"There's something else you should know," Smith said. "Please do not try to call me at the hotel again. Use this number." He gave the Doctor a slip of paper.

"Why not?"

"I moved out this morning. This afternoon I phoned the desk to check my account and they said someone had been in my apartment and gone over it."

"I thought you said nobody could trace you?"

"I did. I left nothing, not even a fingerprint. I suspect it was a thief, or one of my agents looking for me. I haven't told anyone where I am now."

"You had better be right," Doc said, his face grim, "You must not come here again. In any case, I will not be here. Where is Ballance now and that man Ngwenya?"

Smith sipped wine and smiled. "That's the good news. They've both gone to Maputo. A friend at Jo'burg International told us the police put them on a plane this morning."

"What's good about that?"

"It'll be much easier to eliminate them in Mozambique. Being a black country in such a mess you can get away with murder, so to speak." Smith smiled again."I've already alerted our people there."

"No matter," Doc said, raising a hand. "They cannot affect us from there and in any case it is too late. We begin the final stage next week. Which is why I am leaving here."

"So everything's ready?"

"As ready as it will ever be. The country is close to administrative collapse and the public is a hair's breadth from general panic, as you are no doubt aware."

"My work here is finished then?"

The Doctor sipped port and looked thoughtful. The assassin had become dispensable, as they had foreseen when they hired him. The new state could not be born with the millstone of a professional killer around its neck. Blackmail was too easy, he had to be silenced.

But how? Smith was an expert in staying alive. The Doctor had already decided the best way was to set him a task which would kill him in the execution. If by some genius he succeeded, well, it would be two birds with one stone.

"No, your work is not quite finished, Mr Smith."

Smith put down his glass. His eyes glinted with anticipation. He had hoped to be in at the finish. "What must I do?"

"Eliminate the president. That will be your last assignment, and the last straw."

When Smith had gone, the Doctor placed his empty glass on a windowsill and walked to the bare entrance hall. He picked up the telephone from the floor and stabbed the buttons for a private number in Cape Town.

He spoke without using names and replaced the handset on its cradle. The trap was baited and set. The rest was in Fate's hands.

***

On the way back to Johannesburg, Smith was already turning over ideas in his mind. It would not be easy; the President was the best-protected man in South Africa.

His position obliged him to appear in public, especially now that he was an international figure, and by sheer force of personality, was holding together the country's volatile mix of peoples. There had to be cracks in the high wall of security surrounding him.

Smith could take no chances with a target as prime as this one. He would set up alternatives for the kill to improve the odds in his favour.

There was little traffic on the N1 this late. The few cars whose lights appeared in the rear-view mirror soon passed him at his moderate speed, satisfying him that he was not being followed.

He did not know then that from inside the hollow of the Mercedes Benz's chromed back bumper a small transmitter, no bigger than a peppermint, was sending a steady signal.

Stramm had crept into the driveway of the Waterkloof Ridge house to anchor it there while Smith was inside. Now Stramm listened to it beeping on his radio some two kilometres behind the Mercedes Benz, content that Smith was secure as a bird on a string.

***

While they both drove south, the Doctor made his own departure. He turned off all indoor lights in the gabled house except in the upstairs bedroom and left by the French doors into a garden on the side away from the street. The garden, with a breathtaking daytime view across gentle valleys, dropped in terraces of lawns and flowerbeds, to the neighbouring house.

He followed a brick path to a gate in the bottom wall leading into the neighbour's garden and made his way to a double garage. The swing doors had been well oiled and made no sound when he raised one.

Inside stood a black BMW 745i polished to a gleam. His luggage was already in the boot. The Doctor turned the ignition key and the engine purred into life more quietly than a cat. He drove two blocks before turning on the headlights and travelled east to the N1 highway, where he turned north.

CHAPTER TWENTY THREE

The boy was not seeing anything. His eyes beneath the turban of white bandage swathing his head stared at the floral wallpaper. His face was very pale. His underlip quivered as his mind played over and over the memory of the terror-ridden train ride from Muizenberg, the shine on the descending knife blade as he ducked in panic, the slash of searing pain, his headlong flight from the coach at Wynberg. He recalled nothing of coming home, lost in the caverns of his personal horror.

***

The MP sat on the edge of the bed in his son's upstairs room, where the brass-and-teak windows gave an expansive view over the peaceful green sea of Newlands' old oak trees ruffled by the fresh morning breeze, and beyond them to the Cape Flats.

There, past the tall cooling towers of the Athlone power station, the view was not peaceful. Columns of white and greasy black smoke rose from Guguletu, Langa, Crossroads and other townships, and from squalid squatter camps hidden by the dense Port Jackson bush.

South Africa's burning, he thought as he stroked Jannie's arm lying on the coverlet. *Ons Suid Afrika*, our South Africa.

"Jannie?" his father whispered for the umpteenth time.

The boy still did not answer.

The MP ran his hand again through his long, dishevelled black hair. He had not slept at all during the night while his wife, under a heavy dose of sedation from the doctor, had snored in the main bedroom across the passage.

He heard a tap on the door. It was the maid carrying a tray with three coffee mugs and a plate of rusks, which she placed on the bedside table. Behind her came his wife in her dressing gown, a petite woman of middle age, her smooth complexion puffy from deep sleep, but she appeared composed.

She handed her husband a mug and was about to offer one to the boy when her husband shook his head.

"It's no good, my dear," he said. "He's awake, he's been awake all the time, but he's not reacting to anything."

She sat down on the foot of the bed holding her mug in both hands and sighed.

"Dear God," she whispered, "what have they done to my boy? Will he be all right?"

"I'm sure he will," he said although he had no confidence in his own reassurance. "The wound on his head is not serious, it will heal. But there is a wound in his soul."

"When is the doctor coming?"

"He said early. He should be here any minute."

"My husband," she said, "you must sleep now."

"No, I can't. I'm not tired. I want to stay with Jannie."

"What happened yesterday?"

He recounted the news, which she had missed while under sedation, of the insane attack on train passengers. As he spoke, the agony of his secret knowledge gripped him and his face twisted with the pain and shame of it.

It had seemed so bold, so brave, so patriotic a gambit to safeguard Afrikanerdom and the values of Western civilisation against the looming wave of destructive black nationalism.

And now ... his injured son was a result, and the columns of smoke out there. The Coloured people, brown Afrikaners, who injected vivacity into their shared language, were dying in scores, trapped in the spiralling madness he had helped to spread.

His wife saw the distress on his pale face. "Paul, what's wrong?" she asked in concern.

They heard a car crunching up the driveway.

"Nothing. That must be the doctor. Please bring him up here."

She hesitated for a moment then went down the stairs.

While the doctor removed the bandages, examined with satisfaction his handiwork on the long wound and rebandaged it with a fresh dressing, Jannie continued staring straight in front of him.

The doctor peered into his eyes with a small torch, spoke to him, pricked the skin of his forearm with a needle, and drew its point across the soles of his feet.

When Jannie reacted, it was sluggish and his slack expression did not change.

"The shock is more severe than I expected," the doctor said. "He's showing serious withdrawal. I'm afraid I must hospitalise him. Please do not worry yourselves into a state. Jannie will be all right. It will take a little time for him to get over this but the sooner we start treatment the better."

Half an hour later, an ambulance took the boy to a private clinic in Newlands.

In the breakfast room, the tired MP dropped into a chair, propped his elbows on the table and sank his face into his hands.

His wife stood behind him and kneaded his taut shoulder muscles with firm fingers, always soothing to him after a long day in the House. "He'll be all right, Paul, don't worry. Jannie's a strong boy. We'll go to see him later, when you've had some sleep."

"It's not just Jannie," the MP mumbled through his fingers.

"I know. Many were hurt on that awful train. But you cannot bear the hurt of all of them."

"I must, I must ..."

She was confused. "Why, Paul? Has someone else we

know been hurt?"

"No. Yes ... I don't know."

He lowered his arms to the table, dropped his head on to them and sobbed. She moved to his side and raised him to cradle his face against her bosom, warm beneath the soft stuff of her gown and nightdress.

He wrapped his arms about her waist and pulled her close, overwhelmed by guilt and desperately needing comfort. The words came, a few at first, between deep shuddering sobs in jerky strings, half muffled by her gown and then an outpouring of his living nightmare.

***

She did not understand at first, it did not make sense. When it did, she could not credit what she was hearing. It cannot be she tried to persuade herself.

But it was. As he spoke, the television images and the pictures conjured by the blaring headlines leaped into her mind with startling clarity.

Her son, her only son ... good God, how could he!

Her fingers ceased stroking her husband's hair and she clutched, hurting him. Her stomach became a knot of taut muscle. She looked down with disbelief at the mewling head pressed to her and felt the grip of the arms around her. A volcano of revulsion rose in her. She thrust herself from him and rushed to the bathroom.

***

The MP heard her being sick. He sat at the table and stared at the floor, a woebegone figure in creased trousers and a crumpled, tieless white shirt, with tears streaking his face. He was still there lost in misery when she appeared at the breakfast room door fifteen minutes later. Her face was white and mottled and her hands clenched in determination.

"You will go to the authorities at once and tell them everything," she said, her voice low and shaking with loathing, "If you do not, I will go to the police."

214

She turned and ran up the stairs. The bedroom door slammed.

He could kill himself, he supposed, and let her tell the authorities everything, which she would do without doubt. But that would be the coward's way out and he did not want Jannie to remember him as a coward.

He realised then that he might have lost his wife. He had been so sure she would understand his pain, stand by him and console him.

Weary, every fibre of his body weighted by fatigue and self-disgust, he rose from the chair and climbed the stairs to bathe and dress. As an MP, he should talk to his party leader first. He might be able to see the man before Parliament began.

***

In exasperation, Penelope Fox tossed the file she had been trying to study on her desk and stood up to pace the carpet of her office, her arms clasped about her. She could not concentrate.

Every time she tried to, a mental picture of Jeff interfered, smiling down at her in the dimness of her bedroom, muscled arms clamping her close, his face and rumpled hair as he stood in the kitchen trying to scramble eggs, together with unpleasant images of Jeff suffering unknown hardships in strange black countries.

Damn! she thought, I'm coming apart.

Her telephone buzzed. She grabbed it.

"There's a Mr Louw here to see you," said the secretary. "He doesn't have an appointment but he says it's urgent."

Mr Louw? "Send him in," she said.

Superintendent Louw's hand was raised to knock when she swung the door open.

"Superintendent, please come in." Her face was alight with expectation; he must have word of Jeff.

"Good morning, Miss Fox, I hope you're well."

"Please call me Penny, everyone does. Sit down. Would you like a cup of tea or coffee?"

"No thanks, I won't stay long." He perched on the edge of the guest chair and she sat behind the desk.

"What have you heard from Jeff?" she asked.

"From Mr Ballance? Nothing yet."

Penny felt her face fall.

"I'm sorry, but he's just left and I'm not expecting to hear for a few days."

"Oh, well. What can I do for you, Superintendent?"

"Miss Fox, we've had a bit of luck in our investigation into the underground movement. I need your help and I know you'll keep everything I tell you in the strictest confidence."

He told her how they had tracked down the man who had placed the bomb in Ballance's home, Smith, and through him the financier, Dr Gideon van Geyssen.

Remembering Van Geyssen's once frequent appearance in the finance pages, she was surprised.

"Smith turns out to be a very experienced and cold-blooded professional assassin. Politics mean nothing to him, money does. He has worked for many clients. In the Middle East, both the Israelis and the Palestinians have hired him at different times. When things turned a bit hot, he took jobs in Argentina then Colombia, where he is thought to have murdered for a cartel in the cocaine war. He was in the Far East for a while before he went to Rhodesia. He is also credited with the disappearance of certain black leaders. His way of life has become a habit and somehow he hooked up with the CCB. The rest I think you know."

"Where did you learn all this, Superintendent?"

"Interpol. They have a file on him a mile thick."

"And if you know all this, why haven't you arrested him or deported him or something?"

"Because there is nothing positive on him, no hard evidence, not even from Interpol, and because we want to see where he leads us. He made two small mistakes, which just goes to show even the best professionals can be careless. He borrowed a dog as camouflage when he bombed Mr Ballance's house and we found the dog and traced it back to him. We also found fingerprints on the plastic around the light switch outside the bathroom when our men searched his hotel room and Interpol identified him."

Penelope listened, fascinated.

"I'm telling you all this for background, Miss Fox ... Penny." The use of her familiar name came awkwardly. "I'm not asking you to have anything to do with him, he's a dangerous man. His controller seems to be Dr Van Geyssen. I know it sounds ridiculous – he's a well-known philanthropist and reformer, but the evidence is strong. We have the facilities to check on most of Van Geyssen's background and past activities without him knowing about it. The one thing we cannot check is his personal papers."

"I don't see how I can help you, Superintendent."

"His documents are right here. The law firm you work for is the biggest and most prestigious in Johannesburg and he's been a client for years."

Objections rocketed into Penelope's mind; he was asking her to break every ethic in the book. "Superintendent Louw, I don't think I can help. Papers put in trust with us are sacrosanct. Not even his personal lawyer may see them without his approval. I don't even know who his attorney is."

"Look at it this way. Everything we've checked about him so far, much of it open to public scrutiny anyway, is above board. We suspect this man involved in the planning and financing of the assassin's activities and of whatever this mysterious secession movement is up to. It's a thin chance but it's quite possible he has kept something in writing ... few businessmen like him can work without committing something to paper. For instance, he can't be using hard cash so he must have a record of what he is receiving and spending."

Superintendent Louw leaned forward and looked her in the eye. "Miss Fox, this organisation is responsible for a number of deaths already, remember, and seems to be trying to start a civil war. Do you want that? If we have to bend the rules to stop them, they must be bent."

"But superintendent, there might be nothing at all useful in his files."

"Maybe. We won't know until we look."

Penelope lay back in her chair and blew out her cheeks. "Phew, Superintendent! You're asking a hell of a lot."

"I know. Will you help?"

She stared in thought at the angular face, stern even in repose. She stood to lose either way: out of a country if there was civil war, out of work if she was caught with her fingers in the files.

"Superintendent, I'll see what I can do but I promise nothing. I'm putting my job on the line for you. Tell me what to look for."

Superintendent Louw smiled.

***

That evening, like several other of the firm's lawyers, Penelope stayed on late at the office, explaining that she had to catch up on work.

She tapped her computer keyboard for half an hour, pulling onto the screen the names of the firm's partners one by one, before she found the partner with the right list of clients.

Among them was Gideon Jean Tertius van Geyssen. When she tried to bring the files under that heading onto the screen, the computer informed her access was barred without a code.

It was not possible for all his papers to be in the computer alone, she reasoned. There was always the risk of a hard disc crash and no sane firm of lawyers fully trusted files of computer discs. Anyway, computers were time-savers, not a legally acknowledged repository. Somewhere there had to be files containing original documents.

Penelope unlocked the small safe in her office and took out a large double-sided key. Picking up a batch of folders from her desk, she walked through the dim offices occupying a full floor of the building to see who else was working late. The vault needed two keys to open it.

A senior partner was still behind his pigeonwood desk, as was his habit since he had become a widower.

"Please, sir," she asked him, trying to look tired and turn on the charm at the same time, "could you help me open the vault? I must deposit these in their proper places before I leave."

"What's wrong with your own safe, Miss Fox?" he asked, smiling back.

"It's full, and these are not supposed to be left out of the vault." She hoped he would not look at them.

"All right. Come along."

He led the way to the steel-and-concrete lined room larger than her office in the core of the building. They inserted and turned their keys and he took the handle and swung open the massive door. He turned his key back and withdrew it.

"When you've finished, close the door and lock it with your key," he said. "Mine will lock automatically."

Penelope could not believe her luck.

She switched on the stark overhead light and slotted the folders on her arm into their places. That done she scanned the crowded racks filling every inch of wall space.

The Van Geyssen papers occupied several big box files and a locked steel case. No luck there, she thought, when none of her keys would fit it. Hope dwindling, she made a rapid search of the box files, leafing through brittle documents of thick paper with heavy seals, carbon copies of letters, title deeds, and pages of handwritten notes spanning years. Every few seconds she glanced towards the open door, praying nobody would come in.

In the seventh box she found a copy of an unsigned two-page list of place names, some of which she recognised, together with dates, sizeable sums of money and another column that caught her eye. The symbols in it were vaguely familiar: .762 ball, RPG, 9 mm pb, RPD, TMH52 and a whole lot more until she came to one she recognised: AK47. Next to it were the figures 2,000 and 40,000.

That must mean two thousand guns for forty thousand rands. This had to be a list of arms purchases. Near the bottom of the box was a list of freight containers filled with machinery from America, landed at Durban harbour, and railed to different destinations all over the country.

Machinery? Freight containers? What did this stuff have to do with a law firm?

In the eighth box was a letter caught by a paper clip behind an insurance policy. It was typed and dated a year earlier. It began 'Dear Gideon' and the writer said that yes, he agreed,the government had left no alternative and an independent white state was the final solution, so a meeting was being called at the venue near Louis Trichardt. It was signed 'Nico'.

Penelope opened the spring clips of both files and extracted the two documents. She took down a file from the racks, slipped them inside and carried it out. The heavy door swung closed and she turned her key.

***

Although not yet ten-thirty in the morning, the sun's heat was already strong when the telephone rang in the study of a rambling old house, high in the mountains above Louis Trichardt. The Doctor strode in from the porch where he was drinking his mid-morning coffee, lifted the receiver and identified himself.

"Someone has been into your private papers," said the

caller, the lawyer he had used for twenty years and trusted.

The Doctor felt a flare of anger that anyone should pry into his personal affairs. "Go on," he said.

"I thought you should know, especially at the moment. All the important documents are still locked in the box for which nobody except you and I have keys, and it hasn't been tampered with. I don't know yet about the other files, I'm still checking them, but so far I've found nothing missing."

"How do you know then, that somebody was ferreting?"

"Our computer. It logs all attempts to enter certain directories, including yours. This person first tried to get into your files that way, but couldn't, and then went into the vault."

"Someone in your office?"

"Correct. The computer attempt was from the office of a new girl and she later asked one of my partners to help her open the vault."

"Who is she?"

"A young lady named Fox, Penelope Fox." He gave the Doctor her home address.

"Thank you. Let me know if you find out more."

The Doctor felt a chill down his spine. He raked his prodigious memory for what might be in the box files, nothing incriminating, so far as he could tell, but there was always the possibility.

Fox. The name rang a bell: the instructing attorney in the abortive case against Ballance. That affair kept coming back like a bad penny.

He had hoped it might stay away now that Ballance and Ngwenya had gone to Mozambique, but Smith's bungling had opened a can of persistent worms.

There could be but one reason why she was prying, he realised. Someone, somewhere, had stumbled across his name, linked it, and then put her up to it.

The last thing the Doctor needed was anyone inquiring into his connections. It would be disastrous for him if his secret activities were uncovered. He had to find out more, who her contacts were, who asked her to pry. He would have to stop the interference.

For several minutes, he considered what to do, his incisive mind lining up and weighing all the options. He could use the Committee's extensive underground network within the government but word might leak back to the Committee of this compromise and they would cut him out.

He had one option. Smith could find out who was behind her without causing ripples. Once he knew, the Doctor could take appropriate action.

He shuffled through the clutter on the desk until he found the slip of paper with Smith's new telephone number. He was about to dial it when he thought again and replaced the handset.

He told the servant he would be away for lunch and drove into the town of Louis Trichardt, snuggled into the fold where Zoutpansberg mountains meet the plains, pretty in its cloak of flowering trees.

He telephoned from a public call box in a shopping centre. When Smith came on the line, the Doctor spoke without preamble.

"I want an urgent check on a customer's credit rating and business operation," he said. It was a pre-arranged code for a covert investigation into someone's activities and connections, one of a series of codes covering everything from simple identification to straight murder.

"Not the full package?"

"No," Doc said. A 'package' meant assassination. "Just the credit check and in particular what she is delivering and to whom. The customer is a woman who had dealings with those two who have left the country. We need to know all about her. Please do not fail this time. It's becoming bad for trade."

"Who is the customer?"

The Doctor gave him Penelope's home address but not her name.

"I'll check it out right away," Smith promised.

"Good." Doc put down the telephone, confident that Smith would put two and two together, and realise the importance of the task when he learned her name from her address.

***

The police constable in Brixton who was recording the tap on Smith's telephone shook his head in puzzlement when he eavesdropped on the conversation. This was commercial talk; the mark must be some kind of salesman. He turned his attention to the buttocks and breasts in the latest *Hustler* magazine; the officers could sort it out when they went over the tape.

***

Smith felt the prickling on the back of the neck and surge of tension that comes with the sudden knowledge that hidden eyes are watching.

It was three o'clock in the afternoon and he was sitting in the Mercedes Benz in the garage next to the house, the powerful Becker radio tuned to short wave to pick up the BBC news.

Through the announcer's voice, he heard the steady *bip-beep ... bip-beep ... bip-beep* that meant one thing.

He sat through the news as if listening, but did not hear it, his thoughts busy with the problem. When it finished he pulled down the garage's roller door and went into the house. He dug about in his bag until he found a small device the size of an electric shaver and returned to the garage through the small door at the back.

He switched on the device and moved around the car. The nearer he came to its rear end, the faster the tiny bulb on the device flickered. He found the bug with his fingertips but did not remove it.

His mind raced over the implications. One thing it meant was that he could not drive to the address Doc had given him, as he had intended to do after the news, to examine the scene before going there tonight to check on whoever lived there. It would be a complete give-away.

Another was that the Mercedes Benz had become a millstone. He could not use it without his every move known, and he could not remove the bug without revealing that he had found it and drawing even closer attention.

The worst was realizing he had a tail. It annoyed him intensely after he had taken such meticulous care to cover his tracks. He could not believe he had made a mistake; someone, one of the very few people who knew about him, must have talked; perhaps that idiot Basson.

He ticked off the other implications. It was a certainty the house was being watched and his telephone was tapped. The call from Doc must have been overheard. He went over the conversation – little there to give the game away, no names, a quite ordinary business instruction; an address.

He should warn the Doctor but it would have to wait.

This assignment he would handle himself, Smith decided, his ego still smarting from the recent failures.

He would slip out of the house after dark tonight. First he had to meet his two remaining agents, the strong young men who had eliminated that police sergeant, Greeff, to plan the big one, the assassination of the President.

It had to be within the next week, which meant going to Cape Town. He would set it up so that all three of them would go for the man, each working independently from a different approach. That would triple the odds in Smith's favour; there could be no more misses.

Later tonight, after briefing the men, he would steal a car to go to the Illovo address Doc had given. He wondered who the woman was.

CHAPTER TWENTY FOUR

Returning to the Cardoso at lunchtime from a fruitless canvass of friends and contacts, circumspect because they could not afford to arouse curiousity, Ballance and Ngwenya found a hand-printed note waiting for them at the reception desk. It read, *Botequim Pinguim*, 8 p.m.

"Must be Hannes," Ballance said. "Where's the *Pinguim*?"

"It's something of a dive down on the Costa do Sol, near the beach. It calls itself a cocktail bar though nobody drinks anything except beer, *bagaceira* and cheap wine. Tourists go there for a thrill. They sometimes have a stripper."

"Sounds like fun," Ballance grumbled. "Let's eat here before we go."

The taxi dropped them a few minutes before eight. The place had several dozen customers, despite it being a weeknight and still early. Two lurid hostesses, sitting at a semicircular bar just inside the entrance, eyed them as they walked in. Ignoring them, Ballance and Ngwenya wound between full tables, to one with padded benches against the back wall, as far as they could get from the small dais, where a stripper would gyrate later to the cacophony of a local pop group. Smart and Armando were nowhere in sight.

"Give them time, they might have been held up somewhere," said Ngwenya. "Let's have a drink."

They were sipping their second draught Laurentinas and debating who to contact to next, when two men paused in the entrance and glanced around the room.

Not recognising them, Ballance and Ngwenya resumed talking, heads close together. The newcomers moved inside, out of their vision.

The strangers sat down next to them, one on either side.

"I'm sorry, these seats are taken," Ballance said. He felt a nudge against his leg, glanced down and saw a small automatic pistol. He froze.

"What the hell ..." Ngwenya said loudly, raising his arm in reflex when the other man jammed a gun into his side.

"Be quiet!" the man hissed.

Dumbfounded, Ballance stared at them. The one next to him was Portuguese, about thirty, scrawny and nervous. The other was African, short and deep-chested with powerful arms, a bulging belly and grey sprinkling his temples. Both wore loose sports shirts hanging outside their slacks.

Ballance tried to stand up. The table prevented him from straightening his legs and while he was off balance, the white man raised an elbow and shoved him back.

Ballance felt his temper heat up and struggled to control it. He did not want a public scene.

"What the hell d'you think you're doing?" he asked in anger. "Put those damn guns away! Who are you?"

"Shut up," the white man said, poking him with the silencer on the barrel. "With this I can do what I like, and in this crappy country nobody can stop me. Who I am doesn't concern you. What matters is who you are. You're Ballance, aren't you?"

Ballance boiled but kept his temper.

"Strange company you keep," the Portuguese said. "I suppose this must be your fancy black friend, Ngwenya?" He read the fury and frustration on their faces and grinned at his partner. "The gentleman's lost his tongue but we hear they've been busy little boys, meeting all the right people, chirping away ... right?"

The African nodded, grinning. "I think the two of you should come along with us for a nice little chat."

"Get fucked!" Ngwenya growled. "The only way you'll get me out of here is feet first."

The white stranger bared his teeth in mockery of a smile, beneath eyes as cold as a snake's. "Be happy to accommodate you, mister. Let me put it this way, you either come along with me and Miguel here, or you both stay here dead."

At the edge of his vision, Ballance noticed Smart and Armando come in. They glanced around the room, took in the scene at a glance, and sensed trouble. They turned aside to sit at the bar beneath the thatch awning, next to the hostesses.

Ballance said to Ngwenya, "This guy looks crazy enough to do what he says." To them he said, "I'll go along if you leave him."

"Very heroic of you," the Portuguese replied, dripping sarcasm. "And bullshit. Please don't be difficult. We're quite happy to use these."

They stood up, concealing their guns under their loose shirts.

"Move," the man said, grasping Ballance's arm.

***

Watching from the shadow of the awning, Smart and Armando saw the two men crowding Ngwenya and Ballance, whose faces showed anger. Who the hell were they? When the strangers stood, they thought with relief that they were leaving, then saw them force Ballance and Ngwenya to stand. A gun appeared for a moment in the big black man's hand before he concealed both gun and hand under his shirt.

Shit! Smart thought. They're hijacking them! His mind raced, seeking a way to help. Just inside the bar entrance, stood a large fire extinguisher. He hoped to God it still worked; such details were seldom tended to in Mozambique.

The newcomers started to move, pressed close behind Ballance and Ngwenya.

Smart snatched a cigarette lighter from a hostess, flicked it into flame and, to her astonishment, held it against the thatch over his head. The brittle-dry grass caught fire in seconds. Flame bloomed and in seconds blue-white smoke billowed.

"Fire!" Smart yelled and dashed for the door.

The buzz of talk in the bar stopped. Every eye fixed on the smoke. It expanded in a rolling cloud shot with tongues of flame.

People rushed for the door. Glasses and bottles toppled and crashed. The barman, eyes large as golf balls, leaped over the counter and fled with the hostesses close behind him.

Smart pulled the fire extinguisher from its clips. Through the thickening smoke he saw Ballance and Smart being shoved forward in haste. They stumbled past him with their eyes screwed up.

Smart aimed the nozzle and squeezed the trigger. A powerful jet of dense chemical foam shot out and hit the big black man in the face. He screamed with pain, dropped his pistol and staggered back, clawing at his eyes with both hands.

The white man spun in surprise, mouth wide, and the acrid jet filled his throat, drowned the cold pale eyes and covered his head in foam. Blinded and choking, he staggered back, tripped over a chair and crashed to the floor. He let go of the pistol to wipe his face with both hands, roaring with pain and anger.

***

Ballance and Ngwenya dodged aside and snatched up the guns. Through the coiling fumes, they saw Smart whirl to aim the jet at the burning thatch.

The snow-white foam blanketed and stifled the fire in

seconds. The extinguisher's jet died to a trickle and Smart dumped it on the bar.

"Quick!" he said, bending through the smoke swirls to the men on the floor, "Pick them up, bring them!"

"No, leave them!" Ballance objected, "Let's get the hell out of here!"

"We *must* take them!" Smart insisted. "They were after us, they're our lead."

He dashed a full jug of water into the black stranger's face and emptied the dregs of an ice bucket on the white man's.

"Move!" he barked. "We've got your guns."

Blinded, they staggered forward without resisting, as Ngwenya and Armando steered them by the elbows to the door. Customers who had fled outside watched them emerge.

"Let us through, please!" Ballance called out. "We're taking them to hospital!"

The small crowd parted. They rushed the two men along the road, with Smart leading the way to a dented Cressida station wagon. They pushed the two into the luggage space. Ngwenya and Armando sat in the back seat aiming the pistols at them. Tyres smoked as Smart pulled away.

"Where are we going?" Ballance asked.

"To a safe place."

The white man swore, his face in his hands. "I'm blind, I can't see!" he moaned. His partner sat with his hands over his eyes, slumped like a sack of coal, and whimpered.

"How did you know where to find us?" Ngwenya demanded. The man shook his head and said nothing.

"Why were you there so early?" Smart asked Ngwenya.

"You said eight o'clock."

"No. I said nine. Good thing we were also early."

"Yeah, thank God for that. Two more minutes and

these jokers would have had us. We'd be floating in the bay by morning."

"Somebody must have substituted my note at the desk," Smart said. "We're being watched, friend."

"Oh shit! Well, we'll know who's doing it once we've finished with these guys."

Smart turned west and drove fast through the city centre on the Avenida 24 de Julho and at the outskirts turned towards Xipamanine, a fringe suburb of small houses with tiny walled gardens rubbing shoulders in narrow streets. He stopped at a high wall on a corner, Armando got out to open a solid wooden gate and they drove in.

"Welcome to *Casa Mkonto*, the House of the Spear," Smart said. "It's an ANC safe house from the old days. Armando stays here now."

Ballance watched while the others took their two captives indoors and made them rinse their faces in the bathroom. He wondered at the strange circumstances that had led a quiet-living professional into this bizarre situation in a foreign country, then pushed the thought from his mind. He could worry about it later.

The two emerged still part blinded, faces red from the bite of the chemicals. Armando shepherded them to a couch in the tiny living room, where they sat side by side in sullen silence, holding handkerchiefs over their smarting eyes.

Armando stood in front of the Portuguese, holding the pistol in his left hand and with his right grasped the man's bony chin, forcing his head back.

"Who are you?" he demanded. "I know his name's Miguel, what's yours?"

The man batted his hand away and slumped against the back of the couch. Armando reached again and this time seized his chin hard, fingers denting his cheeks. Ballance watched, not comfortable in the presence of brute force.

"Don't mess me around, white filth!" Armando growled, leaning close as a lover. "If I have to, I'll make you talk."

In answer, the man spat full in his face. Armando stepped a pace back and for a moment stood still, body taut and expression impassive, spittle trickling down his nose and cheek. His right fist lashed out and struck the man on the temple so hard, he toppled against Miguel and slid half off the couch.

The Portuguese reached behind to grip the edge of the couch and heaved himself upright. Dazed, he shook his head from side to side and grimaced up at Armando through eyelids screwed up against the light, trickling tears. When he moved, it was so fast, nobody could stop him.

His arm flashed from behind his back at blurring speed with a thin double-edged knife. He aimed just below Armando's ribcage to stab and rip upwards into his heart.

Armando reacted by pure reflex. In the last split second, he twisted and the blade raked up the ribs of his left side like a stick across a picket fence, scoring to the bone. In the same instant, he triggered the gun in his right hand, twice.

It gave a sharp *sput sput* and two .32 calibre copper-jacketed bullets struck the white man in the chest. One penetrated his heart, killing him. He sagged back on the couch, a look of quiet surprise relaxing his angular face.

Smart leaped to help Armando, bent over in pain and dripping blood on the cheap carpet. Ballance was immobilised by the shock of sudden, unfamiliar, violent death.

"Jeff, help us, dammit," Ngwenya snapped. "Get something for bandages, fast!"

Jeff ran to a bathroom, found nothing there, went to a bedroom, ripped sheets from the bed and ran back to the others.

Using the dead man's knife, Ngwenya slit and ripped

the sheets into makeshift dressings, clamped a pad over the long but shallow gash in Armando's side, and bound it tight in place. It would hold until he reached a doctor for stitches.

Armando grimaced but managed to stand straight. He looked sourly at Miguel, still cowering on the couch, unable to see clearly what was happening. "Search him," he said.

Ngwenya and Smart seized Miguel by the arms, hauled him to his feet and poked and patted his clothing. Nothing. They shoved him back so hard he bounced.

"You are next, *amigo*," Armando hissed and held the pistol so close to Miguel's nose, he smelt the stink of burned cordite. "Your friend is dead and you are next tonight, unless you talk."

Ballance was in no doubt he meant it.

Miguel melted into a blubbery heap and his face paled to grey. "No!" he begged, in Portuguese. "No, do not shoot, I will tell you."

"You sure will," Ngwenya rasped and squatted in front of Miguel, balanced on the balls of his feet. Miguel tried to press himself deeper into the couch and focus his weeping eyes, first on the corpse beside him, next on Armando's face, next on Ngwenya's.

"Who is your dead friend here? Who does he work for?"

"He is Chris. I don't know his whole name. He works for a business here."

"Which one?"

"I do not know, *senhor.*"

"Who are you and who do you work for?"

Miguel's reddened eyes flicked across the three faces frowning at him. He licked his lips. Armando placed the muzzle of the pistol against his nostril and pushed.

"Speak, damn you!"

"I am Miguel Salazar, *senhor*, and I work in Maputo for Colonel Manjacane of Renamo."

"Manjacane of Gaza?" Armando interrupted, surprised.

"*Sim*, that one."

"And why did you try to kidnap us tonight?" Ngwenya continued, indicating Ballance.

"It was on orders, *senhor*. Chris told me I must help him."

"Who gave the orders?"

The captive shrugged. "I do not know."

"And what were you going to do with us."

Miguel's eyes searched the room as if looking for a way out. Ngwenya stood up.

"Okay, Armando, he doesn't want to cooperate and he's lying through his teeth. He's all yours," he said and stepped back.

Armando stood spread-legged in front of Miguel, left arm held tight against his wounded side, and extended his right arm to aim the .32 pistol at the point between Miguel's watering eyes. He cocked its little hammer with an audible click. Miguel squealed in fright and held his hands out in front of him, palms forward, as if they would stop a bullet.

His voice rose an octave, "*No! No!*"

Armando squeezed the trigger. The little gun went *sput* again. The bullet singed the hair above Miguel's ear and bored a hole in the cheap upholstery of the couch. Miguel's eyes grew huge and he almost fainted.

"Next one will be yours," Armando said.

"All right! All right! I will tell you everything I know!" Miguel gasped, cowering away from the pistol so he was almost horizontal on the couch, "Please ... put it away."

They sat him up straight; he shivered as if cold. Ngwenya gave him a half tumbler of *aguardente*. He drank it in one swallow, coughed at the burn in his throat and began to talk, unnerved by the nearness of death.

He worked for a Colonel Simião Manjacane, *chefe* of the Renamo base north of Maputo. He had several thousand guerillas, most of the same tribe who wanted their own country.

"They want the land between South Africa and the coast in the Gaza province. Their headquarters are near—"

"We know where it is," Ballance broke in. "Go on."

Fearing he could not go it alone with his forces, Manjacane had approached some of the South Africans who continued to supply weapons to Renamo long after the Mozambique civil war had ended, Miguel explained. In turn, he wanted advice, money and political support when the day came.

They agreed. They were *simpatico*, they said, because they, too, were seeking a cultural home of their own. They had started a secret organisation they called the Free State Society. In return for helping him, they wanted certain weapons from the considerable stockpile the old South African government had sent to Gaza.

"Chris," Miguel glanced at the corpse beside him as he spoke and shuddered, "was one of their men based here to help with the weapon shipments. In the old days, he served with something called the CCB. On paper he now worked for the Maputo office of a South African import/export business."

"What's their name?"

"I do not know but the *chefe* is a *Senhor* Thomlinson."

"The plan is that when everything is ready Colonel Manjacane will make attacks on some places just inside South Africa, while the Free Staters rise to seize part of South Africa for themselves. At the same time Manjacane will declare independence in Gaza."

"Where is this white state going to be?"

"Somewhere in the north or north-east, I am not sure. Maybe close to the Mozambique border, they talk of a federation, one white state and one black."

"Shit," Ngwenya murmured.

"It's bloody crazy," Ballance whispered. "White con-

234

ceit gone rampant. But it is just bold and brash enough to appeal to the right-wing fanatics who yearn to recapture the privileged past. They don't have the sense to see it's impossible. Consider the permutations. All lead to the same conclusion, in South Africa's present jittery, volatile state it would be disastrous, a trigger for civil war. Maybe that's what they want." He turned and asked Miguel. "When is all this due to happen?"

"Next week or the week after."

"*What!*"

"The end of next week is what my colonel wants."

Ballance was stunned. "Jesus Christ! They've got to be stopped. We must go back now!"

"Damn right," Ngwenya said. "But how do we stop them? We don't know who they are yet. If we stir up trouble, they will go into hiding and we might never find them. There is one thing we can do though, we can emasculate this Gaza group before they can act. Without their help the secessionists should have much less chance of success."

"How?" Ballance wanted to know.

"Tell the government here about Gaza."

"Ha!" Armando snorted, still pointing the pistol in Miguel's general direction. "Frelimo would not dare to attack them. Its forces are too weak and ill-disciplined. They cannot even patrol outside the cities. And there is supposed to be peace in Mozambique now, so how can Frelimo start fighting Renamo again? It would restart the civil war."

"There is another way, " Ballance said. "We could just make the whole thing public to blow the scheme apart ..."

"And precipitate the uprising before the South Africans are ready to come rushing in wearing white hats and stop it?" Ngwenya interposed.

They fell silent, considering. Revolution was due to erupt in two countries in one to two weeks and there was nothing they could do about it.

"Except, perhaps ..." Ballance pondered, "... it would be a hell of a risk in terms of international repute, but well worthwhile and it would drive the Frelimo government up the wall with indignation ... listen ... the South African National Defence Force ... why can't they attack this base camp if Frelimo can't or won't? They've got an oversize army of former South African and former ANC men sitting on their butts doing nothing, burning up taxpayers' money, why not use them with good reason?"

"Now you're talking, *bra*," Ngwenya grinned, patting Ballance's shoulder. "There's one small problem though ... we have to convince the whole damn government we're telling the truth then persuade them to attack a friendly neighbour."

CHAPTER TWENTY FIVE

"Ah, Paul, come in, come in."

The Opposition Leader moved from behind his wide desk to a cluster of deep leather armchairs near the tall teak windows of his office, giving a view across upper Cape Town of Table Mountain.

"You wanted to see me," he said with a benign smile, gesturing the little MP to a chair. The man was dapper as usual in a fashionable dark suit, club tie on creamy white shirt, and black crocodile shoes; his black hair brushed as smooth as if it had been painted on. But his face was pale and drawn.

"Are you all right, Paul?" He injected concern into his voice but the last thing the Opposition Leader wanted now was the burden of the trivia of someone's personal problems.

With the entire country teetering on the brink of anarchy with voices being raised louder on all sides, he and the Vice President had their hands full keeping their respective rank and file in check. He had tried to stave off the MP's request for a meeting, but the little man had been insistent.

It was unusual for him. The Opposition Leader knew him as a quiet backbencher who, in the old government, had represented conservative Nationalists in a rural constituency. He was reliable cannon fodder when the division bells rang in the House but otherwise a background figure. Because he did not want to ruffle the conservatives in his party any more than he had to, the Opposition Leader had agreed with reluctance to the meeting.

"No, sir," the MP replied, sitting erect on the edge of his

chair, "I am not all right."

"Is it your son?"

"You know about that?" The MP said, his surprise obvious.

"Yes. I'm very sorry and I hope he'll be all right."

"Sir, it was that which made me ask for this meeting."

"Paul, I don't know what I can do to help him, but if there's anything—"

"No, sir, you misunderstand me. What happened to Jannie was the last straw. May I speak to you in the utmost confidence, with nothing on record?"

"There are no recording devices here," the Opposition Leader said, his expression sober.

"I had to see you for two reasons. First, here is my resignation from our party and from Parliament."

He drew an envelope from his inside pocket and laid it on the stinkwood coffee table between them. The Opposition Leader glanced at it and let it lie.

"The second reason, sir, is also the reason for my resignation. I have been involved with a covert movement to create a separate state for whites. Our objective is to secede with a part of South African territory, declare ourselves independent and to go to arms, if necessary, to ensure our survival."

The Opposition Leader's eyebrows lofted in surprise and the benign expression vanished from his face. "Go on," he said.

"I still believe that an independent white state is necessary and viable and that it can enjoy good relations with black neighbour states. In fact, we already have the friendship of black neighbours.

"But," the MP went on, "I cannot in all conscience continue to support the tactics the leaders of our movement are using to gain our objective. The way they are doing it, we will have a government of murderers. We will have achieved our independence at the cost of destroying the rest of South Africa, which in turn will throw the whole of

Southern Africa into turmoil and, in the end, will destroy us as well."

"What are they doing, Paul?" the Opposition Leader asked, his face grim.

"The plan is to seize independence when the rest of the country is in such conflict and confusion that the government cannot stop us. Up to that point, I find it acceptable. But the leaders, my colleagues in the Free Staters Movement as we call ourselves, have gone too far. In fact, for several months they have been hastening the conflict and the confusion by provoking violence among blacks and between blacks and whites.

"They have given blacks guns, stirred fighting between Inkatha and the ANC, and initiated gang attacks in white suburbs. Worse than that, I have learned that they have hired professional assassins to liquidate leading South Africans of all political beliefs.

"This, sir, I cannot condone. So I have decided to put myself at your mercy and tell you everything in the hope that you can help stop the death and misery. Perhaps you can persuade the government to cede the land for a white state."

The Opposition Leader rose from his chair and turned his back on the MP to gaze out of the window. This was his favourite scene, the magnificent bulk of Table Mountain with its ruggedness, gentled by a tablecloth of soft cloud laid by the south-easter. White and pink houses with bright-coloured roofs clustered in the wooded greenery at its feet, like sheltering chicks.

Now he saw none of it. His mind was wrestling with the vision of horror the MP's confession created.

"Tell me, Paul," he said after a long pause, still staring through the window, knowing the answer he would get, "where is this new state to be, and how will it be created?"

"In the north, sir." The MP was precise. "It will extend from the Limpopo river southwards past Louis Trichardt as far as we can get people to support us, which could be as far as Pietersburg. It will reach to the Mozambique border in the east and to the nearest black border in the west.

"On the day the signal is given, the people there will block all access roads, seize control of all government offices, and announce their independence by radio and through the international media.

"It is not an idle plan, sir. They have brought in enough weapons in secret to arm themselves well. They have the cooperation of Vendas next door, who oppose the ANC and want to retain their independence. They also have the support of the tribe just across the border in Mozambique, in Gaza province. They will seize their own independence at the same time. All have planned this in concert. They will fight."

"What about the police and the army there?"

"I'm not sure, sir. I think many are on the rebel side, maybe most."

"And when will all this happen, Paul? When?"

"Towards the end of next week, when the signal is given."

"*Next week!* Who are the people involved?"

"I know those who are on our Committee, our future cabinet."

The MP's brow furrowed while he dug into his memory and relayed names, ticking them off on his fingers.

The name Gideon van Geyssen, advisor to the government, was one of the first. The Opposition Leader frowned.

The MP told of the meetings at the Chairman's farmhouse in the Zoutpansberg, of the assassination plots he knew about, and of the smuggling and resale of arms.

"Paul, you have done the right thing in coming to me. I suppose I can understand your reasons for supporting secession although I cannot agree with them. I'm grateful that your morals have prevailed against exploiting violence.

"I will not accept your resignation now. If you wish to resign later, when this is all over, that is up to you. Until then please tell nobody about our meeting and go about your business as you always do. I want your promise on that."

Relieved, the MP gave it. He had expected an explosion of temper, and severe castigation at least, prompt arrest at worst. He left the office feeling better with his burden shared. It did not trouble him that he had betrayed his rebel colleagues; what had happened to Jannie had wiped out old loyalties.

When the padded door closed behind him, the Opposition Leader pressed a button on the intercom machine on his desk.

"Sir?" his personal assistant responded.

"Ask the Vice President if I can see him at once," he said. "Tell his secretary this is priority, an emergency. Don't take no for an answer. Suggest he should also have Assistant Commissioner Miller present."

While he waited, the Opposition Leader opened the top left drawer of his desk and pressed the rewind button on a tape recorder. When the tape stopped, he pressed the play button and listened to the voice again, "No, sir, I am not all right ..."

He removed the tape and slipped it into his jacket pocket. Two minutes later his PA called him in the intercom to say the Vice President was waiting for him.

They met in the spacious vice-presidential office in Parliament, a gracious chamber of polished woodwork and furniture whose windows gave views of the Gardens and the mountain. Assistant Commissioner Miller was already there, his blocky body filling a tailored business suit instead of his usual uniform. He carried a brown briefcase.

"Please sit, gentlemen." The Vice President ushered them to studded leather chairs around a low yellowwood table. "Now," he looked at the Opposition Leader, "what is the problem?"

The Opposition Leader took the tape from his pocket and placed it on the table.

"Please listen to this, it will explain everything."

Miller put his briefcase on the table, extracted a small portable tape deck and inserted the tape. They listened to it in silence. As the words spilled out, the Vice President forgot the pipe he had started to light and his frown grew heavier. When the words ceased he nodded to the Assistant Commissioner to play it again.

"I am very surprised," the Vice President said afterwards with some acid in his tone. "This indicates you never suspected that a senior member of your own party was involved in subversion?"

"That's right." The Opposition Leader was irked by the tone. If the man sought to make political capital there would be a fight.

Sensing this, Miller intervened. "Sir, even very senior members of the police appear to be involved and, as you said before, perhaps even members of the Cabinet. We cannot be aware of everything."

"No, I suppose you're right." He busied himself lighting the pipe and exhaled an aromatic blue cloud.

"With this tape, sir, we can nail the people he has named right now."

"No, Mike, we cannot. He's given us less than a dozen names and there must be hundreds involved, maybe many more. I want them all. We'll wait."

"But sir ..." The Assistant Commissioner was anxious.

"Mike, that tape goes into my personal safe in this office now. You say nothing and do nothing. That is an order. I will tell you when to act."

"Sir, you're taking one hell of a bloody risk."

The Opposition Leader smiled at the policeman's unparliamentary language. "I know, Mike, I know," the Vice President said, smiling too. "Trust me."

He looked thoughtfully at the two men with him. He had watched the Assistant Commissioner's career for years and believed him honest. He and the Opposition Leader were already collaborating to uncover the mysterious third force. He came to a decision.

"Gentlemen, there is something you do not know."

They looked at him.

"I have a man inside the rebel movement. He has been one of them from the beginning."

"But—" Miller said.

"Why have I not said so?" The Vice President anticipated him, "Because he is an old and valued friend, because I have not been sure until very recently whom I can trust, because I dare not risk exposing him and thereby putting his life on the line."

"So you already knew what's on this tape?"

"Much of it, Mike. And he will let me know when they will make their move. We can be ready for them and take the whole lot. That's why the tape stays here. He contacted me yesterday," the Vice President went on before anyone could interrupt, "and gave me something you *can* get your teeth into. The rebels have ordered their hired assassin to kill the President, the same man who arranged the killing of the Freedom Front Whip and a number of other people, left and right, black and white."

For once Miller's urbanity cracked. He half rose out of his chair, gripping the arms. "Damn it, sir ... pardon me ... but why the hell didn't you tell me earlier! The man might be waiting for the President right now!"

"It's possible. I don't want to make him sound the foolish hero, in fact I'm quite apprehensive, but to catch a jackal you have to set bait, don't you? And we very much want this man caught, so the President is prepared to be the bait. We are giving him the fullest possible protection without taking him right out of public view, which he refuses to leave anyway, and without making it obvious. It's up to you to make sure the assassin is trapped. I want him and the people who use him brought to public trial."

"Do you have a description of him?"

"No, I'm afraid my agent didn't have the time. I know he's ordinary and inconspicuous, goes by the name Smith, is good at disguise, uses a variety of weapons and has access to official identity documents through the rebels' connections inside the civil service."

Miller leaned back, took a deep breath, and released it in a rush. "That covers just about everybody in South Africa," he said, his voice bitter. "The priority is to make sure that the President is protected at all times, that not so much as his fingertip is exposed. We can't guess how the killer will try, it could be with a bomb, or poison."

The Vice President waved a deprecatory hand.

"Perhaps you're being a little melodramatic, Mike. The staff here and at the Presidential office, the Tuynhuys, are impeccable and his personal bodyguards are outstanding. You selected them, remember? Security is so tight already, I suspect the assassin will try with a rifle, so we'll endeavour to keep him out of exposed places until this thing is over."

***

The idea of using the Head of State as bait for a killer appalled Miller, but there was no alternative. The President himself had agreed. Politicians' ways were too devious for him, a man of direct action. Unhappy, he handed over the tape and left the office with his mind churning.

The first step was the immediate and discreet replacement all the accreditation documents and ID cards of the Parliamentary personnel in the House and in Ministerial offices, up to and including his own. Then his men would be able to filter out any strangers using the existing IDs.

He gave strict orders that he and the security personnel should be alerted the instant anyone used the old documents, but not apprehended; they should be covertly watched to see what they were doing. Some might be innocent, unaware of the abrupt change in the ID system.

***

The Vice President cancelled all appointments for the next hour and sat gazing at Table Mountain, engrossed in convoluted thoughts. It all tallied and confirmed what he

244

knew, but events were moving rather faster than he had expected. The situation was not yet out of control, he would have to step with great care.

***

Detective Inspector Joe Stramm resumed the watch in Orange Grove at five o'clock in the afternoon, this time in a green Nissan Skyline which he parked seventy metres from the house. The detective who had been watching Smith's house for the past six hours gave him a brief wave before driving away. Dumb bugger, Stramm thought, if Smith had spotted that he might have wondered.

Stramm checked the transceiver, picked up the beep from the bug and inclined his seat back to settle down for the night's work. He had chosen this shift because it gave him escape from his wife's steady complaining about the cost of living and his salary, and from his daughters' carping. They appeared to think his bank account was bottomless.

He had slept late after the excursion to Pretoria and checked with Captain Ndzimandze before taking the Skyline. The detective he had replaced had made one report: mid-afternoon Smith had opened the garage and sat in the front of the Mercedes Benz for some twenty minutes, seeming to listen to the radio, and then gone back into the house. There had been no sign of him since.

A few tired people walked past the Skyline on their way homeward from bus stops in Louis Botha Avenue. They were past middle age. Young people were a rarity this suburb of boxy little houses dating back to the thirties. It had been settled mainly by Jews who fled from persecution in Estonia, Latvia and Lithuania during the prelude to Hitler's imperialism and had been welcomed by the settler-hungry South African government.

Dusk spilled into the crevices of the city bringing the street lamps to life and softening the seediness of the suburb. Lights switched on in houses and, in the twilight stillness, Stramm could hear faint voices and the clatter of utensils through open kitchen windows.

At six o'clock he reported in by radio: nothing happening.

After reporting in again at seven o'clock he felt uneasy and restlessness; something niggled at his mind but he could not pin it down.

He expected Smith to emerge soon. He had been indoors all day; he must have business to do. Still there was no a sign of him, no hint of movement against the light behind the curtained front windows.

And then the thing eluding Stramm burst with clarity in his mind, like a slide projected on a screen. The windows, the light behind the windows ...

In the other houses around him indoor lamps had winked on one by one as night approached; one second darkness, the next a bright rectangle in a wall, or a pool of light on a front porch.

In Smith's house, the glow of lights had appeared gradually, becoming brighter as the evening darkened.

They'd been switched on in full daylight and became visible with nightfall. Why? People did that when they went out by day knowing they would not be back before dark, and wanted the lights on to deter burglars.

Or to make watchers think they were still at home.

Stramm looked up and down the street. It was empty of people. He slid out of the Skyline and clicked the door shut, then strolled towards Smith's house as if going to the café on the corner of Louis Botha Avenue.

As he passed, he glanced from under the brim of his hat down the driveway past the garage, at the front windows, and down the narrow gap between the house and the six-foot wire mesh fence dividing it from the next yard. Nothing moved in the half shadows between the patches of blacker darkness.

Past the fence, he again looked up and down the street and, seeing nobody, put a hand on the neighbour's front picket fence and jumped over it. He heard the television in the neighbour's house. There was no indication he had been seen.

He walked alongside the wire mesh fence towards the backyard on the grass to deaden his footsteps. There he peered through the wire at the back of Smith's house.

No sign of activity, all the windows and the back door on a small stoep closed, and all inside lights on.

Now what the hell? Stramm thought. He had to have a closer look.

He tested the wire mesh, found it firm where it was anchored to a pre-cast wall running behind both houses. He climbed up, heaved himself over and descended on the other side.

He stood there for a minute illuminated by faint reflection from a street lamp, his right hand on the butt of the pistol under his waistband. Still no reaction.

Choosing boldness, Stramm ran on tiptoe to the back wall of Smith's house and moved along it until he was at a window. He took off his hat and edged an eye closer to peer over the sill.

The curtains were cotton lace and he could make out the shapes of furniture inside. A bedroom and it was empty.

Next was the kitchen with a blind down. Through the crack under the bottom edge he saw that it, too, was empty. Nothing on the stove.

He was able to see into the living room and, by pulling himself up with his hands, looked through a tiny fanlight into a toilet where the light was also on, with the same result.

He found the rear door to the garage. It opened without sound on oiled hinges. The old Mercedes Benz stood there. The bug was still under its bumper.

Stramm was convinced Smith was not in the house. He walked up the driveway and back to the Skyline, where he picked up the transceiver handset and dipped the button.

Superintendent Louw answered.

"The pigeon has flown," Stramm told him, describing his suspicions and what he had done. "The house is stone empty. Smith must have found the bug, Superintendent. He's supposed to be a pro."

The superintendent cursed their luck. He was pleased Stramm had used his head, otherwise Smith's disappearance might not have been discovered for hours. "You did well," he told the detective. "Stay there until you hear from me, in case he comes back."

He placed the microphone next to the transceiver on the table in his living room, his temporary base, and considered his next step. "Lucky!" he called.

Captain Ndzimandze came from the kitchen where he was making tea.

"Smith's gone." He repeated what Stramm had said. "Call Brixton and ask them to read back the log of the phone taps. There may be a lead there."

The captain used the phone in the hall. He returned five minutes later, looking apprehensive.

"There's this," he said. "The duty constable said it was nothing, just a business call, so he didn't bother to bring it to anyone's notice. I didn't check the log because I was out trying to track down Van Geyssen."

Superintendent Louw read Ndzimandze's scribbled notes and went pale. "God damn it!" he spat. "That's Miss Fox's address, Ballance's lawyer. They're after her! Come on, let's go!"

The superintendent grabbed his jacket and ran for the door then had a second thought and ran back to the transceiver. Stramm was a lot closer to Fox's flat.

"Stramm, write down this address" he said when the detective answered. "Go there as fast as you can. It's a flat where a Miss Penelope Fox stays, a lawyer. I'm pretty certain that's where Smith is heading. He may be going to kill her. Move! We're on our way!"

The superintendent tried to raise Nichols, the constable posted at Penelope's apartment block, but there was no answer. He cursed, maybe the radio was dead

***

Earlier, at about the same time Stramm was wondering what was bothering him about the lights in Smith's house, Smith with quiet expertise was breaking into a Honda Ballade, in a row of cars, angle-parked on the sidewalk in a quiet street in the Berea suburb near Hillbrow. He wore thin rubber gloves so there would be no fingerprints.

He was amused by the ease with which he had left his house unnoticed.

At four o'clock, the time the streets begin to fill with homeward traffic, he had picked up his small suitcase and gone out of the kitchen door, locking it behind him. A gate in the wall behind the house took him into a neighbouring backyard, cluttered with motorcycles in various states of disrepair.

He had picked his way past them and walked along the short driveway to the next street, unconcerned. He would not be coming back here. Nobody noticed him.

In the street, he strolled down to Louis Botha Avenue and caught a bus into town, the last way any sleuth would expect him to travel. At the Jeppe Street post office, he used a public telephone to track down the two men he sought and agreed on a place to meet them.

When Stramm was parking the Skyline in Orange Grove, Smith was already long gone, stepping from a taxi outside a hotel in Berea.

His meeting with the pair had lasted two hours in a secluded corner of the upstairs bar, a venue seldom busy before nine or ten at night ,when the local whores came to sell their wares. They sat in a booth around a pine table and arranged the details of the assassination of the State President over frosted glasses of Windhoek draught lager.

Smith explained in detail how they would carry out the assignment together but independently, each with a different approach.

The State President and his entourage moved fast behind a tight screen of sharp-eyed security men who were
quick on the trigger. One man alone had little hope of
getting him in the sights. This way, at least one of the three
would. The Vice President had less protection, but was
second prize.

He opened the suitcase and handed them two thick
wads of banknotes, half their fees in advance, plus open-
return air tickets to Cape Town.

"I won't see you there," he told them. "From now on
we'll go our separate ways. You know where to find what
you need when you arrive there, it's all been arranged.
Don't make contact with each other and don't recognise me
if we chance to meet. Stay in separate places and avoid the
main hotels if you can."

"Is there a bonus for the one who gets him?" one of them
asked.

Smith studied them for a second. They were so alike in
their muscular fitness and appearance down to their
Sundance moustaches, as if stamped out with an army
biscuit cutter. Sometimes had trouble remembering which
name fitted whom.

"Why not?" he said. "I'll make it a bonus for both of you
if either of you does it."

They grinned at that, pleased.

They would get bonuses, he thought as he left the bar,
whether they made the kill or not, but not the kind they
expected. Smith believed in covering his tracks.

Now, the unfinished business. He had the Honda and an
address in Illovo.

He could not go back to Orange Grove afterwards and,
he realised with regret, he would have to abandon the
Mercedes Benz.

Johannesburg was becoming altogether too warm for
him. It was time to adopt a new identity and move on.

In fact, it was time to leave South Africa, which was going down the same savage tube as the rest of Africa, he

thought, but he couldn't do so until the secession began and he received his fat final payment in US dollars.

After that he would try the new Europe, where there should be scope for his special skills. Meanwhile he would go to ground in Cape Town and finish up with a flourish of presidential assassinations.

It left him little time to find out what the woman was up to. That meant he had to use the direct approach: interrogation, which he was good at. It was amazing how fast pain applied with care produced results. That in turn meant she would have to go.

The Doctor had stressed that he did not want the 'full package', meaning Smith must not kill her, but with time so short and the police on his tracks, he had no alternative. Another liquidation would make no difference either way. Smith's unwavering priority was his own survival. He had to cover his tracks.

He decided he would move tomorrow. All his possessions were in the single suitcase. He would stay the night in her flat, alter his appearance, and fly to Cape Town in the morning.

The Honda hummed into life when he by-passed the immobiliser and connected the ignition wires. He backed it off the sidewalk and turned its shark nose towards the M1 and Corlett Drive, pleased to be active, looking forward to the job ahead.

CHAPTER TWENTY SIX

The drive from his home, high in the Zoutpansberg mountains, to the old stone farmhouse on the northern slopes took the Doctor a little over half an hour. The big BMW easily smoothed the curves and slopes of the highway twisting through valleys, blanketed by monotonous pine and gum plantations and the stretches of indigenous forest in the many greens that he loved so much; African bush still unspoilt by development.

He travelled at a slow speed on the last few miles of dirt road following the mountain contours that hid the farmhouse from view, concerned that the grassy ridge between the wheel tracks might scrape the belly of the low-slung car.

At the high game fence, a tanned young man in khaki shirt and trousers with a Musgrave hunting rifle slung from his shoulder recognised him, and opened the gate.

Good thinking, Doc thought with grudging approval, nobody who might by chance see the man would give a second thought to a hunting rifle, commonplace on a game farm. The AK-47s and American weapons would be issued later, when it did not matter who saw them.

Hearing the car approach, the Chairman came out on to the stoep to meet it, a dignified figure with his erect bearing and snowy white hair, in spite of his faded farm clothes.

"Welcome, welcome," he greeted in Afrikaans, squeezing the Doctor's hand in powerful fingers, "come in and see what we're doing."

Inside, the house was like a military operations centre, busy with men in khaki. Some were in their twenties and thirties and several, men of senior rank, were older and thicker around the middle. Although it was cool and dark in the great living rooms beneath the high-pitched log and thatch roof, some wore bush hats with wide floppy brims.

Most carried handguns in hip holsters; .38 specials, heavy long-barrelled .45 revolvers capable of knocking down a buffalo, magnums, 9mm parabellum pistols. Some had already gathered around a long table covered with maps, listening to a tall angular man with a pepper-and-salt beard.

All stood in respect when the Chairman entered. He introduced them to the Doctor as the Free Staters' operational headquarters team and the section leaders, the men who would command the groups manning the road blocks, taking over government offices, whipping up public enthusiasm, cowing any local resistance that might arise, and spearheading the defences should their new white republic come under attack.

The Doctor surveyed them critically.

"Good," he pronounced. "If everyone is as enthusiastic and disciplined as you, we've won already."

"Good?" the Chairman retorted. "They're damn good, man, and more are coming. We have help filtering in from all over the country, men who have trained and are waiting for the day. But," he went on, "there is much to be done yet. Come and see this."

The Chairman led the way down a passage to a spacious bedroom converted into a communications centre. The grey-enamelled metal cabinets of a powerful transmitter-receiver system squatted on a dining table of carved teak with ball-and-claw feet. A tall antenna had been rigged behind the house on steel poles, a common sight on farms. Two men wearing headsets sat in front of the illuminated dials.

"Here is where we will give the go-ahead."

"Has this thing been tested?"

"Thoroughly. We've distributed portable transceivers

253

already and of course some have cellphones. But the nice touch ..." the Chairman chuckled, "... is that we'll also use the old farm radio network."

It started as the military Marnet, set up in rural areas by the former government for protection against guerilla attack in the apartheid days. With the huge upsurge in crime since the end of apartheid, in particular murders of remote farm families, the network had been upgraded and expanded in many parts of the country.

"Oh? What do the police and army have to say about that?"

"They don't know. We're using local channels and codes they won't suspect. You know how it is, Doc, the wives use Marnet more for gossip nowadays. There's no need to worry anyway, I told you the garrison here won't give us any problems."

"How can you be so sure?"

"The brigadier." The Chairman smiled, complacent. "He's on our side, one of us. He will arrange matters so that his troops can't interfere and those who want to can come over to us."

"And the police? They're transferred around so much these days you have little chance to get to know them."

"They're not a problem. They're scattered, a few here and a few there. Most are on our side and it will be easy to block any who want to make trouble. Come and have coffee."

The Chairman led the way down the long passage to a spacious flagstoned kitchen, dominated by a huge Aga stove against the outer wall.

"All that remains is to distribute the arms," he said. "Those from Mozambique have been taken from the warehouses in Venda to caches in many places and the material from the States has been trucked in. The *veldkornets*, the young captains back there in the house, will issue them."

The Doctor took the earthenware mug the Chairman's

wife handed him, savouring the familiar aroma of chicory. The two big men, typical South Africans of the old school of rugged purists, stood deep in their thoughts while they drank. Doc broke the silence.

"Our friend Manjacane and the others in Venda, are they ready?"

"As ready as they will ever be. That's why we must move within the week. You know these blacks, they lose spirit if they have to wait around." The Chairman refilled his mug from the pot on the stove. "And on the day, Doc, where will you be?"

"Down in Cape Town, fighting our battle within the enemy's ramparts as we discussed. Here, I'd be just an old man getting under everybody's feet. Political pressure in the right places at the right time down there is just as important to our cause as good men and bullets up here."

"*Ja.* You're right of course."

***

Penelope Fox coasted her car down the ramp into the basement of the flats and brought it to a stop with its nose to the wall of her parking bay. She was tired after the long day and still rattled by the experience of pilfering papers from a client's files the night before.

Superintendent Louw had seemed quite excited when he read them over lunchtime hamburgers in a Wimpy bar near her office. For him, excitement translated into the hint of a smile and a glint in his eye.

"That's fine," he had said. "Very good. This one looks like a list of weapons purchases and this one pins him to the secession cause, though there's nothing criminal in talking about it. This one," he picked up the list of containers, "is odd indeed and we'll look into it. They could also be arms."

"I don't know if it will ever come to court," he added, looking at her, thinking, "but if it does I don't suppose you would testify that these came from his personal files?"

"Me?" She blanched. "Good God, no!"

"No, I thought not."

Enough of that sort of escapade, she had told herself, it's too harrowing.

She locked her car and walked to the lift, her high heels ticking on the cement floor. A young man in a denim jacket appeared at the foot of the stairs, looked at her and smiled in welcome.

She knew him as one of the several policemen who rotated the duty of keeping an eye on her safety at Superintendent Louw's behest. He was a good-looking fellow with curling brown hair that reminded her of Jeff's, laughing eyes and a lithe restless body. He seemed very young for the job, about twenty. She assumed he carried a gun.

She smiled back at him and rode up in the lift.

The constable quite liked this stint. It was a break from the routine, she was a hell of a good-looking woman and a bit later, as had become habit, she would ask him in for a cup of coffee and a light supper. They would chat for a while before he took up his station downstairs again. There were worse ways of killing duty hours two or three times a week.

***

Smith parked the stolen Honda around the corner and strolled, hands in pockets, the half block to the apartments and past them on the opposite side of the street. His senses, honed by years of hunting, attuned to anything out of the ordinary as he passed the building, detected nothing.

The foyer, visible through the glass doors, was empty. By coincidence, at that moment the policeman was in the small backyard at the dustbins next to the wall Ngwenya had climbed over days ago to visit Penelope. He was making a routine check before re-entering through the basement to stand in the foyer or sit on a stool at the entrance to the basement parking area.

On his belt beneath his denim jacket, he wore a police-

256

issue Beretta pistol in a blue webbing holster and from his shoulder hung a portable two-way radio with its switch set, as the rules said, to receive.

At the end of the block, Smith crossed the quiet street and strolled back on the apartment side, this time more slowly. Near the basement entrance, he stopped in the darkness under a tree to look and listen.

He waited. Five minutes later a Morris Mini drove in; he heard the slam of its door and the whine of the lift before lights came on in a top-floor flat.

Inside, the policeman heard the car and although it was not necessary, he moved a few steps up the staircase from the basement to the foyer to stay out of sight until the newcomer was in the lift. No point in making the residents wonder, he reasoned.

Smith detected his presence when the policeman climbed the foyer stairs. From his angle, Smith could not see the man, just a shadow cast for a moment against the front door glass when he emerged from the top of the flight of steps, and passed between the wall light and the doors.

He waited. There was no more movement. It might have been a resident going up the stairs to his flat, Smith thought, but where could he have come from? Just the one car had gone in. Must be a nightwatchman.

Sure enough. He saw a dim figure appear a couple of feet inside the basement entrance, outside the scattering of light from a street lamp, and sit down.

Still Smith waited, eyes fixed on the darker shape in the darkness. As his sight adjusted, he thought it had a pale face but dismissed it as illusion; nightwatchmen had black faces.

Then another car came down the street, slowed and turned into the basement. Its headlights swung across the figure, which stood up. Smith saw it was a young white man in blue jacket and pants.

That was not a nightwatchman. He had to be a policeman or a hired security guard. Which meant someone in the building was under protection. And that person must be his target, the woman.

It gave a new dimension to his task. The thought of abandoning it did not cross his mind; he had to question the woman. He could have slipped by a nightwatchman but a trained white guard was another matter.

One answer was to take him by surprise and knock him out. It held the risk of a struggle if the surprise was not complete, or his strike with the butt of his .357 magnum revolver, not the best of bludgeons, it was not hard or accurate enough. Smith knew too that he was no longer in his prime and a fit young man might get the better of him.

The other was to kill him.

His reverie disturbed by the arriving car, the constable stretched and decided to make another inspection round before going up to Miss Fox's flat. He ambled down the slope and through the basement into the backyard, opening the back door with a click of its latch.

As soon as Smith saw him disappear and heard the faint sound, he ran along the sidewalk and dodged across the narrow strip of lawn and garden fronting the building to peer around the edge of the basement doorway. Without the street lamp flare in his eyes he could see cars, no person.

He darted across the basement and stopped with his back against the rear wall between a parked car and the two steps up to the open back door. Raising his right leg, he extracted a knife from an ankle sheath inside his sock. Its three-inch double-edged blade was exceedingly sharp.

Smith sensed the guard coming before he heard him humming to himself. The man paused on the top step and twisted his body to pull the back door shut, and for an icy second Smith thought he had been seen, but the cheerful humming continued.

The guard trod down the two steps and half turned to head for the foyer stairs. Smith jumped forward.

Smith reached up his left hand to clamp over the guard's

mouth and jerk him backwards against his upraised knee. The startled man tilted backwards, off balance, and Smith's right hand whipped around in front of him, slashing the knife blade deep across his exposed neck. In the same swift composite motion as he completed the knife stroke, Smith thrust hard with his knee, propelling him forward.

An unbelievable fountain of blood jetted from the young constable's gaping throat. He crumpled like an empty sack, dead.

Smith stepped back to the wall to be out of the way of any spurts and splashes. A minute was enough, by then the heart had stopped and the fountain slowed to seep into the great patch of blackness on the cement floor.

He wiped the almost clean blade on the man's trouser leg and slid it back into its sheath. With delicate fingers he turned over the corpse and with his fingertips probed the pockets of the denim jacket until he found a wallet, which he placed in his own pocket.

The corpse he rolled and shoved under a car. The pool of blood was large, with no way to hide it, but it was unlikely anyone would notice it in the near darkness. He had to move fast now; he could not stay here for the night as he had intended.

The foyer was still empty. In its light Smith searched the wallet and found the police identity card. He put it in the breast pocket of his tweed jacket and dumped the wallet in the ashbin beside the lift door.

He found the address he sought on the row of post boxes against the foyer wall. The name on it was 'P. Fox'. Ballance's lawyer. No wonder the Doctor wanted her investigated. She would be better dead.

He hurried up the stairs to the third floor.

***

At the knock Penelope thought it was the young policeman coming for his evening visit. She was about to turn the handle when she hesitated and peered through the tiny

259

peephole she had had installed in the door.

The magnifying lens gave a distorted view of a little grey-haired man standing with hands thrust into the side pockets of his tweed jacket. He looked harmless, small and bland with drooped shoulders, but ...

"Yes?" she called through the door. "What do you want?"

"Police, Miss Fox," the man's muffled voice replied. He smiled straight into the peephole lens and with his right hand drew a card from his breast pocket, which he held up in front of him.

She saw the SAP sunburst emblem clearly through the distortion but the identity picture and number were blurred.

She opened the door.

"I'm sorry to bother you, Miss Fox." His accent was very English. "Superintendent Louw sent me to ask you about something. May I come in?" He peered up at her, birdlike, benign, from under wispy grey eyebrows.

"Please," she said and stood aside.

***

Smith took his hands from his pockets and walked into the lounge, glancing about him. His brain was working rapidly. He would first question her, continuing the pretence of being Louw's emissary, and use force if that did not produce results.

Then he would kill her, if possible making it look like an accident. He did not want to use the gun, too noisy, it would have to be the knife or a lamp cord.

"Please have a seat, Mr ...?"

He turned to face her, still smiling. "Smith. Inspector Smith. Shall I close the door?"

"No." She indicated the coffee table set for supper. "I'm waiting for your young watchdog. He always comes up about now for a snack and a cup of coffee."

This disconcerted Smith though his expression stayed

bland. The policeman was no problem; it was the open door.

"Oh good, I'd like to see him myself. I'd love a cup too, please, if I may."

It would have to be force. He must shut the door first.

"Yes, of course, let me get you one. Milk and sugar?"

"Black, please, no sugar."

***

Odd, she thought, that he hadn't seen the young policeman on the way up. The young man checked every visitor.

She was half way to the kitchen when the telephone rang. It stood on a low table at the end of the couch.

"Excuse me," she said to Smith and turned back to pick it up, "Oh, hello, Superintendent. What? No, I'm fine. In fact I have one of your men with me now, Inspector Smith ..." She swung to look at him with realisation dawning on her face.

Smith moved so fast she could do nothing. He hit her hard just beneath her breasts, in her solar plexus.

Penelope gasped and doubled up, all the breath knocked out of her. She opened her mouth wide to scream, a dry retching came.

Smith plucked the squawking receiver from her slack hand and slammed it back on its cradle. He grabbed a napkin from the coffee table and stuffed it in her open mouth. She collapsed semi-conscious on the carpet.

***

Smith stepped to the open door and closed it, then leaned against it and took a deep breath. No time for finesse or questions now, the police would be calling their radio cars already.

Damn! He had minutes, if that. He must finish this here and now. Furious with himself for yet another mistake, he bent to pluck the knife from its sheath.

CHAPTER TWENTY SEVEN

Captain Ndzimandze raced the Corolla through the narrow streets of Melville and hurled it with howling tyres around the curves and dips of Richmond. Once in Empire Road he stamped the accelerator flat, switched on the emergency flashers, and blasted other traffic out of the way with the horn. Superintendent Louw remembered they had a flashing blue light and stretched his arm out of the window to clamp its magnetic foot on the roof.

He picked up the radio microphone. "Nichols, Nichols, Nichols, this is Louw, do you read?" he said again. Still no answer.

Miles away, his metallic voice came from the portable transceiver lying near the pool of blood in the basement. Smith, already at the top of the stairs, did not hear it.

"God *damn* it!" the superintendent swore and switched to the patrol car channel. No car was near Penelope Fox's home but on his order one in central Johannesburg turned on its siren and sped towards Illovo. He switched back to his channel.

"Stramm," he called as Ndzimandze swung the Corolla hard into Jan Smuts Avenue and then into the tight circle of the entry road to the M1 freeway north. The reply was immediate.

"Stramm here, over."

"Where are you?"

"Just, hold on ..." Louw heard the squeal of tyres behind the tinny voice "... just approaching Corlett."

Thank God. He was way ahead of them. "Stramm, be

careful. There's no answer from the duty constable there, Nichols. Something's happened."

"Okay, out."

The superintendent called up the police radio headquarters. "Emergency, patch me through to this number." He gave Penelope's home number and waited for the call to go through, seething with impatience. She answered on the fourth ring.

He must not alarm her, he thought. "Good evening, Miss Fox, it's Superintendent Louw here. I'm just phoning to see if everything's all right."

"Oh, hello, Superintendent. What? No, I'm fine. In fact I have one of your men with me now, Inspector Smith ..."

An icy fist clutched the superintendent's gut, then her voice abruptly stopped in a gasp and he heard a thump before the line was broken.

"Move!" he shouted to Ndzimandze, "Smith's in there!" He clipped the microphone back on its hook. There was nothing he could do now but grit his teeth and pray Ndzimandze did not hit anything. He braced his feet against the floorboards and watched as they streaked past other traffic at a hundred and sixty kilometres an hour, weaving between the lanes.

Far ahead of them, Stramm shot the Skyline through two red lights, skidded around the turn off at Corlett and braked hard on the approach to the street where Penelope lived. He travelled the last block at normal pace and was slowing to stop opposite the building, when on a whim he drove into the basement.

He came out of the car fast, hat firm on his head and his semi-automatic pistol in his right hand, and crouched low for the few seconds it took his eyes to adjust to the dimness. Light spilling down the stairs from the foyer reflected dully from the metalwork of several cars but there was no sign of life.

Stramm rose and sprinted for the stairs. His foot skidded from under him and he fell hard in what he thought was a puddle of oil, until the unmistakeable smell hit his nostrils. Fresh blood.

The hairs prickled on the back of his neck. Jesus, he thought, the bastard's beaten us to it.

He picked himself up and ran, ignoring the blood smearing him from shoulder to knee down his left side. By the time he reached the third floor he was breathing hard.

Penelope's door was the second on the left down the passage. He stopped close to the wall in case anyone should be looking through the peephole, and listened.

At first there was no sound. Then he heard soft bumps, as if something had been dropped on a carpet, and a whimper that rose into a whine, like a small animal in distress.

Without hesitation he braced himself against the wall opposite the door, raised his right foot and drove himself at the door. The sole of his shoe hit it just below the knob with the full power of his right leg. The lock burst and the door crashed open.

Stramm's momentum propelled him through. In the same instant his mind photographed the scene across the room, near the window: a dazed blonde with a short grey-haired man propping her up from behind.

***

As Stramm reached the third floor, Smith was bent over Penelope lying prone on her back. He touched the skin of her throat with his knife to pull it across in a single quick slice, then realised blood would spurt all over him.

He rolled her on to her stomach, twisted both her arms high behind her back and gripped her wrists in his left hand to heave her on to her knees, facing away from him.

The movement aroused Penelope and as she was lifted, knees bumping on the carpet, the pain in her drawn-back arms made her whimper. She tried to scream but with the napkin jammed in her mouth, it came out as a kittenish whine.

The door crashed open. A man in a hat stood in it, swinging his arms down to aim a gun. Smith reacted with feline speed.

He jerked Penelope to her feet by her wrists and held her in front of him as a shield, with the knife in his right hand poised a fraction of an inch from her neck.

Stramm stopped dead, half crouched, his gun held steady in front of him. Neither man spoke, the impasse obvious.

***

Smith thought of the magnum in his shoulder holster; he could not free either hand long enough to reach it. He backed to the window, dragging Penelope, and snapped a quick glance out. Too high, it would have to be by the door. He started to edge around the carpet.

Penelope fainted and collapsed like an emptied sack. Her feet slid from under her, placing her full weight on his left hand. Smith could not hold her. He let go and whipped his left hand around her waist.

In that split second both men acted. Smith's right hand dropped the knife, dived under his lapel with dazzling speed and came out with the gun.

***

To Stramm, everything in the next two seconds happened in eerie slow motion. He saw the knife falling as if through water. Before it reached the carpet, Smith's hand emerged at a snail's pace holding the heavy calibre revolver and the tunnel of its muzzle was swinging to engulf him.

Stramm elevated the barrel of his pistol a fraction to aim above the woman, knowing he had no choice. This was it, one way or the other.

He squeezed the trigger. It seemed to take forever. And then, at last, the huge boom and the firm kickback against his taut fist ... and, to his utter surprise, another

265

boom, heavier, deeper.

The 9 mm parabellum bullet caught Smith just below the throat where his collar bones joined. The copper-jacketed lead drilled in, struck a vertebra, became a miniature bomb and emerged from Smith's back in a flock of jagged fragments, leaving a hole the size of a fist, punching him off balance.

Stramm was lucky. Striking first, his shot diverted Smith's instinctive aim by millimetres. Instead of Stramm's chest, the heavy .357 slug of solid lead hit his left hipbone. Its massive magnum power hurled him backwards, out of the door and slammed him against the wall across the passage.

He slid down it, feeling no pain yet, just surprise through the rush of adrenalin, and watched the dying Smith stagger backwards with the woman. The backs of Smith's thighs struck the low windowsill. He overbalanced and toppled out of sight, still clutching the woman.

A great clangour of metal came from below and then silence.

Oh fuck, Stramm thought, I've blown it.

He was sitting against the wall staring in wonder at his left hip and the blood puddling beneath it when he heard feet pounding up the stairs and the superintendent yelling, "Stramm! Stramm!"

"Here," he called, feeling very tired.

Ndzimandze stopped in shock at the sight of Stramm covered in blood down one side and sitting in a spreading pool of it. Superintendent Louw charged past them into the flat.

"The window," Stramm said, annoyed that his voice was fading.

The superintendent leaned to peer out, spun around and raced down the stairs.

"It's not all my blood," Stramm said, seeing the look in Ndzimandze's face.

A siren *wow-wow*-ed into the street outside.

The fucking cavalry's here, Stramm chuckled to himself, and passed out.

***

Superintendent Louw took the steps three at a stride to the foyer, saw there was no back exit there, and leaped down the stairs to the basement. At the foot he felt the wall for a switch, found one and pressed it. Neon tubes flickered into cold blue life in the concrete ceiling, revealing a door at the back above two steps.

They also revealed a large shiny pool of blood, congealing at the edges, and streaks leading from it to underneath a car.

Oh God, he thought, Nichols.

He did not pause to look and ran to the door.

The cemented yard behind the building was empty. Where the hell were they? Smith couldn't have got away after a three-storey drop.

He saw a steel-framed doorway in what appeared to be the wall enclosing the far end of the yard. It opened into a storage room for brooms, buckets and other equipment used by the cleaning staff. Superintendent Louw shone the beam of a pen torch inside.

Smith lay flat on his back on the floor staring vacantly at the sky, very dead, his face bland in repose, as if he welcomed it.

Penelope lay half on top of his chest also facing skywards with her skirt pulled high above her waist and her long legs hooked over a crushed cardboard carton.

Her head moved from side to side a little and she moaned behind the napkin still in her mouth. The superintendent breathed a gusty sigh of relief and knelt beside her to pull it away.

From a quick check, she seemed not to have broken any bones but was semi-conscious, battered and bleeding from several cuts on her arms and head.

He looked up and saw what had happened. The corrugated iron roof and its supporting two-by-four beam hung concave and shattered. It had broken their fall and Penelope had been further cushioned by Smith's corpse.

He pulled her skirt over her legs, picked her up and walked through the basement to the front of the building, where he put her down on the narrow lawn.

A man from a squad car brought a blanket and spread it over her up to her chin. The driver was already calling an ambulance. A small crowd of onlookers watched, drawn from neighbouring houses by the gunshots and siren.

Superintendent Louw turned back to the basement, knowing he would find young Nichols dead. He felt sick.

***

Assistant Commissioner Mike Miller was in a foul mood. The Vice President's embargo on action filled him with frustration; he could have lopped off much of the head of the rebel movement in a matter of hours by arresting its known leaders. The rest he could have picked up when they started flapping about like decapitated chickens, leaving the security forces to concentrate on the mainline task of stopping the bloodshed between opposing black groups.

Instead, he had to wait with his hands tied, for a rebellion and for a man or men sent to kill the President and, he assumed, the Vice President as well. All he had been able to do was tighten the security system around both of them.

He leafed again through the national situation reports prepared by the office of his immediate chief, the Commissioner of Police, and by the NIS.

They read like an overture to anarchy. The country was so tense it was threatening to snap.

Yesterday afternoon more Zulus, men and women, died in Tembisa on the East Rand, when a crowd of hundreds danced and sang their way to an Inkatha rally. They were peaceful, though many carried their traditional kieries and sticks and had followed the route laid down by the police, well away from ANC parts of the sprawling township.

Four gunmen had opened fire on the crowd at a range of less than thirty yards from inside a small cement-brick house at the crossing of two dusty streets. Shooting for less than a minute, they killed over a dozen and left behind sixty-two empty AK-47 cartridge cases when they escaped unseen from the back of the house.

That was shooting by trained men, not the wild firing of novices, Miller thought. They had to be the third force, or killers hired by them.

Enraged reaction had erupted within hours all over the Witwatersrand. Unsuspecting miners making their way home to their quarters were attacked alone and in groups. Some were necklaced – petrol-filled tyres hung around their necks and set alight.

Several mines shut down, dealing more blows to the cracking economy.

The litany went on. In Soweto, Sebokeng, Alexandra and other townships, as far as Atteridgeville and Mamelodi in Pretoria, anger had flared into murder, rape, looting and burning.

Nearby city centres were strangely empty and quiet, with almost no blacks about and few black taxis running. Those that dared to enter the townships were stoned, rolled over and put to the torch, several with their drivers inside.

The pattern was much the same in all the big centres and through it ran a familiar thread of single, smaller incidents in which obvious experts had used AK-47s, hand grenades and limpet mines: deliberate mayhem to keep the pot boiling.

A well-known white liberal, so old he was no longer active, was shot down in the street outside his small home in Norwood. Miller remembered him as a gentle man of intellect. They took him away still clutching the ANC magazine, *Mayibuye,* he had bought at the cafe up the road.

A black executive in a Johannesburg mining house was blown to shreds with his car, when it exploded coming out of the company's parking garage. In Krugersdorp an outspoken Conservative Party councillor died in a fire in his home with his wife and two small children.

The toll of death for the week was rising. Soldiers had been brought in to help the police enforce curfews – raw youngsters, few of them familiar with the townships and their inhabitants.

God's teeth, Miller thought, I *can't* afford to wait. At the least I can position my people so they can move fast if things get out of hand ... if the Vice President has made the wrong choice and the rebel balloon goes up. When that happens, he thought with gloom, it might already be too late.

He picked up his private telephone and dialled.

***

At that moment in the gracious Tuynhuys Presidential offices next to Parliament someone else advised the Vice President and the Opposition Leader there should be no more delay.

They were alone together. The President, a tall, greying man of great dignity, listened in silence while his deputy told him what had just been learned about the secessionists who called themselves the Free Staters.

The President spoke, his voice calm but with authority, "If we do not act now to find and stop this third force, the destabilisation will drag the country into complete chaos. I see the dilemma." Turning to the Opposition Leader, he said, "You and I must together fulfil our roles to keep the nation stable, you a white man, I black. If we

– black men – initiate action alone the race factor will be like fuel on the flames. We, the ANC, have done all we can to bring an end to the bloodshed but the white public will not believe it because provocateurs have created the impression it is the ANC who are causing it.

"You as a white man and Opposition Leader cannot solve the problem alone, although it seems to have been instigated by white radicals. You must act in concert with us. We must tackle this situation together, not as black or white, but as leaders of the nation. Anything else will tell our people and the world that South Africa is divided forever on race lines."

The President inclined his head and talked straight at the Opposition Leader across the broad expanse of polished table, empty save for three small coffee cups. "Who are these people? Are they Afrikaners trying to show that black people are incapable of civilised government?"

He paused, seeing the thunderclouds gathering on his parliamentary colleague's brow.

"We all have our extremists," the Opposition Leader replied, choosing his words, "people who want to see South Africa reduced to ashes. I am no less aware than you are, sir, that this is the gravest crisis to confront the country. It does not help to point the finger.

"I can promise you this," he went on, tapping the table to stress each word, "that as God is my witness, the third force is not a creation of my supporters and its actions do not have the sympathy of the vast majority of white people. I am using every means at our disposal to find out who restokes the fire every time we try to quench it. When we do, we will join you in crushing them, no matter who they are, black or white."

"There is little time left."

"I know. Please take great care because you are a prime target."

The President shrugged. "So are you." He smiled for

the first time. "It goes with the territory."

***

Three people left Johannesburg in the morning for opposite ends of the country, two south, one north, all impelled by the rising crisis.

It dominated the nation's attention. Newspapers were weighty with grim headlines, blood and bodies were routine on television news, and several thousand foreign correspondents rushed in to compete for glory and feed the international appetite for mayhem in full living colour.

It was of no concern to two of the passengers in the departure queue at the Johannesburg International domestic terminal. Nobody would have guessed they knew each other, separated as they were by half a dozen other people checking in for the Cape Town flight. They were similar only in size and their drooping Sundance moustaches.

One carried a slim attaché case, wore a tailored suit, Cardin shirt, Italian shoes. The other was draped in a loose red and yellow shirt, half unbuttoned to expose a hairy chest above white shorts and Reeboks, a comb stuck into the top of one sock. His eyes were invisible behind wraparound dark glasses.

Waiting to board the plane, the well-dressed assassin sipped coffee and read a book. He glanced once at his partner, with distaste. The casual killer sipped a beer, although it was not yet ten o'clock, and watched the bustle of ground crew serving the huge flying machines on the apron.

One travelled business class and the other tourist class. At Cape Town's D F Malan airport, one hired a car and drove to an expensive secluded hotel in Newlands. The other rode a courtesy bus to a cheap tourist hotel in Sea Point. Well disciplined, they followed their instructions to the letter.

At about the same time as the Boeing flew south, a fifteen-seater minibus travelled north from Johannesburg to Louis Trichardt and Venda.

One of the passengers was Ephesias Mutale, though few of his former comrades in Venda would have recognised him with his untidy beard and worn clothes. Beneath the greasy rim of an old hat, his eyes shone with manic ferocity.

Physically, Mutale had recovered from his ordeal during the night of the massacre. Psychologically, he was scarred by a corrosive hatred he was now on his way to consummate.

He had told the South African Police everything after they brought him out of the Kruger National Park by helicopter and then to Pretoria by light plane. At first sceptic, they had later confirmed his story of the massacre.

But, they said, they could do nothing except open a murder docket for every corpse found. Of course, they would investigate but there were no witnesses to corroborate Mutale's evidence. No-one was talking.

Mutale had sought out his immediate leaders in Johannesburg. They discussed for an hour what to do about the brutal liquidation of most of their structure in Venda.

They ruled out making a public fuss because it would have little impact amongst all the other anarchy. They rejected asking the government to act because the government seemed unable to do anything about all the violence. In the end they reached an impasse; the ANC was weak in the northern parts of South Africa.

Mutale listened to the meeting with growing frustration.

"I am going back," he interrupted them. They looked up in surprise, indicating they had almost forgotten him.

"Let me take back some cadres. I will re-establish the

ANC's authority. I will find who was responsible and see that justice ... that they are brought to justice."

He glared at them. They were much senior to him but he did not care.

The discussion lasted a few minutes longer, with sidelong glances at Mutale. They agreed he would go back with a small team.

He chose ANC members of the Venda tribe. They were the other passengers in the minibus.

Under a false floor beneath their feet lay six AK-47s, fifteen Makarov 9mm pistols, full magazines and a dozen hand grenades, all wrapped in oiled cloth to stop them rattling. That should be enough, Mutale thought. His bosses back in Jo'burg did not know he had taken the weapons.

The minibus turned east on the outskirts of Louis Trichardt and headed for Thohoyandou.

CHAPTER TWENTY EIGHT

Ballance had never felt less comfortable in his life. The new khaki clothes chafed, the sun spewed heat like the open door of a furnace, and the air was soggy with humidity. He was drenched in sweat. Ngwenya looked in no better condition.

They carried rucksacks. Armando and Smart walked with long easy strides and showed little discomfort, although they also had AK-47 rifles and extra magazines.

The rhythm of their stride became hypnotic. Nobody talked. There were no animals and few birds in the monotonous flat veld.

Ballance cast his mind back over the hectic activity of the past forty-eight hours. He had telephoned Superintendent Louw to tell him they had pinpointed the source of weapons. He would fly to Johannesburg, give the superintendent all the information they had, and fly back in the afternoon.

Stay put at the airport, the superintendent had said, he and Ndzimandze would drive out; it was better for Ballance not to be seen in the city.

They had taken him to a private lounge in the transit section, inaccessible to anyone except police, customs, and immigration officers. Ballance talked for an hour, telling them what had happened in Maputo and what they had learned from Miguel, now held prisoner in the ANC safe house. The policemen went over it with him twice more, questioning every detail.

Louw showed uncharacteristic excitement when he heard about the import/export firm run by a Thomlinson for whom the late Chris had worked.

"That has to be the link between the third force here and the arms suppliers," he said, "Good! It gives us a solid line to follow. By the way, what did you do with the body?"

"Me? Nothing. I think the others must have removed it by night after we left." Ballance found himself wondering at his own indifference about the corpse. "I suppose it's floating out to sea by now."

"You've done very well," Superintendent Louw said, a smile erasing the frown of concentration from his face. "Tell your friends we'll start working on the arrangements right away. It won't be easy, there's huge political risk in doing what you ask, but I'm hoping we can persuade the brass that the good will outweigh the bad. I'll call you at your hotel this evening to give you the answer."

He fished in his briefcase and handed Ballance a rectangular, smooth-edged case of hard plastic about half the size of a brick and a slip of paper with numbers on it.

"I thought you might like this," he said, smiling. "It's a compact frequency-hopping transceiver and radio beacon. You'll need it if we get the green light. This is the frequency you must tune to. The battery's full and should give you about eight hours."

"You mean I have to go up there to put this thing in position?"

"That's right." Louw and Ndzimande smiled.

"But ... why not Temba? Or this Renamo fellow, Armando, who knows it well?" Even as he spoke Ballance realised how negative he sounded. They would think he was scared, which he was. "Okay," he sighed, "show me how to use it."

It took ten minutes. Modern electronic equipment was designed for use by the simplest minds.

"How's Penny?" Ballance asked when they were ready to leave him, feeling guilty for not having asked earlier. "You're still looking after her?"

"She's fine." He lied so blandly that Captain Ndzimandze cocked an admiring eyebrow at him. "Quite safe and very much in our care."

"Good. Please give her my love." Ballance felt awkward making the request. It was a new experience for him.

***

In Cape Town some hours later, the Minister of Defence sought an urgent meeting with the Vice President.

"Pretoria has passed me a request from Superintendent Louw of our special investigation team," he said. "It is for help for an agent of ours in Mozambique ..." he glanced at the paper in his hand "... a man named Ballance. When I raised it with the President he told me to talk to you."

"What does it say?"

"He says they have identified, and are preparing to attack, the enemy HQ and ask us for comprehensive air support." He laid the paper on the desk. "What is this all about?" the Minister asked acidly. "On the word of some complete stranger we're expected to risk aircraft and personnel to make covert strikes into the territory of a peaceful neighbour?"

"My apologies." The Vice President smiled. "Things are happening rather sooner than I expected."

He unlocked a steel-lined drawer in his desk and took from it a three-page document, which he handed to the Minister.

It was a top secret report from Superintendent Louw via Assistant Commissioner Miller. The Minister read with growing amazement Ballance's account of the Renamo rebel plan, its link to a secession plot in South Africa, and the proposal to attack the camp in Gaza.

"Why haven't I been shown this before?"

"You would have been today, by the President. It must remain secret outside the special committee because we still have to track down the rebels here."

Mollified, the Minister read the document again. "Well,

what do we do?" he asked.

"For now, give all the help you can to the people in Mozambique. I don't know how, that's your department, but I suggest you arrange it as soon as you are able."

"We have helicopter gunships ready with jets in support." The Minister strode out.

Within an hour four Rooivalk and four Oryx helicopters and a wing of Impala jets fitted with cannon and rockets for ground strafing, took off from the Hoedspruit base in Mpumalanga province for the short flight to an airfield inside the Kruger National Park near Punda Maria.

***

Ballance was pacing the carpet in his room back at the Cardoso when the phone rang at eight o'clock that night.

"It will be the day after tomorrow at seventeen hundred," said a voice he recognised as Louw's. "Try to be there in good time so we don't miss you. Good luck, we'll see you later."

Soon after dawn, Smart and Armando fetched him and Ngwenya at the hotel and drove to the airport where, like tourists, the four of them boarded a light aircraft and flew north to the coastal resort of Xai Xai. They travelled light, except Armando, who carried a large tog bag. Waiting for them at the airstrip, was a driver with a battered diesel Land Rover. Ballance wondered how Smart had managed to arrange it at such short notice.

They drove east to Macia and turned north off the tarred coastal road onto a gravel road to Macarretane, where the railroad to Zimbabwe crossed the Limpopo River on a long barrage wall. Once a thriving irrigation farming area worked by peasants transplanted from Portugal, it had reverted to Africa. This is not a happy place, Ballance thought, it feels as if it's been raped a thousand times and wants revenge.

They crossed the barrage to travel north on a double-track road, so neglected they could not average more than about ten to fifteen kilometres an hour. The scenery was flat and monotonous, dreary grassland and scrub, veined with dry gullies and a few streams, seemingly empty of people. With the summer rains, this would be floodland.

His senses dulled by the constant roar of the old engine, Ballance managed to doze despite the jouncing of springs undamped by shock absorbers. Endless hours later he awoke with a start when the Land Rover jolted to a halt and its diesel clatter stopped, radiator hissing. It was full night and the stars shone with such brilliance he could see his companions clearly in the pollution-free atmosphere.

Ngwenya climbed out, stretching his cramped limbs. The others followed. The air was so crisp and still, they heard the click and rasp of frogs and insects from the vast savannah.

"What's up?" Ballance asked, yawning.

"Nothing," said Smart. "Time for a break. We're north of a place called Dindiza, though there's nothing to show anybody lived there. Next stop is near Chigubo about sunrise, and from there we go into the bundu because we whiteys stick out like dogs' balls."

Two hours later with the first silver sliver of dawn slipping through the crack between horizon and sky, the driver put the Land Rover into four-wheel drive and turned off the track. They jolted across bumpy veld through grass and between low scrub for another two hours until the driver stopped close to a large clump of bush.

"This is it," Smart said. "Welcome to five-star Africa, friends. From here we walk." He grinned at Ballance's dishevelled hair, stubble of beard and layer of dust.

The driver took the Land Rover deep into a patch of thick bush, which closed behind him. He would wait twenty-four hours and if they did not return, go back to Xai Xai. The earth under Ballance's feet was soft; he knelt to touch it and felt damp clay.

There was no sound as they walked, except the swish of grass against cloth. Sometimes they flushed francolins into whirring flight.

Devoid of shade, the treeless plains stretched to distant horizon on all sides.

Now, at midday, they were at their destination near the spongy edge of a swamp that stretched out of sight, north and south, and about two kilometres across. It was very shallow. Short green bushes sprouted all over it and they could see the bottom through the clear water.

Armando made them stop and kneel when they were in shoulder-high scrub some fifty metres from the water. Producing binoculars, he peered across the swamp.

"There," he said, pointing. "That is it, straight across."

Ballance took the glasses after Ngwenya and saw nothing at first until a faint column of smoke caught his eye. Below it, amid low trees, the lines of simple structures of wood and thatch emerged with clarity against the background.

This was Colonel Manjacane's Gaza base.

"Are we not taking a hell of a risk being this close?" he asked, nervous.

"*Não, amigo,*" Armando dismissed the thought. "They feel so secure there they do not patrol the area this side … they would get their feet wet. They stay over there. Perhaps they come this way sometimes to carry arms to Chigudo to be loaded on trucks but I think not. That road is so bad I think they use the shorter road on the other side to the railway."

Ballance eased the rucksack off his back with relief. Ngwenya sat next to him.

"What happens now?" Smart asked him.

In answer, Ballance unzipped his bag and took out the compact transceiver Superintendent Louw gave him. "We wait until we can use this," he said, opening it up and setting the dials to the frequency on the slip of paper stuck inside the lid. "At a quarter to five on the dot, we switch on and wait."

"And then?"

"Then the cavalry come galloping to our radio beacon and we sit back on our grandstand seats to watch the shoot-out. After that your guess is as good as mine." He grinned. "It depends on who wins."

***

Superintendent Louw and Assistant Commissioner Miller talked over bacon and eggs in the dining room of the Town House Hotel near Parliament in Cape Town.

The superintendent had been woken from exhausted sleep in his room at six a.m., after a day and night of hectic activity following his meeting with Jeffrey Ballance at Johannesburg International airport.

From the airport he had rushed back home, written a report and transmitted it to Assistant Commissioner Miller by high-speed scrambled fax, and on Miller's instructions had met certain people from Defence Head-quarters in secret and visited the Zwartkops air force base for an emergency planning meeting. Late that night, he had been whisked to the nearby Waterkloof air base by helicopter. There, anonymous officers in blue had led the weary policeman on board a Mercurius, the South African Air Force name for a Hawker Siddeley executive jet, which sped him to Cape Town.

Now he was pushing a piece of grilled tomato around his plate with a fork, having ceased to wonder at the fate that had him eating supper in Pretoria, breakfast in Cape Town and no doubt lunch back in Johannesburg.

"Miss Fox is okay," he said, finishing his account of the bid on her life. "She has a fractured wrist and cuts and bruises and she was shaken by the experience. It must have been very frightening. She'll stay in hospital with a police guard until she's over the shock.

"Stramm's past the crisis and will live but he'll have a limp for the rest of his life. When this is over, I think you should look at him for promotion. He's brighter than he seems and he did a damn good job."

"A far better job than you realise, Frans."

"How do you mean, sir?"

"He stopped an attempt on the President's and Vice President's lives, and he's saved me a hell of a lot of trouble and a few ulcers besides."

The superintendent looked at him in inquiry.

"In the strictest confidence, Frans, Smith was assigned to eliminate the top three, but your man got him first, thank God."

"How on earth did you know that?"

"The Vice President had a tipoff from an infallible source. It worried me sick in spite of having your description of Smith, because he was so clever at disguise and obtaining faked papers."

The superintendent pushed away his half-eaten breakfast and exhaled in a gust of relief. The President, Vice President and Opposition Leader assassinated ... the thought frightened him.

"Are you sure they're safe now?"

"One can never be sure, Frans. Security will stay as tight as pants on a virgin until this business is finished because there's always a risk. Now, to get back to your friend Ballance, we've had confirmation from an unexpected quarter."

He handed the superintendent a folded sheet of paper. On it was a summary of what the conservative MP, agonising after his son was slashed on a train, had told his party leader about the plans for a breakaway state.

Superintendent Louw read it, dropped it on the table as if it was tainted, and spread his hands in disgust.

"For Christ's sake, Mike, why don't we *move*? With this we've got the bastards on toast!"

"The Vice President insists we wait until the last minute to nail all the rebels and not just those named here. He's got something up his sleeve."

"But damn it, while he sits on his arse—"

"There's nothing we can do about it. We have to position ourselves to act against the third force and their allies the moment the President gives me the go-ahead. This is what I want you to do ..."

Miller's arrangements were straightforward. He spelt them out in ten minutes.

"I'll come up to Jo'burg if he'll let me but I want you to handle that end, Frans. You know the ropes there and you'll have enough trustworthy men.

"This Chairman the MP talked about is a nothing, a figurehead. You can mop him up like that." Miller snapped his fingers. "Gideon van Geyssen seems to be the kingpin. Without him in the bag the rebellion could drag on."

***

The Doctor stretched in comfort and sipped his after-breakfast coffee at a garden table under an old oak tree, its massive limbs sheltering a lawn trimmed smooth as velvet. The morning was bright with sunshine and the air was full of perfume from kaleidoscopic beds of arum lilies, roses, hydrangeas and clivias.

His BMW was locked in a garage on the game farm of a friend in the remote bushveld, west of Louis Trichardt, and all his various residences were closed up or in the care of servants.

Nobody could trace him here. This was the last place anyone would look.

***

On the way back to the airport to leave Cape Town, Superintendent Louw passed within a couple of kilometres of Gideon van Geyssen.

CHAPTER TWENTY NINE

Careful not to tear it, Colonel Manjacane unfolded the map on the rough-cut plank table in his headquarters, where not long ago he had entertained the two big *brancos* from South Africa. He remembered them with condescension; rebels, yes, but old and soft, not hard bush fighters like himself.

The map, narrow and a metre and a half long, creased and cracked from use, dated from Portuguese rule when bureaucrats hung framed copies on their office walls. It still bore the old colonial names.

His staff listened while he gave orders. A young aide wrote them down on a note pad labelled 'Discount Supermarkets'.

When Manjacane finished, the aide took the notes to a signaller in an adjacent office, who began relaying them by radio to the commanders of rebel Renamo groups to the south.

"You," Manjacane levelled his trigger finger at each of the commanders around him, "you will move out now to take up positions on the border here ... and here ... and here." His finger moved to three places on the map.

One was near Pafuri in the hot, forested valley at the confluence of the Luvuvhu and Limpopo rivers, where the borders of South Africa, Mozambique and Zimbabwe met. Remote and wild, it had a few houses and disused buildings on the Mozambique side and a small police camp inside the Kruger National Park on the South African side.

Manjacane had assigned two hundred men to attack it

and did not anticipate much resistance.

The other two places were a little further south. Groups of a hundred men would hit the Punda Maria and Shingwedzi tourist camps in the Kruger National Park and recross the border before the South African forces could react.

"Do not move until you receive my signal the day after tomorrow," Manjacane ordered. "Once you are across, you will stop for nothing, not even elephants. You will destroy the bridge at Shingwedzi and block the airfield near Punda Maria."

The men nodded. They had been over this many times.

An hour later, four hundred laden guerillas left the pole-and-thatch camp in single file, an unkempt yet formidable fighting force.

Manjacane stood at attention and saluted as they marched past. Two hundred yards away, the three columns peeled apart on their different routes.

It left him with about fifty men at base. He was unconcerned; the action would be far from here.

***

The one place in Cape Town where the paths of the two men with Sundance moustaches crossed, was a hole-in-the-wall shop in the old part of Salt River, below Main Road in a side street, between a reject clothing store and a halaal fast food shop, spicing the air with rich Malayan smells.

The one who had flown business class came first, in mid-morning. Wearing a yellow cotton shirt, white slacks, white socks and matching shoes, his eyes hidden by wraparound RayBans, he strolled through the bustle of shoppers and peddlers on Lower Main Road.

He paused at the corner before turning down the side street, just another tourist. At the café he bought a samoosa. It burned his fingers and while he waited for it to cool, he examined the odd collection of junk in the next shop.

It was a pawnshop with windows grimed by the dust of years. Shelves inside held a catholic jumble of relics from other peoples' lives. An old brass naval telescope minus its front element, a cracked Italian mandolin, Benares brass trays and Buddhas, a nest of used Tupperware containers, several leather sandals without their mates, a pile of Taiwanese digital watches surrounding a beautiful old silver half hunter, a stuffed lion's head dribbling sawdust ...

He ate the samoosa, wiped his fingers on the paper napkin and went in. The interior was cool and dim. A woman with long black hair cowled by a tasselled shawl sat behind a counter at the far end. He went to her and spoke three words. She inclined her head to indicate the way past her and parted a heavy curtain for him.

Beyond it was a small storeroom crammed with junk and past that a locked door. He knocked.

"Who's there?" a voice called and he said the three words again.

The door opened. A man of middle age, wearing a crocheted kufi, stood there. He beckoned the visitor to come in.

The room was in total contrast to the front of the shop. Under bright fluorescent lamps, workbenches lined the walls on either side, beneath racks of gleaming tools on white-painted walls. The benches were clean and there was a faint smell of machine oil.

He relocked the door.

"You have identity?" he asked.

The visitor drew a card from a wallet. It was forged and said he was a member of the police.

The shopowner nodded and gave it back.

"Yah," he said, "I am waiting for you two days. There is two of you, no?"

"The other man will come later."

"Good. Which kind you want?"

"Long range."

The man reached up to a rack of tools, gripped a ring spanner that appeared to be hanging on a hook, twisted it, and pulled. The whole rack hinged away from the wall.

In a foam-padded stainless steel cavity behind it hung a variety of firearms glistening with oil. He reached for one and handed it to his visitor.

The visitor knew a great deal about rifles, but at first did not recognise this one. He turned it over in his big hands, frowning with concentration, then whistled in admiration.

It had once been a Musgrave "Ugly Duckling" 308, a very popular hunting rifle, which fired the military 7.62mm bullet with great accuracy. Designed not for beauty but to take hard knocks in the bush, its original stock was rubber-cushioned, carved with a cheek rest and extended into a bed for half the length of the barrel.

An expert had worked on it; the bed had been shaved thinner and the stock replaced with a steel-frame one. The trigger guard had been removed and the back-sloped trigger replaced with one that curved straight down.

"Look," the man said, taking the gun back, "like this ..."

He twisted the barrel hard and unscrewed it from the breech, pushed the hinged trigger forward to lie flat against the magazine base, and folded the frame stock underneath. Now the rifle was not much longer than his forearm. He placed it on a workbench and laid a short telescopic sight and a screw-on flash suppressor beside it.

"See? Now it is small. You carry it anywhere, in clothes, in briefcase." He demonstrated with voluble hands.

It was an ideal assassin's weapon, lightweight, easy to conceal, accurate and powerful.

"Very good," the assassin said. "How much?"

"No, it is paid already. You take it now?"

"I haven't brought anything to carry it in."

"No worry."

The shopkeeper unlocked the door and rummaged in the storeroom. He brought an old tennis tog bag with a pocket on one side for racquets.

"You take this. Ten rand, second-hand. No, no," he went on when the customer reached again for his wallet. "I include in price."

He added an old racquet, a cheap T-shirt and a threadbare beach towel to lie on top of the dismantled gun.

"You have bullets?"

"No. I want five."

They cost fifty rands, also included in the price, cheap for illegal ammunition.

His colleague the economy class traveller arrived at the shop just after four o'clock when the afternoon traffic rush was building up. The owner looked at him in some surprise, at first glance thinking the man in khaki shorts, loose floral shirt and sneakers, was a wayward tourist, until he looked closer and saw the similar moustache and the strong build.

This one chose a very flat and compact FN Browning semi-automatic pistol, stripped down to lighten it and make it more compact. In place of the standard butt grips, were thin strips of hard plastic taped to the frame. The magazine held nine 9mm short cartridges. At the range he would be working from, he did not need parabellums.

He walked out of the shop with the FN nested in a chamois clip holster in the small of his back under his belt, covered by his floral shirt.

The remaining weak point was the shopkeeper, he thought as he made his way to a bus stop. They would sort him out afterwards. There was no point in stirring things now, before the big job.

Thohoyandou was busy because its main thoroughfare was a national highway passing right through it. The day was clean and bright, the orchards and plantations vivid with life, the streets full of people and the roadside shops thronged with tourists.

Bearded and hatted, Ephesias Mutale stood outside the supermarket near the tourist hotel and watched the bustle without noticing it. His mind now filled with a lust so potent it left no place for trivia; a kind of insanity that concentrated on his prey like sunlight through a lens.

He knew who he had to murder, but not their names. Their faces were engraved in his memory from the night of butchery at the abandoned mine. He had seen them in the beams of light from the vehicles, etched in highlights and black shadows, but it was enough.

He was looking for the faces, those of the two men who had dragged him from the back of the van and those who had chopped and hacked and shot.

He alone could do this. He had ordered his team to spread out in the town in pairs, ask innocent questions, and see what they could discover in bars and eating houses.

The butchers he sought would have to come to Thohoyandou some time, the focal point of Venda; the place of bright lights and activity and the kind of political intrigue that could breed massacre.

They had to walk past him some time.

Seated in an office in police headquarters in Johannesburg, Superintendent Louw found it difficult to credit that he had just been to Cape Town, although his ears still buzzed from the Mercurius's rapid descent to Waterkloof airfield.

The document in his hands was proof. It was an order

for the immediate temporary withdrawal of certain policemen, whose names were listed, from stations all over South Africa, north of Johannesburg.

His job was to get them moving, without delay.

"Speed is of the essence but try to do it as unobtrusively as possible, Frans," the Assistant Commissioner had said. "If anybody beefs, and I don't care if he outranks you, wave that order under his nose and tell him to speak to me. Your suspension has been lifted."

There were more than three hundred names of men ranking from constable to director, vetted and selected by Assistant Commissioner Miller and his staff, all deemed trustworthy. There were others but Miller did not want to remove more than two or three men from each station.

Officially, they were to join a special force to subdue the spreading township warfare. In fact, they were being posted to police stations all over the north.

At the same time, a general at Defence Headquarters in Pretoria was withdrawing certain officers from various military bases in the north 'for rebriefing'.

Superintendent Louw did not expect much sleep that night. Later he and Ndzimandze would also go north.

He wondered what Jeffrey Ballance was doing, then brushed the thought from his mind to concentrate on his task.

CHAPTER THIRTY

Major Niall Sutton settled himself into the squabs of the armoured bucket seat and drew the shoulder straps tighter. He looked forward to real action instead of the endless war games they played: it was what being a combat pilot was all about.

The rising whine of the turbine engines was muted by the insulation of his domed and padded helmet. With the visor pushed up, he scanned the square screens of the multi-function displays in front of him, fingers dancing across buttons and switches as he went through the pre-flight checks with his co-pilot and weapons system operator.

Captain Jo van Warmelo responded in monosyllables through the intercom. Enclosed in an almost duplicate cockpit above and behind Sutton, he had a higher view of the tarred Punda Maria airfield and the wide vista of virgin bush stretching to all horizons, already rippling in the heat waves.

It was a novel way to see the Kruger National Park, thought Van Warmelo, whose hobby was photographing wild animals.

He glanced to both sides where the other three Rooivalk (Red Hawk) helicopter gunships, so named by the South African Air Force for a kestrel with impressive hovering skills, were warming up their turbines, their main rotors spinning in flat black lines against the sky, the stabilisers blurred circles at the tips of the tail booms.

Sutton had a special affection for these ungainly yet menacing machines resembling monstrous dragonflies with their long tails, widespread legs, huge eyes in predatory heads, and bulbous noses. In character, they were more like racehorses, powerful and skittish, and winners.

They were flying weapons platforms designed to knock out tanks and bunkers with air-to-ground missiles controlled by a sophisticated target detection, acquisition and tracking system.

Each could also carry a formidable armoury of air-to-air missiles and air-to-ground rockets on raked wing stubs. Under its fat chin nestled its sting, 30mm cannon, which the pilot aimed by moving his head to look at the target. His electronic helmet sight did everything except pull the trigger.

Sutton wondered why four of the deadliest flying gunships in the world were chosen to take on a rabble of guerillas. It was using a shotgun to kill a mosquito. Perhaps, he thought, they want a fast clinical job with no political fuss about forces crossing borders on the ground.

Four Oryx helicopters were warming up behind them, each loaded with men of the Parachute Battalion.

Sutton was mission commander and the small screens said his machine was as ready as it ever would be. He raised his right thumb and spoke into his helmet microphone.

With the delicacy of considerable experience, Sutton lifted the collective lever and eased the cyclic stick forward. The rotor blades whirring overhead canted and bit into the air with a flapping roar. All four Rooivalks trundled a few yards and rose in unison.

Going up, they swept past three straight-winged Impala jets, painted in mottled camouflage above and sky blue underneath, which would rendezvous with them near the target area, just in case something unexpected turned up. Behind them, the pregnant-bellied Oryxes lifted from long take-off runs.

The flight turned almost due east in staggered formation, a comfortable two hundred feet above the undulating carpet of mopani rushing past. Elephants startled by the sudden noise and downwash milled about in the trees, flapping great ears. Roan antelope fled, trailing dust. Zebra stopped in full gallop and whirled to stare back with surprised faces.

It was an easy run of a little over two hundred kilometres to the target zone, an hour and a half at a reasonable fuel-saving speed. They would refuel on the return trip.

Sutton did not need the electronic map unscrolling on one of the screens. There was no radar to duck under and the sole physical hazard was the span of powerlines on tall pylons bringing electricity from the Cahora Bassa dam far to the north in Mozambique. The helicopters passed well above them.

Some twenty minutes into Mozambique, the land dropped away in a series of steps and slopes into the shallow Limpopo River valley. The helicopters slipped down the contours as if on invisible wires. Ahead of them a dark green line appeared, threading through the mopani, the tall riverine forest along the Limpopo.

Sutton aimed for a spot about fifteen kilometres upstream of the Mapai Bridge and in minutes, the broad and muddy ribbon of water flashed past below. He glanced at the digital clock: about half way now.

The target would be somewhere in the Banhine swamp, they had not told him its precise position. "Inside a probable radius of several kilometres, Niall," the CO had said at the briefing, "but in that godforsaken countryside a big camp should stick out like a supermarket and anyway the fellows on the ground will spot for you if their beacon acts up."

Thirty minutes later Sutton touched tabs to put his radio on a new frequency.

***

By mid-afternoon Ballance was in that state of fatigue-induced muscular anaesthesia where the aches had disappeared, his legs moved of their own volition and he had forgotten his discomfort. His mind was focused on what was about to take place, on his role.

Two minutes before 1645 hours, he cushioned the little transceiver on his rucksack in a patch of grass he had trampled flat and sat cross-legged in front of it. He toggled the 'on' switch. He wanted the extra two minutes because he was nervous of making mistakes with the unfamiliar equipment in spite of the explicit instructions and Superintendent Louw's coaching. It blinked into life and confronted him with an array of digital and dial displays. Most of them he couldn't understand but didn't need to anyway.

They waited. Ngwenya, Armando and Smart sat next to him, close enough to see but not to disturb him. Their tension was palpable.

At 1645 the displays twitched. A cheerful voice boomed from the transceiver: "Elephant, Elephant, Elephant, this is Falcon, do you read?"

It was so loud, Ballance hastily turned down the volume. He picked up the small handset and pressed the speak button.

"Falcon, this is Elephant, reading you loud and clear," he answered. "Welcome to the party."

"Elephant, we require description of the target, please."

"Falcon, it is a large camp of pole-and-thatch huts in trees and scrub on the western edge of a swamp some fifteen kilometres west of the Chigubo road. If you follow our signal you should land right on top of it. We're on the eastern edge of the swamp about two kilometres away."

Land on top of it, Sutton thought, he sounds like a novice, but it's enough. "Thanks, Elephant, be there in eight. Keep your head down."

"Elephant!" Ballance muttered. "Bloody cheek."

***

Sutton felt the sudden sharpening of senses that comes just before action.

"All set?" he asked Van Warmelo.

"All set, skipper."

He gave terse orders to the other pilots and lowered his visor. Behind him, Van Warmelo flicked toggles to arm the weapons systems. They were flying very low, almost brushing the short bushes. Ahead they caught a sudden glint of reflection on water.

***

Manjacane donned a clean and pressed camouflage uniform after a lukewarm shower and looked forward to his first brandy. The camp was quiet this afternoon with most of the men away and he intended to relax. From tomorrow he would be very busy.

He adjusted the beret with three stars at a comfortable angle on his head, settled the Makarov pistol in its holster behind his right hip and set off on a stroll around the camp.

The evening would be perfect, cooled by a slight breeze rising off the marsh. Aromatic smoke drifted from the cooking fires and he heard the quiet talk of men around them. The flaw, when the sun set, would be the mosquitoes but they were a fact of life, like heat and ticks and sand in the food.

He paused several times to chat to sentries. They smiled their greetings, relaxed in the cooling afternoon.

The diesel generator coughed and thumped into life as he entered his command hut. He used it usually just to charge the batteries because fuel had to be lugged in by porters, but tonight he wanted to be sure of power for the transmitter. He would also enjoy the luxury of electric light.

He poured himself a large measure of the brandy the South Africans had brought him and took his first sip, feeling its pungency bloom in his mouth and nose.

It would be better with ice. He must remember to ask them to bring him a refrigerator that could work off the generator.

***

The Rooivalk helicopters came in low and fast. Sutton chose rockets on the little MFD screen in front of him and his finger brushed over the trigger on the cyclic stick. The homing blip from Elephant's transmitter was increasing in volume and frequency; his instruments said he was less than a minute from target.

In the last seconds, the helicopters reared up. From about fifty feet they looked down on rows of huts, sheds and roofed shelters, laid out between trees like a toyland. Here and there, men emerged and stared up at them.

They must be mightily surprised, Sutton thought.Well, they're in for a bigger surprise. The head-up aiming display in front of him told him he was on target.

"Firing rockets," he announced, and his finger closed on the button. Pairs of 68mm missiles streaked from all four helicopters on converging shafts of flame and smoke.

There were almost no return shots, just a few wild bursts from terrified sentries. Surprise had been complete.

***

From two kilometres away Ballance looked aghast at what he had wrought. Flame and dust erupted all over the camp in a bedlam of noise as the Rooivalks circled, firing rocket after rocket. Pieces of hut walls and roofs, and sometimes bodies with outflung limbs, spun high in the air above the ragged line of bush. In minutes, flames were roaring through the camp, spouting columns of grey-black smoke.

It seemed to go on forever and looked like Hell. He shuddered at the sight of such pain and death and destruction. Did any men deserve this? Yes, his conscience told him, they would have caused greater pain.

***

Sutton stopped firing rockets and drew his flight back to study the target from a distance. He saw guerillas on the windward side setting up a tripod-mounted machine-gun.

"Circle and use cannon fire," he ordered.

He pressed the switch on the collective pitch lever that

unlocked the cannon. The crosshairs and dot of the reticle sight appeared in front of his eye on his visor.

Approaching low and fast, Sutton lifted his head and squeezed the trigger on the cyclic stick. Under the Rooivalk, the muzzle of the cannon lifted in synchrony to hose shells at men on the ground. He turned his gaze to a group running to his left and the gun barrel followed, obedient, relentless, beating them down. Where he looked, he killed.

Moving around the camp, the four machines spat bursts of 30mm explosive shells into it at a combined rate of twelve hundred per minute. They chewed through trees, buildings, men and equipment, like a rampant chainsaw.

He stopped after half a minute. There was no point in continuing; the camp was in ruin with no visible signs of opposition. He called in the Oryxes.

***

Manjacane had been slumped in his chair savouring his first brandy when a huge explosion rocked the flimsy building, sending things leaping from the walls and enveloping him in clouds of dust. For an instant, he thought the camp munitions store had blown up, but when repeated explosions happened, he realised with astonishment he was under attack.

He could do nothing. The blast of rockets buffeted his hut, hurling him on the floor. One blew out two walls and filled the air over his head with whistling shrapnel. When the hail of rockets stopped, he climbed to his feet, staggering and half blinded by dust, still with the tumbler of brandy in his hand.

The pause was brief, long enough for him to hear the clamour of helicopter rotors thrashing the air. The generator which had blanketed their approach had stopped, blown to bits.

A thundering rain of explosive shells ended the pause. It scythed the camp from end to end, back and forth, chewing it up like some monstrous predator. Shells chopped up walls and trees, punched through the iron stove in the kitchen, exploding Manjacane's precious small store of red wine. One passed so close to his face he felt its wind. Another shattered the half-full bottle on the table, spraying liquor on him.

The roar of cannon fire ceased as suddenly as it began. In the blessed lull the clattering of helicopters increased, then diminished.

Manjacane became aware of the drink in his hand and swallowed it in one gulp. He staggered out of his hut. He could not see much through the acrid fog of smoke and dust. The camp seemed to have gone to sleep. The ferocity of the attack had withered the paltry defence of a few sentries. Men had died, unsuspecting, in showers, around campfires and asleep.

He moved out of the smoke to less contaminated air at the edge of the nearby swamp. There he saw movement. Four figures strung out across the swamp, ploughed knee-deep through the water towards him, and some distance away to his left and right other men in camouflage with rifles zigzagged, half-bent, through the grass.

He looked about anxiously for his own men. There was no sign of any, no movement. Manjacane knew he had lost to the enemy, whoever they were.

They were white and black soldiers, although at first he could not tell the difference beneath the camouflage paint on their faces, and they carried assault rifles. He was mystified.

The first of the four men crossing the swamp waded out. He was an angry, sweating white man, his khaki trousers stained with swamp mud. He stopped in front of the little colonel.

"Colonel Manjacane?" he asked in Portuguese, looking at his shoulder tabs.

"Yes."

"You are a prisoner, sir."

"Who are you?" The colonel was stunned by the effron-

298

tery, thought of drawing his pistol and then decided there was no point.

"Jeffrey Ballance. You are under arrest for planning revolution, Colonel."

Behind Manjacane, the camouflaged soldiers moved through the wrecked camp, fast and efficient, herding prisoners, patching up the wounded. The air stank of burned cordite and the sour fumes of explosive. All shooting stopped; there was no fight left in the camp's small garrison.

A tall camouflage-clad man with heavy shoulders emerged from the smoke and strode up to Ballance, joined by Ngwenya and Smart. Next to him trotted a soldier with nervous eyes, pointing his rifle at them, a 5.56mm R5 with a folding stock. Armando was sitting some distance away at the swamp edge pouring water from his boots.

"Which one's Ballance?" the big soldier asked gruffly.

"I am," Ballance answered, "and this man ..." he indicated Manjacane, "... is the commander of the camp and my prisoner."

"I'm Colonel Steyn, Parachute Battalion, commanding this unit," the big soldier said. "We have a problem."

"What's that?"

"The camp is big enough for a thousand men at least, but there were no more than a hundred or so here. Where the hell are the rest?"

They all turned to look at Manjacane, who glared at them as if they were on parade before him.

"You are a prisoner and you will do as I say," Ballance said. "Where have the rest of your men gone and when will they return?"

"I do not tell you anything," Manjacane said in English. "I have my rights under the Geneva Convention."

Colonel Steyn chuckled. It was not a pleasant sound. "Damn the Geneva Convention. This is not a formal war. You are a terrorist trying to make trouble in South Africa. We will ask you questions and you ..." he stabbed a finger at Manjacane's chest, "... you will answer!"

Manjacane's dismay on learning they were South African was visible. "How did you find me?" he demanded.

Armando had finished draining his boots and joined the little group. At the sight of Manjacane, he smiled.

The instant Manjacane saw Armando's face he guessed how they had found him; this man used to be under his command ... now he was with the enemy. Rage and frustration filled him.

Armando was turning away but Manjacane was quick. His right hand streaked to the Makarov pistol hidden on his hip by his arm, twisted the holster upwards and fired the gun without drawing it.

The crash of the shot was deafening. The 9mm parabellum bullet punched Armando in his bandaged side, bowling him over into the dust.

The little rifleman next to Steyn reacted in pure reflex: he jerked up his gun and triggered a short burst on automatic.

It struck Manjacane in the chest and toppled him backwards against the wall of his hut. He was dead when he slid down it, leaving streaks of blood on the wood.

The South African colonel's face twisted in anger. It was not the soldier's fault; they should have disarmed the bloody commander.

***

Ballance, shocked, stared at the two men who, mere seconds ago were alive and breathing right next to him, but now dead or dying.

Smart kneeled beside Armando, who grimaced in pain. A small circle of parabats gathered around them. With nothing they could do to save him, one bent, inserted a hypodermic needle into a vein in Armando's arm and pushed the plunger, injecting morphine. The stricken man relaxed, closed his eyes and a few minutes later, died.

Smart stood up, sighing. There was no time for emotion now.

Steyn spoke into a handset clipped to his shoulder strap. When he finished he turned to Ballance.

"The gunships are putting down next to our transports to save fuel," he said. Noticing Ballance's expression, he added, "They're safe enough, we have air cover."

Smart was about to search Manjacane's pockets when he noticed the antenna sprouting from the dead commander's hut. He went inside. A minute later he came out pushing a frightened boy ahead of him.

"There's a transceiver in there," he said. "It seems undamaged. The signaller's here too, found him under a cot."

In the hut Steyn picked up a message pad. "What's this?" He handed it to Ballance who studied the cryptic notes in Portuguese.

"Looks like orders to various units to attack something or other at nineteen hundred hours tomorrow,"

"So that's where the bastards went! Ask the signaller when the orders were sent."

Ballance handed the notes to Smart, who questioned the quivering young signaller.

"They were transmitted this afternoon."

"What are the targets?"

Smart quizzed him for some time, going through the items on the notepad one by one.

"These are to outlying units confirming strikes on Maputo, Xai Xai, Inhambane and Moamba in Mozambique."

"Tell him to get that radio working and signal in Manjacane's name that the attacks are called off."

"He says he can't, they're already on the way and won't make radio contact until after the strikes."

"Damn!" Steyn punched the palm of one hand with the fist of the other, thinking hard.

The youngster started talking fast.

"What's he saying?" Steyn demanded.

"For God's sake!" Smart exclaimed. "He says another big group are on their way to hit Pafuri, Shingwedzi and Punda Maria in the Kruger Park!"

"When?" Steyn snapped.

Smart spoke rapid Portuguese. "The day after tomorrow," he translated, "and they are supposed to check in by radio at six tomorrow. He doesn't know more than that."

"Fuck!" Ngwenya breathed. "They must be timing their strike with a UDI by those crazy whiteys!"

Steyn hitched a hip on the edge of Manjacane's shrapnel-scarred table. He was dirty and tired and beginning to taste the hangover of disgust that follows killing.

"Well?" he asked, looking at Ballance. "You know these people, you think they'll go through with it?"

Ballance did not hesitate. "Yes. Call them back under some pretext and ambush them."

Steyn nodded and turned to Smart. "Take good care of that signaller, we'll need him at six tomorrow to tell them the attack is postponed and their boss here wants them back."

He stalked out of the hut and began barking orders. Men ran to do his bidding.

Ballance heard the mutter of the helicopter engines rise to a united howl and one by one, they took off due west.

Half an hour later, Colonel Steyn found him walking around the shattered camp looking at the damage. "I sent the choppers back to base. Can't have them parked here the whole night, we don't know who might be in the area," he said. "We'll call them back tomorrow if we want them. My men are using the captives to clean up the camp and bury the dead. I suggest you get some sleep, it'll be a long day."

CHAPTER THIRTY ONE

To Smart's relief, the transceiver in Manjacane's HQ hut had escaped damage because the signaller, proud of his charge, had packed it in its metal case on the floor. On the table, it would have been shot to scrap.

Early in the morning Smart had sent him on to the roof to rejoin aerial wires cut by shell splinters. Now Smart stood at his shoulder while he tested the set. It muttered and buzzed and the needles swung to normal. It seemed healthy.

Five minutes before six a.m. the signaller tuned it to a channel, and waited. Smart pulled an extra headset over his ears to eavesdrop. He loosened the strap of his holster and looked at the signaller.

Smart doubted he could shoot someone in cold blood but his message was unmistakeable: no tricks or you're dead.

The deception worked. As each of the three rebel units called in, their voices loud and clear, the signaller told them, "The operation is postponed for one week. Colonel Manjacane says you must return to base for new orders and new equipment."

The commandant of the most distant unit, those headed farthest south who had marched hard and far, quibbled until the signaller on his own initiative said, "Our colonel says that is an order. Return immediately."

The commandant refused. He would rest his men today and return tomorrow, he said, sullen. Hearing him, the others said they would do the same.

When the transmission ended, Smart buttoned his holster strap and patted the signaller on the shoulder. He opened the lid of the radio's cabinet and extracted a small printed circuit board to make it useless.

"All cut and dried," he reported to Colonel Steyn.

"You quite sure?"

"Yes. The call signs and identifications all tallied with those we found on the written orders."

Some of the worry drained out of Steyn. "Good. And they're all on their way back?"

"Yeah, tomorrow."

"Tomorrow?"

"One of their leaders got uptight because he'd already hiked so far and said he'd rest up and come back tomorrow, so the others said they'd do the same instead of returning today. That raises another thing ..." Smart paused.

"What?"

"Because they left here at the same time doesn't mean they'll all come back at the same time. They had different distances to travel, so the chances are they'll trickle back separately."

Steyn considered this. "In other words, we can't trap them here," he said half to himself. "We'll have to nail them group by group, and if one happens to be close by when we hit another, or if we use the Oryxes to get close, the others will hear us and – *phffft* – surprise gone."

"And then they'll hunt us."

"Yeah. It could be rough."

Steyn slumped on a bench at an outdoor table to think. Without surprise on their side, in unfamiliar territory, his company stood a fair chance of being overwhelmed.

The Renamos were an ill-disciplined bunch but they had long fighting experience and the instincts of hyaenas. This was their home ground, they outnumbered his men by many to one, and they were geared for battle.

"We'll call in the gunships when we hit them," he decided, "but first we must get moving on foot to find a good place to set up an ambush. Any suggestions?"

***

That same morning, about 3,000 kilometres away in Cape Town, a new waiter presented himself for duty at the Houses of Parliament, where catering was by tradition the duty of the national railway service, Transnet.

He passed the stringent security checks without a hitch when he presented the small green card in laminated plastic with his photograph and the Parliamentary logo that indicated vetting and accreditation by the police. Telephone calls to Transnet confirmed that he was temporary relief for a waiter on leave.

An underground contact in the CID had provided the card and the confirmation.

The new waiter's size and deferential manner impressed the chief caterer. The new man donned his high-collared white tunic with silver buttons and took up his duties right away.

These entailed serving drinks and canapés in the lounges and carrying trays along the carpeted corridors to the offices of government and opposition leaders too busy to use the big dining room.

Like most of the servants in the House he melted into the background, always attentive but seldom noticed. He effaced himself, speaking when spoken to, wearing a bland expression, doing nothing that might attract attention. Once he caught himself reaching up to his face, to stroke a drooping moustache that was no longer there, and stopped the habit.

In the afternoon a small van brought a supply of new catering equipment to the delivery door for the kitchens; cartons of new plates, cups and saucers, pots and wooden boxes of silver-plated cutlery, all bearing the Parliamentary logo.

The policemen on security duty checked the delivery note and examined the goods by hand because the metal detector could not do the job. The new waiter, who was hovering about, offered to help carry them to the storeroom.

He had placed the order the day before using forms supplied by the source of his ID.

Out of sight, he opened the boxes of cutlery one by one. The knives, forks and spoons were nested in slots in felt-lined trays stacked on top of each other. He lifted out the trays to place them on the cutlery shelves.

Fastened under the bottom tray of the third box, wrapped in black plastic and covered by a sheet of thin plywood, was an FN Browning pistol.

This was his precarious moment. Tucking the plastic package under his belt in the small of his back, concealed by the pointed tail of his tunic, he walked the few yards to the pantry.

Inside, he opened the large flour bin, which was two thirds full, pushed the package as deep into it as his arm could reach and returned to the storeroom, dusting himself off.

***

There were four men in the old farmhouse now, the Chairman, two young radio operators and a former Reconnaissance Brigade brigadier who had retired in disgust when the new government gave senior ranks in the defence forces to former ANC guerrillas. He would be in direct command of the young lions of the Free Staters' Movement from the moment the secession was announced tomorrow.

"If at all possible we should avoid violence," the Chairman had told the assembled leaders the previous day before they dispersed. "There will be some people here who will not agree with us and the government might send police or troops to try to stop us.

"Remember that they are Afrikaners too. We do not want to shed the blood of our brothers if we can avoid doing so. We will talk to them and tell them to leave us alone. If they insist then be it on their own heads. But you will not use your weapons until the order is given. Is that understood?"

All nodded, although some thought he was an old fart who would need sidelining once the new state was established.

The group leaders had filtered away to places between Alldays in the west, the Kruger Park in the east and south as far as Zoekmekaar, a small railway station on the Tropic of Capricorn.

Tomorrow afternoon their local groups would assemble, be issued with weapons and wait for the signal to block roads, take over police stations with the aid of rebel policemen and cow potential resistance.

Up north at Messina, near the Beit Bridge over the Limpopo river to Zimbabwe, a large body of troops would come out armed, ostensibly to keep order while the situation resolved itself but in reality to support the secession.

The Chairman was a little tense. At the same time as he made the announcement by radio it would be sent to the local and foreign media in Johannesburg and London.

What worried him, however, was timing: how close would the actions of the others coincide? The opposition party in Venda was to recognise the Free State and demand its own independence.

Simultaneously, Manjacane's people in Mozambique would declare their independent *Republica de Gaza*. To confuse the South African forces, some of his men would make diversionary strikes at places in the Kruger Park and farther south. Near Durban his provocateurs would instigate a shooting match between ANC and Inkatha supporters among the fiery Zulus.

The Chairman smiled to himself. The most difficult part might be shooting up parts of the precious Kruger

Park. It would inflame conservationists around the world.

***

Ephesias Mutale was savouring his next moves with the delectation of a connoisseur. At the shop and hotel complex in Thohoyandou he had at last seen one of the men who had abducted him, together with another man he remembered well from the night of the massacre.

The second was the killer who had wielded the panga and lopped the head off the defiant old man, the face engraved in his brain.

Mutale had followed the first and sent one of his team after the other. He blessed his luck when both met at the same house – luxurious by local standards, plastered and painted and with a corrugated iron roof and a fenced garden – in the hillside suburb overlooking the main road.

Casual inquiries in the neighbourhood revealed it was the home of a senior bureaucrat and that the second man lodged there.

He met his team that evening at the home of one of them. They would make their raid well after dark. Mutale was sure his prey could be persuaded to name names and give addresses. He looked forward to a satisfying night.

***

Superintendent Louw stepped from the Piper Seneca that had brought him to Louis Trichardt from Lanseria airport near Johannesburg. He carried his bag to the VW Citigolf in which Captain Ndzimandze had come to meet him. Both were dressed in casual clothes and would pass themselves off as visiting businessmen.

"There's still no sign of Dr Van Geyssen," Ndzimandze told him on the way to a hotel in the forest, above the town. The big captain hunched over the steering wheel, barely able to fit his lanky frame in the small

308

car.

"And the boss, their Chairman?"

"He's out at his farm now. I didn't go close because the house is inside a game fence with armed guards."

"Did they see you?"

"No, I used binoculars."

"Good. We don't want to make them nervous."

"What's the score, Superintendent?"

"You and I sit tight and wait for word from the Assistant Commissioner. Then we collect some of our men and raid the farmhouse. I'm pretty sure it's their headquarters and if we shut that down, the rest will be easier to mop up. Our men are in place already. Have you seen any of the other Committee members?"

"As far as I can tell none have arrived, if they're coming at all. But there's a whole flock of right-wingers here from all over the country, including some heavyweights from places like Rustenburg, Brits, Klerksdorp, Krugersdorp and Standerton, and as far away as the Orange Free State and the Northern Cape."

"A real teddy bears' picnic. It looks as if Assistant Commissioner Miller's scheme is working ... wait until they're all here then grab the lot."

"Where'd he hear all about this, sir?"

"A Member of Parliament discovered he had a conscience and started singing."

"A politician with a conscience," Ndzimandze muttered. "*Aî* That's an endangered species."

***

Assistant Commissioner Miller was edgier than he had ever been. The Vice President was cutting it damned fine and taking a hell of a risk when the country could least afford a mistake.

Not only was he waiting until the last minute, which he would learn of from some mysterious source he would not reveal, but he had not told all to his special

309

Cabinet committee.

Miller reflected that as the one man who knew how far the Vice President was going out on a limb, politically and personally, he himself was at risk. If the limb broke, the Assistant Commissioner and Vice President would fall together.

Too bad, he thought, I'm over retirement age and I've had enough of all this cloak-and-dagger stuff.

The Vice President was himself showing some signs of strain through the imperturbable facade he had developed during years of political manoeuvring, although he was going through the paces of routine as if everything was normal.

Tomorrow he had to attend a formal function at the Tuynhuys with the President. It would be indoors except for the few moments when the President would emerge on the front steps to greet some visiting African head of state, coming to taste the South African fleshpots, and lead him indoors.

***

The Doctor was at ease in spite of the fact that in something over twenty-four hours he would be at the focal point of a drama that might well result in excess bloodshed, if he did not act with absolute precision.

With the gambit almost played, he thought, he had little left to do. He would speak to the Chairman late tomorrow afternoon, by when the Free Stater forces, strengthened by men from many parts of the country, would be armed and primed for action.

He was satisfied that Smith was off his back. The hired killer had served his purpose but the Doctor had never felt comfortable in the presence of a man to whom murder was as ordinary as shopping for groceries.

However, he thought with satisfaction, his tipoff to the Vice President himself that the assassin was on the way, had sealed Smith's fate.

The President was surrounded by experts who would kill with no more compunction than Smith himself.

The Doctor did not know that Smith was already dead, or that he had assigned two more assassins to the job.

The south-easter was blowing in gusts through the leaves of the old oaks around the garden, making the flowers dance. It fluttered the newspaper on the white cast-iron table and threatened to scatter the pages.

The Doctor gathered them up and made his way across the lawn to the gracious old home where nobody would think of looking for him.

***

Penelope Fox sat up in bed in a private room at the Milpark Clinic with a newspaper propped in front of her and tried without success to concentrate on the running catalogue of disaster. She tossed the paper to the floor in exasperation, her mind too full of worries.

She was over the worst of the shock of Smith's attempt to kill her; sedatives would see her through from now on. Her left wrist was in plaster and her back, shoulders and thighs were blotched with bruises.

She worried that she had not heard from Jeffrey. Never having been to Mozambique, she worried about his safety there.

She worried too about where to go when she left the clinic the next day.

The flat near Corlett Drive was out, she had decided, the memory was too vivid.

She would consult with Superintendent Louw.

Chapter Thirty Two

The village of Ressano Garcia in Mozambique dozed beside the crocodile-infested Incomati River near the South African border post to which it owed its existence. In the civil war the rival Renamo and Frelimo forces had shot, rocketed and mortared it almost into ruin.

That had provided some entertainment for the residents of Komatipoort, a sleepy village on the South African side. But when it resumed this night, the bombs fell into Komatipoort itself.

Most churned up gardens or burst on streets. Nine people were slightly hurt and none killed. The attack lasted a few minutes.

Hot lines to Pretoria and Cape Town hummed. Suspicions and accusations flowed thick and fast. Before dawn military reinforcements were on their way to Komatipoort, which for the next week or two would enjoy a brisk boom in trade.

***

Other Gaza guerrillas made brief hit-and-run strikes at Maputo, on a Frelimo barracks at Moamba nearby, and at Inhambane on a bay of blue water and glittering beaches to the north.

At Maputo, the strike dissipated in the thick perimeter of overcrowded slums. At Moamba, the Frelimo garrison returned such hot fire from behind the thick barracks walls, the attackers retreated.

At Inhambane, they killed two people and looted but the pickings were meagre and they left in less than fifteen minutes.

The Mozambique Government reacted like a stung wolf. Frelimo troops were placed on full alert.

***

In Venda, Ephesias Mutale and his men were busy cutting throats. The first was that of the bureaucrat he followed to his home.

It was so easy. With the local ANC organisation broken, his target was complacent about security. When Mutale knocked on the door at nine o'clock it was opened without hesitation.

Mutale shoved the man back inside with the muzzle of a silenced Makarov pistol in his stomach. The bureaucrat was so frightened his voice failed him.

Two of Mutale's team slipped past, drew pistol-grip AK-47s from beneath their overcoats and moved in silence to the curtained kitchen, where they found the bureaucrat's wife and the lodger sipping tea.

They tied all three to straight-backed chairs and gagged the wife and the lodger with rags stuffed in their mouths and broad strips of masking tape.

Mutale took off his hat and recognition dawned on the husband's face. With it came real terror: this ANC commissar should be rotting in a mineshaft in the hills.

"I want the names of all who were with you that night," Mutale told him. "The names of the men who seized us and killed everyone ... and I want to know where they live."

The bureaucrat, slack-mouthed and grey with fear, shook his head in a last flicker of courage.

Mutale bent forward to speak, so close the man could feel his breath against his cheek.

"You will tell me," he said, his voice gentle. "First, we will cut your friend here, and next we will cut off your wife's breasts and then we will cut you. Oh yes, I am sure you will tell me."

He took a spring knife from his pocket, pressed the stud to shoot out the double-edged blade, and handed it to one

313

of his men. To demonstrate its sharpness, the man angled the blade against the cringing woman's forearm and shaved some hair. Then he placed the flat of the blade against the soft curve of her throat and waited.

Their captive talked for ten minutes, while the third man wrote down names and addresses in a wire-bound notebook with a stub of pencil. There were thirty-one. He did not know all of the men who were there, he said, some were strangers.

Of the thirty-one, seventeen lived in and around Thohoyandou. One had been a member of the Venda Cabinet when the homeland was independent and still had an official guard.

When the bureaucrat could think of no more and stopped talking, Mutale put his hat back on his head and smiled, altering his grim expression. The bureaucrat smiled back. With relief in his voice, he said, "Now you will spare us."

Mutale held out his hand for the knife. With a vicious backhand whip of his arm, he slashed the blade across the bound man's neck, slicing it through almost to the spine.

The man jumped and jerked in his chair for the few seconds it took him to die while his lifeblood gushed from his gaping throat. His lodger vomited inside his gag, choking himself, and his wife's eyes bulged like eggs as she tried in vain to scream through hers.

Mutale handed the knife back to his assistant, who slit both their throats.

They closed the door behind them and joined their colleagues in the minibus outside. They drove from address to address, visiting those nearest first and extending their hunt wider.

The first eight were easy. Not expecting trouble even this late, they opened their doors when Mutale said he had brought a message from the bureaucrat.

He killed six of the men, and their women, with the knife, leaving the children. Two he shot with the silenced

Makarov when they became suspicious and tried to resist.

By the time they reached the ninth address, the alarm had spread. Coming home late, the bureaucrat's son had found the bloody mess in the kitchen and called the police.

Children of other victims ran for help and the police became very busy.

It was when a policeman who supported the pro-independence group recognised the names of the dead and made the connection, that the pattern become clear.

He explained to the chief of police what was happening. The chief, who opposed independence, decided to pursue the killers with more caution and less haste.

Six of the people Mutale sought were not at home. The former Cabinet Minister was.

Two armed policemen stood slack in boredom at the iron gates and a bodyguard lounged at the front door. Mutale abandoned finesse.

The ANC men gunned down the sentries, shot open the lock on the gates, and charged in. The bodyguard fired his pistol at them until a burst from an AK-47 hit him.

They smashed down the front door but the ex-minister and his wife were already running out the back in their pyjamas and escaped into the night.

Mutale spilled a can of paraffin and a bottle of benzene on the kitchen floor. He tossed a phosphorous grenade from the doorway and felt the whoosh of heat on his back as he ran.

As the minibus pulled away, flames were reaching through the kitchen windows.

Mutale considered visiting others on his list and decided against it. The risk was not worth it; he had eliminated the core of the opposition. He had left an unmistakeable message in Venda tonight.

A routine homicide investigation was launched. The motive for the spate of murders was not yet known, the chief told the newspapermen, who came like flies to dung. It could be anything from money to witchcraft.

CHAPTER THIRTY THREE

Colonel Steyn led his men out of Manjacane's ruined camp, leaving the few surviving Renamo guerrillas to their own devices, taking the young radio operator and his transceiver. His men had heaped together all the arms and ammunition they could find, poured diesel fuel and paraffin on them and lit the pile. It burned fiercely until ammunition and grenades blew up with crackling explosions.

"You keep an eye on the young fellow," Steyn said to Ballance, "we might need him to talk to the groups we called back. Our signalman will handle our routine operational traffic but we'll use your set to bring the flyboys in because they're already tuned to its beacon."

The colonel had spoken to his headquarters the previous evening when a clipped voice said air support would be given and quizzed him about map coordinates, enemy numbers and weapons.

"I cannot give details and won't know the precise positions until we are there," he said. "We'll use the same homing signal used yesterday."

"Understood," the voice replied, metallic and impersonal. "Try to give us good advance warning when they are near the bridge at Mapai. It's where the Limpopo can be crossed easily so that's where they'll show up. Set up a stopper group."

The bridge was perfect for an ambush, Steyn saw. A handful of men could hold off hundreds, but they had to move fast to reach it before the rebels.

They left camp before dawn. Refreshed by sleep, the parabats settled into a distance-eating stride through bush and grass across a dusty floodplain. It gave way to a monotonous red sea of head-high mopani with oily, butterfly-shaped leaves infested with small flies that crawled into ears, eyes and nostrils.

Mid-morning, an eroded, overgrown railway embankment came in view, a long low mound of packed earth a little higher than the mopani.

"The railway line from Zimbabwe," Steyn said, examining a map. "We've made good time."

Ballance climbed the embankment and peered over. The view extended into flat infinity where sky and veld merged into one. West was the low escarpment of the Limpopo valley. Nearer, a long thin line of dark green wandered almost north-south: the Limpopo.

The dirt road to the Mapai Bridge, little used in recent years, was rutted by erosion. They followed it with the lift of spirits that comes from reaching a river. Two hundred yards from the bridge, they approached in a skirmish line, but there was nothing to shoot.

The ruins of a few buildings stood in the shadow of riverside trees whose massive limbs rose like cathedral arches, tall jackalberry and nyala, the pale green domes and flying buttress roots of sycamore, figs, and the pale luminous yellow of fever trees.

What astonishing beauty Africa hides in its remote places, Ballance thought, gazing at the shafts of sunlight slanting through leafy canopy. How inappropriate to kill here.

The river slid past, a hundred metres wide. Its serene mud-brown surface seemed still as a pond until Ballance saw a piece of wood sweep past on the invisible current.

The bridge stood on square concrete pillars. Steyn positioned his men amid the trees at both sides of the bridge to cover the approach with raking crossfire.

"This is our temporary HQ," he said, pausing beneath a giant fig tree and turning to Ballance. "Get the signaller to call up the rebels and find out where they are. Make sure he doesn't try any tricks. If he does, hit him and take over."

More fearful of his captors than of combat, the young signaller tuned to the right channel and began intoning a call sign. In less than a minute, a voice crackled back in Portuguese.

Smart translated for Steyn. "They're suspicious. Those guys are foxy as jackals. They want to know why we're asking, when they're already on their way back. One said they're a few kilometres from the river, the second an hour away but the third is being coy. He's the bloke who bitched when we told him to hold off the attack. He won't say."

"His group is the one sent to attack Shingwedzi," Steyn said, "which puts him the farthest from us. I would guess he is ..." he made a quick mental calculation "... about six to ten kilometres south of the others."

He touched Ballance on the arm, "Your turn now."

Ballance placed his compact transceiver on a low wall and switched it on.

"Falcon, Falcon, Falcon," he intoned. "This is Elephant."

The now familiar voice responded. "Elephant, Elephant, Elephant, this is Falcon, how do you read?

"Falcon, this is Elephant, reading you strength six," Ballance replied.

"Elephant, we are thirty to forty-five minutes distant and will move when you signal that a target is available. Describe target area please."

Ballance gave their position in relation to the Mapai Bridge. "One bunch suspect something's up," he added, "the group farthest from the river. They might decide to head in another direction."

"Understood, thanks. Stay on this frequency."

Ballance acknowledged, sighed, and sat down on the dusty ground. Soon men would die.

"There's no option," Steyn said, divining his thoughts. "Think of what they would do if they were not stopped. They are cold-blooded killers, bandits. Not disciplined soldiers defending their country."

"That doesn't make it feel any better. Do you have anything to guide the planes when they arrive, like a flare?"

"A Very pistol with red and green flares and you can use the bridge as a reference point. We'll hold them off until the choppers arrive."

Ballance and Ngwenya sat on the wall next to the transceiver. They might have been alone on earth except for the faint snick and click of rifles and machine-guns, checked by unseen men nearby.

***

"Falcon, first target is a loose column a few kilometres west of the bridge. Second target unspotted but believed to be six or more kilometres farther west. There is a third farther away but we don't know exactly where. Our observer says those nearest are spread out along a path and do not appear to have been alerted. The parabats will engage and when you are close we will fire a green flare to indicate our position."

"Roger, Elephant, got that. We are airborne and on our way."

***

The two groups returning from the aborted strikes on Pafuri and Punda Maria had already joined forces, a straggled line of some three hundred hot and thirsty men. They were making for the river to drink and soak themselves in its cool water.

Unlike the leader of the larger group south of them, they were unsuspicious though disappointed by the delay in hitting a fat target with good prospects of loot. They would make camp that night under the riverside trees and cover the last short stretch to the camp in the morning.

The column leader sent four men out on point when he saw the green treeline ahead. He was not anticipating anything. It was routine. The four trotted about a hundred metres ahead, pleased to be the first to reach the water.

They paused on the riverbank to splash water on their sweating faces then strolled onto the bridge, two with their rifles slung from their shoulders.

Steyn allowed them to reach the near end before he fired his 9mm Beretta pistol at them. The shot triggered a huge, withering fusillade of projectiles at the entire column strung out for some three hundred metres – rifle and machine-gun bullets, grenades and rockets from shoulder tubes.

The men on point shrivelled like straw in flame. The blast of fire stripped holes all along the column but the guerrillas were seasoned fighters, whose first rule was survival. Those who lived through the first barrage melted like snow into the tall grass on either side.

Within seconds, they gave return fire, ragged and erratic at first but soon rising to a steady stream of bullets and a few rocket-propelled grenades into the trees on both sides of the river. Their aim was random. The guerrillas could not see the well-concealed ambushers, but the hail was thick and disconcerting.

It began to look like a stalemate: a handful of men in a commanding tactical position holding the bridge against hundreds. It could not last long. The guerrillas had a mobility the ambushers did not and could wait for night-fall.

"Elephant, Elephant, Elephant, this is Falcon," the transceiver muttered.

"Reading you loud and clear, Falcon," Ballance said, "you're in good time."

"We are approaching along the river under cover of the trees, Elephant, be there in two. Can you give me a visual on your position?"

Visual? Ballance wondered what he meant, then it clicked. "Falcon, we'll fire a green flare when you tell us. Enemy will be almost due south of it, range two to three hundred metres from us."

"Roger, Elephant, fire flare ... now!"

Colonel Steyn aimed the Very pistol up through a gap between the trees and pulled the trigger.

The reverberation of gunfire smothered the drone of the approaching Rooivalks flying a few feet above the Limpopo's slick surface behind the screen of riverside trees. The first the guerrillas heard was a sudden drumming of rotor blades. The gunfire dwindled as they looked for its source. It seemed to come from the general direction of the river but they could see nothing.

A streak of white smoke soared high from beyond the river and burst into brilliant green light. An instant later the Rooivalks leaped straight up from the concealment of the treeline like toys on strings, four in a row.

They angled their noses down and charged.

Some gunfire winked at the helicopters from the ground. Niall Sutton knew he would have to act fast before the target scattered. He snapped commands and swung his machine to rake the path from the bridge. The others veered to attack from the sides.

His subconscious mind had switched to a state of detachment cocooning him for the slaughter. From a hundred feet up, he and Van Warmelo stared down the ragged line of men milling about in panic or fleeing. Some stood their ground and aimed at the mechanical raptors. Bullets rattled on the Rooivalks' armour.

Sutton pressed the switch on the collective pitch lever that unlocked the cannon. The crosshairs and dot of the reticle sight appeared in front of his eye.

"Circle and use cannon fire," he ordered and squeezed the trigger on the cyclic stick.

The helicopters moved around the milling men like lazy hawks spitting 30mm explosive shells. Explosions flowered on the ground, wreathing men in dust. A body revolved in the air with arms and legs stretched out like Leonardo da Vinci's sketch.

In less than a minute, the path and the bush on both sides became a charnel house.

Sutton stopped the barrage. There was no point in continuing; dead men and weapons littered the scene.

A computer beeped a message in his earphones and a signal flashed on an MFD screen: a bullet had passed right through his helicopter, no serious damage. He left it to Van Warmelo to handle.

With light movements of hands and feet, Sutton took the Rooivalk sideways and down almost to the mopani scrub. The powerful downdraft from the rotors raised a roiling cloud of dust.

He sped forward and when almost on top of the guerrillas he jumped the machine thirty feet up to sweep down the length of the path. There was nothing to see except dead and wounded, no return fire. Dark faces with wide white eyes flashed past below.

At the far end, he hoisted the machine high, looked back and saw the other pilots chasing men fleeing into the bush.

"Break, break, break," he ordered. The shooting stopped and the machines peeled away. Below them survivors scattered like panicked ants.

"Mop them up, skipper?"

"No," he said, feeling slight nausea. "Look for the others."

Seven kilometres southwest, the other party of two hundred rebels were walking in single file when the roar-and-slap of rotor blades and the tattoo of cannon fire warned them.

Their leader ordered his men into the cover of the mopani scrub on either side of the winding game path they were following. They crouched low and stared up through the leaves.

The searching pilots did not find them until bullets rattled on the belly of one machine. The pilot lunged it away and a billowing brown smoke ball from a rocket-propelled grenade filled the space he had just vacated.

The four machines lofted high to look back like young hawks assessing a prey that bites, then swooped in low, firing rockets, sowing a crop of explosions for a hundred metres.

The guerrillas dissolved into the bush. Sutton reconnoitred with caution. Here and there a few men ran like rabbits, intent on putting distance between themselves and the gunships.

"Leave 'em be," Sutton ordered. "They'll tell the others."

***

Watching the lethal aerial ballet, hearing the *daka-daka-daka* of the cannons and the *whump* of rocket bursts, Ballance thought of men dying and was thankful he was on this side.

"Elephant, Elephant, Falcon," a metallic voice called. He grabbed the microphone.

"Standing by, Falcon."

"Both targets found and routed. Some survivors may head your way. We're going home now."

"Falcon, many thanks, you've prevented a lot of grief."

"Our pleasure. Stand by for pickup."

The four helicopters climbed higher and disappeared to the west.

Pickup? What did Falcon mean?

"Watch out for strays," Steyn called from his position near a machine-gunner covering the bridge. Eyes turned to the far end of the bridge. Nobody appeared. It was finished. The silence was so intense they heard the chuckle of the river around the bridge pilings. A burst of sound from the transceiver startled Ballance.

"Elephant, Elephant, Elephant, do you read?"

"Receiving you loud and clear."

"What is the situation now?"

"The show is over. The gunships have left."

"Casualties?"

"None here, lots on the other side."

"Stand by."

Ballance looked at the colonel in puzzlement. Steyn shrugged.

The radio came to life again. "Elephant, be ready for pickup in ten minutes. We will land on the railway embankment. Acknowledge."

"Pick up who?"

"The parabats, sir, and you too. Your presence is required."

Ballance glanced at Steyn, who nodded.

"Affirmative. We'll be there."

"Roger. Over and out."

The transmission died.

The plump Oryxes came on time, escorted by two pugnacious Rooivalks, signalling their coming from afar with their noise. They settled in a tornado blast of dust and gravel on the railway embankment, straddling the tracks, with rotors whirling while the gunships patrolled in a wide circle.

An airman in blue overalls jumped down from the open door.

"Mr Ballance?" he shouted above the whistle of the turbine. "Get aboard right away, please."

Hands reached down to help Ballance, Ngwenya and Smart into the Oryx.

"What about him?" Ngwenya asked.

Ballance saw the young Renamo signaller watching them with dismal eyes.

"Come!" he yelled in Portuguese. They dragged him aboard.

The crewman slid the door shut and talked into his microphone. The turbine whine swelled to a banshee howl, the rotor blades slammed the air and the machine heaved aloft.

Peering out of a small window, Ballance felt a touch of sadness. All that violence and bloodshed, for what? The Limpopo and its trees and the veld blended into uniformity as they rose higher, swallowed up by Africa.

CHAPTER THIRTY FOUR

In a rare outburst of temper, the Vice President glared at the men around the table, his inner circle of caucus confidants, and shot to his feet. Startled, they watched him in silence. The public had not seen this other side to his laid-back mien but his colleagues knew it and feared the ruthless will it exposed.

"We will *not* take *any* action until the moment is right!" he growled, resting his knuckles on the table and weighting each word, "I am *not* going to be persuaded to go off at half-cock now. Nor, if you value your positions, should any of you."

The angry frown swung from face to face, as intimidating as an aimed gun.

"If any one of you acts unilaterally at this most delicate stage, it will negate everything that I and the others whom you have entrusted with this task have done. You do so at the nation's peril, and your own."

He sat down. The Minister of Defence coughed and said it was time to break for tea. The sudden rustle as they all rose signalled their relief.

The Vice President heaved a sigh of relief. He had been holding his colleagues, some of them strong-willed characters, in rein for weeks. The stress was telling, he could not restrain them much longer while South Africa plunged further into chaos. He was not sure he had held all of them now. He was not even sure he could fully trust them anymore.

When told what the special investigation unit had uncovered, all of them had demanded immediate and decisive action including a full state of emergency or martial law. He argued that either step would spell disaster; the government had to keep its cool.

He couldn't blame them, he thought gloomily. The pressure from the ANC MPs, dismayed by spreading violence, was becoming almost intolerable. The President understood the Vice President's dilemma, but had warned that not even he could contain his supporters' anger for much longer.

Newspaper posters in doomsday type, sombre headlines, television news clips which many people were too frightened to watch, and a climbing toll of dead and injured were the indicators of ferocious disorder and intense public disquiet. Suspecting inability by the security forces to act with force, or perhaps unwillingness, many people on both sides of the political fence were yelling for heads to roll.

Time. His need was desperate, a few more hours if his inside source was right. If not, his political life was at an end.

Today the media were screaming about last night's mortaring of Komatipoort. Although no one had been killed, they gave it more prominence than the deaths of scores of people in other violent eruptions all over the country, most of them random massacres in townships. Like the politicians, the media were becoming punch drunk and losing perspective.

Five minutes after the meeting broke up, there was a knock on the door and the Minister of Defence walked in.

"News has just come in from DHQ in Pretoria," he said.

The Vice President lifted his eyebrows in question.

"The air strike in Mozambique was a success," his colleague said. "Helicopters routed the terrorists identified by your Mr Ballance. We have no count yet of enemy casualties but we believe any threat of attack in the Kruger Park has been eliminated."

"Thank God for some good news," the Vice President sighed, "and thank you, too, you've done very well."

"Was the Komatipoort attack part of this?"

"I suspect so but cannot be sure. There were other raids in southern Mozambique last night and the government in Maputo is calling us rude names."

"Is there anything more you want to tell me about all this?"

"I've told you and the others as much as I know. The groups the air force broke up were supposed to help the South African rebels. We don't know who they are yet." The Vice President rose and stood with his hands behind his back. He looked very tired.

The Minister felt sorry for him; there could be no heavier responsibility in South Africa at this moment, except the President's. "Well if you need me ..." he said, moving to the door.

"Thanks. Stay close by today. I might well need you soon."

***

At twelve-thirty, the African head of state would come through the tall ironwork gates of the Tuynhuys in the big black Mercedes Benz provided by the Department of Foreign Affairs.

It would stop next to the colonnaded portico where the President would emerge, smiling, to greet him at the top of the broad steps and usher him indoors.

There he would be guest of honour while the President presented several medals for meritorious service to distinguished citizens.

In the climax of the ceremony, the two heads of state would bestow upon each other the most grandiose decorations they could find in their jewel boxes and retire to a lunch of bean soup, rock lobster mayonnaise, medallions of kudu, all washed down with Cape wines.

The sommelier would take care to fill the President's

glass from wine bottles containing pure grape juice. The Vice President would have something stronger.

Fifteen minutes before the African leader was due to arrive, a burly plainclothes policeman carrying a briefcase presented his Parliamentary identity card at the security desk in the cheerless block of government offices across Parliament Street from the House.

The uniformed policeman scrutinised it with meticulous care, checked the man against his picture and tapped out the details on the keyboard of a computer which immediately relayed the information to a security office inside the building.

The visitor's face was new to him and the ID was one of the old ones. He had been ordered to look out for IDs like this and to enter the details on his console, then admit the holder. He had no idea why, he just obeyed orders. Others would deal with the visitor inside. Without expression he ushered the visitor in.

The visitor walked through the metal detector arch after handing over his briefcase to be passed through the X-ray machine. The arch detected nothing except a belt buckle. The X-ray revealed a blank; unbeknown to the policeman the lid, sides and bottom, inside, were lined with thin sheets of lead.

The visitor rode the lift to the fourth floor at the Table Mountain end of the building. He walked down the corridor past small reception rooms and offices where secretaries tapped word processors. Nobody gave him a second glance; his grey suit was the uniform of the civil servant.

Near the end, he pushed open a door bearing a stylised figure with spread legs, the quaint symbol for a men's washroom. It contained two basins beneath a large mirror, a stainless steel urinal and two toilets.

He chose the cubicle in the corner and latched the door. The bowl, flushed by a button on the wall, did not have a cistern. Above it, a narrow fanlight window, hinged on top, opened outwards.

By standing close to the back wall between the toilet bowl and the side wall, he could look out on the sun-washed suburbs below the cableway end of Table Mountain and Lion's Head and, nearby, the peaceful greenery of the Cape Town Gardens and the front of the Tuynhuys.

The angle was a little steeper than he had expected, he would have to stand on tiptoe. He stroked his thick Sundance moustache in thought.

He glanced at his watch. Twelve twenty-three.

Placing the case on the toilet lid, he unlocked it and began assembling the Musgrave 308. On the end of the barrel he screwed the ten-inch tube of a crude but effective silencer. It would reduce the gunshot to a dull thump. It would also reduce the velocity of the bullet but the range was so close that did not matter.

Before he attached the telescopic sight, he held it to his eye at the window and measured the distance to the Tuynhuys portico. A little under two hundred yards; no problem for a marksman of his experience.

He had tested the gun with three of his five bullets. With the first two, he found it to be shooting a fraction to the left and adjusted the scope sight to compensate. The third was right on target.

The air was warm and still and he would be shooting down, so he would have to aim a little high.

He hung his jacket on the hook behind the door. Taking off his shoes, he placed them on the floor in front of the bowl where anyone peeping through the narrow gap under the door would expect to see a pair of feet.

At its full stretch, the brass arm of the window did not hold it open far enough. He took an eighteen-inch plastic ruler from the briefcase and by standing it on the outside sill, propped the window open almost horizontally.

The briefcase he placed against the back wall. He looked at his watch again. Twelve twenty-seven.

Stal Plein and the streets below were quiet, closed to traffic. A man in uniform pacing behind the Tuynhuys gate glanced at his watch.

The washroom door opened and sighed closed on its hydraulic arm. A steady splashing sound came from the urinal. He rested the rubber-edged butt of the rifle on the toilet lid and leaned against the wall to wait out the last few minutes.

***

When the policeman at the security desk entered the details of the visitor's identity card on his keyboard, it triggered a buzzer in an office on the first floor.

A young man sitting in front of a monitor screen there read the details and saw that the ID was one of the old ones. Everyone else's in the building had been changed yesterday. It galvanised him into action.

He pressed the transmit button of a handset radio. "Stranger coming in," he said, agitated. "His ID is invalid."

Four men lounging in the next room jumped to their feet and ran out. All wore blue shirts and trousers tucked into rubber-soled combat boots. They carried Uzi machine pistols, with holstered Beretta pistols and two-way radios clipped to their web belts. They sprinted to the stairway next to the bank of lifts.

Assistant Commissioner Mike Miller heard the message in his third floor office at the same time. "Keep talking," he ordered into his radio. "Don't stop him, I want to see what he's doing." He grabbed the hand radio and hurried out.

The young man turned from the monitor to the screen of a closed-circuit television system. It showed a picture from a wide-angle lens high in the granite-walled ground-floor foyer of the burly visitor walking to the lifts, where he touched a panel and the grey metal doors slid open.

"He's going into Number Two lift," the young man said and flicked a switch beneath the screen. It changed to a picture relayed by a lens concealed behind the control panel in the lift and showed a large man with a drooping black moustache wearing a suit and carrying a briefcase.

"He's pressed the fourth floor button."

The four armed men took the steps two at a time to the fourth floor and paused a few steps below it, out of sight around a corner, moments before the lift arrived. In spite of the exertion they were not breathing hard.

The ceiling eyes of the CCTV followed the man out of the lift and down the passage, walking briskly but not fast enough to attract attention, and tracked him into the washroom.

There was no camera in the washroom, a concession to privacy.

Assistant Commissioner Miller came puffing into the passage to find the four men against the wall next to the door, one on one side, two on the other, holding their Uzis erect. The fourth held his machine pistol level and was about to fling the door open and rush in.

"Wait!" Miller hissed. The policeman paused. Miller beckoned him and they moved several paces back in the passage.

"He might have a gun," Miller said, "and we don't want anyone shot if we can avoid it, least of all him. We have a little time, the President won't appear for another eight to ten minutes. Let him get ready in there and think he's getting away with it, then we'll grab him."

They waited five minutes, turning away two men seeking relief.

"Give me your pistol," Miller said, "and come in behind me if all's clear."

He held the Beretta under his jacket and pushed the washroom door wide. Nobody was in sight but the door of the cubicle at the end of the small room was closed. He walked in without attempting to conceal the sounds of his presence.

The four men slipped in behind him without making a sound. He nodded at the cubicle, stepped up to the urinal, and unzipped his fly.

Miller had no urge to urinate. This is a hell of a time to let me down, he thought in wry amusement, and summoned his reserves to produce a satisfying drum and splash against the steel. It would help disguise any slight sound of movement.

He raised his right hand and chopped it down.

***

The assassin watched the gates swing open for the big black limousine gliding across the flagstoned courtyard. He relished the fascination an imminent kill always brought: a sense of unstoppable power, like a leopard about to pounce on a buck.

He rested his left hand gripping the barrel on the windowsill and put the crosshairs of the sight just below the front edge of the portico roof. As usual, the State President or Vice President would emerge from there to grasp the visiting dignitary's hand in the sunlight, for the benefit of the handful of photographers.

Through the ten-power telescope he could see the weave of the red carpet and the dust gathered on the plasterwork facade of the portico.

He settled the stock against his cheek and laid his forefinger on the cool steel of the trigger.

Propelled by the rubber sole of a boot, the cubicle door crashed open behind him.

The assassin whipped in the rifle and whirled in one swift movement. The barrel knocked out the ruler and the fanlight banged shut.

He looked straight into the round black mouths of two Uzis.

"Don't move!" a voice pitched high with tension

shouted.

He was holding the Musgrave straight up in front of him. It was surrender, or ...

He moved very fast. In the fraction of a second, he jerked the rifle down to aim the muzzle at the face of the man nearest him.

What saved the man was the length of the rifle. In the cramped space of the cubicle, the steel-frame stock hooked on the window ledge as the assassin pulled the trigger.

Even with the silencer the shot was loud in the confined space. The high-velocity bullet went over the policeman's head and buried itself in the opposite wall. The policeman fired by reflex. The 9mm Uzi bullets hit the assassin in the face, spraying the window and wall behind him with the contents of his head.

Miller pushed in to see the body crumpled in a heap in the corner with the rifle across his chest.

"God damn it!" he exploded, then said to the policemen, "Sorry, it's not your fault, you did what you had to."

He squeezed into the gap on the other side of the toilet bowl, pushed the window wide and peered out. He was in time to see the President usher a tall fat black man with a leopard-skin cap and a knobby cane, walk from the top of the steps into the Tuynhuys.

Miller stepped back and looked at the corpse, a big man with a drooping black moustache. Who the hell could he be, and who was he working for?

**

A few minutes before two o'clock, the Doctor drained his glass of white wine and dabbed his lips with a crisp napkin. Rising from the long, mirror-polished dining table, he strolled into the large panelled hall, picked up a telephone and dialled a code and a number.

A phone rang in the farmhouse more than a thousand

miles to the north. On the eighth ring it was picked up.

"Yes?"

Doc recognised the voice as the Chairman's. "Everything is fine for tonight," Doc said, "Nineteen hundred, as planned."

"Good, and thank you."

"Good luck."

Doc cut the connection and dialled again, this time the private Cape Town number. The phone was picked up on the first ring.

"It's me," he said before the other party could speak, "it's all set for seven p.m. tomorrow."

He replaced the telephone on its cradle and returned to the table. His hostess smiled up at him and poured black coffee into a small porcelain cup. "Is everything going well?" she asked.

"Perfect, my dear. The perfect end to a lovely lunch."

He decided to take a nap. There was nothing to do but wait.

***

"Signal the commandos to start moving into position at seventeen hundred to be ready for action at nineteen hundred tonight," the Chairman told the former Recce brigadier, "That should give them enough time."

"Yes, sir!" the colonel said, grinning. He gave the order to the two radio operators, who began going through a list of code names, calling each in turn, speaking in Afrikaans.

"Dad says he's coming home at five o'clock this afternoon and wants to eat at seven." Innocuous enough, the kind of message the farmers passed over their local network.

The atmosphere of anxious waiting, that had pervaded the farmhouse for days, evaporated in excitement.

***

"Frans? This is Mike Miller."

"Afternoon, Assistant Commissioner. Any word yet?" Superintendent Louw transferred the phone to his left hand to reach for a ballpoint pen with his right.

"*Ja*, at last. It starts at nineteen hundred tonight."

"That's cutting it a bit fine."

"It couldn't be helped. We picked it up on the phone tap ten minutes ago. The call came from down here in Cape Town but it was too short for us to trace the recipient."

"Okay, sir, we'll get on to it right away."

"I am not coming up, Frans, there's no time, but you know what to do."

"Yes, sir. Everything's ready and everyone's in place."

"Good. And Frans, keep it cool, try to avoid bloodshed. We don't want any more Jopie Fouries." The name of an Afrikaner martyr.

"We'll do our best, Assistant Commissioner, but I hope someone tells *them* that."

"Yes, well, you can but try. Keep me informed, superintendent, I want to know everything that happens, when it happens. And good luck."

Louw put the telephone back on the bedside table and glanced at Captain Ndzimande watching him expectantly from the hotel room's armchair.

"The rebels make their move at seven o'clock tonight, Lucky. We'll make ours at six. You get on to this phone and the radio now and pass the word to everyone."

***

Far south in Cape Town, Miller put down his phone and it promptly rang again. He picked it up and heard the voice of the Vice President.

"Mike," he said, "I've just had word from my man … you know who I mean?"

"Yes, sir."

"The launch is at seven o'clock tomorrow night, nineteen hundred hours. It's in your hands now, understood?"

"Yes, sir, but ..." Miller paused, confused.

"What is it? Is there a problem?"

"We're all set but, er ..." Miller hesitated to correct the Vice President's infallible source, "... you're sure he said nineteen hundred *tomorrow* night, sir?"

"Yes, tomorrow. It's over to you, and good hunting."

The Vice President must have misheard, Miller thought. According to the taped phone tap it was tonight, not tomorrow night.

***

"You can't walk about like that, somebody will shoot you," a cheerful air force captain said. He looked at Ngwenya and grinned. "Especially you, being black. We'll have to find you some civvy rags. About time too, I'd say."

He gave an exaggerated sniff, smiling to show he meant no offence.

Their clothes were stiff with swamp mud and sweat. Ballance felt they were part of him.

"Thanks, Captain. We'd appreciate a shower and shave if you could lend us the necessary. I'm afraid all our gear is stuck in Maputo."

"No trouble, except the toothbrush part. You'll have to use a finger. I think we can find you some overalls. Come with me, you haven't much time."

"Where are we going?"

"At first, Cape Town, then we were told to drop you at Louis Trichardt, which is just around the corner, so to speak. Some policeman wants you." He raised a quizzical eyebrow. "Been up to no good, have you?"

"Yeah, you could say that. Can I phone Jo'burg from here?" Ballance wanted to talk to Penelope, to grasp a straw of normality in the sea of chaos he had been plunged into.

"Rather do it from Trichardt, old man. Time's short."

CHAPTER THIRTY FIVE

Captain Ndzimandze stopped the police van on the gravel track close to the tall game fence. The gate to the Chairman's farm was out of sight behind the next curve of mountainside

Two policemen in mottled camouflage and carrying Uzis dropped from the open back of the van and ran to the fence. One used cutters on a section of the mesh wire and folded it back. They both ducked through.

The time was a quarter to six.

"Give them ten minutes then drive to the entrance," Superintendent Louw said. He turned in the front passenger seat to talk to Ballance and Ngwenya sitting among the eight constables and a sergeant, most of them black, all of them African. "I shouldn't have let you come with us, there might be shooting."

Ngwenya laughed without humour. "Superintendent, after where we've just been, I wouldn't worry."

"There's no way you could keep us from being in at the finish," Ballance added. He was in a grim mood.

Earlier in the afternoon Ndzimandze had met them when the SAAF light plane landed at Louis Trichardt's small airfield and raised his eyebrows at the sight of the two men in SAAF flying overalls, all the officers' mess at Hoedspruit could find for them in a hurry.

"I want to phone Miss Fox," Ballance said as they got into the car.

"I think you'd better speak to the superintendent first," Ndzimandze replied and would say no more, leaving Ballance to worry all the way into the small town.

"What's happened to Penelope?" he asked before Super-intendent Louw could greet him.

"Miss Fox? She's in hospital," he answered and added, seeing the anxiety on Ballance's face, "but don't worry, she's fine, nothing but a fractured wrist and mild shock."

He sat Ballance down in the single armchair and told him about the assassin's murder of her young police guard, his attempt to kill her, the shoot-out with Inspector Stramm, and her fall from the window.

Ballance paled at the thought of the terror she must have felt.

"Which hospital? I want to phone her now, from here."

The clinic said she had checked out the day before. She was not back at work yet. Ballance tried her home number; there was no answer.

"Damn!"

"Look, I said she's all right. You can go and find her to-morrow after we've finished here."

"How the hell did she get involved, superintendent?" Ballance asked.

Superintendent Louw spread his hands in embarrass-ment while he explained how he had asked Penny to delve into the private files of the suspected Free Stater leader, Gideon van Geyssen, and that Van Geyssen must somehow have discovered this.

Ballance's first reaction was anger, most of it aimed at himself for involving her from the outset.

"Van Geyssen?" he asked. "You mean the industrialist, the fellow who gave money to the old National Party?"

"The same."

How deep did the rot reach? Ballance wondered.

They went over what they had learned and done since they had flown to Maputo a four-day aeon ago, looking for missed leads, anything that might help them wrap up the incipient rebellion.

"For a pair of amateurs, you've done pretty well," the superintendent said; high praise from him. With their help the air force and parabats had eliminated the threat of reinforcements from across the border. Louw could concentrate his resources on the rebels at home without worrying about his back.

Venda remained a problem; something was going on there nobody could fathom. At a pinch, troops could go in.

"Tonight you two wait here while we clean up this end," he told Ballance and Ngwenya at five o'clock, when he and Ndzimandze made ready to leave. They had refused point blank, so here they were, on a mountainside waiting to raid a house.

Superintendent Louw sighed and watched the lowering sun draw blankets of shadow over the flanks of the mountains for the night. The time was five to six.

"Move," he said.

The sight of a police van coming around the slope of hill a hundred yards away, alarmed the young guard in khaki behind the security gate. He unlimbered his sporting rifle and drew back the bolt to ram a cartridge into the breech while he ran towards the gatehouse telephone.

"Stop or we shoot!" a voice ordered from behind him. He spun around to see two men in camouflage less than twenty paces away, half hidden in bushes, aiming machine pistols at him.

For a moment he vacillated. Standing brave guard with a big rifle and bold ideas was one thing; confronting reality was another. His will collapsed and he held both arms high over his head, still holding the rifle.

One man took it from him, the other handcuffed him to the steel gatepost, went through his pockets to find his keys and unlocked the gate to let the van through.

Ten more men jumped from the back. The superintendent and the captain led four men towards the farmhouse, the others spread out. Ballance and Ngwenya followed a short distance behind.

**

"I can't understand it," the ex-Recce brigadier said, worried. "We've been trying to raise Manjacane's units and the people in Venda for the last twenty minutes and there's no response. We can't even get Manjacane himself, he seems to be off the air."

The time was ten to six.

"Are you sure the radio is working? Have you tried all the frequencies we've been using?"

"The whole lot, sir. And there's nothing wrong with the transceiver. We tested it umpteen times."

The Chairman frowned; the last thing he needed was a communications breakdown. The arrangement was to give his black allies ninety minutes' notice; they should have been in position and listening long ago.

He had heard the frantic newscasts of the attack on Komatipoort and in Mozambique and assumed the Renamo mutineers were also striking at Pafuri, Punda Maria and Shingwedzi as they were supposed to.

The Venda revolutionaries had reported days ago they were ready and waiting.

"Keep trying, for God's sake. We *must* tell them! We have to make the announcement at seven p.m. on the dot."

A single shot went off on the verandah outside, startling them.

The brigadier's hand dived for the gun at his hip.

"Wait!" the Chairman snapped. "It's probably some young fool shooting at shadows."

The brigadier slid the heavy .45 calibre Colt semi-automatic back into its holster.

The Chairman strode across the wide lounge to the front door. He had never reckoned on trouble coming here; the place was so secret the perimeter guards were a formality. So his astonishment was great when he saw one of them lying on the verandah with blood leaking from a hole in his leg and his face screwed up in pain.

It was still greater when he saw the police van down at the gate and two men in casual clothes but with "policeman" written all over them coming up the front steps, walking well apart and holding Uzis. Beyond them in the dusk stood four combat-uniformed constables, also with Uzis and ready to use them.

"Dr Nicolas Albertyn?"

The stocky greying man on the steps spoke Afrikaans politely, as if at a formal meeting, but the gun in his right fist pointed impolitely at the Chairman's middle.

"Who are you," the Chairman demanded with an authority he did not feel. "What the devil are you doing here? This is private property!"

"I am Superintendent Louw of the South African Police Service and this is Captain Ndzimandze. We would like to talk with you."

To his right Ndzimandze twitched up the muzzle of his machine pistol. "*Don't!*" he said sharply. "There are others aiming at you!"

Behind the Chairman, the brigadier hovered for seconds on the brink of death, then re-holstered the Colt. His face twisted with the realisation he was too old for this sort of thing; it was suddenly important to live.

Superintendent Louw turned his back on him. "Smit! Matsebula! Moloi! Around the house!" he ordered. "Johnson, see to that man on the stoep."

He strode up the steps and inside, brushing past the deflated brigadier. The Chairman followed with a dignity he struggled to muster; his world was teetering.

"What is the meaning of this?" he blustered with resonant indignation. "You cannot walk in here, into my home, waving guns."

Superintendent Louw paused halfway across the big entrance hall and turned back to face the senatorial old man. His stare was bleak. "I most certainly can, Dr Albertyn," he said. "I have every right to enter premises where assassination and mass murder and treason are organised ..."

A brief flurry of shots echoed outside, most of them the

quick flat chatter of Uzis.

"... and as for guns, you appear to have too many here already, a remarkable number for the protection of even so eminent a professor of theology as you."

"Oh, Nico ...!" a woman's voice wailed and the Chairman's plump wife came running through the passage from the kitchen, apron flapping. "There are people out there shooting at us! They've shot Hansie!"

The last shreds of the Chairman's confidence drained from him. His leg muscles turned to jelly and he groped for an armchair and sank into it. His wife ran to him and he buried his head in his hands.

Ndzimandze entered, the Uzi in his right hand and the brigadier's Colt .45 in his left, and walked down the passage. A minute later he returned, shepherding the two radio operators. They held their arms straight up over their heads.

He made them stand against the lounge wall with a policeman guarding them.

"There's a big new Varcom C21H in there you could talk to Mars with," he told the superintendent. "These two characters were under the table, they're the signallers."

"Dr Albertyn," Louw said, "you will use your radio now to call off your stormtroopers right now and cancel this whole uprising."

"No." The Chairman's face was haggard but his voice was determined. "No. We have worked too long for this. Do what you wish with me, there are many more of us. It is too late to stop now."

The superintendent stalked across the room, placed his hands on the arms of the chair, leaned forward and thrust his face close to the old man's.

"Dr Albertyn," he said, his voice low and urgent, "where are your famous Christian principles now? If you do not stop this stupid rebellion, a great many people will die, young men, the pride of your people. And it will be a terrible waste because they will all be *your* men. You see,"

342

he said, half in truth, "we know all about your plans, we know where your men will strike tonight, and we know they will do it at seven o'clock, in less than an hour.

"And we are ready for them, doctor. So if you want to save their lives, talk to them. Cancel the operation. Tell them to give themselves up and hand over their weapons. The government is not vengeful, it is ready to talk and it will be generous if you come to your senses. There has been too much killing."

Louw stepped back when two more short bursts were fired outside. The captain came in the front door with Ballance and Ngwenya trailing behind him. His face was beaded with perspiration.

"We have rounded all of them up, superintendent. Another three are wounded in the legs but not seriously."

"And our men?"

"All fine, sir. The resistance was less than we expected. There was not much heart in it."

An unexpected ally came to the superintendent's aid.

"Nico," the Chairman's wife urged, kneeling at her husband's feet and grasping his hand, "please do what he asks. Four of our beautiful young boys have been hurt already ... through God's will they are not dead. If you let this thing go on now, when they know all about us, God may not be so kind."

For a long moment, the Chairman closed his eyes as if in prayer. When he opened them, he spoke with resignation. "I will do what you ask. I am not betraying our cause by trying to save lives if the battle is lost before it has begun." He pushed himself erect.

Louw sighed and said to the captain, "Perhaps we can round up the rest without a shot being fired."

The clap and concussion of an explosion shook the house. Thick grey smoke and debris erupted into the passage. Things crashed in the kitchen and dust drifted down from the thatch.

Ndzimandze ran into the passage masking his nose and

mouth with a handkerchief. In seconds he emerged from the smoke, coughing. "The radio," he spluttered, "Gone ... blown up."

The sudden burst of laughter was as surprising as the explosion. Louw spun around to see one of the two signallers backed against the wall laughing in hysteria.

"You can do fuck-all now, you fucking coward!" the other one shouted at the Chairman in Afrikaans, and spat on the floor. "It's just a bleddy pity you and these fucking cops weren't in there when the bomb went off!"

Shocked by the language, the Chairman's wife covered her ears with her hands.

Ndzimandze reached the signaller in three strides and smacked him so hard with an open hand he was lifted off his feet and fell in a heap on the floor. The other one stopped laughing when Ndzimandze hit him in the stomach.

"Pigs," the captain muttered.

The Chairman was stunned; without radio communication he was powerless to do anything.

"Do you know how to call up your people?" the superintendent snapped.

"We are using the Marnet frequencies."

"Marnet! The bloody cheek!" Superintendent Louw turned to Ndzimandze. "Take the good doctor here to the van, switch our radio to the Marnet frequencies and put him on the mike. Quick man, there's no time to spare. Captain, handcuff all the prisoners and lock them up in a room under guard. Bring Mrs Albertyn with you."

Ten minutes later, as night settled on the peaks and valleys, the van raced out of the gate, leaving the sentry handcuffed to it coughing in their dust.

The time was six-fifteen pm.

While the superintendent hurled the van around the curves on the way back to Louis Trichardt, Ndzimandze switched from frequency to frequency and the Chairman spoke into the microphone.

344

"Commandos of the Free Stater Movement, this is your Chairman speaking ..."

None responded because he had left out the pre-arranged identification codes.

***

The time was five minutes past seven p.m.

Pieter-Dirk, age nineteen, virgin, son of a prosperous rancher, first-year university student , was one of ten men manning an improvised road block, just south of Louis Trichardt past the junction of the Venda road and the N1 highway, which led to Pretoria and Johannesburg, enemy territory, home of the liberals.

In the centre of the roadblock stood a massive Caterpillar bulldozer in bright unwarlike yellow, its huge shiny steel blade resting on the tarmac. Big farm tractors filled the gaps on either side and harrows and multi-disc ploughs covered the grassy shoulders.

It looked impregnable, an obstacle to stop a tank. In the ten minutes since the procession of farm machines had trundled down the highway behind the bulldozer and assembled into the road block, scoring the road surface, half a dozen cars had approached.

They had slowed for the battery of winking red and blue lamps and turned to speed away, when their headlights picked out the wall of machinery and the men with guns.

Cocky and confident, the rebels saw a pair of very bright lights approaching in the distance.

"The man must be using his spotlights or maybe it's a tractor coming to join us," joked the young captain in charge.

The lights came at a steady speed. The men could not see what they belonged to but heard an unusual drone of engine.

"*Ja*, it's a tractor," Pieter-Dirk said, anticipating the surprise its driver would get.

The lights were fifty metres away when the men could

discern a bulky angular shape. Several of the rebels recognised it from their national service days. Their flesh went cold.

It was a Ratel, the six-wheeled, high-speed armoured personnel carrier and combat vehicle as tough as its namesake, the honey badger. It carried a 30mm cannon and 7.65mm machine guns. The shadowy shapes of several more appeared in the dimness beyond it.

The big squat vehicle glided to a stop thirty paces away and rocked on giant tyres, its halogen beams brilliant on the makeshift roadblock. The drone of its Rolls- Royce engine fell to an idling thrum. The small rectangles of bulletproof windows set in the sloped planes of its matt green front reflected the winking red and blue lights like the eyes of a spider.

It was pure menace. For the first time Pieter-Dirk had a niggling doubt about the good sense of what he was doing.

But not the *veldkornet*, the young captain, a fanatic sustained by his faith in white nationalism. "Fire!" he yelled from behind the shelter of the thick bulldozer blade, and loosed off a burst from an AK-47.

A fusillade came from the assault and sporting rifles of the others. Bullets pinged and caromed harmlessly from the Ratel's steel nose, leaving little shiny streaks of copper and lead.

Watching this futile effort from inside the Ratel, Captain Etienne Rossouw felt sick in the stomach. He did not want to shoot at his own kind, or anybody for that matter.

But his orders were unequivocal: clear road blocks, suppress all resistance, shoot if there is no alternative.

There was no alternative here. His driver could take the Ratel through the bush around the barrier with ease but that was not removing the barrier.

He could not afford to delay. If they had AK-47s they might well have an RPG-7, a tank killer.

Rossouw had long admired the old British colonial tactic for suppressing mobs: shoot the ringleader.

"That man in front, behind the 'dozer blade," he snapped into the intercom, "cannon, fire one round."

The rebels' ragged fire continued. The captain ducked behind the bulldozer blade to load a fresh magazine.

He did not see the black hole of the big gun come down to bear on him. The other rebels did and stopped shooting. Eight scrambled for cover behind the machines. Awed by the sight, Peter-Dirk stayed where he was on top of the bulldozer.

The 30mm armour-piercing shell punched a neat round hole through the thick steel of the blade and blew up the young captain. Much of him was spread on what was left of the Caterpillar's flat radiator grille. The rest flew high like rags in the wind.

The impact jolted the Caterpillar back on its locked tracks. Pieter-Dirk dived in panic from the bulldozer, broke an arm when he hit the road seven feet below and raced back along it yelling in pain and fright.

It was the last straw for the other young men. They jumped down and ran after him.

Two soldiers climbed out of a hatch in the Ratel's top and under the protection of its guns, they started the bulldozer and tractors and drove them off the road.

They climbed back in and the Ratel cruised past on huge tyres to look for more trouble.

**

In Louis Trichardt, four khaki-clad men startled passers-by outside the closed post office when they tumbled from a kombi at seven o'clock, brandishing pistols. They were escorting a fifth, a telephone company employee with a bunch of keys.

Inside, the employee found a relay switch and pulled it down, cutting power to the automatic telephone exchange and thereby cutting Louis Trichardt's main communications and those of a number of smaller communities whose phone systems channelled through it.

The job done, the five men boiled out of the post office door waving their handguns, paused to lock it while a few curious onlookers watched them, and roared away in the kombi.

Five minutes later another telephone company employee emerged from a darkened office inside the building where he had been waiting with a policeman, and switched the power back on.

***

Ten raiders jumped from two 4x4 trucks, which stopped in front of the police station with screeching tyres and rushed up the steps, not noticing that two streetlamps were out.

The black policeman at the door did not attempt to resist when they seized his shotgun. Four raiders stayed there, crouching, aiming AK-47s up and down the empty street.

Another jabbed his gun at the constable controlling the security gate and ordered him to open it, which he did. They ran inside.

In the charge office, Captain Ndzimandze in shirtsleeves lolled in a wooden chair with his heels on the edge of a desk, and a uniformed constable stood at the charge counter with his head bent over paperwork.

The constable glanced up, showing no surprise at the bristle of guns. "*Ja*, what can we—"

"Shut up! This is a raid!" shouted a man with a three-legged swastika on his shirtfront.

Captain Ndzimandze slid his feet off the desk, stood up and shambled to the counter, imposingly tall. Two rebels levelled their rifles at his chest.

"Put down those guns before you get hurt," he said in a conversational tone.

"We are taking over this station," the rebel leader blustered, unsettled by his calmness.

"No, you are not."

Doors slammed open at the side of the room. The rebels whirled and stared down the gaping tunnels of six semi-automatic twelve-bore shotguns in the hands of men in camouflage.

Two more rose from behind the counter on either side of Ndzimandze. *"Don't think of it!"* he shouted at the rebels. "They're a SWAT team and they'll kill you!"

The leader spun back in rage, swinging his AK-47 towards Ndzimandze. Before he could complete the turn, a shotgun boomed and a concentrated load of SSG hit him in the chest, obliterating the bastardised swastika, killing him and hurling him against the counter.

For aching seconds the other five and the policemen faced each other, taut as sprinters in the starting blocks.

Moving with slow care, one of the rebels bent at the knees, placed his gun on the floor and straightened. The remaining four looked at each other and then they too laid down their weapons. The tension drained from the room.

Outside, the four on the steps heard a voice say, "Don't move or we'll shoot." They turned to see eight shotgun-armed men emerge from the darkness at the sides of the building, just as a shotgun roared inside.

The choice was stark: open fire and die, or give up. They dropped their weapons.

The SWAT team locked the captives in the police cells. Two constables rolled the corpse in a blanket and dumped it on a stainless steel table in the mortuary room at the back of the station.

Ndzimandze went into the radio office and called up Superintendent Louw.

"All secure here, sir," he reported. "One of them's dead and the others are behind bars."

"Thanks, Lucky. I'll be there as soon as I've mopped up here."

***

The eight men on the main road at Dendron, south-west of Louis Trichardt, had enjoyed an easy evening at their barrier of two ten-ton trucks overlapping across the road so vehicles had to slow and turn at right angles to zigzag between them.

By seven-thirty they had stopped nineteen cars coming from the south and allowed all to enter their new republic. All the occupants were local people or innocent travellers. No traffic had come from the north.

At eight-thirty p.m. a voice called to them in Afrikaans through a loud hailer from the north, their home ground.

"Paul! Theo! Johnny! Cornelius! Fanie! And you other three! Put down those bleddy guns and come out with your hands up!"

The surprised rebels turned to look for its source but could see nothing. The night was made darker by the flashing lights they had put on the trucks, which also illuminated them like stage lights.

"I said stop this nonsense, you bleddy fools! There are twenty of us here, all armed, and you haven't got a cat's chance!"

The voice continued at a lower volume, aimed at people unseen, "If we have to shoot, aim for the legs. We don't want to kill the stupid buggers."

Rooted by astonishment, the rebels stood fingering their AK-47s and peering unseeing into the night, until one reacted.

He dived flat behind the big wheels of a truck and started firing wild bursts through the narrow gap between two double sets of tyres. It galvanised the others, some followed him underneath the trucks, three started running off the road.

"Jesus Christ!" the voice in the dark exclaimed, as bullets whistled down the road and clipped twigs from the scrub. Then the fire was returned in heavy double-taps from R1 rifles and snapping bursts from R4s.

The running men were hit first, all in the legs. Two lay prone on the tar, the third tried to crawl away, screaming.

Bullets punctured the tyres in front of the man who started the shooting. They deflated, trapping his gun barrel and his left arm against the road in a crushing grip of hard rubber.

"Stop! Stop it!" a rebel yelled at the top of his voice.

The gunfire sputtered out. He emerged from beneath a truck with his hands high. Three more followed him.

"Dammed fools," the voice in the dark said. "Okay, men, you can come out now but be careful."

The men who walked into the flashing light were a police sergeant and nineteen farmers and farmers' sons, all members of the local citizen force commando.

They tended the three wounded men with tourniquets and bandages.

The sergeant, owner of the voice and the neighbourhood policeman for many years, knelt to watch while two men with a truck jack lifted the punctured tyres off the trapped rebel's numb arm.

"Yussus, Theo, but you're a lot of bleddy idiots," he said, shaking his head sadly, "Nobody likes a black government, man, but this is not the way to change things."

***

By seven forty-five, the two men in the bar of the Holiday Inn at Thohoyandou were becoming agitated.

"Something's gone haywire," the larger one said, looking at the clock on the wall for the twentieth time, "they should have been here at seven, maybe seven-fifteen at the latest."

"So what are we going to do?" asked the other, who was on his third beer.

The big man thought for a moment.

"You stay here in case they turn up," he said. "I'll use the radio."

In the double-cab truck parked outside he turned on the transceiver under the dashboard, checked the tuning for headquarters and pressed the transmit button.

"Tabernacle, Tabernacle, Tabernacle, this is Number Seventeen. Come in please."

He released the button. Nothing came over the speaker except the hollowness of empty ether. In the Chairman's house the big Varcom transceiver was spread over the communications room in thousands of broken pieces.

He returned to the bar and drained his brandy and soda.

"Come on, we're getting out of here," he muttered. "The bloody Vendas have either pulled a fast one on us or they've been stopped somehow."

On their way out they saw no extraordinary activity, no indication of anything unusual. The people were going their way as usual and the few policemen about looked relaxed, with none of the ant-nest commotion they expected.

One thing was sure: the promised back-up from Venda was not materialising.

At Ratombo they came to the road block the rebels had been setting up when they passed on their way to Thohoyandou over an hour earlier. Maybe the fellows here have heard something, the big man thought, and stopped the truck.

"Mr Pieterse and Mr Jonas?" a voice asked at the side window.

He looked out and his jaw dropped. The man wore a police uniform.

"Please get out," the policeman said. The Uzi in his hand made it a command. "We know who you are and what you are doing. You are under arrest."

***

Superintendent Louw arrived at the police station in a yellow police truck with Ballance and Ngwenya riding in front with him and seven men in the wire-caged back.

The seven, all past middle age, were shepherded into the now crowded cells and their handcuffs removed.

"They're all the local ringleaders we could find," the superintendent said to Ndzimandze. "The others weren't at home, maybe they got wind of us. But they won't get far, there's an alert out for them."

"Superintendent, it's eight o'clock. Don't you want to speak to the Assistant Commissioner?"

The superintendent had forgotten; the Assistant Commissioner would be pacing a hole in his carpet.

He went into the station commander's office, vacant since Ndzimandze had arrested the man at a quarter to seven, and tried the telephone: it was working. It rang once before the receiver in Cape Town was snatched off the cradle.

"Yes?" Assistant Commissioner Miller snapped.

"It's Superintendent Louw, sir—"

"Where the hell have you been? Why haven't you called?"

The superintendent could see the Assistant Commissioner's frowning red face in his mind's eye.

"I'm sorry, sir, we've been very busy, but it's all just about wrapped up now."

"Tell me."

"We've picked up more than two hundred rebels so far, sir, not counting those in Messina and a couple of small places we haven't heard from yet. Five dead at the last count and maybe a dozen wounded, none serious. There was little resistance when they saw we had them taped. No casualties on our side. A little bit of public disturbance but we managed to keep the operation pretty quiet."

"You expecting any more trouble?"

"I doubt it. Their heart's not in it. They fizzled quickly when they saw what they were up against and realised their leaders were in the bag."

"I thought that whole damn region was fascist, superintendent. What happened to the public uprising they expected?"

"We caught the boss man before he could broadcast a public announcement and spread the news, so nobody knows what's happening right now. But our people will be on full alert through the night and tomorrow, just in case.

The air force brought Ballance here, as you asked, and he told me about the Mozambicans, but I don't know what's going on in Venda."

A long silence followed on the phone. Superintendent Louw wondered if the connection had been broken.

"Assistant Commissioner?"

"I'm here, Superintendent. I'm just enjoying the first good news I've had in a bloody week. You needn't worry about Venda, that's been sorted out. An ANC man, the one who escaped the massacre there, he went in on his own bat and did us a favour by liquidating the heart of the opposition in a personal vendetta."

"And the army, sir? What about the brigadier up at Messina?"

"That's also sorted out. The officers DHQ sent there locked up the armoury and arrested the brig before he could get started. Half the troops are under arrest by the other half."

The superintendent's shoulders sagged in relief. That left a few loose threads to be tied in the immediate area.

"Thanks, Assistant Commissioner. I'll stay a few more days."

"No you won't, Frans. The SAAF will have a Mercurius at Louis Trichardt tomorrow morning to bring you to Cape Town. Bring Ballance with you and that ANC fellow ... what's his name? ... Ngwenya."

"But sir, there's a lot of cleaning up to do, and what about all the other places like Pietersburg, Tzaneen and Warmbaths ...?"

"There are others to handle all that. You come here. That's a presidential order, Frans. You've done a bloody fine job."

CHAPTER THIRTY SIX

"We're stopping at Jo'burg, we can't meet the President looking like this." Superintendent Louw looked down at his clothes creased by a long night's work. "A car will meet us at Waterkloof and I'll drop you at your place in Sandton and pick you up in an hour."

He looked Ngwenya up and down.

"I don't know what we're going to do with you. We'll have to try and fit you out in Cape Town."

"No problem, Mr Policeman, I'll just wrap a tablecloth around my waist and stick a feather in my hair and go as a Swazi in full dress."

Ballance smiled at the superintendent's frown. "Some of my stuff should fit you, Temba," he said. "We can find you a suit at Sandton City on the way out."

"I've got no money."

"You can pay me back when you become minister of education."

The executive jet was arrowing through the high sky at top speed, racing its own sound. The three sat in swivel chairs at a low table in a tubular lounge that smelt of leather and panelling.

He could get used to this sybaritic life, the superintendent thought, sipping coffee. He felt relaxed for the first time in weeks, since the day something had niggled at his mind about the body found in a Hillbrow basement.

He had been reluctant to leave Louis Trichardt but by dawn the police, army and SWAT teams he had positioned, backed up by trusted members of citizen force commandos, had brought in more than seven hundred and fifty rebels for the loss of several dozen lives. The captives were under guard at the army base at Messina and the air base at Pietersburg south of Louis Trichardt. They had come from all over South Africa.

Scores were surrendering, dispirited without leadership and disillusioned by failure, and handing in a formidable armoury of weapons. They were being charged and released on bail.

There had been two serious clashes.

One was in a mining town where five soldiers died in a heavy firefight with khaki-uniformed members of an ultra-conservative private army, all with battle experience with the South African forces in Angola. The rebels had quit after they witnessed fifteen of their number shot dead.

The other was in Pietersburg, where seven government men died in a night-long conflict with the same illegal army, who only gave up when their ammunition ran out and they had lost twelve men.

The back of the rebellion was well broken. All the members of the Free Staters' Committee had been found in various parts of the country ... except one, the elusive Dr Gideon van Geyssen.

But he alone could do nothing.

The superintendent had left the clean-up to Ndzimandze, the SWAT leader and the army commander at Messina.

Less than an hour later the slender jet touched down at Waterkloof and taxied to a huge grey hangar away from the terminal. A police driver waited for them in a big black Camry with tinted windows.

***

Ballance was uneasy about returning to his townhouse. The neighbours had been far from amiable on the night of the bombing.

"One hour," Louw said as they stopped outside the

familiar brick-walled complex. He was wearing a broad smile.

Ballance and Ngwenya walked up the path. The front door and its shattered jamb had been replaced. Seeing it, Ballance realised he had no key. He ran to the kerb but the Camry was already rounding the corner.

"Damn!" he swore.

"What's up, *bra*?"

"I don't have a key." Ballance was staring, hands on hips, after the departed car.

"You don't need one, man."

"What do you mean?" Ballance turned around and his eyes widened in surprise.

The door was open and Penelope stood framed in it, waiting. Her brushed golden hair fell about the shoulders of a pale blue summer dress. She was smiling in delight and her eyes shone.

"Penny!" he yelled, so loud pigeons fluttered from the roof, and ran to her, "Penny!"

They hugged each other and they kissed until she gasped for breath, and he lifted her off the ground and buried his face in the sweet-scented softness of her hair, the rest of the world forgotten.

"Thank God," she whispered into his throat, "oh, thank God. I thought you were never coming back."

"Hey," Ngwenya said, bringing them back to earth, "we've got one hour."

They went inside. Most of the bomb damage had been repaired. The windows had new glass and the walls patched and repainted. The lounge suite was still full of shrapnel holes.

"Your neighbours did this," Penelope said, "with some insurance help. The man across the garden there, Mr Cartwright, said they were ashamed of the way they reacted that night."

"How come you're here?"

"I couldn't go home when I left the clinic. Joe Stramm,

the policeman who saved my life and is still in the clinic, suggested I come here. He said it would be safe with that awful Smith dead."

"Coffee," said Ngwenya, emerging from the kitchen with a tray, "and then you'd better pack, Jeff."

Ngwenya took Penelope's wrist encased in a light plastic cast in his hand and looked at it.

"You had a rough time, madam, but it's all over now."

"I hope so, Temba. I don't want to go through anything like that again. What have you two been up to?"

"We'll tell you all about it on the plane."

"On the plane?" Ballance's gaze switched from one to the other. They were grinning.

"Yeah, *bra*. I guess I've blown the surprise. The superintendent's fixed for Penny to come with us to Cape Town. Figures you need someone to look after you because you're always getting your ass in a trap, and I can't be nursemaid all the time."

"You lovely great bastards!" Ballance laughed. "That's terrific! Come on Penny, help me pack."

They could not help touching each other. In the bedroom Ballance wrapped his arms about her and kissed her, feeling her slim firm body pressing against his, the softness and warmth of her through the thin dress. The bed was right behind her and they still had thirty-five minutes.

She felt his desire and stepped back. "Not now," she purred in mock disapproval, "you'll crease my dress."

"That's right," Ngwenya called from the living room and Penelope blushed: he had heard every word.

Sighing, Ballance pulled clothes from drawers and cupboards which she packed into a soft case. Her own things were already packed. Ngwenya selected several of Ballance's shirts and socks, a belt and a tie and found a pair of comfortable black slip-on shoes.

Louw knocked on the door on the hour. His tailored suit was charcoal grey with a faint stripe. His grin was huge.

"Superintendent, I owe you," Ballance said with one arm around Penelope.

At Sandton City, he took Ngwenya, still wearing the pilot's overalls, into a men's shop and emerged half an hour later with him transformed by a dark blue off-the-peg suit.

"If the president doesn't like this I'll break off negotiations," Ngwenya muttered. "It cost a goddamn fortune."

Flying level at high altitude, the Mercurius was as stable as a mansion. The co-pilot emerged through the curtain separating the crew deck from the mini-lounge, extracted bottles, glasses and ice from a cupboard concealed in the panelling and served drinks and little triangular sandwiches.

"Compliments of the airline," he said. "Help yourselves if you'd like another."

Ballance had already heard about the assassin's attack on Penelope from the superintendent, but demanded that she tell the story again. The telling revived chilling memories and she shivered in spite of the cabin's air-conditioned warmth.

The Karoo slipped by far below in an abstract of browns, greys, whites and random lines. The jet slanted lower until the earth became real again and rocky crags of towering mountains reached up, then fell away to the patchwork quilt of the Cape winelands. Table Mountain stood like a monument across Table Bay.

When the government wants to it can lay it on thick, Ballance thought as the stretched Mercedes Benz 500 carried them from the airport. No wonder people competed to become cabinet ministers. It stopped at the Vineyard Hotel in Newlands.

"We'll be collected at five-thirty," the superintendent said. "We meet the president at six p.m. He wants to hear the whole story, including yours, Miss Fox ... Penelope. So I suggest you have a rest. It could be a long evening."

Ngwenya grinned at Ballance. "Rest well, *bra*."

Ballance glared at him.

The French doors of the room opened on to a small, low-walled patio and emerald-green lawn shaded by gnarled old oaks. Beyond it steep, tree-cloaked suburbs rose to the awesome crags and shoulders of Devil's Peak, sharp against the clean blue of the sky.

Penelope kicked off her shoes, bounced on the floral cover of the double bed and flopped on her back, arms stretched above her head.

"Who wants lunch?" she said.

Ballance closed the French doors and drew the curtains across them, leaving the room dim.

"I do," he said, "and you're it."

She stuck out her tongue at him and shifted to make space on the edge of the bed. He sat and buried his fingers in the silky mass of her hair, stroking it. Penelope closed her eyes dreamily, pulled his other hand to her and kissed the palm.

They stayed like this for a long time, he sitting and she lying with her head against him, savouring the simple pleasure of being in each other's presence again, knowing a whole afternoon lay before them, a whole lifetime. He bent to kiss her on the lips.

He tried to undo the buttons of her dress and she smiled at him.

"They're for show," she said, trickling her fingers up his back, "The zip's behind."

It slipped off. She pulled off her underwear and lay back. Ballance sat still, admiring the gentle curves and swells and long strong legs. He traced his fingers over her and felt her tauten.

"You too," she whispered, sitting up to undress him, tossing his clothes on the carpet.

They lay down and wrapped their arms around each other, not moving for long minutes until neither could wait any more. He freed himself from her arms and

360

pushed her on to her back, then rested on one elbow for a moment to admire her, her blue eyes watching him through half-closed lids. Then he leaned across and lowered himself into her. Immediately they lifted into rapture. She cried out and folded her arms and legs around him, skin hot against skin.

He tried to prolong each second, but their hunger took control. "Now," she whispered. "Now!" Eyes shut, he felt weightless, borne on a cloud of sensation, as they lunged and rocked until they shuddered to completion and collapsed exhausted.

She looked into his eyes from inches away. "I love you," she said.

He kissed her, just touching her lips. "I love you." He hugged her and she squeaked.

They lay coiled together for a long time, silent in their thoughts.

"Jeff," she murmured in his ear, "Don't you dare leave me."

"I won't. I couldn't. Besides ..." he raised himself on an elbow and grinned down at her, "... where else would I find a lunch like this?"

"Pig!" She hugged him, gripping with hidden muscles, feeling him filling her, moving again. "And we still have two hours ..."

***

Dr Gideon van Geyssen listened to the morning news with dismay.

"An uprising by a group of rebels wanting to create an independent state in the Northern, North West and Mpumalanga provinces was squashed last night by security forces within hours of beginning .... number of fatalities not yet known but not expected to be high .... the leaders, including a prominent theologian, have been detained ... police expect to round up the rest within a day ... many armed rebels arrested or have surrendered

... the rebellion has been described by the State President as a futile effort by a handful of misguided fanatics ... the government is not concerned about the effect on the future ... praise for the firm action has come from all parties in Parliament ... the extra-Parliamentary conservative alliance has condemned the brutal repression and reiterated demands for an independent white state ..."

After the first shock of the news, the Doctor's mind moved into high gear, revising his tactics to meet the situation. Something had misfired. They had been stopped before they had a chance.

He wondered what had happened to the backup they had organised with meticulous care from Mozambique and Venda. The news had mentioned nothing about them. Either they had reneged at the last minute, or they, too, had been beaten before they could begin. He had no way of knowing.

The Doctor believed there was no alternative to independence for whites. Multi-party democracy meant black majority rule, plain and simple, which had proved to be the formula for political, economic and social calamity throughout Africa.

The Free Staters debacle was a serious setback. His plans would have to go into temporary storage.

It would take a little time to regenerate the right conditions for the birth of a separate white state. His mind was already working.

CHAPTER THIRTY SEVEN

They arrived together at the Tuynhuys, Superintendent Louw, Penelope, Ballance, Ngwenya and Assistant Commissioner Miller. The Vice President met them at the top of the steps behind a screen of watchful security men.

Familiar with the procedures at the Presidential residence, the Assistant Commissioner Miller was relaxed and confident as he introduced the four to the nation's number two.

Surrounded by the protocols of power, Louw was nervous but concealed it behind the kind of wooden expression he wore when questioning suspects. He noticed that Ballance and Miss Fox were also tense, although Ngwenya appeared as phlegmatic as always. He hoped the whole business would be over with soon.

Recognising the nerves, the Vice President turned his charm up full.

"Miss Fox, I am delighted to meet you," he said, bowing and raising her hand to his lips with old-fashioned courtesy, "I hope you have recovered from that terrible ordeal."

In a kingfisher blue dress that accentuated her pale hair and ivory skin and did full justice to her slim figure, Penelope was luminous beside the men in their dark suits.

"Thank you, sir," she smiled, with an inclination of her head that swung her hair.

The Vice President shook Louw's hand. "Welcome, superintendent, I'm glad to see you looking so relaxed. Ah, Mr Ballance and Mr Ngwenya," he beamed, shaking their hands, "It's a pleasure to meet you at last. I've been sharing your adventures vicariously with great admiration."

He ushered them into a long reception room decorated in warm shades of muted pastel with comfortable armchairs arranged at the far end.

The President stood there in an elegant dark suit, his cropped grey hair striking against the dark of his lined face, his black eyes smiling a welcome. He radiated benign charisma.

Beside him towered a tall, broad-shouldered white man with granite features, also in a dark suit. Even across the length of the room, they felt the impact of his personality.

They stopped in surprise. All recognised Dr Gideon van Geyssen, the financier, philanthropist and advisor to the President, the shadowy figure behind the rebels. The very man every policeman was looking for.

Louw stood anchored, his face a picture of shock and bewilderment. "It can't be ... Van Geyssen? Here? It's not possible ..." he breathed, not taking his eyes off the man, who stared back almost with contempt.

Assistant Commissioner Miller's face was grim.

The Vice President watched with amusement.

"Ah yes," he said, enjoying the moment, "I believe you've been looking everywhere for our good friend, Dr Gideon van Geyssen. Well, gentlemen, here he is."

His obvious pleasure at the surprise he had caused confused Louw even more. Miller composed his features into a semblance of calm.

The President greeted each in turn in his gentle modulated accent, now familiar to millions.

"Miss Fox," he smiled, his voice gentle, "it is always a pleasure to meet a fellow lawyer. Ah, our academic friend," he turned to Ballance, eyes twinkling. "Your periodic papers and essays have kept me entertained and informed. But," the twinkle disappeared, "now I am very much in debt to you."

Ballance flushed with embarrassment and mumbled his thanks. While the President was talking to Ngwenya, Dr Gideon van Geyssen was greeting the superintendent.

"I must compliment you on a fine job," he said. He did not offer to shake hands.

Obviously still bewildered, Louw moved on to make way for Penelope, murmuring as he did so, "This is not going to be an easy night."

Intrigued to meet the man whose personal files she had raided, she replied, "He must have sent that bloody little killer to my apartment." She looked up at van Geyssen's face, parted by a smile like a crack in rock, as he greeted her with a platitude, touching her hand.

When the little rituals of etiquette were completed, the President beckoned a thin, uniformed steward hovering in the background, a familiar figure in the lounges of Parliament for many years.

The man poured their drinks at a stinkwood cabinet and served them on an antique silver tray balanced on the fingertips of his right hand, then left the room.

"I ... I don't understand ..." Superintendent Louw muttered, half to himself, unable to keep his eyes off the *eminence grise* of the Free Stater movement, the man he had hunted so hard. The man who had set in motion the attempt to murder Miss Fox, in which one policeman was killed and another grievously wounded.

"I'm beginning to," Miller, standing close, muttered, "and I don't bloody believe it."

The President looked around the small group and cleared his throat.

"The reason you are here is for me to express my heartfelt thanks, both for myself and on behalf of the nation, for what all of you have done to stave off disaster," he said. "I will ask the vice president, who has been dealing with the situation on my behalf, to explain why we are doing it in this way."

He stepped to one side and the Vice President, glass in hand, stood with his back to a flower-banked fireplace.

"The president should have been hosting a full-scale function tonight to honour all of you for what you have done for the new South Africa," he said. "But I am afraid your actions must remain secret for the time being. While you deserve public recognition, the publicity could very easily exacerbate the still volatile national situation. If what you have done became public, your actions would be exploited without any doubt by political opportunists to cause friction between the races.

"My regret is deep because all five of you, and most of all Dr van Geyssen here, deserve high reward, but we, the government, cannot bestow it without destroying secrecy. Perhaps it will become possible later. You will not be forgotten.

"You have no doubt heard the latest news? No? Of course, you've been rather busy today. By good fortune the fuss over the attack on Komatipoort is being dismissed as a mistake by bandits, not an attack on South Africa. Nothing has leaked out about the air strike into Mozambique, your little adventure," he nodded at Ballance and Ngwenya, "nor has any word come out of Venda about the extent of the coup and counter-coup there, details of which are still vague.

"None of those aspects of the secession attempt have surfaced and they are not likely to for a long time, if ever. We could not prevent its suppression in the north from making headlines but the harm is not irreparable.

"In fact, our official spokesmen were the first to announce it and cooperated with the media, giving them enough information to satisfy them but of course, not all. Very few people apart from us here know its scale and details.

"So the rebellion is being treated as an ill-conceived effort by a small illegal army, tragic and pointless but in the long run of less importance than our many other challenges."

The Vice President paused to glance at the two police officers.

"This brings me to my good friend, Dr van Geyssen. The

reason you have been unable to find him is because he has been my guest at Groote Schuur. No, Superintendent Louw, in spite of what your investigations indicate, he is not a fanatic or a rebel. As you know, he is a valued advisor to the government on economic affairs. He is a loyal South African as dedicated as I am to a free and open society. Let me explain.

"He joined the right-wing underground eight months ago *at my instigation* and worked his way into the rebel movement's hierarchy as my personal agent and informant when it began. They did nothing that he did not tell me about. His rôle was known to nobody else but me. Now all of you know too. I owe you that.

"Asking him to infiltrate and spy was a most awkward and unpleasant thing to ask of anyone, but necessary. I had to have an inside source to know what the rebels were plotting so we could nip the plot in the bud."

In his armchair the Doctor nodded his large head in confirmation. The Vice President went on.

"You have seen the damage even these amateurs caused by stirring conflict and by selective murder. You can imagine what they would have done with efficient leadership and better backing.

"We knew most of the third force leaders, but we had to bring their rank-and-file out into the open to identify and seize them or they would have remained as a running sore for years. We waited so long because we were balancing the risk of more violence by them against the risk of acting too soon and missing most of them.

"However, we have defeated and discredited them thanks to you, our Fourth Force."

His gaze travelled over all of them.

Superintendent Louw put his glass on a side table and stood up, his face bleak, his nerves seething. "Mr President," he said, looking at each in turn, "if I may, with all due respect ..."

He paused and they watched him in expectation. "Sir,"

the superintendent went on, "Dr van Geyssen here was part and parcel of the plot. He not only condoned the killing, which makes him an accessory to it, he in fact ordered killings himself, which in my book makes him a common murderer."

The atmosphere in the room turned electric as if a switch had been thrown. Miller looked at the superintendent in delight and then confused everyone by grinning.

The Vice President's brows lowered like thunderclouds. Ballance and Ngwenya stared at the superintendent, fearing for him. The President, sitting with crossed legs and hands resting on his knees, wore a puzzled frown. Penelope sat erect, smelling battle.

Dr Van Geyssen lifted his granite face and stared at the superintendent.

"You have to break eggs to make an omelette, superintendent," the Vice President said, his voice very cold, making it plain he was affronted by the policeman's blunt accusation. "Some casualties are inevitable in a thing like this, which we did not start, by the way. A few have suffered for the sake of the majority."

"Dr van Geyssen could not escape being involved. If anyone is to blame, I am because I ordered him into that impossible position. He was an accessory technically, in reality he was there to help stop the secession and the killing. He did his utmost to thwart bloodshed without revealing himself."

Louw sighed and plunged deeper. It was all or nothing. "I am sorry, sir, I cannot agree. Dr van Geyssen is a hard-core supporter of the Free Staters movement and he is a murderer."

The Vice President glared at him. The Doctor's face turned red.

The President's keen eyes flicked across them, taking it all in, like a watching wolf.

"Superintendent, I will make allowances for your feelings in view of what you have been through," the Vice

President said, his anger now open, "but I know the facts and they are not to be contradicted. Dr van Geyssen has proved his loyalty and does not deserve those remarks. I request you withdraw them and apologise."

"Sir," Miller intervened, "I suggest we hear what Superintendent Louw has to say."

"No!" Van Geyssen said, standing up to loom over everyone, "My life has been so disrupted already, do I now have to endure this insult from some obscure policeman?"

"Be quiet and listen!" Assistant Commissioner Miller retorted. He rose to his feet, a dominant figure.

Everybody stared at him. The room was charged with tension.

Stunned, the Vice President glanced from one to the other, sensing he was losing control of the scene. "What?" he asked. "What is it, Mike?"

The Assistant Commissioner nodded at Louw to continue. "We have proof that Mr van Geyssen knew of the scheme to kill Mr Ngwenya here and place the blame for the murder on Mr Ballance," the superintendent said. "It caused the death of an innocent man."

"Of course I knew of it, but after the event!" Van Geyssen interjected. "I did not plan it!"

The superintendent met his eye for a moment and went on, controlling his own temper, gaining courage from it. "He told the rebels' ruling committee in person that he had ordered the death of one of my men, Detective Inspector Greeff."

"I ordered his demotion!"

"Same thing. He admitted to a meeting of the rebel committee at his own home in Pretoria that he himself made the decision to assassinate the deputy leader of the Freedom Front with a bomb."

The others were shocked into silence.

The Vice President broke it. "Gideon?" he asked, his voice sharp.

"That too is utter rubbish! I had to say that to convince

the committee I was one of them. Do you think I enjoyed it?"

Louw's frown deepened. Staring at van Geyssen, he continued. "All of this we learned from our own inquiries, from your old friend the Chairman of the Free Staters committee, Dr Nicolas Albertyn, and from some other members who are talking non-stop now that they see the error of their ways. We also learned from them that you were the go-between for the committee and their thugs.

"We began to investigate your activities after we discovered your connections with a curious Englishman named Smith, a professional assassin, and we found some interesting information, Dr van Geyssen."

At the mention of the little grey-haired killer's name, Van Geyssen felt his stomach lurch.

"Yes," Penelope said.

They looked at her as if they had forgotten she was there. She placed her glass on a side table, opened her small white handbag and brought out a folded sheet of paper.

"The vice president says he asked you eight months ago to infiltrate the rebels, Dr van Geyssen. We have this letter ..." she flourished it, it was from her mother but nobody knew that, "... in which Dr Albertyn, who was later elected the Free Staters' Chairman, wrote to you a *year* ago agreeing with your proposition that there had to be an independent white state because the government had left no alternative."

She put the paper back in her bag. Ballance eyed her with new respect; a formidable woman.

"It is interesting, though perhaps not incriminating," she went on in a matter-of-fact tone, as if addressing a judge, "that we also found a list of a large quantity of Eastern Bloc weapons among your papers – interesting because the Free Staters were smuggling large quantities of weapons from Mozambique – and a list of freight containers from America."

"Which contained weapons," Louw added.

She folded her hands on her bag and looked at Van Geyssen.

"As I have already explained, Miss Fox," the Vice President interrupted, attempting to re-assert his authority in a situation that was fast running wild, "Dr van Geyssen had to be in the thick of things to establish his credentials. I am sure that what you say can be explained."

"There is another thing, sir," Miller broke in. "The question of the assassin sent to kill you and the President."

"Oh, I know all about that. Gideon warned me several days ago and I told you," the Vice President said, exasperated.

Miller faced Van Geyssen: "Can you describe Smith, sir?"

"Smallish, middle-aged, grey hair and a grey moustache, very ordinary," Van Geyssen said after some reluctance.

"Yesterday we caught an assassin as he was about to shoot the President from the offices across the road, a big strong fellow built like a rugby prop, with black hair and a drooping black moustache."

Van Geyssen looked blank. Miller and the superintendent exchanged glances.

"He cannot be Smith," Louw said, "because one of my men shot Smith dead days ago when he tried to kill Miss Fox here. But you wouldn't have known that because we kept it quiet."

Van Geyssen maintained his apparent calm by clasping his hands together to stop them shaking, but he paled. "What has this to do with me?" he demanded. "Who is this man?"

"He's telling us all he knows," Miller lied, "including what Smith told him. Yes, you sent Smith to assassinate both the President and Vice President and you deliberately sent a warning because you wanted Smith killed in the attempt. You set a trap to get rid of him and, with luck, both the national leaders too.

"It was pure good luck for us that Superintendent

Louw's man shot Smith dead when he tried to murder Miss Fox here, on your instructions—"

"Absolute nonsense!"

"... but you also assigned a second killer to make quite sure these two were murdered. It would have plunged the country into the kind of anarchy in which you could seize your white homeland and declare yourselves independent. Right?"

Miller knew that he was now far out on a thin limb of guesswork and fabrication. He waited for the inevitable denial as Van Geyssen again shot to his feet.

"That is a damned lie!" he shouted, his fists clenched in rage. He knew nothing about this second assassin, whom Smith must have sent contrary to instructions, but there was no way he could prove it. It was his word against the assassin's.

"Gideon ..." the Vice President said, white with shock, and Van Geyssen whirled to face him "... is this true? Are you one of them?"

"No, it is *not* true!"

"And there's one more thing, sir."

Everybody looked at Miller. "Dr van Geyssen," he said, "when you telephoned the vice president yesterday to tell him when the rebels would start their revolution, you said seven o'clock *tomorrow* night, that would be tonight ..." glancing at his watch "... about now. But just before phoning him you phoned Dr Albertyn, your Chairman, and said at seven o'clock *tonight*, that was *last* night, when the rebellion started.

"No, wait!" Miller held up his hand to forestall another outburst. "There's no doubt about this because we were tapping Dr Albertyn's telephone, which you obviously didn't know. Minutes after we overheard your call to him, the vice president called me to say the attack would be *tomorrow*.

"Your purpose was to mislead us and give the rebels a full twenty-four hour start, wasn't it?"

CHAPTER THIRTY EIGHT

Dr Gideon van Geyssen realised he had been trapped, denial was pointless, and the mounting fury in him erupted.

"*Yes! Damn you all!*" he roared. "You have brought the country to complete and utter ruin! You ..." he aimed his outstretched right arm and rigid finger at the Vice President "... you are destroying the country and the Afrikaners!"

The President watched, his dark, lined face impassive, still seated with legs crossed, listening, saying nothing.

"Yes, I *am* a supporter of a white state and I always will be," Van Geyssen thundered, "and you won't stop us! You can take me to court, you can do what you like, but be sure our cause will live! I am but one, there are many of us! Your ridiculous dream of a rainbow nation is no more than that, a dream! You have delayed us this time," he sneered, "you will not do it next time."

He turned on his heel and stalked towards the door, stiff with rage. Miller made a move to stand in his way but the President stopped him with a swift motion of his hand.

***

The door opened before Van Geyssen was halfway there. Through it came another uniformed parliamentary steward with a silver tray of canapés balanced on his right hand. He was a big man with black hair. Perspiration beaded his upper lip.

He used his left hand to steady the tray because underneath, between it and the palm of his right hand, nestled a Browning 9mm pistol.

He took in the scene in an instant: a tall heavy man whose face was filled with anger advancing on him with clenched fists, beyond him the President, the Vice President and several other people; all but the President looking shaken.

Something had gone wrong, they were expecting him.

He dropped the tray with a crash, scattering stuffed prunes, asparagus in bacon and vol-au-vents across the pile carpet.

In the same movement he levelled the Browning.

The tall man stopped three paces away, between him and the President, eyes fixed in disbelief on the gun.

The steward pulled the trigger.

The shot boomed. The bullet went straight into Van Geyssen's heart. He toppled over backwards like a felled tree with an expression of total surprise on his face. The explosion drowned the thud of his fall.

The steward tugged the gun down from the kick of the recoil to aim into the tableau in front of him, at the President, who was still sitting unmoved. For a tick of time he stared straight into the black eyes levelly returning his gaze.

Before he could pull the trigger again, two shots crashed almost as one.

The two bullets struck the steward in the head and chest and hurled him back against the door. He was dead before he hit the floor.

***

Assistant Commissioner Miller and Superintendent Louw stood like crouched statues, arms extended, guns still aimed.

A screech of alarms shattered the ringing silence and the smack of running feet came from outside the room. Double doors at both ends of the room burst open and suited security guards rushed in waving pistols. They saw the President seated, calm and unhurt, and the Vice President standing near him, also unharmed, and levelled their guns at Louw and Miller.

The superintendent and the Assistant Commissioner bent to place their weapons at their feet. A security guard picked them up and stepped to van Geyssen's body. A glance showed him both the men on the carpet were dead. Runnels of blood were leaking into the pile.

The Vice President covered his face with trembling hands.

Penelope's face paled as she gazed at the two corpses lay in front of her. "Hell," she said. "I'd never seen one in my life and in one week I see three."

Ngwenya, ever practical, went to the Cape Dutch armoire where the liquor stood and poured neat scotch into two glasses. He tossed one drink down his own throat and carried the other to Penelope who swallowed it in a gulp then picked up her first drink from the side table and drank that too.

Ngwenya filled another glass and offered it to the President, who shook his head with a slight smile. He gave it instead to the Vice President, who downed it without hesitation.

"It is all right," the President said to the security men, "It is all over."

"Are you all right, sir?" Miller asked him.

"Yes, thank you, Mr Miller, but I think my colleague here might need help."

"Is Gideon dead?" The Vice President's voice was unsteady.

"Yes," Miller answered. "It's better that he is."

"Is it true, Mike, was he a genuine traitor?" the Vice President asked. "Did he truly want to kill us?"

"I'm afraid so, sir."

"Mike, who can I believe? Gideon was one of my most trusted friends."

The President rose from his seat, shaking his head. "So

much stupid killing," he said. "How in heaven's name can we progress if we cannot trust. We *must* learn to trust. What sort of life can we have without trust? What kind of country?"

He glanced up at the others watching him. "Will you please excuse me," he said. He half-raised a hand in farewell and walked from the room with a slow tread.

The Vice President pushed out of his chair and walked to Van Geyssen's body. "Poor Gideon," he said, "such a big man to choose so small a cause. Who's the other man, the waiter?"

"Another assassin. He comes out of the same mould as the one we caught across the road."

"But Mike, what's he doing in a Parliamentary staff uniform? I thought we screened everybody?"

"We did, sir, and that ..."

"... that," the Vice President completed the thought for him, "... means they penetrated our tightest security."

"I'm afraid so, sir."

The Vice President looked at the people around him: his guests and the security men, all watching him.

Who *could* he trust?

"Mike, Superintendent Louw, I don't think it's over yet. I still need you two. I thought we'd stopped the rot but maybe it's just beginning."

The bodies, zipped into plastic bags, were carried out on stretchers.

"You're right, sir," Assistant Commissioner Miller sighed, watching them go, "There's a long way to go."

We hope you enjoyed *The Hidden Third* by Wilf Nussey. Please turn the page for a preview of another great book from the author, *The Machiavellian Affair.*

The Machiavellian Affair
Wilf Nussey

Chapter One

MAY 25TH, 2000

"What a strange monument," the South African president whispered to his Foreign Minister standing next to him.

"Yes, is it not?"

The precise but Portuguese-accented English surprised them before she could reply. They turned to see the president of Mozambique smiling at them, a small, neat man who radiated authority like warmth from a fire.

"Not many people know what it is," he said.

"The nose cone of a rocket of some sort?" his guest ventured. "It looks like those we saw at the May Day parades on Red Square." He turned to his Foreign Secretary. "Remember?"

She nodded.

"Ah, of course." The president of Mozambique inclined his head in acknowledgement. "This one is in fact Russian and some were on show there."

The South African was intrigued. In the fight against the apartheid government, his African National Congress had used some pretty sophisticated light weaponry but never anything approaching a rocket that could carry a nuclear warhead. And he was certain Mozambique's rebels, who defeated the Portuguese colonial rulers, never had them or would have dreamed of using them.

The Mozambican president read his thoughts.

"Now it is just part of the junk of war we want to forget, to commit to the past. But it also marks an incident few people know about that may well have started another, much bigger, war than ours."

He paused and his hypnotic black eyes fixed on the South African's.

"At the very least it would have wiped out our subcontinent as we know it." He stopped and glanced at the crowd on the plaza.

The South African president remembered nothing about any incident involving a weapon like this, the playthings of the Big Powers. He was about to ask, when the band below struck up a deafening fanfare of brass with Afro-Latin zest.

The two leaders and their entourages stood at attention for the national anthems. They were on the tall-pillared balcony of the Maputo city hall, a baroque relic of Portuguese colonial days when the city was named Lourenço Marques. It looked down on the Praça de Independencia and the Avenida de Samora Machel sloping to the ship-lined harbour in the great three-river estuary flowing into Delagoa Bay. Colourful thickets of suited civil servants, officers in vivid uniforms and wives over-dressed despite the steaming humidity filled the plaza below.

The nose cone, the centrepiece of a war memorial created by some Mozambican with more welding enthusiasm than artistic skill, arose from a pedestal in the middle of the black-and-white paved plaza.

The triangular panels of the nose cone were splayed open like the petals of some huge, bizarre lotus in the dull military green favoured by the Soviets. It was empty inside where the nuclear warhead would have nestled. Once it had sat on the high tip of an SS-X-25 intercontinental ballistic missile, part of the SS-20 series built by the now-defunct Soviet Union. This one had been designed to deliver any of a variety of warhead combinations. None of these missiles were supposed to still exist, scrapped by agreement after the Soviet collapse.

Surrounding it was a twisted mass of old, big and small gun barrels, brass shell cases, rifles, iron-wheeled recoilless cannons, mortar tubes and other paraphernalia of warfare, tangled and bonded by the welder's exuberance.

Now the whole construction was almost hidden by the panoply of flags, bunting, immaculate soldiers all from the same mould, a battery of aged 25-pounder howitzers, hundreds of scrubbed schoolchildren and a mass of interested spectators. They crowded the sidewalks, gazed down from the windows of apartment blocks and festooned the trees around the plaza like fruit. The occasion, the start of a formal visit by the South African leader, to mark the 25th anniversary of Mozambique's independence, was free entertainment.

Speeches were made, fortunately short because the schedule was running late. The 25-pounders roared, bounced and belched blue clouds in a 21-gun salute, frightening small children out of the trees above them. The dignitaries retired indoors from the balcony for sherry and thick, strong coffee.

In a quiet moment the South African president, stuffing fresh tobacco in his pipe, said to his counterpart, "I'm fascinated by that rocket head out there, by what you said. I thought our Truth and Reconciliation Commission and other inquiries had opened wide all the secrets of the apartheid regime and its allies, but I've heard nothing about this. I mean ..." he hesitated "... you said a *world* war?"

"It is a fascinating story," the Mozambican president said in his careful, enunciated English, "but a long one. It will be my pleasure to tell it to you when we have time to relax with our wives after the function this evening."

"I look forward to it."

After dinner, the two men sat down in buttoned-leather club chairs, in the study of the presidential palace behind high white walls and guard houses in Maputo's well-heeled Polana suburb. A waiter poured healthy measures of a rich old Portuguese aguardente into snifters and withdrew.

"You are the first person outside a very small circle to hear this," the Mozambican said, swirling the brandy. "Feelings still run high in certain quarters."

The South African inclined his head in tacit acknowledgement.

"You will remember that when Mikhail Gorbachev launched perestroika and glasnost, he severed bonds tied by the Cold War, freeing many nations from ideological obligations so they could at last give their attention to their own priorities.

"We have both prospered from that freedom. Our future in Mozambique is beginning to look good, thanks in great measure to your support, but also to the generosity of others with funds released by the end of the Cold War. Everyone is sick and tired of fighting. People want peace and food on the table.

"But all this almost did not come about. Some individuals did not like the change Gorbachev started. It cost them power and wealth. Some tried to turn the clock back and came very close to succeeding. Had it not been for a handful of young people with a great deal of luck, all of Southern Africa might have been plunged into a conflict that would have destroyed us and perhaps started another cold war, even a hot war.

"That was in 1988 ..."

ABOUT THE AUTHOR

Wilf Nussey was a newspaperman for forty years, all but four of them in Africa. He was the foremost foreign correspondent for the Argus group of newspapers for many years spanning most of Africa's transition to independence and its continuing upheavals. Before that he was a freelance correspondent in Kenya for British and North American media and lived and worked in Britain and Canada. Assignments have taken him to the Middle East, Far East, Europe and New Zealand.

Five years after becoming editor of a small newspaper, he quit to live in the bush and write books and has produced four successful documentaries. Now he and his wife live a few metres from the sea at Simon's Town in South Africa's Cape.